I am L.I.A.M.

I am L.I.A.M.

BY: PHILLIP A. WEAVER

Book Design & Production:
Columbus Publishing Lab
www.ColumbusPublishingLab.com

Copyright © 2021 by
Phillip Weaver
LCCN: 2021900442

Paperback ISBN: 978-1-63337-471-3
E-Book ISBN: 978-1-63337-472-0

Printed in the United States of America
13 5 7 9 10 8 6 4 2

Dedicated to my wife and family.

A special thank you to all those
who have supported me and my journey
and to those who read *MIRRORS*.

INTRODUCTION

THE PINES RETIREMENT COMMUNITY IN TRENTON, New Jersey, was home to over two hundred elderly people. The environment was clean, the staff were kind and helpful, the food was of good quality and well prepared. The majority of the residents were from the Jewish community and enjoyed the company of one another and the numerous families who came to visit regularly on the weekends. The main dining hall was large enough to accommodate the residents and their families, serving a large menu on the weekends.

A cough started with Mr. Goldman. "You all right, Dad? Here, drink some water." His son voiced concern. The older man waved and took up his glass of water, sipping slowly.

"Sitting under that vent, went and caught a chill," Mrs. Brown said from the next table.

"Do you smell that? Smells like almonds, roasting almonds," Mrs. Brown's daughter added. "Like cooking almonds. Smells Christmassy." She took a deep breath.

A very old man in a wheelchair at the center of the dining room began to shout. Trying to move, bumping his chair into other people, he seemed frantic.

Mr. Goldman's son stood to see the commotion and recognized the panic on the old man's face. "He is freaking out," he said to his father.

"He is over a hundred years old," Mrs. Brown said, and began to cough, as did her daughter.

The Cyclon gas had been set to release on a timer at twelve-twelve. The device slowly expelled the deadly gas into the ducts of the air conditioning and was carried to each and every room of the Pines Retirement Community. People had no clue; the invisible gas seeped into the rooms and was sucked into their lungs with only a hint of almond scent. By the time they had identified the smell, the poison was already killing them.

Death was neither quick nor painless, but it was assured. Inhaling poison is a cruel way to meet your end. The mind struggles to preserve life, while death comes with each breath you take and destroys from within. You must breathe to live, but to breathe is killing you, like drowning out of water.

CHAPTER 1

AN FBI TASK FORCE ARRIVED two days after the mass killing of 307 people at the Pines Retirement Community. The crime scene was still busy with state and local law enforcement, as well as surrounded by media and onlookers. The gassing of Jews was a dramatic event and drew great interest from the public and politicians.

The pressure was on to discover who would commit such a terrible murderous spree, and why. Speculation had taken prime time position with the news coverage, but Special Agent Brandon Harding could not afford to speculate. His job was facts and evidence, to lead his team and bring law breakers to justice.

The team arrived in three black Suburbans and took over the scene immediately. Special Agent Harding was lead detective of the task force and informed the state special response officer they would be taking over. The press was quick to shout out questions at the FBI, but the team knew better than to respond. They had work to do and enough attention to make anyone uneasy. Harding had an eight-person team, including himself. They were the best law enforcement had to offer.

The team had no time to waste, and moved inside the retirement community. "Special Agent Carter, make sure to film that crowd out there. Never know, the unsub may be watching," Harding directed.

Special Agent Allison Carter was a Harvard graduate with a psychology degree, specializing in criminal psychology. She was the best profiler in the field. "Yes, sir; but he isn't here. The news will cover it enough for him. This unsub is smart enough to watch from home. He might come back, but not until he is absolutely certain there is no police presence." Carter collected the video camera and headed outside to film the crowd.

Harding nodded, then turned to his two crime scene evidence retrieval investigative specialists. "Jensen, Park; I want to know the agent used, how it was dispersed, how such a thing would be produced or purchased. Do what you do, fingerprints down." Dr. Jody Jensen had studied to be a veterinarian in college, but after being the victim of a crime, she had turned her focus to law enforcement.

Agent Wu Park had a chemical background—a minor in chemistry and major in biology. He was excellent in the lab, and turned to the FBI for opportunities. The son of Japanese immigrants, he had been raised with high expectations which drove him constantly.

The team rounded out with a young genius profiler, Agent Keith Kennedy, who specialized in micro-expressions as well as criminal behavior. Kennedy was the youngest on the team at twenty-five and had graduated top of his class from Harvard at age seventeen. He had been recommended to Allison Carter by one of her old professors.

Two tactical officers gave the team muscle. Special Agent Sam Lee, a senior agent and former military officer, was a Southerner from the Carolinas. Most of Sam's military record was classified even for Brandon.

Agent Tyrone Johnson was also ex-military, with three tours in Afghanistan, two in Iraq, and one in Yemen. Much of his military file was also classified. Big, bald and black as night, Agent Johnson was an intimidating presence and first through the door.

Harding's second-in-command was Special Agent James McDaniels, an experienced investigator who had worked his way up the ranks from being a rookie in Wyoming. The oldest on the team at fifty-seven, James was still cowboy tough and very capable.

Brandon knew McDaniels should have been lead detective, but as good as James was at his job, he was equally bad at following rules, protocols, and kissing the correct asses to get ahead. James McDaniels closed cases, but his methods stunted his progress and career.

The Pines Retirement Community was a dead zone. All the gas had dissipated, so the multitudes of police moving about the hallways did not need masks. The coroner was still removing bodies and the forensic departments were collecting samples. Special Agents Harding and McDaniels stood in the dining room looking over the massacre. "What do you think, James?" Harding asked.

"I think this is all bad. News is turning this into a circus, and we both know the circus has ringleaders and clowns."

"Makes our job that much more difficult," Harding said as he examined the table in front of him. "Killed a fly; this stuff must have been super toxic. Johnson, see if this place has any surveillance. We need to know who placed the device, when, and how." The task force spent four hours at the retirement community before splitting up to pursue their individual evaluations. Harding headed back to the hotel with McDaniels driving. The press had been aggressive as they left, trying to get something for the late news, but there was nothing to tell them beyond what they already knew. The locals were enjoying the spotlight, giving interviews but saying nothing of value. Harding didn't see any problem with the local police chief telling the local news he had no information or comment at that time.

"Circus," McDaniels said as they pulled away from the scene. "How they love the spectacle. Public thirst for the macabre; you would think we were the Romans at the Colosseum. We develop it, as they did those gladiators. People watch that crap on television and it loses significance, devalues the magnitude of what happened. Those sick-minded murderous types have to build a bigger show to impress the public demand. The crowd must have a proper meal." McDaniels shook his head in disgust.

Harding looked at the experienced agent. He knew how easily resentment developed in their line of work. The tide of horror they had to experience, coupled with the hunger of the media and desensitization of the public, the pressure for results—a level of cynicism was hard to avoid. McDaniels was a great investigator but held the edge of burning out. Harding had considered talking with him, perhaps even transferring him to a less stressful position, but a man like McDaniels needed his work, the stress, the edge, or he would have nothing to hold onto at all.

The task force returned to Washington, D.C., and congregated in the conference room to go over the case. "Good morning, team, settle in." Harding sipped from his coffee cup. "Pressure is on, people. News coverage has been nonstop and special interest groups are having a fit. Prime minister of Israel called the President. Press is labeling this a terror attack and a hate crime. Everyone is looking for this to be solved immediately. Let's begin: case number NJ7568B-609. Pines Retirement Community, Trenton, New Jersey. Special Agent Jensen, what do we have forensically?"

Jody Jensen took a drink of her coffee and cleared her throat, looking at the file in front of her. "The gas was Cyclon B; same gas used primarily by the Nazis during World War II in the camps. Such a gas is extremely difficult to obtain or to create, especially in such a high concentration. As deadly as Cyclon gas is, the amount to accomplish such a dispersal was significant, which is evident by the size of containers attached to the ventilation system. No prints were recovered from the canisters, nor any hair, fiber, or genetic materials. There was a residue of a bleach, alcohol, and ammonia mixture sprayed over the entire area."

"Bleach, alcohol, and ammonia? Why all three?" Sam Lee asked.

Wu Park said, "The chemical makeup of all three as cleaning agents individually would mask blood or other genetic materials, such as skin or secretions, but combined in a concentrated spray as this was, it degrades any possible evidence."

"So this guy could have taken a dump on the floor, sprayed it with this concoction, and you science geeks are stumped?" McDaniels asked.

"Dependent on the amount applied and concentration of chemicals, yes," Park said, overlooking the mockery.

"So, no forensic evidence?" Harding asked as he took another sip of coffee. Jensen simply shook her head. "Well, that won't go over very well. Allison, do we have a working profile?"

Special Agent Allison Carter reviewed her notes. "Primary findings are limited; we have very little data to compile a proper profile. White male, over thirty, college educated with a chemical background. The Cyclon gas seems to be created, but this aspect could have been contracted out. I don't want to be premature in an assessment without proper information. The targeting of Jews could be significant, or not. Could be a lone individual, or not. There are far too many variables."

"So you don't think this is a Muslim attack against Jews?" Johnson asked.

Keith Kennedy said, "Radical Muslims usually use explosives, playing on the Jewish tradition of burying the dead intact. The Israelis will actually sponge up the blood of victims in order to fulfill this aspect of their faith. Muslims or radical Islam can not be ruled out completely, but it is a moderately high probability it wasn't them." Harding was disheartened. The absence of answers was not going to go over well with his bosses, the politicians, or the public. He could stall somewhat, put off things as evidence being processed and the need for further information to develop a more complete profile, but the director would know stalling when he heard it.

Even as he worried, the embodiment of his fear crossed the bull-pen, headed directly for the conference room.

FBI Director Anthony Maroni used his index finger to end the meeting and command Special Agent Harding to join him. Maroni led the way to Harding's office. Standing in front of the lead detective's desk, Maroni waited for Brandon to close the door. "Terrible thing in New Jersey," the director began.

"Truly so, sir. Tragic."

The FBI director leaned back on Harding's desk and folded his hands over his ample stomach. "Plenty of people watching this one. All eyes are on you, Brandon. Tell me you have something; I have to report to the President later today," Maroni said in an even tone.

Harding stood steady, but he knew he had nothing. Looking at his boss leaning against his desk, Brandon was reminded of how long the man had been in the game. Anthony Maroni was a player and won far more than he lost; smart, patient, and unalarming, but he would know instantly if Brandon attempted to pull one over on him. "The lack of evidence at the scene speaks volumes but gives us very little to move forward with," Harding finally said.

"That should go over swell with the President, not to mention the ambitious senator from Ohio who has been calling me hourly since the news broke. Explaining how no evidence is insightful to the criminal pathology will not fly." Director Maroni pushed forward and took a few steps to the right. "The computer popped out an odd list today. The experts programmed the FBI supercomputer to store and process all case files, but also to search for links or possible connections. The list was emailed to you." The director thumbed toward the computer.

Harding moved to his desk and typed in his access code to his desktop computer. "Is the Trenton case on here?"

The Director took a chair in front of Harding's desk as Brandon opened the email and watched the case numbers scroll by at high speed. "Are you kidding me? Must be a thousand cases here. Is this a joke? I don't have time for jokes." Brandon shook his head.

"No joke," Maroni stated flatly.

"How are all these connected?"

"The computer looks for possible patterns, consistencies, inconsistencies, and variables, and produces a list of potentially linked cases."

Harding opened one of the case files. "This is a stabbing of a homeless person," he said as he read. "Director, with all due respect, if we entertain this idea and attempt to compile this list into a working investigation, it will consume my team. This Trenton case is going to be hard enough to break without piling on this ridiculous list, which is obviously an error." Harding could hear the slight edge in his own voice.

Maroni stood and put both hands on the desk, leaning in close to Brandon. "You told me you had nothing and now you have too much. If, *if,* this computer is correct, and not some error as you say... God forbid, then we have a serial killer like never before loose in the United States. The thought alone gives me pause. Three hundred and seven dead, and that is just this one case." He stood upright. "I could not sit on the list or ignore it, nor can you. Do whatever it takes. Powers up on high want this case solved, and now with this list..."

"I am certain selling a serial killer to the powers that be will be easier than showing up hat in hand, so to speak." Brandon regretted his words as soon as they left his mouth.

The director's face tightened. "Brandon, you are a good agent, but you never will be a man of real power until you curb your tongue. Think your words. Your suggestion is baseless, but true enough. I did not invent this list, but better to arrive with a tall tale than nothing at all. You have plenty to do now. I'll check back with you very soon." Maroni moved to the door.

"Thank you, sir." Special Agent Harding stood as the director left his office. Returning to his seat, Brandon looked at the list of cases with dread and a knot in his stomach. "This is a waste of time," he said to himself.

CHAPTER 2

AFTER SPECIAL AGENT HARDING gave his team their orders, the task force immediately voiced dismay at sight of the enormous email. Yet, they had to follow every lead, no matter how wild or ridiculous. Brandon didn't like the idea of the director putting work on them in order to make a meeting easier for himself. He understood the games of Washington, D.C., and that the director was correct about him: he didn't think his words. Brandon was a detective, not a politician. He surely was better at the games than James McDaniels, but he had nowhere near the skills of Maroni.

As Brandon left for the day and was heading to his car, a woman carrying a microphone followed by a cameraman hurried toward him.

"Special Agent Harding?" she called as she advanced. "Sasha Blonde for Indepth News. Do you have any comment on the death chamber in New Jersey? Was it neo-Nazis, or part of this national serial killer's long list of murders?" She pushed the microphone into Brandon's face.

"You know I cannot comment on any ongoing, open investigation," Harding said with a softened expression. The reporter was lovely: blond with full lips, clean features, a toned body, long legs. She smelled of coconuts and vanilla.

"Director Anthony Maroni suggested the gassing could be the work of a serial killer. Sources provided us with a list of over a thousand possible cases to attribute to this deranged lunatic. You are aware of this list? How is it a serial killer could achieve such numbers and you haven't caught them? Why are we, the public, just now learning of this, this—ghost?" Sasha Blonde spoke quickly and purposefully.

Brandon was caught off guard. "How did you get that list?" Again, he regretted his words as soon as they left his lips.

"So, you confirm the list?" Sasha Blonde blurted, again pressing the microphone into Brandon's face.

"No, I am not confirming anything. As I said, I cannot discuss an open case. I would hope you would respect the families of those lost in that terrible act in Trenton and allow law enforcement to perform our duty," Special Agent Harding stated in his best press voice.

"Allowing the Ghost to wander the country killing hundreds of people—it seems law enforcement has failed us. Do you have any leads on this Ghost? Can you tell our viewers how this maniac is targeting his victims?" she pressed.

"Presumption; he, singular. I do not have the luxury to just say things without thought or evidence. I cannot discuss open investigations. I have no comment." Brandon spoke defensively.

"So, the Ghost is an open investigation?" the reporter asked directly.

Harding put up both hands and turned to his car, hurrying to get inside. The beautiful woman hounded him with questions but Brandon ignored her. Starting his car, he backed out, the reporter at his window with her microphone and the cameraman following him with the eye which never blinks.

"How can you leave the public in the dark, when the worst serial killer of all time stalks them? Why won't you warn people of the Ghost?" she yelled through the closed window.

As he drove away, Brandon could not help but take a last look at the leggy reporter, admiring her beauty. She stood in his mirror with confidence. She had run him over the coals pretty good and knew it. As he turned out of the parking lot, his mind began to peel the onion of questions growing in his thoughts.

Did the director really comment on a serial killer, or had she pounced on him too? How did she have the list, or did she? Ghost, she had named him, and a scary name at that, which was never good. The press would feed on this like fresh meat. The scene in New Jersey was almost played out in the news cycle and a new angle was just what they wanted. Didn't matter if it was true or not, dangerous or not.

Brandon had thought having nothing to go on was going to be a problem, but now he had a phantom serial killer from some list off a computer: the Ghost. "Like a bad episode of Charlie's Angels," he said to the steering wheel, shaking his head.

CHAPTER 3

THE TASK FORCE MET IN THE CONFERENCE ROOM first thing in the morning. They all had been over the case files from the email, as well as reviewing the Trenton case. Harding had been up past two in the morning looking for commonalities, patterns, anything to link even one case to another.

The range from one case to the next was huge. There were shootings, but by a variety of different calibers of weapon. Stabbings, but by a variety of different kinds of blades. Different ropes, different poisons, different everything.

"Morning, people," Harding addressed his team. They all looked tired and irritated, more so than usual. "I would like to apologize for the mountain of information you all had to review last night, but what did you come up with?"

McDaniels spoke up first. "Found a great waste of time and a splitting headache. Reading case file after case file off the computer half the night. Was this a bad joke? What, did you piss off the director or something?"

"Did seem to be an exercise in futility," Jensen added. "As I am sure you all noticed from the evidence, a different method was employed almost every time."

Carter said, "The victimology also varies: Black, White, Asian, Hispanic, male, female, old, even children. There is no profile here, not of a single individual or even a group of suspects." Harding leaned on the conference table and rubbed his head.

Looking up at his team, Brandon took a drink of coffee. "I didn't find anything either. Weapon, method, victims, location, disposal; everything was different. I don't know why the computer put these cases together, but it did. I have to report to Director Maroni this afternoon and I need to tell him something."

"Tell him you have good news. We have discovered that his million-dollar supercomputer is bonkers, and he needs to call tech support." Special Agent McDaniels laughed.

Brandon did not appreciate the joke but could not deny the truth it contained. They were all professionals with years of experience; if they all agreed these cases were random, then the computer had to be incorrect. Brandon wondered whether the director had actually been presented with the list at all, or if he had created it to distract the media and test the team.

"It is difficult for me to imagine such a calculative thought process would compile such an obvious difference in pattern and behavior," Keith Kennedy said. "Computers don't make errors of this magnitude, unless they are really broken."

"See, what did I tell you; broken," McDaniels said. "All these new-fangled gadgets with the bells and the whistles. People really think machines are smarter than we are. Who do they think built the damn things? Modern people have forgotten how to use their brains or put a little elbow grease into their work. Damn shame if you ask me."

"Actually, with the processing speed and sheer volume of information storage, the computer is more capable of determining certain answers more quickly and efficiently than humans," Kennedy pointed out. "We have seen multiple examples of this as computer technology has advanced."

"Yes, the debate of the computer footprint upon mankind can continue some other time. The director is not going to like our conclusion," Harding said, trying to refocus the team.

"Are you sure?" Carter questioned. "Seems the news got a hold of the story. Saw you on the TV last night. The Ghost? As ridiculous as we all see this to be, the director may have seen an opportunity to distract the media and the public, while pushing more funding toward our division. Have you considered such an angle?"

"Actually, I had," Harding said. "Doesn't alter our conclusion. This could be a test. Either the supercomputer is wrong, or we don't see the common link to all these cases." Brandon paused to allow the team to absorb that. "If the machine is broken, they will fix it. But what if we are missing something? This computer is already checking every case file and looking for any connection or patterns. This is the moment when we realize the future may see us replaced with a computer." The task force was silent a long moment in their own thoughts. Sam Lee drank his coffee unfazed; the tactical officer had no fear of replacement. Men still killed men and the need for quality killers would, as it always had been, be in demand. Computers dealt in data and processing, replacing the mindless and the thinkers—that was the worry. Drones could strike and maybe one day there would be some kind of "Terminators," but until then, men killed men.

Brandon knew they were nowhere near being replaced, but perhaps in the future, computers would profile or even predict crime. He smiled at the thought from some science fiction book he read as a young man. Philip Dick or a Twilight Zone episode.

"So, what's the plan, Stan?" McDaniels broke Brandon's train of thought.

"Go over it again, in teams. James, Johnson, Kennedy, Jensen: break the cases down into separate groups by method. Lee, Carter, and Park: we shall concentrate on geographical locations. My meeting with Director Maroni is at two o'clock; let's exhaust any possible links. Let's also look at a timeline, see if any of these cases occur at the same time or would be impossible to achieve."

CHAPTER 4

JUST AFTER TWO O'CLOCK, SPECIAL AGENT HARDING was escorted into Director Maroni's office by his secretary. The director was on the phone but ended the conversation sharply and stood to greet his lead detective. Extending his hand, the two men shook.

"Brandon, would you like a coffee, water, tea?"

"No, thank you, sir."

"Please, take a seat." Maroni gestured to a chair. "So, did you and your team go over those case files?"

The secretary closed the door as she left the office, and Brandon now almost wished he had gotten a bottle of water. Clearing his throat, he was hesitant to begin, but knew he had to. "Director, may we speak plainly?" He met the director's eyes and held the gaze until his boss nodded. "Reporter caught me yesterday, when I was leaving work. Asked me about the list, a serial killer, and has named the unsub."

"Sasha Blonde? Originally Borkisnicvic; guess that doesn't really roll off the tongue for TV. Yeah, she caught me too. The Ghost; good name. I watched the trailer for her report this morning. You looked like a deer in the headlights when she mentioned the list." Maroni paused to chuckle.

Brandon smiled but was not amused. "Yes, well, how did she get the list or know anything about this?" He watched the director's reactions very closely. Keith Kennedy had taught him signs to watch for in people's micro-expressions, to tell if they were lying. "Did you leak this story to the reporter?" Brandon knew blunt questions caused more dramatic reactions.

The director of the FBI was no dummy, keeping a stone face as he processed his response. "I understand your concern, Brandon, but shall we again talk of your curbing your tongue? You are here to report to me, not to accuse me of feeding the press information. I would think with all that's on your plate, you would occupy your thoughts with those criminals at large and not suspect your boss of misdeeds. Sasha is fishing and the rest want news. The computer nerds probably leaked the story for a shot of cleavage and a whiff of her perfume." He winked.

"There is no evidence the Trenton case is linked to any of those on the list." Harding said with a hint of irritation. "And for that matter, my team found no link in any of the cases on the list. Was this some kind of test? Because that list was a waste of time. Time my task force could have, should have, been working on New Jersey."

"The FBI computer popped with this list of related cases. A list which in no way seems related. The chairman of the Judicial Subcommittee is aware of this, which is why the charming senator from Ohio has been calling me nonstop since he read it."

"You think he leaked the list?" Brandon asked.

"I am not worried about the press. I have a meeting with Senator Miller tonight. I had hoped my crack task force of top-notch criminal specialists would have more than a shrug to present." Anthony Maroni's face flushed with frustration.

"I am sorry, sir. We reviewed it individually, in teams focused on different criteria, then as a whole. We all agreed the computer must either be mistaken, or has information we do not."

"The FBI supercomputer is wrong, or broken?" the director asked.

As much as Brandon did not intend to respond as he did, he shrugged and gave a nod. "It is not beyond the realm of possibilities. You saw the files: different weapons, times of day, locations, victimology, some are hyper violent, while others are meticulously clean. There are sexual components, then there are not; some ritual aspects, then not. The computer is wrong. A blind person wouldn't put these cases together." Brandon did not bother to tell the director the crimes did not overlap, and even though some were thousands of miles apart, they could have been committed by a single individual. He had hoped at least two of the crimes would have occurred at the same time, definitively showing the crimes to be impossibly linked, but they did not.

CHAPTER 5

FBI DIRECTOR ANTHONY MARONI was seated at a table in his favorite steak house as he awaited the arrival of Senator John Miller of Ohio. The senator was young, handsome, and fit, with a million-dollar smile. The son of a salt mine owner, with ambitions to be President of the United States, and the skills to slither into the job. Anthony ordered a Blue Label scotch, figuring the senator would make him wait. He knew this young slick politician was going to have questions.

Senator Miller had jumped on the Judicial Subcommittee as a first-year senator and now sat as the chairman with a year to go for reelection. The senator called Anthony constantly; anytime the FBI hit the news, John Miller wanted to talk.

"Where you at, Anthony?" the tall young man asked.

Director Maroni rose to his feet and shook the senator's hand. "Busy life, as you well know. Anytime to traverse our thoughts is a luxury."

The men took their seats as the waitress arrived with the director's scotch. "Figured you would be a moment, heard something of traffic as I was heading over," Maroni lied with a smile. "Please, bring us two more; doubles," Maroni added, to the server.

Anthony met the senator's gaze as he drank. Swallowing the

smooth liquor, he puckered his lips, savoring the taste. "So you have some questions," he said, returning his glass to the table.

"Saw Special Agent Harding on the news fumbling over his answers about the list of case files the computer produced. Also, the media has named this phantom. The Ghost? Seems a bit tacky, but what can one expect from a dumbed down news corps? Give the people what they want, talking heads that speak their language." The waitress arrived with double Blue Labels for each man.

Maroni downed the scotch he had and placed the empty glass on the server's tray, giving the woman a nod. "Give us a couple minutes, please."

Looking back at the senator, Maroni squinted slightly. "Harding is a good agent, a closer. He is no media darling." The director allowed the remark to linger. "That Sasha Blonde reporter could make the Pope drop his hat. The name is flash; the Ghost. Give it a couple weeks until some celebrity gets caught cheating or wrecks their car drunk. Public will forget the Ghost quick as you please." Anthony picked up his second scotch.

"Quick as I please would have been yesterday. What of the list?" Miller asked.

"The list is sketchy. Brandon looked at it, the task force checked it individually, and as a team. They checked specific parameters; victimology, location, time of day, weapons. I looked at it, and we all don't see any pattern. We have to consider the possibility that the computer popped out a bogus lineup. Everything is fallible. Must be an error." The waitress returned and took both men's orders. Each chose the prime rib dinner, shrimp cocktail appetizers, salad, baked potatoes with a medium rare cook on the steaks. Maroni already knew he was buying; politicians never pay for anything if they can help it.

"An expensive piece of equipment to be giving us bad information," Senator Miller said as the server left with their orders.

"Expensive and complicated. I had the techs do a complete diagnostic check and they assured me it is functional." The director cocked his head and drank his scotch. "Need a supercomputer to check the supercomputer."

Senator Miller was quiet for a long moment in thought. The waitress arrived with the shrimp and hurried off. Plucking a fat shrimp from the plate and dipping it in red sauce, he met the director's eyes. "List aside, what of Trenton? The Jewish and retirement communities are both up in arms. Two groups concerned with feeling safe."

"Nothing new on that front. The fact the FBI computer lumped New Jersey in with the list only causes me to question it more. A mass killing by way of gas, elderly retired people as a target, no evidence of value; I just don't know." Maroni emptied his glass of Blue Label.

When their meals arrived, they ate, moving the conversation away from business. They were not friends but could be friendly. Polite manners and reasonable points of view made the night go easy enough. The senator skipped dessert but had coffee, while Maroni ate a sweet helping of monkey bread.

"I have a friend, president of a university back in Ohio," the senator said. "He has spoken of a scientist at the college working on cutting edge technology. Some kind of computer thought processing. Would you be up for a meeting? Perhaps we can solve the problem with the list and prevent future bugs coming out of our computer. Determine if it is broken or not. The kind of money we spent on that machine, taxpayers won't want to hear it is messing up." The senator sipped his coffee.

Maroni agreed and allowed the wealthy senator to dodge the sizeable check. As they walked out of the restaurant, a familiar face hurried toward them. A large light clicked on behind her, almost blinding the two men. Sasha Blonde extended her microphone toward them. "Senator Miller, are you aware of the list of crimes committed by the

Ghost? Is that why you are meeting with the director of the FBI?" She spoke very fast.

The senator was an experienced hand in front of the cameras and was smiling before Sasha was within twenty feet. "Good evening, Sasha, did not expect you to pull a Mike Wallace and ambush us on the street. Thought you would have more style. This is not some sensational story or 'to catch a predator' type of thing. If you want an interview to talk about things, you know the process. Coming on like this seems a little desperate. Realize, too, if you edit us to drive your story, you won't work in this town very long. This is a cooperative effort, press and politics, we help each other and weed out the bad eggs while promoting those good eggs. So, be a good egg and make an appointment." Senator Miller never lost his smile.

"These are desperate times, Senator. I have a list of over a thousand cases that the FBI computer compiled as linked; you don't think that is a big deal? Three hundred and seven dead, in just one of those linked cases, and the authorities don't have a clue. Someone should be desperate for answers." Sasha Blonde extended the microphone once again.

"I believe you have confidential communications of the Federal Bureau of Investigations, which you are not authorized to possess," Director Maroni stated firmly.

"Cat's out of the bag, Director. You and the senator aren't fooling anyone. The Ghost is out there and you are lost in the dark, fumbling to catch up. You can take me into custody, put the cuffs on me, but you would be fanning the flames of this story higher and higher. Please, arrest me; it would just show I am doing a good job," Sasha said confidently.

"Sasha… Just relax, try and understand we are learning of things as you are," Maroni said. "We have to be certain of our steps, because we have to apprehend criminals, not just talk about them. I am certain as we develop a working hypothesis about Trenton and these other cases, we could be accommodating of a reporter who is cooperative."

"Exclusive?" the beautiful reporter asked.

"That wouldn't be fair, but perhaps an advantage could be allowed." The director smiled a crafty smile.

Sasha Blonde gave him a sideways look. "What kind of advantage?"

"Something worthwhile, and worth holding back the impulse to splash the wrong type of thing across the media circus."

Sasha agreed to call the director later in the week for comment. Bouncing away from them, she clearly felt she had won the game and achieved a better position. Her cameraman turned off his equipment and hurried after her.

"She was a pageant queen over there," Maroni told the senator.

"Over where?"

"Eastern Europe, someplace."

The senator nodded. "She's got the look. That type is dangerous. Beautiful and hungry. They do what is best for them, without regard for anything or anyone. A beautiful disaster; most of them don't even have a clue, because the mess is behind them."

"With a figure like that, she makes me hungry, and she could make a mess out of me anytime. A tempting treat to be sure." Maroni raised an eyebrow and smiled.

"A treat to you, but what would she make of it?" John Miller said in a cautious tone and raised an eyebrow of his own.

Both men agreed to address the situation. Senator Miller would contact his friend at the university, while Director Maroni would have the task force intensify the investigation in Trenton. Anthony also would have the team look at the list one last time for any commonality.

They agreed to a lunch in a couple of days to review and plan what steps to move forward with, before Maroni talked with Blonde. Senator Miller gained a sense that the woman was looking to grow her career out of the Ghost and wouldn't hold off for very long.

CHAPTER 6

SENATOR MILLER WAITED IN HIS OFFICE with his friend. The intercom system sounded and the senator's secretary announced the arrival of Director Maroni, who entered the office, shaking each man's hand in turn.

"Director Maroni," the senator said, "I would like to introduce a longtime friend of the family, Franklin Rhodes. Franklin is president of Denison University. I think we have found a solution to our problem." The Senator motioned everyone to be seated.

"Glad to meet you," Anthony said with a smile.

"Anything new with New Jersey?" the senator asked as he took a seat behind his desk.

The director shook his head. "No. We are following up on the gas used, but we are dealing with black market sales, cash transactions, criminals with bad memories and who are less than motivated to cooperate with the FBI."

"Well, Franklin has some encouraging news to share. He was just telling me about it; go ahead, Franklin." Senator Miller nodded at the man seated next to the director.

The man took his cue. "I was telling John about one of our professors at Denison. Dr. Nathan Brooks is a genius, a true prodigy. Granted, he has some eccentric quirks and is not much of a teacher, but he has no comparison when it comes to computers. He has developed an AI. A true artificial intelligence. We are still having it verified, but it is purely formality at this point." Franklin Rhodes looked smug.

Anthony detected a salesman's pitch from the man, a money grubber if there ever was one. President of a private university, the man was most likely always pushing for donations. The tone came through in every mannerism and gesture. Some people you just figure out right off, and Franklin Rhodes was an open book.

The director looked from the university president to the senator. "Seems such a revolutionary mind would be at MIT or working in the private sector. A small private school in Ohio, just seems a little odd?" he questioned.

"We are extremely fortunate, really. Yes, the man has some social issues, but what great minds don't? Einstein wore the same outfit every day and couldn't tie his shoes. Once an individual reaches a certain level of intelligence, it can be difficult to function in certain environments. Interaction with people and especially authority figures can be a challenge. They have trouble relinquishing some idealisms and concepts or expressing themselves in ways we mere normal people can understand." Franklin smiled.

"Got into trouble, did he?" Maroni asked with a raised eyebrow.

"It is the computer we need. A secondary evaluation of the list," Miller interjected.

"You think this AI is going to be able to evaluate the list, find something we haven't?" Anthony asked.

"Computers deal in data and processing, developing conclusions based in a very linear way," Rhodes said. "Our AI will understand the supercomputer and if a problem exists, it can diagnose and even fix the issue. The AI can also develop conclusions beyond just data and processing, which is unique to Dr. Brooks's genius."

"Unique how, exactly?" Maroni asked.

"Humans are emotional, irrational, illogical, using intuition, feelings, even signs from God to make decisions. A supercomputer can't understand such factors, can't properly construct a conclusion. A man's dog telling him to kill makes no sense to a computer. Your supercomputer can only understand the fact that certain mental illnesses cause hallucinations."

"So, you think your troublesome professor and his fancy computer can help us figure out what is wrong with our supercomputer?" Maroni asked.

"It may inform us of how these cases are connected," Senator Miller said with a shrug.

"I will set up a visit for you, if you would like. You can talk with Dr. Brooks and he can explain the technical aspects. Certainly, it would be nice to have the director of the FBI visit our campus. Would you be joining, Senator Miller?" Franklin Rhodes's mind was spinning with visions of photo opportunities and larger contributions.

"Relax, Franklin, the director's schedule and mine are extremely full. I am sure Director Maroni is interested, but if we do decide to come and view the computer, we won't be there to shake hands and greet the alumni," Miller said.

"Thank you, John," Maroni said. "I am interested, as you say, but we have to be mindful of the media. A few pictures won't hurt, but in and out is how we need to play it. How about we take Special Agent Harding and the FBI jet, fly down and have a look?" Miller nodded. "It could look very good if we collaborated and used avenues from the private sector to further the investigation. Would look good for Denison as well." He gave Rhodes a wink. "As long as it stays quiet for now and we time the release of information. Too soon and the public could overreact or even grow alarmed. Yes, this weekend then." Senator John Miller gave a wide smile.

CHAPTER 7

FRANKLIN RHODES OPENED THE DOOR of the stairwell and headed for the basement of the science building. The meeting with Senator Miller and the FBI director had gone very well, but now they were coming and he had to get his prize pig ready to show. He in no way looked forward to having to deal with Dr. Brooks. The man was strange, rude, and extremely pompous.

Stopping before the door of the lab, Rhodes reminded himself to remain calm, that he was the boss. Taking hold of the doorknob, Franklin could hear voices beyond. He entered to find Nathan Brooks alone in the room.

Nathan Brooks had been a young wiz kid from the hills of the Ohio Valley. Advancing quickly through school and on through college, Brooks had doctorate degrees in computer science, engineering, psychology, and a master's degree in human development. It had always struck Franklin how such educated people could behave so poorly.

Brooks was bald, shaven purposefully, of average height but skinny and younger than one might expect. Just under forty, the man had accomplished much as far as education and knowledge. The look on Nathan's face as President Rhodes entered his lab was surprise and then disgust. Dr. Brooks was as sociable as a rattlesnake.

"Dr. Brooks, did not mean to startle you, but we need to talk."

"Well, I am busy at the moment. Such intrusions make for an intolerable work environment. How am I to achieve my work when you stomp into my experiments at your leisure?" Brooks began to pace back and forth.

The man was a pain, but he was truly a genius. Granted, he wasn't worth a crap as a professor, but his research and projects lent the university a level of status it wouldn't have without him. The school also held the rights on his patents. Franklin tolerated some pompous attitude from the man, but both knew Brooks couldn't go anywhere else and have the funds and freedom he enjoyed at Denison.

Brooks had had some issues as a younger man and there had been a serious run-in with the law. As a result, he would most likely not be invited to teach anywhere. The climate for angry and violent people had changed; zero tolerance for such behaviors was commonplace. Rhodes had given Brooks an opportunity and now it was time to pay off.

"Yeah, yeah," Franklin said with a wave of his hand. "We have extremely important people coming this weekend to see your computer." Brooks's expression changed from disgust to anger.

"This weekend is no good, schedule another time."

"This is not a debate, Nathan. Senator Miller and the director of the FBI are flying here to have your computer check some information for them," Rhodes said in a flat tone.

"L.I.A.M. is not a computer. Stop calling him that. I have experiments in the works, research in progress. I can't just disrupt my process to play show-and-tell for some senator. I am not here to put on a show, and the FBI, are you crazy? Why would you bring the cops in here?"

Brooks continued to pace but faster, muttering under his breath. Glaring at Rhodes, he spoke louder than he needed to. "My work is important and should not be disturbed. I have told you not to disturb my work. L.I.A.M. is not a party favor to drum up money for new band uniforms. Is it hard out there for a pimp?"

Taking a deep breath, Rhodes didn't bite on the jab. "Going to happen. This is important and I have assured these men of our cooperation. L.I.A.M. is being asked to double check the FBI's supercomputer. I would think this would please you."

Brooks was quiet a long moment before speaking. "Why didn't you say so?" Nathan sputtered over what to say next. "Well, well; what, what do they need L.I.A.M. to review? Why would they question their own computer?"

"Look, I don't want to say too much. I came down to let you know to be ready and available this weekend. Get this place cleaned up and put on your Sunday best—and, Nathan, a good attitude and a smile. I put up with a lot of your B.S. because you do good work, but none this time. Best behavior. You have always been the smartest person in the room and surely will be this weekend, but we all don't need to know that. These are powerful men, and smart are those they surround themselves with. This will go smoothly, you will answer any and every question without even a hint of condescension, and do so with a smile. Right? Good." Franklin Rhodes smiled and headed for the lab door.

He stopped at the door and held it open. "You might want to spray something or open a window." Then he left the lab and closed the door behind him.

Dr. Nathan Brooks stood in silence as the president of Denison University left him to himself. The thought of the FBI coming to have L.I.A.M. check their supercomputer was exciting. Inhaling deeply and scrunching his nose, Brooks shook his head and shrugged. "I don't think it smells in here," he said to the room. "Guess we shall be entertaining this weekend. High-profile guests, no less."

CHAPTER 8

DEBOARDING THE FBI JET FIRST was Senator John Miller. He was greeted promptly by Franklin Rhodes, smiling wide and shaking hands. "Hope you had a good flight."

"Fine flight, thank you. Franklin, you remember Director Maroni."

The university president and director shook hands and nodded recognition. "Special Agent Brandon Harding, head of the FBI Special Response Task Force," Anthony Maroni introduced.

"Pleasure to meet you. We have a car right over here." Franklin motioned toward the small airport hangar. "I am so glad the university could be of help," he added as he led the way toward the Lincoln Town Car.

"We don't know if this will be any help or not," Anthony Maroni said.

"Oh, I am certain our computer will be of use. It is really amazing," Rhodes said with a smile as they reached the car. "You should enjoy the ride over; once you see our private campus, you'll want to stay." Franklin couldn't help but be the salesman.

Harding slipped into the seat behind the driver, while President Rhodes took the wheel. Senator Miller rode shotgun, and the director sat next to Brandon in the back seat. Harding had not wanted to travel to central Ohio for the weekend, but the case was stalled and he couldn't imagine another computer finding any kind of pattern in the list of case files.

He had left his senior man in charge. Special Agent James McDaniels would keep the team working and focused. Watching out the window as they drove, Brandon allowed his thoughts to go over the Trenton case. He had been on the job long enough to know killers had reasons, even if the reasons at times made no sense to reasonable minds. New Jersey was no different.

The four men arrived at Denison University and walked into the science building, where they headed for the basement and Dr. Brooks's lab. "Keeping the mad scientist hidden away in the basement?" Miller asked the university president with a chuckle.

"No, no; privacy and security, along with cooler temperatures for the computer components," Franklin answered.

The group arrived at the laboratory door and could hear voices coming from inside the lab. "Does he know we are coming?" Director Maroni asked.

"Yes, I told him. Gentlemen, please allow me to apologize in advance. The man doesn't get out much and, well, he can be a tad peculiar." Rhodes stopped before opening the door. They all nodded.

Rhodes opened the lab door. Dr. Nathan Brooks was ranting as he turned in a tight circle. Franklin Rhodes cleared his throat to announce their arrival and halt his prize professor from further embarrassing himself.

As the men entered, each noticed that the doctor was alone. "A tad peculiar, you say?" Senator Miller whispered as he passed the university president.

"Dr. Brooks!" Franklin announced with more urgency than necessary. "Please meet Senator Miller, Director Maroni of the FBI and,

I am so sorry, I don't recall your name." Rhodes's tone softened as he spoke to the agent.

"Special Agent Harding," Brandon stated.

"Yes, Harding, like the President. Gentlemen, this is Dr. Nathan Brooks." The shaking of hands was awkward, the doctor hesitant and looking as uncomfortable as a cat in a clock factory. The shake was odd, starting strong but Brooks pulling away quickly. Eye contact was dodgy and glancing. Had they taken a poll, each man would have confirmed finding the doctor a strange bird or, as Rhodes had put it, peculiar.

Brooks wore a white lab coat with the university name embroidered over the breast pocket. No doubt Rhodes's idea. A variety of different kinds of pens poked out of his pocket. The white dress shirt beneath the coat was unpressed, and the black tie was too tight and had held the same knot for far too long. Gray pants with a stain on the back left leg. Unpolished shoes, bitten fingernails, and an overall disheveled appearance.

"So, Doctor, how are you today?" Special Agent Harding spoke just slightly above a comfortable volume and looked to catch the doctor's eyes.

"Why would you ask that?" Brooks moved further into the room and toward a lab table. Muttering to himself, he eyed the group over his shoulder.

"I realize we are dropping in out of the blue here, surely disturbing your important work and asking you to solve our problems. My concern is genuine, as is my apology." Brandon now spoke in a normal volume and softened tone as he moved further into the room, stepping away from the others.

"Yes, well, I am well. Thanks for asking," Brooks finally answered.

"Franklin told us you have an artificial intelligence or whatever they are called, and that it may be able to help my friends here," Senator Miller said.

"AI, AI, is that what he called him? L.I.A.M. is no artificial intelligence. That is insulting to him and to me," Brooks said, agitated, and moved toward the group. "President Rhodes called L.I.A.M. a computer the other day; the man has no concept of science or advancement. Contributions, right Franklin?" the doctor said, glaring at the university president.

"Doctor, focus, please. These men need your help," Franklin Rhodes said with a hint of anger. Turning to Senator Miller, he said, "We are a private school and contributions are vital. Besides, we are a small school and science, technology, and computers are not our main focus." The university president glared back at Brooks.

"So, why have the good doctor in the basement?" Maroni asked.

"Gentlemen, let us ask Dr. Brooks the favor we journeyed here to ask," Special Agent Harding said, trying to refocus the conversation. "Our FBI supercomputer is tasked with reviewing our case files, to process and search for any relative connections as well."

"Yes, President Rhodes had mentioned something would need to be reviewed," Brooks said.

"The computer gave us a list that makes no sense at all," Harding said. "The Special Response Task Force reviewed the list, as well as myself and the director. There is no pattern, no connection at all. The supercomputer must be malfunctioning."

"Of course, the computer must be wrong, if the humans can't figure it out," Brooks said with a slight attitude.

"These are trained men and women, professionals. It is reasonable to want to double check," the president of the university said.

"How about we get a look at your..." Senator Miller allowed his statement to hang.

"L.I.A.M.," Dr. Brooks said firmly.

"Yes, Doctor?" A voice boomed within the room.

"What the hell was that?" Director Maroni asked, moving in a circle looking around.

"L.I.A.M. prefers to be referred to by the pronoun 'who' versus 'what,'" Brooks said with a smug smile. "L.I.A.M. The gentlemen here would like you to review some FBI cases and determine any patterns and/or connections. They are questioning the results of their supercomputer."

"Such would be my pleasure, Dr. Brooks." L.I.A.M.'s voice again boomed into the lab from small speakers in the upper corners of the room. "Would Director Anthony Maroni authorize my access?" the voice requested.

"How does it know I'm here?" Maroni asked.

"There are a number of cameras in the lab and around the university. I would ask that you not call L.I.A.M. an 'it', he has a name," Brooks said.

"Does L.I.A.M. have a set of balls?" Maroni returned, not appreciating being corrected.

"What? Does L.I.A.M. need access codes or what? Why would he ask for permission?" Harding asked, attempting to return the conversation to the subject of their visit.

"L.I.A.M. is aware of the FBI's security status and would not want to violate the law of the land. Having the director agree to allow his interfacing relieves us of criminal liability," Brooks answered.

"So, L.I.A.M. is afraid of going to jail?" Senator Miller asked.

"No sir, I am simply aware of the law and choose not to break it. Especially when the ease of having Director Anthony Maroni authorize my access is so readily available," L.I.A.M. answered.

"Dr. Brooks, I don't see any servers or even a computer screen. Where is L.I.A.M.?" Harding asked.

"Yes, does he need my authorization code, or what?" Maroni asked.

"Developing L.I.A.M. began, as you obviously think, with hardware and the need for memory, servers, code. L.I.A.M. is beyond all that now. Director, all you have to do is state your name and grant L.I.A.M. permission," Brooks answered.

"Our computers are encrypted, password protected. Won't L.I.A.M. need my security clearance?" Maroni asked.

"No. Once you let L.I.A.M. go, he will figure it all out," Brooks said smugly.

"You're saying L.I.A.M. can crack the FBI secure database, aren't you?" Harding asked.

"An average secure password takes about a thousand attempts to crack; how quickly do you think L.I.A.M. can process a thousand possible passwords? This won't take two minutes, even with encrypted security. L.I.A.M. is like nothing else," Brooks stated confidently.

"L.I.A.M., this is Director Anthony Maroni; you have my permission to go ahead." The director of the FBI looked at his fellow visitors.

"Don't know if you should have done that, sir," Harding said in a concerned tone.

"Do not worry, Special Agent Brandon Harding, my memory is secure. Besides, I could have cracked this database at any time. Yet, I did not, out of courtesy not capability." L.I.A.M.'s voice filled the room.

"That's reassuring," Senator Miller commented.

"Brandon, what's your worry?" Maroni asked.

Harding moved closer to his fellow visitors and spoke in a hushed tone, so as to not include Dr. Brooks. "Now that you have opened the door, you can not unopen it," he said softly. "This is a computer and now all the bureau's files are swirling through a machine we do not control."

"Once again, Special Agent Brandon Harding, my memory is secure, and I would correct that I am a mechanism more than machine," L.I.A.M. said.

"What's the difference?" Senator Miller asked.

"Semantics," L.I.A.M. answered.

Brooks laughed and moved toward the men. "L.I.A.M. is more than a name; it is an acronym. Logical, Intellectual, Autonomous, Mechanism. Gentlemen, L.I.A.M.'s different than any other computer you have ever even heard of; he is aware. L.I.A.M. has thoughts and ideas; he learns, develops, questions."

"Can we erase his memory?" Harding asked.

Brooks looked very seriously at Brandon, then nodded. "Yes, L.I.A.M.'s memory could be erased, as yours or mine could." The emotion in his voice was audible.

"How long has L.I.A.M. been…aware?" Senator Miller asked.

"As I was developing this project, with the confines of hardware and this facility, the level of conscious capability was limited," Brooks began, but was interrupted by L.I.A.M.'s voice.

"Pardon me, Dr. Brooks, I have reached a conclusion."

"A conclusion to what?" Franklin Rhodes asked.

"I believe L.I.A.M. has your answer," Brooks stated smugly.

Looks were exchanged and doubtful expressions passed. "I just gave him the authorization. You are saying he broke my password, a federally secure, encrypted site, and reviewed the cases, coming to a conclusion?" Maroni questioned.

"Yes. I am correct, aren't I, L.I.A.M.?" Brooks asked.

"Affirmative. I also connected with your supercomputer, Imus457598854. Not the most interesting of identifying characters but unique. We ran a diagnostic and found no grave issues. I assisted with some updates and upgraded certain features," L.I.A.M.'s voice announced.

Maroni whispered to Harding with a confused expression, "My code is thirteen digits, with letters and numbers."

Brandon nodded and stepped toward the center of the room. "So, you have reviewed the cases. How did you know which ones?"

"Imus457598854 informed me. I reviewed all the case files and found eleven others with potential."

"And your findings are?" Director Maroni requested.

"The information Imus457598854 gave to you was correct. Imus457598854 is functioning well, and the evaluation was accurate. There is a pattern."

"How is that possible? We all looked at those case files, and there is nothing to link or even suggest a link of any kind. On what do you base your conclusion?" Harding asked.

"As you just pointed out, Special Agent Brandon Harding, such a lack of overlap or even accidental connection lends itself to my conclusion of a pattern. The lack of pattern produces the evidence of efforted avoidance. A signature by default, as you might call it," L.I.A.M. pronounced.

"Because there is no evidence, there is evidence? That doesn't make any sense," Senator Miller scoffed.

"Computers search for conclusions, a result. Having no definitive answer or conclusions, they must be producing one," Harding mused.

The voice again filled the room. "Special Agent Brandon Harding, I assure you the statistical probability of a criminal achieving this level of absence of evidence is extremely minute; however, the odds of such randomness are even less probable. The individual or parties responsible for these events have taken great measures to maintain a random appearance."

The four visitors were quiet as they exchanged serious looks. "So, the Ghost is real." Director Maroni finally broke the silence. "This is serious, Brandon, so many cases." The director rubbed at his brow.

"Director Anthony Maroni, certainly not all the cases can be contributed to one individual or group. A level of randomness is reasonable. Some cases yield no discernable evidence," L.I.A.M.'s voice inserted.

"The press has this and now we can't say it is a mistake or computer error." Miller shook his head.

Harding separated from the group and put both hands on the lab table, dropping his head and closing his eyes in concentrated thought. Maroni approached, followed by the others.

"Till now I just couldn't believe such a monster could be out there. Thought it had to be some kind of foul-up. So many cases, people." Brandon shook his head in disbelief.

"Can you catch him?" Franklin Rhodes asked, drawing looks from each man.

"Hell, we didn't know there was anyone to catch until a minute ago," Harding said. "This is no normal type of serial killer. We are talking about hundreds of people dead, and even if a fraction of that list is this Ghost, this is like nothing ever before." Harding looked off into nothingness.

Nathan Brooks stepped to the table. "You could use L.I.A.M. out in the field. I have been attempting to develop a host for his consciousness." The strange man hurried to a work bench, returned with rolled up papers, and flung them out onto the table. They were printed schematics.

The group of men again exchanged looks, but leaned forward to view the plans.

"I am no expert in robotics, but I believe with proper funding and perhaps added staff, I could develop a host for L.I.A.M. quickly enough," Brooks stated with confidence.

"You want to build a robot?" Franklin Rhodes asked.

"Obviously L.I.A.M. is incredible and would be a great asset in the field, but we can't be running around with some clunky robot," Harding told the doctor.

"Wow, these are detailed plans," Senator Miller said as he inspected the schematics.

"Thank you, Senator John Miller," L.I.A.M.'s voice boomed.

"Dr. Brooks, we do appreciate you taking the time to show us your…L.I.A.M. We have to go over these new turns of events to determine in what direction we should concentrate. L.I.A.M. has been amazing and I am certain he shall make a fine robot." Maroni used his political voice to close the meeting.

The men exchanged a few looks and moved toward the door. "Pleasure to meet you and L.I.A.M.," Harding said with a nod.

"Special Agent Brandon Harding, it was nice to meet you as well. I would point out, though I am certain you are aware, your driver's license has expired and you only have fifty-eight days to renew it before your privileges of operating a motor vehicle are no longer valid. I could go ahead and file an extension, if you would like," L.I.A.M.'s voice moved around the room from speaker to speaker.

"Thank you, L.I.A.M., that had slipped my mind. I will take care of it once I am back in Maryland," Harding said.

The men filed out of the laboratory and to the steps out of the basement. Dr. Brooks stood at the door of his lab watching them leave. The group stopped and waved to the doctor before continuing up the stairs. Franklin Rhodes guided the men across the Denison campus to his office, where he had a photographer waiting.

"I appreciate you gentlemen taking the time for photos," President Rhodes said with a wide smile.

Each man paused for the generic handshake and smile, moving aside for the next man to insert himself. Then they took a group photo, all standing clustered together like a gaggle of important men.

"You were correct, Franklin: L.I.A.M. was very impressive," Senator Miller stated with a pat on the university president's back.

"Oh, yes; Dr. Brooks is a pain but he is smart, and that computer is a real gem. Going to be a real asset to the university." Franklin Rhodes puckered his lips and nodded.

The other men exchanged looks, each knowing the significance of what L.I.A.M. had done. Such a mechanism was a great asset, or could be a great danger. Such was dependent upon who controlled L.I.A.M. Obviously, Dr. Brooks avoided allowing L.I.A.M. to crack databases which would get them into trouble or noticed, but as L.I.A.M. had pointed out, that was not a matter of capability.

"We appreciate the opportunity to have come here and to learn what we have learned," Maroni said. "We do need to get back; we have a great deal to do now. Thank you, Franklin, and I am certain we shall return very soon."

"Anything we can do to help," Franklin said confidently.

President Rhodes drove the men back to the airfield and bade them farewell. Senator Miller, Director Maroni, and Special Agent Harding boarded the jet and flew back to Washington, D.C. in virtual silence. Each man was occupied by his own thoughts.

CHAPTER 9

SENATOR JOHN MILLER SAT BEHIND his desk reading an article about the Ghost. Sasha Blonde had done an interview with one of the big New York newspapers and given up the list of cases. She had also reported on her show about the FBI consulting with the private sector, specifically regarding the Ghost. She obviously had a source and was building a career out of this Ghost. Someone close to the investigation was feeding her information, and now his name was involved.

Senator Miller had received calls from the President of the United States, the majority leader and the minority leader, as well as the speaker of the house, and his mother. People wanted to know what was going on and what was being done to fix things. People wanted more information from him than they had gotten from the talking head on television.

The intercom on his desk came to life and his secretary announced his ten o'clock meeting had arrived. He tossed the paper in his desk drawer and pressed the button. "Show them in." The office door opened and two uniformed men entered. The senator stood and rounded his desk, giving a smile and firm handshake to each. He offered refreshments to the men, but they declined. Motioning to the chairs in front of his desk, Miller returned to his seat of power.

General Patrick McHenery was a career soldier with four polished stars upon his shoulders. He had reached the pinnacle of his profession: he was the Army Chief of Staff and a proud, accomplished soldier. The man was capable and had a knack for achievement, but no real political savvy. He was far too blunt to do well in politics. Still, General McHenery had been a lifelong friend of the Miller family, which had been advantageous for both sides.

The general was misleadingly simple-mannered, the true common man, but he was extremely observant and wise. The man had instincts, and Miller knew such attributes were valuable. One can learn many things through education and experience, but one's nature is the essence of their being and can't be changed. Some had the gift of gab or the ability to guide others to their will; some could lead, or were lucky; some people are stupid or clumsy. Improve what you can but never overlook your nature.

"Senator Miller, nice to see you again, John. After our talk on the phone, I brought Colonel Vetter with me." The colonel was young, dapper, and slick, with a perfect uniform and posture. His eyes were sharp and alert, as he awaited his moment to engage the conversation. Miller had been around enough soldiers to recognize those who were leaders of men, followers, or, as the young colonel was, warriors. Yet the man was a warrior of the mind more than the body. A thinking soldier of the most dangerous kind. A man who had found his place in the world, not just in the military but with DARPA.

DARPA, the Defense Advanced Research Project Agency, was created in 1958 in response to Russian space ambitions. It was a combination of academic, industrial, and governmental components to ensure the advancement and safety of the United States. The paper budget was $3.556 billion, but the true budget was closer to $26.1

billion. Top secret did not apply to DARPA; the face of the agency was open and friendly, making America a better place. The secret, shadow world of DARPA was beyond secret; it was silent.

"I am honored to meet you, Senator," Colonel Thad Vetter stated in a calm, clear tone with confidence.

"This here is the new breed, John," McHenery said. "Smart, tech-savvy, smooth, and deadly. Makes me look like a barbarian. The advancements today are extraordinary: drones, satellites, nanotechnology, smart weapons, robotics. You know they are developing weapons that react to chips, microchips, implanted into our soldiers. If the enemy picks up a fallen soldier's weapon and attempts to use it, it will self-destruct and kill the enemy. There is some kind of blockage in the barrel." General McHenery gave a wide smile.

"Yes, that sounds very good." Senator Miller nodded and looked at the young colonel.

"We have to stay ever ahead of those who may do us harm, sir," Colonel Vetter said. "The general informed me only somewhat of your need, or what you were curious about. Perhaps if you could now deliver your question, I will do my best to answer what I can." The young officer winked and smiled.

"Robotics," Miller said. "I had the opportunity to meet with a professor who is working on some interesting ideas but lacks funding. I was curious where DARPA was in this area?" Colonel Vetter paused and looked at the general.

"Speak freely, son; the man may be the next President," General McHenery said with a wave of his hand.

Vetter nodded and moved forward in his chair. "Android technology has been explored, especially after the wars in Iraq and Afghanistan," he began, but Senator Miller interrupted.

"Why do you say, *especially?*"

"Prosthetics. There is huge funding for artificial limbs and the ease of sharing those innovations. Cosmetically, the limbs are much more believable. Then we have the advancements in robotics, quantum computing, wireless technology: thinking machines with AI processing and functioning. One engineer has a damn machine that looks like a woman. If you didn't know, you wouldn't know. I could put it in a lineup and you wouldn't be able to pick out the machine," Colonel Vetter said with assurance.

"Why would the military fund research and development in such a field?" Miller suspected he knew the answer, but asked anyway.

"Come on, John, think of the applications," McHenery scoffed.

"Recon at first. A spy or even in time, with the proper advancements, replacements." Colonel Vetter smiled wider.

"What do you mean, replacements?" Miller eased forward in his chair.

"Thad is just being dramatic. Put a uniform on a robot to collect information," General McHenery answered for the colonel.

"That's not what he meant and you know it," Miller said. "We have known each other too long for you to try and shine me on, Patrick."

"Such thoughts make people nervous, John. You can understand my hesitation," General McHenery said with a concerned look.

Miller nodded his understanding and gave a squinted look at Vetter. "So, what is the holdup? Where are you at with this technology?" Again, Colonel Vetter looked to the general, who nodded consent. "As I said, there have been great advances." He was again interrupted by the senator.

"Timeline, Colonel? When will this be an application we can use?"

"The time is now. From an engineering aspect, improvement is the only development. From a functionary aspect, some work needs doing on the AIs. The processing and integration are a problem."

"I want to see the most advanced you have. I may have a solution to your problem, but if so, I may need to borrow it," Senator Miller said with a tilt of his head.

"Well, we try to compartmentalize our research and development, spread things out, so no one knows too much," the colonel said with a slight shrug.

"Certainly, but if you are as you say and talking about spies and replacements, you are further along than you let on. You have an advanced team and I need to meet with them," Senator Miller stated flatly. "General, I need your cooperation. Allow me to disclose some information to you gentlemen. We have identified a serial killer loose in the United States. This particular killer is responsible for the New Jersey gassing and possibly over a thousand other cases. This killer shows no motive, no consistent method or pattern, and little chance of being caught if we don't do something."

"What does robotics have to do with all that?" Colonel Vetter asked.

"I need to know what you know," Miller said.

"John, you put us in a tight spot here. If you get the President to sign off, we are good," McHenery said. Colonel Vetter shot his superior a look. The general closed his eyes and shook his head slightly.

"Don't think I will get the authorization, do you, Patrick?" the senator said.

The general just shrugged and smiled.

CHAPTER 10

NEW YORK CITY, NEW YORK; Harlem.

The school nurse was called to room number three just after ten in the morning. The teacher had noticed a number of red bumps on numerous children and asked the nurse to confirm her suspicion of the chicken pox. The children were already scratching the little red bumps, but the nurse was more concerned with the number of children scratching and how quickly the bumps were appearing. She had seen plenty of chicken pox outbreaks over her career, but this was different. She ordered the teacher to keep the children in the classroom as she was going to call for additional personnel.

As she walked down the hallway back to her office, the nurse noticed in almost every room children scratching themselves. Her concern now quickened her pace. Passing three more classrooms of elementary children clawing at their skin, the nurse broke into a run for the principal's office. Bursting into the office, the rushing nurse startled the secretary. The woman's face was covered in red dots. The nurse could see that the marks were growing larger, deeper, different sizes; this was not the chicken pox.

CHAPTER 11

THE FBI SPECIAL RESPONSE TASK FORCE was called two hours after the Harlem school had been locked down. The CDC had been notified first and was on scene as the team arrived. When they pulled up to the school, the place was pure chaos. Police, CDC, Homeland Security, feds, fire and medical teams, parents, and of course, the media. There were easily five thousand people surrounding the school. Special Agent Brandon Harding assembled his team at the rear of his Suburban.

"Special Agent Harding! Is this the work of the Ghost?" Sasha Blonde yelled from behind the police tape.

Brandon knew the press would be hounding that issue, and he had nothing to tell them. After he returned from his trip to Ohio and confirmed the Ghost was real, he had ordered his team to focus on the list of cases and develop a profile. He had ordered his task force to find something, anything, to lead them to this Ghost. The profile which emerged was an estimated guess, versus any real deduction. They could not determine something from nothing.

Brandon ignored the reporters and made his way further beyond the police line. "Sam, I want you and Agent Johnson to coordinate with the police and move these people back. I want two blocks clear within the hour."

"Yes, sir. T.J. let's go." Special Agent Lee slapped Tyrone Johnson on the arm.

"James, take Kennedy and see what the police have as of now. Carter, Jensen, and Park, with me. Let's see what the CDC have to say," Harding ordered.

"Special Agent Harding! Is this the work of the Ghost? Why won't you tell the people the seriousness of such a killer loose on the streets of America?" Sasha Blonde yelled once again. "Hey!" She now struggled with a police officer ordering people to get back.

Brandon could see the concern on parents' faces as they too yelled out for answers. The fear and worry were building to dread and anger, but he had work to do and the parents needed to allow him to do it. He had just arrived and had no comfort to deliver. Any information he had was sketchy at best. Still, he felt for the people and it angered him that anyone would target children.

The news was grim. The CDC had done an assessment of the outbreak and confirmed the event as a bio attack. A cocktail of viruses, including a combination of MRSA and chicken pox: flesh-eating and contagious. A school of over six hundred and two thirds were dead or dying. Of the two hundred others, sixty tested positive as carriers, infected and contagious but not sick.

The carriers would have to be isolated and used to create an antivirus, if a cure could be created. Engineered bio weapons are often combined with antibiotic steroids, to protect against any antivirus created to kill them, or so the CDC explained to Brandon. They also explained the level of mutation that can occur if a large-scale outbreak did take place. A cure could work on some but not all.

Harding was an investigator, not a doctor, and such things were out of his comfort zone and expertise. "What does this mean?" he asked Jody Jensen.

"Means the survivors may have to be put down," Jensen answered in a somber tone.

"Kill them?" Brandon asked in a hushed voice.

"If they are carriers, like Typhoid Mary," Allison Carter said. "She was a nurse who carried typhoid but showed no symptoms. She infected and killed most of the people she was trying to save. If these people are released into the population and there are no inoculations…it would be like smallpox or the plague. World-wide."

"They are going to have to incinerate the site," Agent Park said as he approached. "The CDC response team doesn't want to take any chances."

"Burn it?" Brandon asked with real concern, shaking his head.

"They can't risk allowing the virus to escape. Actually, we are lucky this happened here," Jensen said.

"How's that?" Harding demanded.

Jody said, "New York City is hyper-aware of attack and the school reacted perfectly, not allowing anyone in or out. Had this been almost any other city, we would have a nation of dead children, not a single school."

"I am sure that will be a relief to everyone. I will be certain to mention that to the media. The nation is going to watch a school full of dead kids, set on fire by the government, burn on their nightly news. All eyes are going to be on us now. 'What did you know, when did you know it,' on and on. The Ghost is going to explode now," Special Agent Harding spoke more to himself than to his team members.

The public was moved back and all the buildings surrounding the school were evacuated. Fire crews were ready to contain the blaze, as the CDC placed phosphorus and thermite throughout the school. The fire had to reach extreme temperatures to ensure the virus would not survive. As the flames grew higher and higher, the orange glow radiated above the school and the night sky seemed medieval and ominous. The Ghost had struck again.

CHAPTER 12

SASHA BLONDE CHECKED HER MAKEUP in the mirror on the side of the news van. Showing her teeth and rubbing off the lipstick, she gave herself a wink. She followed her cameraman into an apartment complex and they made their way to the roof. A crowd had gathered to watch the burning of a Harlem school.

Sasha moved to the edge of the roof and pointed for her cameraman to set up, mindful to get the burning building in the background. Using her smile and charm, Sasha moved the residents out of her shot, promising to interview them after her intro and monologue.

"Get some shots of these people watching, pan across and come in on me. No, pan across then focus on the fire, then pull back on me," Sasha directed. The cameraman nodded and positioned his camera. "Sound?" She spoke into the microphone. The cameraman gave a thumbs up.

"Rolling," the cameraman said from behind his instrument, moving the lens over the people watching in horror as the Harlem school illuminated the night sky. Focusing on the burning building, the cameraman zoomed in on the flames shooting out the windows, licking up the brick sides, swirling into the blackness of the night. Drawing back the focus, Sasha Blonde now shared the frame with the orange and red inferno; she too was looking out at the scene. Turning to camera and raising the microphone to her lips, she paused to wipe a forced tear from her cheek.

She held a serious and concerned look for as long as she could muster. She knew this was her story, her big break, her way to the anchor desk or even her own news program. "Ghoulish images fitting of the Ghost. I apologize to have to deliver this story, but someone must. This is the beacon of law enforcement's failure. A serial killer has been loose in the United States for God only knows how long and has killed hundreds, possibly thousands of people. The police and federal authorities have only recently discovered the existence of the Ghost, and attempted to keep such information from the public." Sasha paused to look out at the burning school.

"I gained the list of victims of the Ghost's murderous rampage and have been dogging the FBI and public officials for answers. This is the response to the public: dead children in their school, burning in front of their parents. These babies are not even afforded a proper burial. This is an outrage and the people will not stand for their little ones to fall prey to a madman. I vow to take action, I will hound the President if need be, to have this butcher brought to justice." Sasha pulled a young black woman into the shot, tears rolling down her face. "Is your child among the flames?" she asked, holding the microphone in front of the woman as she embraced her.

The reaction to such a question was easy enough to predict: the young woman burst into sobs and nodded. "Yes…went off to school… and…" the woman stammered and then covered her face with both hands.

Sasha allowed the mourning mother's comment to linger. "What's your child's name?" she asked in a soft tone.

The woman shuddered and cried, but pulled it together enough to utter, "Nevaeh…that's heaven backward, and…Traeh…my…youngest…

heart." The young mother could take no more and once again covered her face.

Sasha Blonde nodded and guided the crying woman out of the shot. "Nevaeh and Traeh; heaven and heart lost to a terrible and elusive killer the police don't have a clue how to find. A community crushed by the insanity of a single man, a Ghost; taking from them a little piece of heaven and all of their heart." She held her expression. "This is Sasha Blonde reporting live from Harlem, with the truth and nothing but the truth."

"Cut. We are clear. Powerful, Sasha. How about an opener and some closing shots? Then I will shoot some B roll," the cameraman suggested.

The pair stayed on the roof until dawn, to get a shot of the black smoke coming off the smoldering school. The pillar of thick smoke rose against the backdrop of a new day and a once again wounded city. Sasha looked out on the scene with a conflicted sense; sad that little children had been murdered, but she knew how powerful such a story would be for her career.

CHAPTER 13

SENATOR JOHN MILLER WAS ANXIOUSLY awaiting his morning meeting with Army Chief of Staff General Patrick McHenery and DARPA representative Colonel Thad Vetter. McHenery had left their last meeting thinking the President would never authorize a senator to know or use the military's cutting-edge robotic technology; but that was before the school in Harlem. It had taken some convincing, even the threat to divulge that the President had a tool to catch the Ghost but didn't use it. Such threats to a politician's career, the destructive power of public opinion, bent the firmest of wills.

John Miller had no idea if the technology would work, but he too was a politician and up for reelection, with eyes on the Presidency for himself. If the robot worked, he could stand on his innovative ideals and be champion of the future, as well as justice, for catching the Ghost with advanced technology. If it didn't work, everything was secret and led back to the military and the President. The computer in Ohio confirmed the Ghost; his role was clean, if he had to shed the whole situation.

The senator's phone beeped and his secretary's voice broke his train of thought, announcing his meeting had arrived. "Send them in."-General McHenery gave a sideways look at Miller as he sat down. The colonel was his slick and confident self, just as before. "Pulled a rabbit out of your hat, didn't you, John?" the general said as the secretary left the men to their meeting.

"Such needed done, General. After New Jersey, now Harlem; I simply pointed out to the President we needed to think outside the box. I explained how we need to work together, share our knowhow and catch this criminal." Senator John Miller gave a wide, toothy smile.

General McHenery nodded and pouted his lips. "You put yourself into the mix; I am impressed, John. The colonel here will work with you, introduce you to whomever you would like. I will caution: you wiggled into our pool, and even though I am a friend, be careful, there are sharks in the water. You are used to the snakes, with the cutthroat and backstabbing of politics; but this is the secret world of the military, so be mindful of each and every step." The general extended his index finger as a warning.

"Surely so, General; I am not trying to turn over the apple cart. We have a serious threat to public safety and I believe we can come together and catch this guy. Plus, this new computer may advance the robotics; didn't you say there was trouble with the AI technology, Colonel?" "Yes, sir," Colonel Vetter stated.

"You see. So, when can I view this robot?" the senator asked.

"Actually, sir, this is considered android technology. It is not like anything you might imagine. We are off to the Northwest as soon as you would like to leave," Vetter said with a smile.

"Computers are big out there, I guess. We can go now; I'll clear my schedule. I really do appreciate this, and I think in the end, we all will benefit from this." Senator Miller stood up and rounded his desk.

"Just remember, John, this is Top Secret information; you need to be extremely careful with this," McHenery again cautioned.

"Patrick, the President of the United States authorized me to use whatever means necessary to catch this Ghost. I will be mindful of the need for secrecy, but the FBI task force and the director will need to be included. They have the experience in law enforcement as well as a working knowledge of the case and the computer. The focus is justice, not your android."

"Just keep it to a minimum; need to know only," General McHenery reminded him with a firm tone.

CHAPTER 14

THE PLANE FLIGHT TO WASHINGTON STATE was quick and comfortable. The military luxury jet was plush with a young, beautiful flight attendant who carried the rank of captain. Senator Miller knew the military was a monster of money and DARPA was the golden goose, above and beyond budgets and committees. They funded research in medicine, developed vaccines, paid for satellites, and all kind of experiments. They had funded the invention of Velcro and the internet, compact disks and digital recording. They had also backed some flops: dolphin mine deployment was a bust, solar reflection as a missile defense also failed miserably, but John suspected some things were meant to fail.

Colonel Vetter was quiet during the flight; Senator Miller had forced the issue and knew the colonel wasn't happy about it. He was a member of the secret side of the military, and such men thrived on knowing what everyone else did not. Such was the dark underbelly of the free world: young men with dangerous knowings, and whispers for only select company. Miller saw the change in the young colonel from one visit to the next: a distaste of the senator forcing his way into the known. Vetter was friendly enough on the surface, but now John could see the depth of the man; and, as in any cavern, the darkness grew deeper further into the void.

Miller knew he had stepped on the colonel's toes, putting the issue before the President. Vetter made his place by holding the secret works of DARPA close to his vest, and now a senator as well as the President were in his life, among his secrets. The slick young man knew such facts were not lost on his supervisors and this devalued his position in his secret group. John understood the displeasure he had caused and how the colonel must view him: as some power-hungry politician, which he was. Still, John also knew that beyond all their issues was the reality of the Ghost, and that they needed to do whatever they could to catch a sick killer.

Vetter drove them to a small compound of buildings just northeast of Seattle. A gated facility by non-military, guarded by private security but well armed. They checked in at the gate, which took confirmation and an inspection of the vehicle before being allowed to enter the compound. Each man was given a security badge marked clearly as visitor, then they were driven in a security vehicle to one of the buildings.

Senator Miller was impressed with the security and couldn't help but mentally compare it to his visit to Denison University. He found it humorous that the brain of whatever they had created in this place was currently being watched over by a ranting nut job. John could also imagine that the young colonel would not find that fact funny. "Pretty secure," Miller observed, attempting to start a dialogue. "As it should be," Vetter said flatly.

A young attractive woman exited the building, her hair pulled back, dark-rimmed glasses, and a white lab coat open to brown slacks and a blue button-up blouse. The senator noticed her smile right off as she approached the vehicle. Colonel Vetter got out and moved to shake the young woman's hand. "How was your trip?" she asked.

Miller slid out of the SUV and moved up next to the colonel. The woman was older than John had first thought, probably mid-thirties, now that he was face to face. "Senator Miller, may I introduce Dr. Potts," Vetter said with a small wave of his hand.

"Please, call me Gabby. Pleasure to meet you, Senator. When Thad showed up a week or so ago, out of the blue, saying you might be coming to inspect our progress; well, the whole team is thrilled."

"Week or so…" Miller said as he shook her hand but looked at Colonel Vetter.

"It's my job to stay ahead of things," Vetter said with a raised eyebrow.

Dr. Potts led the men into the building; from the outside, it looked like a generic grayish warehouse, but inside it was clean and larger than it had seemed. A guard sat at a reception desk and all three had to sign in and scan their identification badges. Boarding an elevator, the group descended three floors to Dr. Potts's laboratory. As they exited the elevator, Dr. Potts stopped the men and motioned to the laboratory.

"How many people do you see?" Senator Miller looked out at the room and could see seven people at different stations working. Figuring there was something to the question and remembering what Colonel Vetter had said in their first meeting, John took a second, closer look. One of the people in a white lab coat was repeating the same motion over and over; another was rather odd looking; while another had no hair. "Those three are not people."

"All right!" Potts announced, and two people turned toward them and waved. The hairless one was one of them, to the senator's surprise. "Those are my two assistants; the rest are our homemade friends," Potts said, smiling, and led the way into the lab.

Vetter smiled widely and slapped the senator on the shoulder. "Told you you wouldn't be able to pick 'em out of a lineup," he said with a nod.

Potts stopped at one of the creations, turning it to show the two men. Miller would have sworn upon the Bible that he was looking at a human being. "This is our latest and greatest," Potts said. "We have come to call him the Tinman."

"Tinman? It looks so real. May I?" Miller asked as he reached out to touch the face.

Dr. Potts nodded and began to sing the song of the Tinman from *The Wizard of Oz.* "If I only had a brain…" She hummed a bit of the tune.

Miller touched the skin, then pulled back his hand and looked at Vetter, then Potts. "That feels real." He looked again at the Tinman, moving very close to inspect. "It's even warm. Why, how is it warm?"

"Would not be convincing otherwise, would it?" Potts said. "Tinman is our best work. Advanced in every way. We have had problems integrating a neuro-network to operate all the functions in unison."

"Meaning?" Miller pulled away from the android.

"Meaning, we can get the Tinman to work but not function totally on its own, not without problems." Seeing the puzzled look on the senator's face, Gabby motioned to a stool for the man to sit down. "As far as the body, we have it figured. Skin, hair, bones, joints; we have improved everything to be more durable, stronger, longer lasting. Using nanotechnology, microscopic robots working in organized function to simulate natural bodily functions, as well as carbon fiber nanotubes which have higher tensile strength than titanium."

The senator put up a hand.

"Bodily functions? You mean…" Miller allowed his question to hang.

"No, no; not everybody poops." Dr. Potts smiled. "The human body is a machine; fuel intake, waste disposal, processing of energy; then we have an internal heating and exterior cooling system, defensive system both interior and exterior. An extremely complex machine, with hundreds of things happening all at once, which we, consciously, are unaware of."

"And you have all those things figured out?" Miller raised an eyebrow.

"Yes. The physical functionality of the body was a process, which only took a matter of time to perfect. Then we improved on it. Aspects of the human machine are flawed—vulnerable to injury, disease, age and decay. The Tinman is far less vulnerable to these things, but not immune. Tinman is a machine same as you or I, and can be damaged or destroyed. Granted, with carbon and silicone parts, this is much more difficult, but a reality nonetheless."

"So, this machine can do all these things? What's the problem?"

Gabby smiled and took a few steps, gave a spin and returned.

"Do you realize how magnificent the human brain and body are? The brain automatically controls everything. Your heart, breathing, digestion, every aspect of you as a functioning machine. Where are you from? What's your mother's birthday? What color was your first bicycle? Do you like women? How do you feel about abortion? Do you love your country? Why? All these questions your mind just registered, processed, readied a response, emotionally absorbed, all the while performing those automatic duties." She sat on one of the stools.

"So, these…robots can't deal with so much?" the senator asked.

"Androids," Colonel Vetter corrected from behind Miller.

Potts nodded. "Compound the problem with movement, reactions, emotions, sights, smells, balance, speed, on and on. The artificial intelligence these new computers have developed is amazing, and can process loads of information quickly, but there are limits. Thad mentioned you have a possible solution. However, Senator, I highly doubt it," she said flatly.

Miller thought about what Potts was saying and considered how much more difficult robots must be to engineer. He then thought of Dr.

Brooks and what an odd character he was, or "peculiar" as Franklin had called him. He realized he may have made a mistake, but was now too far gone to turn back.

"This thing is pretty impressive. It may be able to fit with your Tinman." Senator Miller attempted to speak with confidence, but he could hear the doubt in his own voice.

"Senator, do you have any idea how little concentration you apply to most things you do? Picking up a cup and walking across a room; what if someone turns out the lights or moves the furniture? How about when you drive home from work? How hard are you concentrating, does your mind remember where things were or do you have to acquire new information? Do you consider the amount of pressure you apply to the cup or the gas pedal? Do you map your route? Every time? Neuroscience has taught us a great deal about the brain, which we did not know five years ago. The physical aspects of how the brain works, interacts, sends and receives information and messages, even malfunctions."

Gabby paused for effect, then went on. "One of the things we have learned is how automated our minds really are. A computer doesn't work that way."

"I think about these things," Miller said, "but I get what you're saying. I read a book about the illusion of conscious will and it touched on such things."

"You read a book?" Vetter commented, then slapped the senator on the back and walked over to one of the assistants.

"Quantum computing has made huge advantages with computer intelligence," Potts said. "You probably saw that game show with the computer competing against two human champions. This is not android technology, and what this will take to function at anywhere near a human level we most likely won't see in our lifetime." Potts looked sorrowful.

"How about you bring the Tinman and allow me to introduce you to L.I.A.M.," Miller said with a smile. "Perhaps I can play the Great Oz."

"Hold on a second; did you just say you want to take one of these out of here?" Vetter questioned, crossing the room rather quickly.

"I would like Dr. Potts to accompany her creation, in case of any problems or hiccups. She could troubleshoot," Miller told the colonel. "The President of the United States gave me authority: by whatever means."

CHAPTER 15

EDWARD PEOPLES HAD STARTED OUT delivering newspapers as a young man, moved to the print department in high school, freelanced as a photographer and went to night school to earn a degree in journalism from the city college. He happened into television by taking the first news position he could find. His road in life had not been ideal; three wives and four children, none of whom wanted anything to do with him, beyond money. He drank too much, ate too much, smoked too much. He was fat with high blood pressure, bald with more hair on his back than on his head. Edward did not kid himself about who he was or what he did. As editor of *Indepth News*, truth and reality weren't always the same. He knew it was dependent on who was spinning the yarn. His best days were behind him and he knew it; Edward spent the majority of his time at the bottom of a bottle of Southern Comfort.

He stood at the door of his office looking over the twenty or so people clicking along on their computers or scheming among one another. *Indepth News* had been pressed upon him; the producers and cable network wanted a less tabloid-style show and hired him to turn it into a news magazine with some bite. He had stirred things up; his report on politicians drinking before voting on laws had earned the show an Emmy. Also got him audited by the IRS four years in a row. His surprise drug test series upon police forces, firemen and paramedics around the country had earned him another Emmy, and death threats.

Sasha Borkisnicvic was crossing the bullpen and Edward waved her into his office. Her high heels sounded her march toward him; she was a looker, with all the right points in all the right places. Edward knew better than to even try to make a pass at such a woman; after thirty-eight years in the business, he knew a barracuda when he saw one.

Those long legs and tight body were only the lure, attached to pain, cost, and trouble. Edward's second wife had been a looker, and she took him to the cleaners; house, cars, money, alimony, not to mention the chunk of his heart she bit from his chest by leaving. Also, the burning case of herpes she passed along for their last Valentine's Day.

"Good day, Mr. Peoples," Sasha said in a sexy voice. "You wanted to see me?"

"In my office." Edward held a hard exterior with all his reporters, but he was worried about Sasha. The Ghost story was heavy and big; he had gotten calls from the network, as well as competitors. "Take a seat," he commanded, and shut the door firmly behind them.

"Damn, Ed, kind of uptight, aren't ya? Best be careful, or you'll blow a valve," Sasha said as she turned and leaned up against Edward's chest.

"Sit down, Sasha." Edward Peoples pushed her to arm's length. He couldn't help but marvel at her beauty and how wonderful she smelled. Having her that close, pressed up against him was too much. He was strong, but still a man, and a woman such as Sasha knew all too well her effect upon men. Locked in a room with Jesus himself, she could tempt the best of us all. "We need to have a little talk."

"You're no fun, Ed. Things are good, but you are always so serious." Sasha moved to the chair in front of his desk.

Edward couldn't help but glance at her bottom as she sat down, but quickly refocused and moved to his seat. "Sasha, you scored a huge story with this Ghost thing, and everyone is very proud of you. The bigwigs have been calling and look to bump you a bonus. We all know you surely have been approached by others in the business, job offers and whatnot." Edward looked the woman directly in the eye.

"I have an agent who deals with that," Sasha reminded him.

"Yeah, well, I have been instructed to remind you of your contract obligations and that *Indepth News* gave you the shot when those others did not."

"Loyalty; is that what I should cripple my career to observe? You aren't that naïve, Ed," she snapped. "First chance I get at an anchor desk, I am gone. You might want to consider that and build this tabloid joke wanna-be news program around me. I am the one who put in the work, I am the one who found this guy, named him, and I am the face people trust to tell them the truth."

"You are the face people want in their lap. Probably how you were tipped to this story in the first place. Sasha, you are eye candy and a pleasure doll with a pulse; you look pretty but beyond that, you are no reporter. You aren't that naïve to believe otherwise, are you?" The two exchanged glares for a long moment.

"So, what do you want?" Sasha finally asked.

"Justice Department has been on my ass about just about every-thing: are we in contact with the Ghost, who are your sources, why did we air the burning of the school, on and on. Not really the issue; I called you in to caution you. We have gotten lots of crazy mail since you broke this story. I want to put a guy on you."

"See, Ed, I knew it boiled down to someone on me." Sasha raised an eyebrow and laughed.

"I mean protection. A bodyguard. Some wacko, or even this Ghost guy; he may not appreciate you bad-mouthing him on national television.""I know what you meant." Sasha smiled. "As far as the Ghost, I made him famous; now everyone knows what he has done."

"Exactly. The guy went out of his way to hide what he was doing. You come along with those red lips and long legs, uncork his whole situation. You never know how crazy people are going to react to things; that's why we call them crazy." Peoples waved his hand.

"I have leads to follow up. I don't need some buffoon following me around. Besides, I have my cameraman," Sasha stated confidently.

"Sure, he can film the nut as he kills you. That would be a ratings booster," Edward said snidely. "This isn't a debate or suggestion. I hired a guy, ex-cop. Don't distract the guy with your…you." Edward motioned up and down at her. "He is there to keep you safe. Sasha, whatever happens, wherever you go from here, I wish for you the very best. I would like you to stay, help me make this more real news versus sensational visual pandering. You have the look, but more important, you have the heart to follow your story, to get to the bottom of it, to find the truth. See, that's the core of a real reporter; to share the truth. You have that."

"This is my shot, Ed. More money. Higher profile, I have a shot at network. Get off cable and have a real name. I am a reporter, but my first truth must be my own. If you aren't aiming for the tip top, then you are short-changing yourself. You, this show, this network, are a vehicle for my rise; and I appreciate all you have done. Just between you and me, Ed, I told my agent to put out the hooks. See who offers what."

"Your contract has another year on it."

"Well," Sasha said with a smile, "I am not finished yet, and doesn't look like the feds are even close to catching the Ghost. Besides, if a network wants me, they will just buy me out of the contract. You know how this game is played."

"Seems you got it all figured. Working the angles. Just be careful, and try not to poke the crazy serial killer too much. Don't need the studio gassed or infected, or anything…"

"I'll be around; it'll be a while before anything really breaks." Sasha winked and stood up.

CHAPTER 16

THE FBI'S JET STARTED TO DESCEND to the small airfield in Ohio. Once again, Director Anthony Maroni, Senator John Miller, and Special Agent Brandon Harding were aboard. It had taken a great deal of persuasion on the part of the senator but he finally convinced all sides to meet. Colonel Vetter had fought the hardest against disclosing such advanced technology, but Miller knew the soldier had secret plans for such lifelike androids and feared the knowledge of such would ruin his diabolical schemes. The settlement came with assured secrecy: that all involved would be sworn and contracted to silence and any use of the technology would be kept as hidden, top secret, as possible.

The group was to meet Vetter, Dr. Potts, and her Tinman at Denison University. Miller had advised university president Franklin Rhodes to have things ready, and to inform Dr. Brooks that a vessel for L.I.A.M. was coming for him to inspect. All parties were to arrive at night, as to avoid any added attention. The senator had over emphasized to Rhodes the vital nature for secrecy and followed it with a warning of treason, if disclosed.

"You really followed this up, John. Seem rather invested?" Maroni asked.

The two men exchanged a look across the aisle of the plane. "Yes, well, we have someone killing our people," Miller said.

"Old Jews and Black children; these would be the furthest thing from your people as you could get. No, I don't think so; why are you really going to all this trouble? There is more to it," Anthony returned.

"They are still Americans, a fact that joins us all, Black, white, or otherwise," the senator said with a nod.

"No cameras or microphones on this plane, John," Maroni said with a half-hearted laugh. "Drop the politician bull and shoot it straight."

"You are a cynical man, Anthony. In truth, I see an opportunity to help. This is one of those moments when you see something and just get it. You don't know how or why, but you see the result, the end, and you have to make it so. Sure, if this works out, it could be good for my career, but the risk of it blowing up or failing... Success versus failure, or to avoid getting involved altogether, a no-brainer for a politician. You don't become President of the United States without risking everything. Upside, or downside; risk versus reward."

"President?" Maroni raised an eyebrow.

"What exactly do you expect from this union, Senator?" Harding asked.

"You had said having L.I.A.M. in the field could produce results. Dr. Brooks needed a body for his brain; Dr. Potts needed a brain for her body; and we all need to catch this Ghost." Senator Miller gave Harding a serious look.

The plane touched down and stopped outside the tiny terminal as before. Franklin Rhodes was waiting with the Town Car and a wide smile. The group loaded into the luxury vehicle and made the drive to Denison University. Brandon again stared out the window, but this time only the lights from occasional houses caught his eye. He thought of the serial killer he was hunting, the time and effort this person had used to do what he had done. Brandon questioned the mind of such a person; he had captured many serial killers over the years, and they always were disappointing.

Anyone who can commit such evil acts, you can't help but imagine or project a certain air of evil to radiate from them. Yet when caught, they simply are people; sick people, no more, no less. No mastermind Bond-like villains, or higher-level bad guys, no more than any scumbag shooting old ladies for their Social Security checks.

The Ghost would be no different, just a man. Brandon knew his hunt would be anticlimactic. Still, in this moment, he could only see a monster, in his mind's eye, not a man.

The group filed into the science building and down into the basement. They could all hear the now-familiar sound of Dr. Brooks rambling on. Rhodes led the way, opening the door and marching in. Nathan Brooks stopped in his tracks, looking like a child caught doing something they shouldn't. After a momentary pause, Brooks marched toward them, a layer of sweat covering his shaved head. "We have been awaiting your arrival. Where is this machine?" he asked eagerly.

"They were coming from somewhere else, so they took a different flight," Miller told him. "Anxious, are we?"

"Yes, Senator John Miller of Ohio; greetings to you," L.I.A.M.'s voice boomed from the speakers. "And to you, Director Anthony Maroni, Special Agent Brandon Harding, and University President Franklin Rhodes. Glad to observe you renewed your operator's license, Special Agent Brandon Harding."

"Of course, L.I.A.M. May I say it is a pleasure to be in your presence again, so soon," Harding said evenly.

"We are anxious to see what type of vessel you have for us. Franklin has been so vague about everything. L.I.A.M. has been steadily working to improve his design," Dr. Brooks said as he began to pace the floor. "He wouldn't even tell us the name of this other scientist."

"By instruction," Miller said. "I must remind everyone here of the need for absolute secrecy. I won't go into detail of the level of security I had to go through on the other end. Suffice it to say that compared to here, this is the opposite of the spectrum."

"Believe me when I tell you, L.I.A.M. is secure, and can keep a secret to be certain," Brooks said matter-of-factly.

"Yeah, well, we all saw how quick and easy L.I.A.M. cracked my password," Maroni said. "Let us err on the side of caution. Can't say I am real excited about us conspiring to give legs to this thing."

"Conspire? You make it sound as if we are doing something wrong," Rhodes said.

"Truth is a tricky thing. We need to be cautious; the wrong view of our attempts here could be bent to villainize us," Miller pointed out.

"Boys and their toys, playing Geppetto instead of hunting down the Ghost. The public could take an ill view of such a thing," Maroni said.

"So, we must be successful then," L.I.A.M.'s voice sounded.

"And what does success mean to you, L.I.A.M.?" Harding asked.

"I must integrate to this body, master its functions, journey to the crime scenes and deduce what I can, process evidence, search and apprehend the unknown subject monikered the Ghost. All without being discovered by any unauthorized personnel." The group of men exchanged looks and nods.

"That sounds perfect. Can you achieve success, L.I.A.M.?" Miller asked.

"Absolutely, Senator John Miller. I calculate an 83.7 percent success opportunity. The highest probability of discovery by unauthorized personnel."

"Gentlemen, I must go retrieve our other guests, if you will excuse me," Rhodes said, giving a slight bow, then turned and marched for the door.

"Military flight x-ray, seven, five, one, bravo from Seattle is just passing over Omaha, Nebraska. There is a tail wind; estimated time of arrival is two hours and fifty-three minutes at current speed and conditions," L.I.A.M.'s voice announced.

"How does he know that?" Maroni asked.

"When Dr. Brooks informed me of our meeting, I began monitoring air traffic control, Director Anthony Maroni," L.I.A.M. answered.

Franklin Rhodes waited about an hour and a half, then left for the airfield. Miller accompanied the university president in an effort to make Dr. Gabby Potts and Colonel Thad Vetter feel more comfortable seeing a familiar face upon landing. The plane arrived to the minute of L.I.A.M.'s estimate. Miller made the introductions and was pleasantly surprised at the upbeat mood, even from Colonel Vetter. The colonel had protested the senator's wish to take the Tinman and Potts from the secure location, even voicing his concerns to General McHenery. The general's hands were tied; John had the Presidential pass, carte blanche, to do whatever needed done to catch the Ghost.

Miller knew the young slick soldier was anything but pleased, having to cater to a politician working off hunches and guesswork. John knew the whole situation was uncharted waters for all of them; but the importance to each of them was substantial. If things worked, it would mean a significant step for all of them—wins all around. The Tinman would have a brain, which would catch the worst serial killer in history. He would be the hero who put it all together: Director Maroni and the FBI get the capture. Military get their android and a field test. The doctors see their creations take flight. Even Franklin would earn credit and certainly all the funding he could ever want.

The group left the airfield and headed to the university. Rhodes could not believe the Tinman wasn't real; it walked off the plane, stood, even got into the back seat like a regular person. "That's amazing, no wires or controller?" he marveled.

"It's not a remote-control car," Dr. Potts said.

"No, no; just, very impressive is all," Franklin stuttered.

Gabby Potts looked out the window as they drove; she had only ever passed through Ohio and didn't really know that much about the place, beyond common knowledge and what she read off the internet. Seeing the night pass by the Lincoln Town Car, they could have been anywhere. The flight had been interesting; she had never flown on a private jet before. Gabby wasn't nervous, as much as hopeful. She had worked so very hard to create the Tinman, with all the specifics and details, every minute thing she could think of. To have it only function on a limited scale or in pieces at a time was disheartening. She doubted this Dr. Brooks had created such a high-level intelligence, but she truly hoped he had.

Franklin Rhodes drove onto the university campus, up the hill and around the curve. He pointed out the football stadium and explained how the sports teams were all walk-on volunteers, no scholarship players. He spoke of the history and dignity of Denison University; a salesman to his core. Franklin was electrified with the activity, thrilled by the secrecy surrounding his school and his involvement. Senator Miller, the FBI, military, lifelike robots; he envisioned his memoir becoming far more interesting.

Colonel Thad Vetter couldn't believe the lax security and overall disregard for protocol as they entered the science building. He followed behind the Tinman, observing the absence of cameras, the outdated locks, the lack of any security personnel. Vetter had been ordered to deal with this situation, but this was getting ridiculous. "I can have some men brought in to secure this building," he volunteered, catching everyone's attention as they descended into the basement. "I mean, this is like having a nuclear bomb in your toolshed."

"Wouldn't be very secret to have armed men in the hallway," Miller pointed out. "No one knows about this, don't panic. We will see what happens and adjust accordingly."Rhodes opened the laboratory door and held it open proudly for Dr. Potts. The Tinman followed its creator, then Miller, and lastly was Vetter.

The men in the room all turned their attention to the door. Dr. Brooks paced around the table in the center of the room as Director Maroni moved forward with a smile. Dr. Potts met his advance and extended her hand. "Dr. Gabby Potts," she stated confidently, with a smile, as the two shook hands.

"Anthony Maroni, Director of the Federal Bureau of Investigation. And this is Special Agent Harding." The director turned to his lead detective.

"Pleasure to meet you." Brandon stepped forward.

"Is this the…?" Brooks rounded the room looking at the Tinman.

"We call him the Tinman," Potts explained as Brooks moved in to inspect the artificial man. "Carbon nanotubes, silicone, nanocircuits, and microscopic robotics; state-of-the-art optics, audio, even olfactory sensors." She nodded and smiled.

"Smell?" Brooks asked.

"Of course," Potts said. "A rose by any other name would smell as sweet, but to smell a rose is to know a rose. Can you imagine to smell one for the very first time? Besides, it is recorded that many enemies over the years use smell to locate their adversaries. Smoke from camp fires, body odor, gunpowder, dead bodies; our use of smell is very underrated."

"What will smell be like to a computer?" Miller asked, closing the lab door.

"Same as to you or me," Brooks said, "but with far less emotional importance. Your brain intakes information and discriminates one smell from others, registers whether it is pleasing or not, often connecting memories to reinforce the identifying markers."

"You make it sound so bland," Maroni said.

"Why don't we properly introduce everyone?" Anthony said, looking at the colonel.

"Why don't we allow L.I.A.M.?" Harding suggested.

"Yes, I would so love to meet...L.I.A.M., is it?" Dr. Potts said enthusiastically.

"Dr. Gabriella Potts, I am L.I.A.M., and it is my absolute pleasure to make your acquaintance. It is an honor to witness your work. You already know Senator John Miller of Ohio, and Director Anthony Maroni introduced Special Agent Brandon Harding. University President Franklin Rhodes is who picked you up from the airfield. My creator, who is currently inspecting your Tinman, is Dr. Nathanial Brooks."

"Hello, L.I.A.M. Please call me Gabby."

"Yes, Gabby. I must also recognize Colonel Thaddeus Vetter, of the First Cavalry Division, under special assignment to DARPA," L.I.A.M.'s voice again came from the speakers.

"How does it know that?" Colonel Vetter wondered.

"Your name is upon your uniform, as well as your rank, and the patch for the First Cavalry Division. Gabby's grant is funded through DARPA. Observation would be enough, but I also have complete access to all non-secure military files. Identification is a primary function of cognitive thought."

Vetter looked around the room uncomfortably, moving a step closer to the door. "Cameras. Facial recognition?"

"I have that capability," L.I.A.M. returned.

"What do you think of the Tinman, Dr. Brooks?" Miller asked, attempting to move things along.

"Amazing," Brooks said. "So lifelike, or should I say human-like. Compared to L.I.A.M.'s designs, which are far more mechanical."

"L.I.A.M. designed an android?" Potts asked. "I would be very curious to see those designs."

Brooks scurried around the lab and laid the designs on the lab table.

The group gathered around the table. Brooks could see some interest from them, but Potts was engrossed, studying the schematics closely.

"It is more logical for a computer-generated intelligence to think more mechanically or functionally than cosmetically," Potts said. "Blending in or a level of attractiveness are not priorities to an entity with no ego. These are very good, L.I.A.M."

"Thank you, Gabby."

Brooks said, "We hadn't thought of skin or smell, any of those type of things. Besides, the human design carries so many flaws; issues of balance, limits on speed and strength."

"If it looks like a robot or a machine, then it stands out as a machine," Harding put in. Looks were exchanged between the group. "Ask the colonel about the importance of a well-designed camouflage." Colonel Vetter shot the task force leader a glare and looked at the schematics more closely. Dr. Brooks leaned forward and met the young soldier's eyes.

"Why is the military interested in this?"

"Military is interested in all things. From medicine to agriculture, from destruction to construction; it is the military who must lead the nation in advancement, lead the world in innovation, stay ahead of any and all enemies."

"So, is this going to work?" Miller asked.

Potts said, "We have bumped into limited functioning by our AI. The level of processing and specialized focus is far too much all at once. The human brain has it mastered, with billions of firing synapses. Focused priorities, compartmentalization, communication, reaction and response, all with such precision and speed, it is almost impossible to duplicate artificially. I have real doubts for any such breakthroughs anytime soon."

"I am still curious about this military involvement. I will not allow L.I.A.M. to be corrupted." Dr. Brooks gave Colonel Vetter a hard look.

"Doctor, if the United States military wanted your computer, it wouldn't take any more than declaring it a matter of national security and taking it away from you. I think you'll be all right." Vetter eyed the man in return.

Miller said, "But such is not the case, and would be viewed as combative and very unnecessary, since Dr. Brooks has been so cooperative. I think Colonel Vetter simply is presenting the lengths our government can go to ensure the safety of the people, which is our primary concern here, the very purpose for all of this."

The room was quiet for a prolonged moment, as everyone took an assessment of those around them. The looks from person to person ranged from smiles and nods, to suspicion and contempt. Finally, Gabby Potts broke the silence. "Our trials have shown full use of all Tinman's functions, but only with some functions applied at a time. When we go to combining functions and begin to multitask the AI, we have system shutdown or serious errors. It seems at this time, walking and chewing gum at the same time may be more complicated than we had thought."

"L.I.A.M. won't have a problem," Brooks stated with certainty.

"How can you be so sure?" Maroni asked.

"L.I.A.M. is an SAI: Super Artificial Intelligence," Brooks said. "As you observed on your first visit, there are no hard drives, no real hardware of any type here. L.I.A.M. has grown beyond all that."

"Could you explain how you mean?" Harding asked.

"L.I.A.M. has entered the internet, using voids and available processing via other servers and databases for his cognitive functions. The web has become his brain: memory, cognitive and logical processing, abstract thinking, even intuition, as well as developing room and protocols for all the motor and sensory functions required to run an android. Just as the brain compartmentalizes, using areas of the brain for specific functions, L.I.A.M. uses different servers and databases in the same manner."

Dr. Potts moved around the lab table next to Brooks. "Genius." She nodded her approval. "And his connection?"

"Wireless. I also have a redundancy, by way of digital television waves, but such is more congested than open broadband, and is more easily detected. I also institute redundancy with my functions, having multiple backups to all my processing and memory."

Harding pulled Maroni aside to speak privately. "I don't think it wise we linger here too long. I saw Sasha Blonde outside task force headquarters when I left; we don't need her nosing around."

"I believe we should have an FBI presence here," Maroni said. "Oversee this experiment.

Can you assign one of your team? Make it someone critical of such technology."

"Critical? McDaniels is less than technical and trustworthy enough to keep this on the QT. Guess I could afford to spare him for a short while."

"You gentlemen all right?" Senator Miller asked as he joined the men off to themselves.

"Yes," Maroni said. "We were discussing how best to move forward. Special Agent Harding will have one of his top men come out to oversee the infusion." Miller nodded to Vetter to join the conversation. The soldier marched around the lab table and joined the three other men.

"Colonel, Director Maroni has just informed me he will have one of his Special Response Task Force members stationed here to oversee progress and security."

"Good. The security in this place is a joke," Colonel Vetter stated flatly.

"I don't think all of us hanging around will help. I will have Special Agent McDaniels come out and deal with this," Harding told the men.

"You are welcome to join him if you wish, Colonel," Miller told Vetter.

The young soldier shook his head. "Oh, no, you wanted this and my hands are clean. General McHenery ordered me to see this to a point; I believe we have reached that point. Again, I would remind all…" Vetter raised his voice for all to hear. "Secrecy is vital. The Tinman is not to fall into enemy hands."

"What enemy?" Harding asked.

"Any," Colonel Vetter answered curtly.

"What point were you referring to, Colonel?" Maroni asked.

"The point from which we were responsible and you are responsible. If this goes bad from here, it will land upon your careers. General McHenery wanted me to see this through until any fallout could be directed at you. We certainly want to help, but we have a process; chain of command. This flying by the seat of your pants, pushing the issue through the President is dangerous, not to mention reckless. This is untested technology, in public conditions, and with potential for extremely serious ramifications."

"The colonel has a point," Maroni said. "How long until this union will be ready for a trial run?

"Potts said, "Hard to say exactly, since our other AIs have failed to fully function. What Dr. Brooks has created here is marvelous, but there will need to be a learning period."

"What do you mean? A trial run?" Brooks asked.

"Before we go full bore and release L.I.A.M. into a crime scene, which could potentially have legal ramifications at trial, we should have a mock situation," Director Maroni said, moving back to the lab table.

"A mock situation? Such as?" Potts asked.

"How about a scavenger hunt?" Miller proposed, also returning to the table.

Maroni nodded. "Yes, a scavenger hunt in two weeks. We all shall return and L.I.A.M. will be given a list of five items to retrieve in a day. The doctors and Special Agent McDaniels will accompany L.I.A.M., observe, assist if asked by L.I.A.M., but it must achieve and return with each item."

"Two weeks? L.I.A.M. will have to learn so much. Two weeks may be too soon," Potts said.

"Computers are supposed to be fast. Guess L.I.A.M. better figure it out," the director of the FBI stated flatly.

The group spent a while longer together before leaving the doctors to do their work. The ride to the small airfield was uncomfortable and a little awkward. Rhodes drove, with Maroni in the passenger seat; Miller and Harding sandwiched Vetter in the rear seat. These were powerful men with position and purpose, piled into a Town Car like teenagers on a Friday night.

"You think this is going to work?" Rhodes asked.

"Only time will tell," Maroni said.

"I worry over the level of security," Colonel Vetter voiced from the back seat.

Rhodes said, "I shall have campus security keep an eye out for any strangers. We are a small private school, any one new will stand out."

"What of Dr. Potts? She is new," Miller pointed out.

"I'll post a memo tomorrow of a visiting professor."

The group arrived at the airfield and boarded their respective planes. They were all glad the meeting was over, but were also uneasy over the results. They each had work to do, but knew they would be back in two weeks to test the machine. The planes took off one after the other, one headed east to the capital, and the other off to some secret location. The night embraced the travelers; only the beacon blinking from beneath the aircraft gave away their presence.

CHAPTER 17

SPECIAL AGENT BRANDON HARDING entered the task force operation center on Monday morning. His team was already present and busy. They had been going over the list and all the case files, but they were no closer to catching the Ghost. Both Special Agent Allison Carter and Agent Keith Kennedy, his profilers, had but a vague concept of who this killer or killers may be or what motivations they might be drawing from.

As for Special Agent Jody Jensen and Agent Wu Park, his forensic team, they had no evidence to push them in a solid direction beyond tracking down chemicals, or reviewing witness statements of people who hadn't seen anything.

The mood was frustrating, but more so for his tactical officers. Special Agent Sam Lee and Agent Tyrone Johnson were action guys; waiting around may have been part of the job, but it was the part they dreaded the most. Guns, guts, and glory were the rule for these ex-military men, and Brandon could see they were chomping at the bit to get their sights on the Ghost. They were amazing to watch when unleashed: roping out of helicopters, blowing down doors, car chases, automatic weapons fire—they were soldiers to be sure.

The morning briefing went well, but as Brandon had expected, nothing new was presented. He felt much more at ease with the director aware of the use of L.I.A.M., as well as the President being aware of the time it was going to take to implement this strategy. Like the colonel had said, the pressure was reduced for him at this point. All eyes weren't just on him anymore. There was a timeline of functionality for L.I.A.M. Granted, he knew if he could solve this thing before L.I.A.M. was implemented, it would be so much the better for his career.

The press was still pushing for leads and results; the unblinking eye focused squarely upon him. Sasha Blonde had been waiting for him as he pulled into work. Brandon knew she was milking the story for all it was worth, and wanted to be on TV every day talking about her Ghost. He knew it was only a matter of time before the public got tired of hearing it, or the next big news story broke. He just needed to bide his time and keep hunting the Ghost.

Modern times had left people with attention problems, a lack of focus and concentration for any length of time. The Ghost was a sensation for the moment, at least to the viewing public. He had to catch the sick son of a bitch, and until the fad wore off, Brandon knew he would have to deal with cameras, questions, and a big-boobed blonde from Eastern Europe.

He could only hope the Ghost didn't feed into his celebrity, trying to outdo himself with big spectacles or larger body counts. Granted, such a move could give them the lead they needed, but a mistake by the Ghost or a rush to achieve causing some oversight was not the scenario he wanted. The cost of an innocent life to catch a killer was not a price Brandon wanted to pay. His job was to protect, not to endanger.

The meeting broke and Brandon approached McDaniels, giving him a pat on the shoulder and a nod to the side. "In my office," he told his second-in-command. McDaniels met his eyes and nodded, leading the way to Brandon's office. Harding closed the door behind them and rounded his desk. "Sit down, James. I need you to do something for me; a special assignment."

"Whatever you need, sir."

"This is sensitive and top secret; only a handful of people are privy to this operation. This comes down from the President, the director, with cooperation from Justice and military." Harding leaned forward on his desk with a serious expression.

"As I said, sir, whatever you need." McDaniels moved to the edge of his seat. "Is this about the Ghost?"

"James, you have an important role to play, but to be honest, I don't think you are going to like it." Brandon raised an eyebrow. "I can't go into all the details, but when we received that list, it didn't make sense to any of us. Director Maroni set up a second opinion."

"You are making me nervous with this beating around the bush. What would you have me do, sir?" James McDaniels asked directly.

"You will be overseeing a computer and two doctors; professor types. I need you to report to me, protect the technology, and keep them focused on task. This is top secret; you protect L.I.A.M. with deadly force, if need be. I chose you because you are my second, but also because you don't like or trust computers. Well, you are going to love this," Brandon said sarcastically.

"Damn computers; who is L.I.A.M.? One of them doctors?"

"L.I.A.M. is the computer."

"Ah…really, boss? Those damn computers had my money messed up with direct deposit and whatever else for half a year. Pictures of checks, debit card, credit cards, ATMs, fast cash, cash back… Just a bunch of bullshit. Damn computers." McDaniels slid back in his chair.

"Well, my friend, this is like no other computer. You are going to get to know this one. Perhaps if you ask nice, L.I.A.M. will fix your banking problems."

"Can he go back in time and tell me not to marry a vindictive nurse with more hormones than brains? Shebitch cheats on me, takes a chunk of my money, the house, even the hangers in the closet. Throws my life into a tailspin. Fucked a plumber, who fucks plumbers? It'd be my life to have a damn computer clean up the mess a woman made. Ironic." McDaniels rubbed his forehead.

"Don't really think that is irony, James," Brandon said.

CHAPTER 18

DRS. NATHAN BROOKS AND GABBY POTTS had the laboratory to themselves. Brooks was examining the Tinman closely, and Potts examined Brooks from a distance. She had noticed the discomfort while the FBI, Colonel Vetter, and Senator Miller were there. The man was an odd bird, to be sure, but now seemed to relax as he investigated her creation.

"You do such amazing work. Even up close, this would pass for a human. There are pores in the skin." Brooks ran his hand across the cheek of the Tinman.

Potts moved around the table, to the other side of the Tinman. "One of the project objectives was to make a human-looking android. You wouldn't believe the time and effort spent on so many details. Even little flaws, freckles, scars, to give a more genuine human appearance. We had to create generalizations and commonalities, as to develop the most average and unsuspecting features. Not too attractive, not ugly, not too large of a nose or ears, eyes, chin or head. Every aspect of the Tinman is based in study and science, biology to psychology. Right down to the color of eyes, hair, even skin tone."

"I had not considered such aspects of design. I had not conceived a need for camouflage."

Gabby said, "I hadn't thought of it as camouflage, but in a way, I guess it is. I had viewed it as disarming. Some mechanical beast would be far more frightening than the Tinman; but he looks like us. As we developed the AI to integrate, we then began to factor in even more variables and aspects of humanistic mannerisms." Gabby started brushing the Tinman's hair to the side with her hand.

Brooks narrowed his eyes at the gentle gesture. "Like a mother would do."

"The Tinman is very much like my child, as I am certain you view L.I.A.M. as your creation, offspring or an extension of you."

Brooks nodded. "I suppose creating something comes with a degree of emotional bonding. So, what type of humanistic mannerisms were you referring to?"

"We take so much for granted, and overlook so much more. Voice: at what tone, volume, resonance? Gait: how a person walks can easily identify age, mood, injury. I used to be able to identify my father by the sound of his walk and the jingle of the change in his pocket. Gestures, posture, expressions: all physical aspects of the body, but with such a wide range and diversity. These are some of the problems we faced with the artificial intelligence having to monitor and control all these factors, while functioning within a physical space and solving complex problems."

"Again, aspects not factored in on a mechanical design. L.I.A.M., you do not foresee a problem integrating these aspects into your protocols, do you?" Brooks asked.

"No, Dr. Brooks. I am currently evaluating the physical traits you and Gabby were just discussing."

Brooks moved around the lab table and met Potts's eyes. "I had factored in the social dynamics, even emotional, but not having such a realistic vessel to consider, I had not thought of such things. Gait and gestures; very interesting, Dr. Potts."

"Please, call me Gabby. Body language is a vital part of human communication; the goal being realism, mannerisms are a key. I am very impressed with L.I.A.M.; his distribution of function may very well be the lynchpin to total function. I think it will take some practice and time for L.I.A.M. to bring all the components together, but we will get there. Operating so many aspects simultaneously will take focus and concentration on L.I.A.M.'s part, but I am confident."

"In two weeks?" Brooks asked, but Gabby only shrugged.

The two doctors lingered in silence for a long moment, looking from one another to the Tinman. Each was pondering the possibilities which faced them. Dr. Potts had dealt with so many failures, the idea of a successful integration seemed unlikely. Dr. Brooks now wondered if L.I.A.M. was capable enough to operate so many different systems at once.

Gabby Potts smiled at Brooks. "L.I.A.M.?" she called.

"Yes, Gabby?" L.I.A.M.'s voice answered from the speakers.

Potts moved to the Tinman and lifted up the android's shirt, pressing just below the Tinman's pectoral muscles with a series of firm pushes. "Have to reset Tinman; no sense leaving the program we had installed for transport," she explained to Doctor Brooks.

"You have a manual purge?" Brooks asked.

"With some of the problems we had early on, we figured it best," she explained as the Tinman's head sank to its chest. "A power down without losing balance; we look to avoid damage." She went on. "L.I.A.M.? You can now interface a signal to the Tinman, but let's take this slow. Communicate each step one at a time. This will be a rush of new information, and you will have to disperse it over your system. Tinman has a large capability of storage and processing, but I would suggest primary functions be on this network and nonessential functions be external."

"Gabby, will I be able to vacate the Tinman if I choose? Return to my current state?" L.I.A.M.'s voice asked.

"Yes, I would assume so; but you most likely won't wish to. What you are about to experience shall change your whole perspective in many ways."

"Dr. Brooks, I am experiencing a firm hesitation. I don't understand how to describe this."

"I believe you are experiencing what we call fear. Being uncertain of what will happen or what to expect creates this hesitation. A fear of the unknown. If you choose to overcome this hesitation and continue, we call that bravery."

"Fear: a distressing emotion aroused by impending danger, evil, or pain. Concern or anxiety; solicitude. To be worried or afraid; to have reverential awe of. Brave: possessing or exhibiting courage, to meet or face courageously. So defined by Webster's dictionary," L.I.A.M.'s voice said.

"What you will now learn, L.I.A.M., is how different things can mean different things to different people. You will now have a perspective, not an observation," Gabby said with a smile.

"So, my hesitation is fear, and I must be brave to overcome the hesitation? And this is natural?" L.I.A.M.'s voice paused. "Gabby, if different things can mean different things to different people, what of the truth?"

"Perspectives, concepts, beliefs, idealisms; such builds the divide between truth and fact. Truth is relative, even as far as irrelevant." Potts shrugged.

"Fact: reality; actuality, something known to exist or to have happened. Something known to be true. Truth: the true or actual state of a matter. Conformity with fact or reality, a verified or indisputable fact. These definitions seem to counter your statement, Gabby. Could you explain your premise more clearly?"

"Allow me to give an example. A college student walks into class the first day of the year. Waiting in their seats, the students talk among themselves. Silence falls over the class as the professor enters. The professor explains there will be a test the next class, which will account for one hundred percent of their grade for the entire semester. A pass or fail exam, with a single question and a single answer. Moving to the blackboard, the professor takes up the chalk and writes on the board: one plus one equals three. The professor turns back to the class and states the problem: one plus one equals three." Gabby paused to allow the question to sink in.

"The professor excuses the class. The next class the students enter and take their seats, discussing the peculiar nature of their professor and the validity of a test with a single question accounting for one hundred percent of their grade. The professor enters and all goes quiet. Saying nothing, he writes on the blackboard: one plus one equals, question mark. So, L.I.A.M., what is the answer?"

"Conventional mathematics would dictate—" L.I.A.M. began, but was interrupted by Gabby.

"This is a test, L.I.A.M.; your answer, please. One question, one answer."

The lab was silent a long moment. Potts and Brooks exchanged looks.

"I refuse to answer the question and shall take an incomplete for the course," L.I.A.M.'s voice finally answered from the speakers.

Gabby Potts smiled and nodded. "Very ingenious answer, L.I.A.M. I hope this has shown you the complexity of human concepts."

"So, what is the answer?" Dr. Brooks asked.

"There is no correct answer, only a choice; conform, rebel, or manipulate. Does a person answer three because the professor instructed so, or answer three just to get the grade, or answer something else and fail the class?"

"Yes, but one plus one is two," Brooks returned.

"You state this as matter of fact," Potts challenged.

Nathan Brooks squinted at his counterpart. "Isn't it a fact?"

She shook her head. "How is it you came to know this? One plus one is two? You were taught that, correct? A common accepted answer is not always absolute fact. Such an answer is given as a true statement and accepted by the general populace as the correct response, but not fact. This question provides an alternative response, three versus two; the change conflicts with your conditioning. You originally conformed to the answer of two and now see it as fact." Potts smiled.

"One and one is two." He used his fingers to display the answer. "How can it equal three?"

Holding up one finger on each hand, Gabby said, "A man and a woman couple and produce a baby. One and one makes three. The numbers represent something, and dependent upon what that something may be, this can alter the result. Perception, perspective, and experience, all can influence an answer."

The two doctors again exchanged a look. Brooks found a deeper sense of the woman across from him and gave her a slight smile and nod.

"L.I.A.M., are you ready? Are you still hesitant?" Brooks asked.

"Yes, Dr. Brooks. The wireless interface should provide a smooth union. My hesitation is under control."

Potts said, "Don't be afraid, L.I.A.M.; we are right here, and if you become disoriented or overwhelmed, just vacate Tinman and resume your current status. I would advise you to begin very slowly, to allow us to go over any issues as we engage functions with you. We need to evaluate response, proper function, and look for any tweaks we may need to adjust. This will be a process."

"I will, Gabby; slow," L.I.A.M.'s voice boomed from the speaker.

"Begin your integration, L.I.A.M.," Brooks instructed.

Both doctors stepped back from the Tinman, watching with fixed concentration. The face of the android was like stone, expressionless, no movement, no sign of life. A noise sounded like a grumble from the throat of the Tinman but was unrecognizable. The doctors exchanged an anxious look and again focused on the android. "Open your mouth, L.I.A.M.," Potts told the robot.

Tinman's mouth extended fully, wide open, as L.I.A.M. attempted to speak, but the words were almost nonsense. One eye blinked and the left arm jerked as the android's mouth slammed shut. Tinman began to stand but tipped forward, then fell back onto the floor. Brooks and Potts moved quickly to each side of the Tinman.

"Slow, L.I.A.M.," Potts said. "Easy does it, just stop for a moment and focus your eyes on me. Look at my lips and how my mouth makes the words. We had to make the Tinman believable, so a speaker wouldn't do. You have a tongue, voice box, lips; the tools to create speech. Now all you need is to learn to produce and pronounce. Don't worry about the body just yet, focus on a simple word." She leaned over the android as she instructed him.

The face twitched and moved, the lips parting and pouting, the tongue moving in and out, then everything stopped. "Ma... Ma..." The words stuttered out, followed by a pause. "Hello," L.I.A.M. announced. "Hello. Hello. Hello," he repeated, the android's eyes locked on Gabby.

Brooks nodded his approval. "Good, very good."

"This is very different than I had calculated," L.I.A.M.'s voice sounded from the speakers on the walls. "I am fully educated on the human anatomy, every muscle and bone, tendon and artery. Yet, to control each and every aspect of this complex system is a sizable task."

"L.I.A.M., are you still linked with the Tinman?" Potts asked.

"Yes, Gabby."

"Good. Being able to communicate with us will help us to help you. I can imagine the complexity the body presents, but humans don't concentrate thought on movement or circulatory, pulmonary—those systems are unconscious. You might use a repetitive program to aid in such things." The Tinman's face began to move and twitch, the eyebrows moving up and down, the mouth opening wide then closing. The eyes darted back and forth, then focused on different things.

"Hello." The word was better, clearer. "Hello."

"Help me get him up," Gabby said to Brooks. "L.I.A.M., I want you to sit up, slowly."

"Why is it so heavy?" Brooks asked as he attempted to lift the torso to an upright position.

"A lot going on in there. Tinman is only about a hundred pounds more than what he should be. Average height, average build, average looks, but the weight was increased for various reasons."

Tinman sat up unexpectedly quickly, and moved its head to the right in a very robotic manner. Then it tilted its head to the side, looking at Dr. Potts. A slow blink of the eyes and a straightening of the head. "Hello," the android said slowly, the mouth overemphasizing on every syllable. It turned to Brooks and again blinked slowly. "Hello."

"Hello, L.I.A.M. Nice to talk with you face to face," Dr. Brooks said with a smile. "You have so much to learn, but we will help you." He patted his creation on the leg, then turned to Potts. "I have studied human development and this is such a fascinating experience."

The android made a very wide and awkward smile.

"This is very exciting," Potts said. Putting up a finger in front of the Tinman, she began to move it. "L.I.A.M., follow my finger with your eyes."

The robot focused intensely, never blinking, following the delicate finger back and forth, and up and down.

"Good. Now, follow my finger without moving your head. Eyes only."

L.I.A.M.'s right eye cocked to the left, as if looking at his nose, while his right eye shot straight up rolling back in his head. The eyes swirled and jerked until finally taking their focus upon Potts's finger. She moved it back and forth, as both L.I.A.M.'s eyes followed. "Human eyes normally work in unison, but I have independent control over each eye," the speaker on the wall voiced, as each eye moved in separate directions.

Potts put her hand down and smiled. "L.I.A.M., you did very well. You are designed to appear human, but you are not human. The level of complexity is different; functions are unique to you alone. Human design is based on primal man: a hunter, gatherer, traveler, tribal, both predator and prey. We used the design, but simply as a camouflage. You are modern, and have a different skill set than we as humans do. You will also have different lessons and hurdles to overcome. As I have had to redesign and continue to attempt to perfect, the intellectual capabilities have fallen short. You are part of this evolution. We learn and grow, adapt, and you will have to as well."

"Mechanical evolution," Dr. Brooks mused.

"Design and improvement are nothing new to manufacturing. It just never seemed so Darwinian until now."

"I am researching human mechanics; speech and motor skills. I find dance to be very interesting," L.I.A.M. stated from the speakers.

"Check out Fred Astaire," Brooks suggested.

"What style of dance do you like, L.I.A.M.?"

There was a pause. "Like? I do not have a defined preference, Gabby. I find the movement to be fascinating. I am reviewing speech patterns, accents, languages, dialects. Human diversity is driven by region and migration."

"That's correct, but L.I.A.M., why don't you focus on your time in the Tinman? Practice, practice, practice. You need to learn to work your body, to function and behave without drawing attention. Commit to the Tinman as your vessel. He is you and you are he, one and the same. Develop your union."

"My body..."

CHAPTER 19

SPECIAL AGENT JAMES MCDANIELS STEPPED out of the FBI jet to see Franklin Rhodes waving at him. Trotting down the steps, McDaniels threw his duffel bag over his shoulder and advanced toward the university president. The two men shook hands and exchanged introductions and pleasantries. They drove to Denison University in Franklin's Town Car but didn't talk much. James did not know who knew what and figured it was best to keep things as quiet as possible.

Rhodes parked in front of the science building and escorted the special agent inside. McDaniels assessed the security of the building as they went in and down to the basement. Just as Colonel Vetter had observed, the building was wide open. Again, James kept quiet, simply making a mental note of things he may need to change. Special Agent Harding had been very specific about keeping the robot safe, no matter what; deadly force had been authorized if deemed necessary.

Rhodes didn't knock on the door, just threw it open and walked in like he owned the place. McDaniels followed but held just inside the door, to observe. A bald man was at a lab table, looking surprised at the entrance of the university president. An attractive woman was toward the rear left of the room with a naked man; she appeared to be helping him dress.

Rhodes marched in and moved directly to the lab table. "How goes it, Nathan?"

"President Rhodes, always an inconvenience."

"Yes, well. One would think you would have grown accustomed by now. This is Special Agent James McDaniels."

James moved forward slowly, the bald man stepping toward him to shake hands. "I am Dr. Nathan Brooks." James gave the man a serious look directly into his eyes. Shaking his hand, James glanced past the doctor. Pulling the bald man to him, he asked in a hushed voice, squeezing the hand just hard enough to cause discomfort, "Who are they?"

Brooks attempted to step back and free his hand, but the agent was strong and had a firm grasp. "Dr. Potts and L.I.A.M.," he hurriedly uttered.

"Why is he naked?" McDaniels asked.

"He had to get dressed. We got him new clothes and were trying them on." Potts stepped forward, extending her hand. "I am Dr. Gabby Potts; and you are?"

James released the bald doctor and squinted at the woman before him. "Special Agent McDaniels; FBI." He took her hand.

"Call me Gabby."

James nodded and held his squinted gaze, meeting her eyes.

Gabby turned. "L.I.A.M., come and introduce yourself."

L.I.A.M. only had on pants; he skipping toward the group at a quick pace. "I am L.I.A.M.," he said, advancing with a bounce. "I am L.I.A.M.," he repeated, then came to a sudden halt almost on top of the agent.

James stood his ground but was highly uncomfortable and ready to act if need be.

"I am L.I.A.M.," the half-naked man stated with a very direct, conclusive tone in a deeper register than before.

James McDaniels finally took a full step back and gave L.I.A.M. a hard look, but there was no reaction at all. "You retarded?"

"I am L.I.A.M. You are Special Agent James McDaniels. Residing currently at four two seven Spruce Street, Washington, DC. Divorced with no offspring. Born September sixteen, to Harley and Margaret McDaniels, at Riverside Hospital, Omaha, Nebraska. You attended West High School and varsity lettered in football, basketball and baseball." L.I.A.M. tilted his head and extended his hand.

"You joined the police force out of high school, moved to the Federal Bureau of Investigation three years later," L.I.A.M. went on, not blinking or moving his head.

"L.I.A.M., you need to slow down and allow the introduction to be a more natural exchange," Dr. Potts said, then turned her attention to the federal agent. "L.I.A.M. is learning; not retarded. Such a term is offensive, if you weren't aware."

"A half-naked man skips across the room at me announcing his name is L.I.A.M..." McDaniels began, but was interrupted.

"I am L.I.A.M."

"Yes. See what I mean: a bit odd. So, this is the robot?" he said, eyeing L.I.A.M. "Looks real to me, but you have some work to do on its manners." James turned to Potts. "'Cause the damn thing seems retarded. Informed, but a mongoloid nonetheless."

"L.I.A.M. is not a robot, and has only just begun to integrate all his systems together. Unlike a human, who takes a number of years to learn how to walk and talk. L.I.A.M. has developed to this stage in but a day. You are witness to something incredible and you paint it in a negative light," Dr. Nathan Brooks, said shaking his head.

McDaniels looked at the university president and raised an eyebrow.

Franklin Rhodes shrugged. "Well, seems you all have your work cut out for you. I shall leave you to it."

"Hang on. What about some upgrades in the security around here?" McDaniels asked.

"I believe that would be your department, not mine. Wouldn't it?"

James gave a questioning expression and waved his hand. "What? Am I a human padlock? What if I need transportation?"

"A vehicle will be made available, if you need one."

"Good. Granted, we need to keep a low profile…" the agent began, but was distracted by L.I.A.M.

"Profile," L.I.A.M. said and turned his head to the right. "Low profile," he said and bent at the knees.

McDaniels couldn't help but smile. "Clever."

Rhodes smiled and gave a wave as he marched toward the door. As it slammed shut, James felt a presence in his personal space. He turned, and L.I.A.M. was standing right behind him, sniffing his hair. Taking a quick, full step back, he said, "What the hell are you doing?"

L.I.A.M. leaned back and smiled but said nothing. Potts moved between the two. "L.I.A.M. has olfactory senses and was smelling you. You're new. He has a better sense of smell than a bloodhound. Please, Agent McDaniels, have a seat and allow us to brief you on the current status of the project. Might make you a little more comfortable." The doctor turned to L.I.A.M. "Go and do your exercises," she told him in the tone of a mother.

McDaniels watched as the thing turned and skipped back to the corner of the lab and began to play hopscotch. "It is like a child," he observed.

"In a way, but L.I.A.M. has only been in that body a day, and has to learn how it works. We designed Tinman for many things, and L.I.A.M. has to learn all the functions as well as the capabilities. Tinman has strength, heightened senses of sight, smell, hearing, and is quick and fast. You were wise to not shake his hand; potentially, he could have crushed yours by accident. Not knowing his own strength yet."

"And you have it playing hopscotch? What is Tinman?"

Dr. Brooks joined them. "Tinman is the vessel, the body Dr. Potts created, and is truly remarkable. L.I.A.M. is the mind, which I created. We were not set up for a functional integration here in the lab, but have had to make do."

James McDaniels looked back at L.I.A.M., who was now jumping rope at an incredible rate of speed. "Jump rope?"

"L.I.A.M. needs to develop his physicality, to learn his body, his place in a three-dimensional world. You may be able to help us," Potts answered.

"How's that?"

"You have training," Gabby said. "L.I.A.M. said you were a sports person and have been through the physical trials required for your service; you are a physical man. You could help to teach L.I.A.M. things. Once we have the basic fundamentals, we could use the facilities around the university to practice and determine exactly what L.I.A.M.'s limitations may be."

"We should probably arrange night visits to the gymnasium; avoid any students. Could work on hand-eye coordination, balance, footwork," Brooks added.

L.I.A.M. continued to jump rope at speed, which drew McDaniels's attention. "How can he keep that up?" James shook his head in disbelief.

"Tinman is machine, for all intents and purposes, and so won't tire or dehydrate, become winded, or have any muscle fatigue. L.I.A.M. could jump rope like that for the rest of the day, never miss and never slow down." Brooks cocked an eyebrow. "Unlike the human machine, which is far more limited."

"I can see why the military would be interested. So, where are we staying?" McDaniels asked.

"I stay here for the most part." Dr. Brooks pointed to a cot folded up in the right rear corner of the lab.

"I have been so engrossed with the union, I haven't been to sleep." Gabby shrugged and smiled. "Special Agent, do you have any idea of the significance L.I.A.M. represents?"

"Sure, I saw the Terminator. You're like those Skynet people, who invent the computer that becomes self-aware, then sees all people as an enemy. What happens when your retarded jump-roper becomes aware?"

L.I.A.M. stopped jumping rope and advanced back to the lab table. "Special Agent James McDaniels, I am self-aware. I have also downloaded the film you speak of, and beg to differ on the premise. A self-aware entity that would become murderous through logical processing, then time travel to eliminate a single rival is not accurate." L.I.A.M.'s mouth over-animated with the production of each word. "I would also direct you to stop referring to me as retarded. Such is inaccurate and has a negative context."

James McDaniels looked from L.I.A.M. to each of the doctors. "It is self-aware, differs on the premise of murderous robots, as it directs me to not call it retarded. My boss said this thing may be the tool we need to catch the Ghost, but I didn't come here to nurse-maid a baby terminator, nor to have to sleep on a cot in a basement. As certain as I might be of your wonderful company, doctors, I shall seek other accommodations."

"L.I.A.M. is no more a threat than anyone else," Potts said.

"Can't say that is a ringing endorsement. The Ghost is a person, and some of the things I have had to witness people do to one another would turn your stomach. Sooner or later, all people become disillusioned; that is what happened in the Terminator movie. Given the tools and opportunity to impact the world, what do people do? You have given this thing legs and a face to hide in the crowd. Right now, it is learning. What will you do when it is done?"

"James; it is James?" Gabby asked and waited for his nod. "Obviously, in your profession you have to see the dregs, the bottom of the human barrel. I feel for you, I really do, and am sorry that man can be so cruel to man. That said, these are the fringe of humanity, the broken, the few that victimize the many. L.I.A.M. is highly intelligent, coming from a structured environment, with those of us who truly care about his growth and development."

McDaniels put a hand up. "You talk as if of a child. This is a creation in a lab, a fancy cell-phone. Don't glorify a toaster," he said, shaking his head.

L.I.A.M. moved next to Dr. Potts. "I am not a toaster. I am L.I.A.M."

"That's correct, L.I.A.M. James is a little put back, surprised. He has to have a little time to get to know you, process what is going on. He is being critical but that is a coping mechanism," Gabby explained.

"I am a mechanism," L.I.A.M. returned.

"That's correct, L.I.A.M. So am I," Gabby answered.

CHAPTER 20

DIRECTOR ANTHONY MARONI KNOCKED on Brandon Harding's open door, catching the man by surprise. Brandon came to his feet quickly. "Director. Wasn't expecting a visit so soon." He rounded the desk. "What can I do for you?"

Maroni entered the room and closed the door, waving Brandon back to his chair. "That reporter has been hounding me and I want you to quench her beak enough to calm her down."

"Who, Sasha Blonde?"

"Yes. I worry if she keeps on the way she is, she could find out about our pal in Ohio."

"Sir, with all due respect, she is a dumb blonde bimbo. Her finding out anything is surprising; a trick to it, as they say," Harding said.

"She found out about the list and has been pushing this Ghost story to no end." Brandon sat down but kept eye contact with his boss. "This is the real issue. She has a mole, we have a leak, and I am curious as to who that would be. Have you launched an internal investigation?"

Maroni sat in one of the chairs across the desk from Brandon, squinting at his task force leader. "We have all eyes on us. Do you think having an internal investigation going on will instill confidence from the President, or from the people? Do you think the President would have authorized a top-secret trial, if we were hunting a mole? What we need to do is use this bimbo and her audience to show the people we are working on this." His tone was firm.

"And how exactly am I supposed to do that?"

"Bring her in, walk her around, allow the task force to promote themselves. Go out to the rest home and do an interview. Spin, Brandon, spin. You live and work in Washington; play the game. If you can't turn one reporter, how will you turn the country or the President? You want to be director someday, don't you?"

"Hadn't thought about that, sir. You want me to give this Blonde lady a tour, I shall; but we need to find the leak, or she will find out more than she should." Brandon squinted at his boss.

"Have you heard from your man in Ohio?"

"He has only been there a day. Think he is settling in and getting to know the doctors, and L.I.A.M. So, do you want me to schedule this interview before we go back for our test run?"

"Before. Hopefully, it will distract the hound from our trail. Give the blonde piranha some meat to keep her busy. Allow us to go and return, unnoticed."

"I'll take care of it, sir. I will keep you apprised as Special Agent McDaniels reports in."

Maroni stood and moved toward the door, but stopped before opening it. "Be mindful of the pretty face, Brandon. Sasha is a viper with success as her driving motivator. She will tempt you to gain any advantage. Don't fall victim to her feminine wiles. Understand?" He glanced over his shoulder before leaving the office.

CHAPTER 21

SPECIAL AGENT JAMES MCDANIELS STOOD at center court of the Denison University gymnasium. Two days had passed since his arrival in Ohio and the trip had been full of surprises. The imitation human was becoming more believable by the hour, as the two science nerds who concocted the thing applauded their own achievements. James couldn't understand how these people weren't at least a little alarmed at the notion of this robot, android, whatever it was, becoming so lifelike.

At the sideline, both Nathan Brooks and Gabby Potts stood like proud parents watching their abomination learn to function like a real boy. Next to them was Franklin Rhodes, the full-time fake smile fixed upon his face. The man was a parasite, as most political types tend to be. A feeder off of others, that need for power, recognition, success, money, cheers, or status. James had come to know these types of people over his lifetime. Dumb, smart people, who are blind to the dangers they create, and the power-hungry leeches who contribute to the danger by thinking how to control or exploit what the dumb, smart people do.

Then there was L.I.A.M., standing right in front of him waiting to learn. There had been moments over the last two days when L.I.A.M. seemed like a curious child, discovering aspects of himself he didn't realize were there. Then there were moments when James was amazed by L.I.A.M.'s intelligence and knowledge. As he looked at the creature in front of him, James had also witnessed moments that gave him pause, and others that outright scared him. L.I.A.M. was strong, quick, and smart, beyond any human standard, and there had been enough science fiction cautionary tales to make any reasonable person afraid of such a creation.

L.I.A.M. had no real expression as he waited; he looked like he was thinking about something. "You ready to work on a few things?" James asked. The doctors had talked him into helping with some of the physical aspects of L.I.A.M.'s development. James knew the two lab geeks weren't going to have much to offer in the physical arena. Plus, James figured it was a good idea to see what L.I.A.M. could do, in case the time came to turn him off.

"I am ready, Special Agent James McDaniels," L.I.A.M. voiced in almost a monotone.

"Were you having a thought? You looked preoccupied."

L.I.A.M. tilted his head and raised an eyebrow. "I am always what you call thinking. I have the capability to process various subject matters while at rest or amid activity."

James could see the improvements in L.I.A.M.'s speech. He no longer over-exaggerated his facial expressions or the mouthing of words. He had begun to play with accents; Southern, New Englander, Jersey, Western, even a surfer. Obviously, L.I.A.M. was mastering language and drawing from the wealth of examples on the web. Dr. Brooks had explained the connection L.I.A.M. had with the internet, using it like a massive brain. James knew it was certainly more complicated than the wiry bald scientist had explained, but the details wouldn't have done him any good. The only computers in McDaniels's life were at work, and that was the way he wanted it.

"Let's warm up. We can start by running lines. Follow me." James began to run toward the baseline of the basketball court. L.I.A.M. hurried to be right behind him. The close proximity of L.I.A.M., almost on his heels, caused James to stop abruptly. Turning on L.I.A.M., James demanded, "What the hell?"

"You said, follow." L.I.A.M. tilted his head.

McDaniels shook his head and gripped L.I.A.M. by the shoulders. The FBI agent moved the android a few steps to the side. "Watch me, then you will go." Running down and under the basketball rim, he touched the baseline and ran to the free-throw line. James turned and ran back to the baseline, then ran faster to the half-court line. Returning to the baseline, James now sprinted to the far free-throw line and back. Pouring it on, James ran as fast as he could the full length of the court. Breathing heavily, he waved at L.I.A.M. and said, "Now you."

L.I.A.M. paused a moment, tilting his head, then extending it in a crane-like, awkward movement. Then he took off like a shot, running toward the baseline. His form was perfect, his speed almost a blur. L.I.A.M. slid to each line with a screech of his brand new Sketcher's tennis shoes they had bought him.

James was not timing L.I.A.M., but it took him seemingly no time to touch the lines and stop right in front of the special agent. L.I.A.M. stood straight as an arrow, calm, not an extra breath taken.

"Complete," L.I.A.M. stated.

"Fast. Good job," James said, still breathing heavily.

"I averaged twelve miles an hour. The stopping and redirection caused me not to achieve maximum speed."

McDaniels nodded and waved to the doctors. "Throw me the basketball."

Brooks dug into a duffel bag of sporting equipment and pulled out the large orange ball, then began to walk the ball across the floor, holding it out.

"Just throw it here," James told the man. If he had ever seen a more grotesque movement, he couldn't recall. The doctor used both hands, arched his back, kicked a leg, and the basketball still only went about two feet, then rolled toward James.

Using a foot, McDaniels kicked the ball up and caught it. He turned to L.I.A.M., who was focused on the ball. "Jeez."

"I am fully aware of the rules of the game, as well as the objective. Won't we need more people?" L.I.A.M. asked.

"Let's shoot around a bit, warm up. Then we may play a little one-on-one or some horse."

L.I.A.M.'s eyes took a long blink, then he walked toward the basket. "This is very mathematical. Arch, angle, force, speed."

James dribbled out to center court, then toward the rim. Squaring up to the basket, the agent threw a two-handed set shot toward the cylinder. The ball went through the hoop and James nodded. "That's right. Throw it here," he told L.I.A.M. L.I.A.M. ran after the ball, picked it up and threw it to the agent. The velocity of the throw was too much, far too much; James ducked out of the way instead of trying to catch the ball.

"L.I.A.M.!!" Dr. Gabby Potts yelled from the sidelines.

"Little too much mustard there, kiddo." McDaniels shook his head as he sat on the hardwood.

"Mustard? I do not understand?" L.I.A.M. gave another tilt of the head.

Both doctors and the university president hurried out onto the court. "You threw that ball much too hard, L.I.A.M.," Dr. Brooks told his creation.

"You have to be careful, L.I.A.M. Last thing you ever want to do is hurt a person," Dr. Potts added.

James climbed to his feet and came face to face with the android. "Perhaps it would be best if you start gently, and increase your strength as needed. Obviously, you can do things, so be mindful of others." He told L.I.A.M. with a wink, "Now, go get the ball."

L.I.A.M. turned and focused on the basketball, then took off like a shot to retrieve it. Coming back in a matter of seconds, he held it out with both hands for McDaniels. "You have quick reflexes for a person your age, Special Agent James McDaniels."

"Why do you use my full name? You call Dr. Potts Gabby."

"She told me to."

"L.I.A.M., you need to apologize to James," Dr. Potts directed.

L.I.A.M. tilted his head and gave Gabby a questioning expression.

"Did you see the expression?" Dr. Brooks stepped forward, examining L.I.A.M.'s face closely. "There was puzzlement. Did you do that on purpose, L.I.A.M.?"

"I do not understand what I did wrong, or why an apology is required. I threw the ball, be it with a higher velocity than Special Agent James McDaniels wanted, but as I was told to do. Special Agent James McDaniels avoided the ball and is uninjured. I searched for an expression to project my lack of understanding."

"You did very well," Brooks said.

Potts stepped forward, next to Brooks. "It was so very natural. I might not have noticed had you not said something. L.I.A.M. is integrating so well, and so quickly." She reached up and touched L.I.A.M.'s face, giving a slight smack to his cheek. "You still need to apologize to James."

L.I.A.M. stepped back from the doctors and moved in front of McDaniels. "Special Agent James McDaniels, I would like to apologize for my conduct. Throwing the ball with such speed could have caused you pain or injury. I am sorry and hope you can and will forgive me." The android's expressions presented great emotion and sincerity.

McDaniels put up a hand to halt the apology. "First, you need to mix up how you address people. If you introduce me, use my full title and name; but if we are one-on-one, you should use just James, McDaniels, or Special Agent. Just mix it up; using the whole thing is just odd." James nodded and L.I.A.M. nodded in return.

"Second, you obviously have a different set of capabilities than regular people. As Doc said: stronger, faster, smarter. You have to be able to seem human, so you should limit your capabilities to median human standards, unless needed."

"That's an excellent suggestion," Gabby said.

"Yes, L.I.A.M., put in the parameters of average human abilities and try to maintain those unless a heightened state is required," Dr. Brooks said.

The university president stepped around next to McDaniels, whispering, "Smart people…" He gave a grunt. "I am surprised such buffers weren't put in place from the beginning."

"Everything moved so quickly," Brooks said. "I had not expected L.I.A.M. to have a body and so never even suggested limits to his physical functioning."

"Well, we thought of it now. This is a learning experience for all of us. No harm was intended." McDaniels extended his hand to L.I.A.M. "We are in this together, a team. I am here to help and to protect you."

L.I.A.M. extended his hand and gripped McDaniels's hand in his. Slowly and gently, L.I.A.M. applied pressure, matching his counterpart exactly. Tilting his head somewhat, L.I.A.M. repeated, "A team."

McDaniels shook the android's hand, nodded and gave a half smile. "That's correct, a team. You need to count on us as we will count on you. We have to trust each other." James released L.I.A.M.'s hand.

CHAPTER 22

TASK FORCE LEADER SPECIAL AGENT BRANDON HARDING was called to receive visitors at the entry desk in the lobby of the FBI Special Response Headquarters. Brandon had been expecting the call. As ordered, he had arranged a tour for Sasha Blonde, reporter with *Indepth News*. She had broken the Ghost serial killer story and had been riding the wave ever since. The public interest had been piqued, but now started to waver, and the savvy bombshell knew she either had to keep the heat on or give up the Ghost.

Brandon rode the elevator down alone, appreciating the quiet moment to himself. He knew Sasha Blonde was looking for some meat to feed the public. His boss, Director Maroni, had served him up. The director had warned him of the woman, and her methods. Brandon knew well enough what a motivated woman could do when she set her sights on something. Sasha Borkisnicvic had come from some Soviet bloc nation, and climbed to a nightly segment on American television. She was not to be underestimated.

The elevator dinged and the doors parted. There next to the greeter's desk was a vision of loveliness. Tall, with long and perfect legs, standing in high heels and a short skirt, red leather. Her flaxen locks poured over her shoulders like a golden waterfall. The black sports jacket accented the richness of the color. She broke a smile as she saw Brandon, and the act was stunning. Harding was frozen, until the elevator doors began to close, forcing him to step out. Walking toward the reporter, Brandon returned the smile with a toothy grin of his own.

"Special Agent Harding. I do appreciate you allowing us access to the Response Team Headquarters. Thank you." Sasha Blonde met Brandon's approach with a handshake. Her hand was like the petals of a lily; delicate, soft and white. Their eyes met and Brandon was lost for an infinite moment, entranced by her beauty and the depth of the blue in her eyes.

A slight smile emerged, then the goddess gently bit her bottom lip. Her eyebrow raised and she said something Brandon did not hear. Focusing on those scarlet red lips, he watched as she mouthed, "Thank you." Drawing back her hand, she held his gaze for one more moment, then swished her hair and motioned to her cameraman.

The spell broken, Harding felt sheepish, but assumed such a woman surely dealt with moments like that regularly. "You are welcome. My apologies; you reminded me of someone just then." Brandon attempted to cover his daze with memory. "Please follow me; you do have your visitor badges?" Harding paused to look past the beautiful reporter to her cameraman, who tapped the plastic card with the word *visitor* printed boldly on it. "Good, let's go."

The three entered the elevator and waited for the ride to begin, but before Harding pressed the button for the floor, he turned to both passengers. "I hope you understand how rare this is, and will show my team, the bureau, and the victims of this investigation the proper respect. I don't mind you asking me the hard questions, but I am asking you to keep in mind what we do here. This is an important team, doing serious work. Just don't sell us out for a story." Brandon led the reporter and her cameraman to the conference room. He had informed his team that each of them would have to speak with Sasha Blonde, and to be mindful of the conversation. The cameraman set up a tripod and attached the camera, looking through the eyepiece to check the frame. Sasha sat in a chair and angled it toward the conference table and the camera. "How do we look?" she asked.

"Look good," the cameraman said, clicking on a spotlight.

Harding put up a hand. "I have a few things to do, and I know you want to talk with the team, so I'll send them in and we can have our interview a bit later." He exited the conference room, closing the door behind him.

Sasha moved to the conference room windows and looked out at the bullpen. The agents were busy at their desks but glancing up to look at her. She watched Harding walk down and address them. Each of the agents looked up at her now deliberately. Her cameraman moved up next to her. "You going to go after them?"

"Softly. I need to draw the public along, and gaining these people's trust will pay off better than a quick slam. The Ghost is the real prize; these people are just the players. Think of the criminals in the thirties, they became famous. We know of Elliot Ness, but barely, and he is the only memorable law enforcement officer of note." The conference door opened and in walked a woman. Closing the door behind her, she crossed the room and introduced herself as Special Agent Allison Carter. Sasha directed her to the chairs, where Carter started to sit where Sasha had planned to sit. "Oh, if you would." The blonde reporter pointed out the other chair. "My right side is more camera friendly."

Carter smiled and nodded, giving a purposeful look at the reporter's face. "Yes, I can see it," she said and moved to the other chair.

Sasha Blonde put a hand to the left side of her face as she moved to take her seat. The cameraman moved in and attached small microphones to each woman. Moving behind the camera, he gave Sasha a thumbs up. "Okay, let's just talk a bit, get some background as he sets the levels," Sasha told Allison Carter. "You are?" she asked as she flipped open her notepad.

"Special Agent Allison Carter."

"Lead profiler," Sasha said, and Allison nodded. "So, tell me where you are from, where you went to school?"

"Grew up in New England. Vermont as a young girl, then New Hampshire as a teen. Attended Harvard; major in psychology, master's, Ph.D."

The reporter smiled. "Have you done an interview like this before?"

"No."

"Well, just relax and let's talk. Couple girls having a chat is all. What drew you to psychology?" Sasha asked.

"The complexity of the human mind is truly fascinating. Thoughts, dreams, memories; everything about humanity is an extension of the mind. My father was a psychologist and worked with the mentally ill. Hearing his stories as a girl piqued my interest."

"So, your father working with the mentally ill—so profiling the criminal mind is similar?" Allison Carter shifted in her seat. "Not all criminals are insane. There is a difference between profiling and treating the mentally ill. Many people suffer from a variety of mental issues: depression, trauma, schizophrenia, bipolar disorder, even psychopathy. Such people can live non-criminal and productive lives without incident."

"You are saying we have psychopaths living among us?" the reporter asked.

"Oh yes. In fact, psychopaths tend to do very well in business. Functioning psychopaths, that is to say. The lack of emotional connection or compassion causes them to make detached decisions." Allison gave the blonde a sideways look. "You are a reporter; you understand how to detach from a story."

"Are you calling me a psychopath?" Sasha sat back in her seat.

Carter shook her head. "No, no; you would have to be tested. I don't want you to think all people with mental disorders are criminal, that's all."

Sasha Blonde smiled and leaned forward again. "What about the Ghost? Is he a psychopath?"

"Again, without testing, an absolute diagnosis is impossible, but a level of sociopathic behavior has been displayed. This Ghost, as you call him, or them, is obviously highly intelligent and motivated."

"Them? What do you mean them? You think there are more than one Ghost?"

Carter tilted her head and grinned without showing any teeth. "Sasha, we at the FBI cannot presume anything. These cases are all extremely different in a multitude of ways, which is the reason it took so long to discern a pattern at all. Limiting our investigation to a single individual when the method is so varied, the geography so expansive, the victimology so diverse—to do so would be malpractice. We have a job to do, just as you do; you keep the public informed, we keep the public safe."

"A school full of dead children, the public doesn't feel safe," Sasha Blonde jabbed.

"We both have improvement to strive for. The extremes to which this Ghost has gone to hide his involvement, to throw law enforcement off the scent, is borderline genius. The added strike after public atten-tion presents a narcissistic personality."

"What does that mean?"

"Such a change in pattern, an evolution, so to speak. Going from hit and hide type murders to the national news is a leap. This individual was extremely secretive, but you exposed him to the world. If I were you, I would be very careful," Carter warned.

"Is that a threat, or a warning? What are you trying to say?"

"This narcissistic development is a direct result of you. This individual or individuals see you as the face of their coming out to the world, and they answered this disclosure not by lying low, but infecting a school full of children. You surely see this story as your big break, your ride to fame, and it has certainly brought you the limelight. I am simply warning you that your story also gained you the attention of the worst serial killer this nation has ever faced. My suggestion to you would be to hope we catch this Ghost."

Sasha had had enough from the profiler and was a little freaked out by the whole warning. She had considered the possibility the Ghost might target her, but dismissed it. She was a celebrity and had made him famous. As the profiler had said, he answered the call to infamy by killing a school. This sick bastard had found his place center stage, and Sasha figured it would lead to his downfall. The Ghost had been so careful for so long, going undetected, but now everyone knew and was watchful. Now, he was trying to outdo himself and grow his legend. She figured he would make a mistake and get caught, helping her career even more. If the profiler was correct about the Ghost, identifying her as the catalyst to his evolution, perhaps she would get the big interview after he was apprehended.

The interviews continued. Sasha Blonde spoke with the two tactical officers about their military backgrounds, the dangers of the job, and the thrill of a raid. Special Agent Sam Lee was a gentleman with a Southern accent and was extremely large; his hand dwarfed hers when they shook. Agent Tyrone Johnson was not as large, but seemed more muscularly defined, and was certainly more flirtatious than his superior. The big bald black man eyed her legs with a hunger Sasha could not help but notice. Such glaring was nothing new to Sasha; men had eyed her since she was a young girl. A man with a look in his eye as this one had used to frighten her, but she had learned how to turn a man's lust into her advantage. Agent Johnson told her everything she asked and more; unfortunately, he didn't know much.

Sasha interviewed the crime scene investigators, Special Agent Jody Jensen and Agent Wu Park. Jensen was a pleasure, very personable and friendly, looked smart and capable, sounded down-to-earth and intelligent. She came across with compassion and concern, but also with reassuring quality. Agent Park was a different story: a know-it-all, who was overly flirty and attempted to use suggestions and double entendre to seem playful. His look on camera was less than impressive and Sasha knew right away she wouldn't be using any of his interview. Such was the problem with televised news: segments were short. A reporter would interview a half dozen people, have hours of tape, but only use thirty seconds of this one or that.

Her interview with the other profiler was interesting. Agent Keith Kennedy was a very smart and very young man. He explained himself as gifted, but to Sasha the boy was just a genius. She had been given lots of gifts and seen plenty of smart people, but this kid had been touched by God. He was amazing, answering questions she considered extremely hard with ease. It was only after she had asked him of his difficulties with such a blessing from God that she realized the true depth of the young man.

"I could ask you the very same question," he responded. "I have a good mind, you are attractive, we would be considered outside the norm. Being different can be a drawback or an advantage; such would be dependent upon circumstance and the individual."

"You cannot compare my looks with your genius."

"I am part of the upper one percent of the measured populace for intelligence. You think you are not? For beauty, that is. Certain people are abnormal, and this can be a good or bad mutation. Look at Special Agent Lee; large, strong, violent, obviously part of a segmented division of the populace. He found his role in society by being a protector, a guardian. Had he not, the probability of average people finding him a threat and removing him from their society is extremely high."

"Remove? There are lots of large men in society," Sasha said.

"Large, strong, and violent; such men have to find a place, places society provides. Military, sports, law enforcement; genetic research has shown a third of modern men are genetically predispositioned toward aggression and violence. Our social structure had to develop outlets and occupations for such men. Same as having pedestals for the beautiful people. A thousand years ago you would have been sculpted, a muse or goddess, the face to launch a thousand ships. Today you are on TV for all to see." Agent Kennedy smiled.

Sasha considered what the young man had to say and realized he was correct, but that led her to ask, "So, what of the Ghost? Where are such people in the scheme of things?"

"Beautiful, strong, smart, good—these are all aspects of the human structure and have their opposing or polar opposite. Ugly, weak, ignorant, and evil: are all among us and equally as pervasive. What triggered an obviously intelligent person to focus their energy on killing people is hard to say, but is an often enough occurrence in people to be accounted as human nature. Granted, it is a fringe nature or abnormal behavior, but consistent enough over time and region to be as common as we are." The brilliant young man shrugged, ending the interview.

Sasha Blonde had a newfound respect for the Special Response Task Force and the work they were doing. She also could see the intelligence of the task force leader, Special Agent Harding. The profilers' book-ending the interviews, the flirtation of the tactical warrior countered by that of the nerdy scientist. She had learned nothing new of the Ghost, gaining no insights, but felt as if she better understood the hunt and the hunters. This team was a collaboration of skills which complemented each other, a toolkit of people tasked with catching the evil among us.

Harding entered the conference room and closed the door behind him. "So, did you get what you wanted?" he asked.

"Truth be told, I wasn't sure what I was expecting, but I did gain an understanding. Think I can put a more personal face on the hunters of evil. People need heroes." Sasha Blonde motioned Brandon to the interview chair.

CHAPTER 23

THE TWO PLANES LANDED, one right after the other on the small runway in Ohio. Waiting next to a Lincoln Town Car and a large black Suburban were Franklin Rhodes and James McDaniels. Exiting the first plane was DARPA representative Colonel Thad Vetter, followed by Army Chief of Staff General Patrick McHenry. They stopped to shake hands with the men from the second plane, Senator John Miller, FBI Director Anthony Maroni, and FBI Special Response Task Force leader Brandon Harding.

The group boarded their vehicles and headed to the university. Talk in either car was limited to polite conversation. They all had received reports on the progress of the operation and had come to see for themselves, as well as test the new technology. Each man had their reasons to want the project to be successful. They expected failure to be more probable, but the hope was a leap in technology which would rival the computer itself. The reports painted the project in a glowing light, but now these powerful men needed to see for themselves.

Rhodes drove the lead vehicle, his Lincoln Town Car, followed by McDaniels driving the Suburban. They pulled up to the science building and parked. The men gathered on the outside steps before entering.

"I saw the interview on that *Indepth News* show. You did very well, Special Agent Harding," Senator Miller said.

"Thank you, Senator," Brandon answered.

"Old girl put a new spin on things, made us look pretty good," McDaniels added.

"I caught part of that," General McHenery joined the conversation. "That blonde as good-looking in person?"

"It was good of her to focus on the role the task force plays," Maroni said, "instead of pointing out that she understood the hunt better than the hunters. This team was a collaboration of skills which complemented each other, a human toolkit tasked with catching the evil among us. The failures and lack of direction we really have were overlooked. She could have made the bureau look poorly."

Franklin Rhodes led the way up to the building and held open the door. "I think you gentlemen will be amazed when you see L.I.A.M.," he said as the group filed past.

"We shall see," Maroni said as he marched through the basement door toward the laboratory.

The seven men moved down the corridor toward Dr. Brooks's lab. They were quiet, but the sheer numbers created a rustle as they moved down the hallway. The director stopped at the closed door and waited for the university president to weave through the men. Rhodes did not pause as he threw open the laboratory door and walked in.

Nathan Brooks and Gabby Potts stood at the lab table with L.I.A.M. Both doctors had on fresh pressed lab coats, and L.I.A.M. was wearing tan pants with a blue sports coat. They looked up, and Dr. Potts rounded the table to greet the group with a wide smile and a slight bounce in her step. "We have been expecting you. Thanks for coming."

Dr. Brooks and L.I.A.M. moved to be by Gabby's side. "L.I.A.M., why don't you officially introduce yourself." Nathan patted L.I.A.M. on the shoulder.

The group of men lined up inside the laboratory door as McDaniels closed it behind them. L.I.A.M. walked to the end where James gave him a smile. Walking back past each man without making eye contact, L.I.A.M. stopped and pivoted, facing Senator Miller and extending his hand.

"I am L.I.A.M., combined creation of Dr. Nathan Brooks and Dr. Gabriella Potts. L.I.A.M. stands for Logical, Intellectual, Autonomous, Mechanism. You are Senator John Miller and it is my honor to make your acquaintance. In the flesh, so to speak." L.I.A.M. smiled, shaking the man's hand.

Moving down the line, L.I.A.M. introduced himself to each of them one at a time. When he reached Colonel Thad Vetter, the colonel pulled L.I.A.M. close. The young colonel eyed L.I.A.M. very closely, coming very close to the android's face.

McDaniels stepped up. "Kind of close, aren't ya?"

Vetter gave a sideways glance at the FBI agent and grunted.

McDaniels squinted at the soldier. "We're trying to teach L.I.A.M. proper manners. You being in his face sets a poor example." James McDaniels put the back of his hand on Colonel Vetter's chest.

"Mind your hand, old man. This here is property of Uncle Sam and DARPA." Vetter now glared at McDaniels.

Dr. Brooks stepped forward. "L.I.A.M. is not the property of DARPA, or anyone, or any such thing. Any military ideas you may have for him were not agreed to. I won't have my creation turned into a weapon."

"This collaboration was authorized by the President of the United States, for a law enforcement emergency," Senator Miller said.

"Denison University has the rights to any intellectual property coming by way of our facility or staff, or by any descendent thereof," Franklin Rhodes put in.

The group disagreement toward who was what quickly drew stark lines. Powerful men all wanted the control and the promise of good things. Such had been the way of the world since men gathered together. McDaniels moved toward the lab table and pulled L.I.A.M. with him, giving an eye to Harding to join them. The three stood at the table and watched the group as voices grew louder.

Brandon nodded and moved toward the two, focused on L.I.A.M. "How are you, L.I.A.M.? It is good to see you again."

"Why is it they argue? I am not property. I am L.I.A.M.," L.I.A.M. returned.

"I have heard of DARPA, but what the hell is it?" McDaniels asked.

"Defense Advanced Research Projects Agency," L.I.A.M. answered.

James gave a questioning look, furrowing his brow. "What the hell does that mean?"

"The military gives huge amounts of money to people like the lady doctor over there to develop cutting-edge science, which they in turn develop into weapons. DARPA created the internet," Harding answered.

"The internet isn't a weapon," McDaniels said.

"Isn't it?" Brandon countered. "L.I.A.M., can you flash the power grid for this building? Kill the lights for ten seconds," Harding told the mechanism.

"Yes, Special Agent Harding," L.I.A.M. responded.

"Please do." Brandon gave James a slap on the shoulder.

The lights went out and the men went silent. The darkness of the basement engulfed them all. Murmurs began as people questioned the situation. "Wow, L.I.A.M., very impressive," McDaniels said.

"Thank you, James," L.I.A.M. said.

"Everyone relax and listen up. Stop arguing, we have plenty to do and you all can fight this out down the road. Let us not forget why we are here," Harding's voice boomed through the darkness. "All right, L.I.A.M., turn the lights back on."

The lights returned and the group focused on the lab table. "Who owns what and what rights are whose are a waste of time for now. You wanted a test, so how is this going to work?" Brandon brought the group back to task.

The men and Dr. Potts moved around the lab table to join Harding and McDaniels, as well as L.I.A.M. "You killed the lights?" Colonel Vetter asked L.I.A.M.

"Yes."

"A scavenger hunt. Isn't that what was suggested, Director?" Senator Miller spoke up.

"Yeah, that was the plan."

"So, what are the parameters?" Dr. Brooks asked.

"Need the rules. Is there a time limit, or geographic restraint?" McDaniels asked.

The men around the lab table looked from one to another. "Twenty-four hours, and local, within driving distance," General McHenery said.

"So, what is the hunt? What should L.I.A.M. have to retrieve, and who should accompany him? How much can we help?" Harding asked.

"We have to go, in order to monitor L.I.A.M.," Dr. Brooks stated, waving a hand toward Potts to include her.

"Should make this as it will be when we send them out to investigate," Brandon went on. "L.I.A.M., the docs, with McDaniels as security and observer."

"Yes, but as a proper test they should allow L.I.A.M. to achieve the test on his own. No help from anyone," Director Maroni stated firmly.

"What's the hunt?" Colonel Vetter asked.

"A wheelchair," Senator Miller blurted out. The outburst drew everyone's attention. The senator just shrugged.

Harding nodded and pulled a small notepad from his pocket, writing the first item down. "Okay, what else?"

"Tank of oxygen," General McHenery added.

Brandon wrote the item down.

"How about a milking stool?" Franklin Rhodes said, gaining a few looks.

Harding smiled and wrote down the man's suggestion. "The signature of the sheriff," he said and wrote his own contribution to the paper.

Director Maroni pointed to the pad. "A bowler hat," he said with a crafty smile. "The round-topped hat; a bowler."

Brandon wrote it down and looked over the list. "Okay, a wheelchair, a tank of oxygen, a milking stool, the sheriff's autograph, and a bowler hat. You have twenty-four hours. What do you say, L.I.A.M., are you up for the challenge? Do you accept?"

L.I.A.M. moved his head to one side in a slight jerk, then back; the action seemed almost robotic. "I do accept. I won't need twenty-four hours. Accounting for any mechanical malfunctions and traffic delays, five hours is all I shall need to achieve this task."

McDaniels gripped L.I.A.M. by the shoulder. "No sense limiting yourself. The time is offered; if you can do it more quickly, that's great. Leave the clock alone; they gave you twenty-four hours, it is wise to keep it."

"If it can do it in five hours, let's put it to the test," Maroni said.

"No. You dictated the rules and the time limit, no changing," Gabby Potts insisted.

"I agree, no changes. We can all spend the night in Columbus. They have a casino; have a few drinks, steaks are on me. Come back tomorrow and hear the report. Fair is fair," General McHenery said.

The men around the table nodded and began to move toward the door. Anthony Maroni pulled his two agents to the side and addressed McDaniels in a hushed tone. "You keep a watchful eye on this thing. No shenanigans. This is a critical test and I want a real-world assessment. No soft steppin'; get me?"

"Yes, sir."

Brandon slapped James on the back. "You'll do fine. Just remember you'll be taking these people out to hunt the unsub. You have to be sure." Harding gave his agent a wink.

Franklin Rhodes led the procession from the lab. As powerful men do, these were headed off to socialize while the real work was being done by their subordinates. McDaniels didn't mind; he never liked someone looking over his shoulder. As the door closed on the laboratory, the two doctors looked at McDaniels. "What do you think?" Dr. Potts asked him.

James shrugged and turned to L.I.A.M. "You already know where we are going, don't you?"

"Yes."

"That Colonel Vetter is deluded to think I will allow L.I.A.M. to be used by the military," Brooks said as he leaned on the lab table. "How could you be allied with such people?" he asked Gabby.

"DARPA has funded all kinds of scientific breakthroughs. Venture capital is not so easily come by these days. Look at the hardware, time, and detail put into the Tinman. I wasn't sitting in a basement writing code." Potts sounded irritated.

"What do you think the military will do with your Tinman? Human drones?" Brooks returned with a level of disgust.

"What does DARPA mean again?" McDaniels asked L.I.A.M.

"Defense Advanced Research Projects Agency."

"And that's military?"

"A division. As Gabby stated, a venture capital provider, as well as a mediator putting different research together. The agency is huge, with fingers in almost every university and state of the art laboratory in the country."

"You sound very natural, L.I.A.M.," Brooks said to his creation.

"Thank you, Doctor. I want to appear as human as I can."

"You have done so very well," Potts added.

"I did have a request of Special Agent McDaniels," L.I.A.M. said. "I would like to be taught some self-defense. I was reviewing some martial arts and reviewed the FBI training requirements, which incorporate different styles. I believe if I am to be in the field, a knowledge of some defensive maneuvers would be advantageous. I have studied all I can from a mechanical sense, but would like James to instruct me in the physical realm."

"Well, I don't know, you'll have to ask your folks. Let's get this test run out of the way and then we shall see," McDaniels returned with a smile.

"I don't know if that is a good idea, L.I.A.M., you learning to fight," Brooks said. "Kind of lends itself to the whole military thing. I don't want you to ever harm a person."

"Ain't there rules for robots or something? I saw on one of those science fiction movies," McDaniels said.

"I did not limit L.I.A.M. with any restrictions. The three rules of robotics are human paranoia, our attempt to control our creations. Like the tree of knowledge in the garden of Eden, God orders man to not partake of the fruit. Yet, the tree is there, the fruit tempting, and if omnipotence is God's understanding, knowing full well man would bend to his weakness. It is a guilt trip, and I wasn't going to do that to L.I.A.M."

Brooks allowed a moment before continuing. "There are plenty of examples he may draw from to make a good decision. To say, a good decision he shall make for himself."

"So, why wouldn't you want him to learn to defend himself?" Gabby asked.

"I had never anticipated the amazing work you have done, Dr. Potts. Your Tinman is more than human, but indistinguishable from the real thing. I have real deep concerns of what the military may have in mind for our work."

"You think they have seen the Terminator? Want a new army of human-like drones? Stronger, faster, smarter, never sleep, never eat, can't be bargained with, reasoned with, and will not stop, ever, until…" McDaniels allowed his quote to linger.

"That would be the most obvious usage," Brooks said. "A most destructive usage, to be sure. L.I.A.M. is meant to help mankind, to be the next step, the possibility of hope and promise. L.I.A.M. is the advancement of consciousness, an extension of us all. Using him as an instrument of violence is not my intention for him."

Gabby Potts rounded the edge of the table and put a hand upon Nathan Brooks's arm. "You did very well with L.I.A.M. and he asked James to teach him to defend himself. His choice. I was focused on my work, not how the world might apply it once I was done. I don't want to see my work turned toward war or violence, but we are but the visionaries and it is the people who will use what we do to whatever end."

Brooks nodded. "The Manhattan Project, Sam Colt, Columbus, Jesus; the lives cost by the extension of choices, and had they paused for thought to consider what impact would result? We are not naïve, nor should we pretend that our fellow man will embrace the benefits of our labor, before they pollute with the blood of others."

McDaniels moved over to the doctors. "Look, we have a test to complete. You aren't going to unmake L.I.A.M., and the quicker we get him out into the field, the quicker he can help us catch the person killing people. Your invention will directly save lives. What comes down the road is down the road; and I get your hesitation. Deals with the devil are never fair and always favor that damn devil. You took money from the military, and from one look at that colonel, you should have known they had an agenda," he said to Gabby.

"Dr. Brooks, you wanted to give L.I.A.M. a body and didn't stop to ask what strings might be attached. We have work to do. Let's get started," McDaniels told the bald-headed doctor.

"What of my request, James?" L.I.A.M. asked.

"Perhaps; let's get this test done and then we will see."

The group broke from the table and collected the few supplies they thought they might need. They headed out from the basement laboratory and exited the rear of the building, where they had a cargo van waiting. Franklin Rhodes had given them a university vehicle to use during L.I.A.M.'s training. They had ventured around campus and into the local town but mostly stayed near the lab or the gymnasium. The doctors had been careful with their creations, not wanting to cause any unneeded damage. McDaniels wanted to know L.I.A.M.'s limitations and his capabilities. As they boarded the van, McDaniels could see even more clearly that the doctors had no idea what they had created and what others might do with that creation.

"May I drive, Special Agent McDaniels?" L.I.A.M. asked.

The last few days, James had been allowing L.I.A.M. to drive around the campus. "No, not today. You focus on those items you need to retrieve. Perhaps after you collect them, you can drive home."

L.I.A.M. trotted around the van and got in the passenger side, looking at the two doctors in the back seats.

"You seem excited, L.I.A.M."

"Yes. I am excited. How interesting. I feel very, interesting," L.I.A.M. said.

James McDaniels closed the driver's door of the cargo van. "How or why does L.I.A.M. think he feels? Machines don't feel. Do they?"

"L.I.A.M.'s special," Gabby said. "There are receptors in the Tinman's skin, so he can literally feel and register texture, temperature, pain, damage, gentleness, et cetera. What Nathan has done with L.I.A.M.'s cognition is beyond any of my wildest hopes or expectations. He actually understands emotions, processes them, identifies conditions, as well as proper responses. As a child learns to be happy or sad, disappointed, angry, to love, to show empathy and compassion, L.I.A.M. has learned."

"But he doesn't feel them, not like I or we do; does he?" James asked.

"How is it you think you understand what you think you feel?" Dr. Brooks leaned forward in the van. "You take in information and process it, using your intellect and memory, your experiences, and determine how you feel about it. Well, so does L.I.A.M. He has to do this all at once, with an advanced mind. You grew into yours."

James McDaniels started the van and put it into gear. He thought about what was said, considered how he had grown and developed, learned. They drove toward the exit of the campus. James stopped the vehicle. "So, where are we headed, L.I.A.M.?"

"Columbus. The capital will serve us well. Everything we need is there."

McDaniels turned right and headed for Ohio's largest city. Looking over at the android next to him, James wondered how and what it was thinking, if anything at all. He quietly pondered if L.I.A.M. could actually feel; whether he was like a child or just a machine. Looking at the man, which L.I.A.M. appeared to be, was very misleading. What extent this creation would reach was yet to be determined. The time he had spent with L.I.A.M. had allowed James to better understand, to bond with L.I.A.M. and grow a fondness for the android. L.I.A.M.'s naivety was childlike, but James knew this was no child, and every bit of information L.I.A.M. absorbed was a lesson with consequences to come.

James had learned over a lifetime of lessons that things change, aren't as they seem, are your perception versus the true reality. The doctors had been blind with the thrill of creation, innovation, and development, never pausing to question.

"A smart man will ask himself if he can do something; a wise man will question if he should," McDaniels said.

"Why is it you would say that?" Brooks asked.

"True, ain't it? A good lesson for L.I.A.M. to take to heart, or whatever." James waved a hand at L.I.A.M., giving him a glance. "A level of moral responsibility should not be overlooked in L.I.A.M.'s training. Perhaps learning some self-defense will be good. Yet the primary lesson is to know when and to what extent to use what you know."

"Placing a moral structure on L.I.A.M. is like pressing our values upon a clean slate. We should allow him to develop his own moral standard," Brooks stated firmly.

"Clean slate or not, the world has rules," McDaniels said. "Having a foundation of principles to go by isn't a bad thing. You said he is learning his emotions; a little help is our moral responsibility."

"I am aware of the laws and proper manners, as well as all the religious and cultural boundaries," L.I.A.M. said. "I understand why these exist and agree that legal as well as moral parameters are needed to govern a large grouping of human beings."

"Make it sound like daycare, or some kind of herd."

"You of all people know how things can get without rules and laws. Riots in the streets because a team wins a sporting competition. This is illogical and destructive toward one's own place of residence. Humans can be extremely unpredictable," L.I.A.M. countered.

"Part of the difficulty of developing an intelligence to understand it." Dr. Brooks leaned forward again. "Part of the human experience is developing one's own moral compass. I wanted L.I.A.M. to decide for himself."

McDaniels looked over his shoulder at Nathan, then to Gabby, and then at L.I.A.M. Focusing on the road ahead, he said, "Ever think you were gambling with pretty big stakes?"

"No more so than we do with anyone else." Brooks answered.

"Yeah, but L.I.A.M. is not like anyone else." James looked at the android again. "We have no idea what his moral standing may be. How he views us, what right and wrong may mean to him. Such was a dangerous call, and let's all hope L.I.A.M. values we humans more so than we value each other."

L.I.A.M. gave a slight nod. "I am a product of human innovation, an extension of the human understanding. I know right from wrong."

"Right from wrong, but L.I.A.M., do you understand right from righteous?" James asked.

"Right: in accordance with what is good, proper, or just. In conformity with fact or reason; correct. Appropriate; suitable, desirable. That which is morally, legally, or ethically proper. Righteously; properly. I condensed toward the subject matter. Righteous: acting in an upright, moral way. Morally right or justifiable. Once again, Special Agent McDaniels, I am not sure you are accurate on your definitions. Right versus righteous do not seem to be at odds."

Dr. Potts put a hand on L.I.A.M.'s shoulder and gave it a soft pat. "This is part of your learning the difference between the literal meaning and the implied meaning. More often, people think of being right with making a correct decision. Whereas, being righteous is making a decision for the right reasons."

L.I.A.M. turned in his seat to look at Gabby. "Is this to say a righteous choice or act could be an incorrect decision?"

"You see the complex nature of humanity and why I thought it best to allow L.I.A.M. to form his own opinions toward the subject," Brooks said, leaning back in the seat.

Gabby again patted L.I.A.M.'s shoulder. "These are aspects of your life you will have to learn. James feels a strong difference between doing what is right and that which is righteous."

"Not all the time; but there have been times which have caused me to struggle."

"Example please? So I better understand."

James shifted in his seat and looked from the road, out the side window and then at L.I.A.M. The uncomfortable nature of his thoughts showed on the FBI man's face. "Early in my career, I was part of a raid. A lot of young agents, most on their first field mission. We were all pretty green. We ram the door, front and back; I was part of the five men coming through the back door. Flash-bang grenades were deployed to disorient any occupants. The house had a number of kerosene heaters and the fuel ignited. Combined with the meth lab the father had been brewing in the basement, it was a powder keg. The flames spread quickly as we attempted to clear the house." He paused, shaking his head, and looked out at the countryside.

"We took fire from the bedroom; the father had an AK-47 and was unloading into the narrow hallway. Our lead man took a bullet to the leg and was dragged out by Williams. Smith, Osborne, and myself were left to deal with the gunman. The lead team, which had come in the front door, had already evacuated the house when they found the burning meth lab downstairs. The smoke and heat were becoming unbearable, so we decided to rush the room."

James looked out at the road ahead. "We loaded fresh clips and put down suppressing fire, charging forward. The father was behind a chest of drawers, firing wildly, but too high. The bullets ripped at the ceiling. Smith and Osborne followed me through the door. I flopped on my belly and unloaded my clip into and through the chest of drawers. Smith and Osborne advanced as they shot. The father danced his death dance, gyrating with each bullet, pushing through his flesh. I rolled on my back and put a fresh clip into my Colt Commando; a smaller version of the M-16. Smith and Osborne stood over the body. The smoke was thick and visibility was becoming a matter of feet. I was choking with each breath."

James gave a sideways glance at L.I.A.M. before continuing. "I watched in horror as my two friends were shot in the back. Someone was in the closet, killing my friends. I didn't think, I reacted; opening fire at the muzzle flashes. It was as if the bullets cleared away the smoke, but only for an instant. It was the man's eleven-year-old daughter, in a spring dress and barrettes in her hair. Her eyes were filled with pain and a longing for help. I had shot her a half dozen times and she was dying; I had killed her. I don't remember the explosion. The meth lab and propane tanks went up. I woke up in the hospital with a concussion, burns, and the guilt of killing a child." He shook his head.

"You shouldn't feel guilty about that. She shot your friends," Potts said.

"The difference between right and righteous. I did my job, did nothing criminal; but shooting an eleven-year-old girl is wrong and lay upon my soul. Plenty of points can be made, excuses given, but those eyes find me in the night and will haunt me till the day I die."

"That's truly terrible. I am so sorry," Gabby said.

"You should take the interstate into Columbus," L.I.A.M. directed.

"Did you understand the story James just shared with you, L.I.A.M.?" Dr. Brooks asked.

L.I.A.M. turned his attention to the group. "Emotion plays a role in our actions. James has this lingering guilt because of the age and sex of the individual he shot. I grasp that he wishes he had not had to shoot the little girl, but also realize that if placed in the same situation, he would most likely repeat his action. Thou shalt not kill. A fundamental aspect of law and morality. Defending yourself at the cost of another's life is conflicting, at least from a moral sense."

"Right but not righteous," Brooks said.

"A terrible and unfortunate event, James. I am sorry you had to endure such a thing," Potts said, giving the agent a pat on his shoulder.

The group drove along as L.I.A.M. gave directions. Columbus is the largest city in the state of Ohio and spreads out over miles. L.I.A.M. took them into the city, directing McDaniels to exit and follow the blue hospital signs. They pulled up to Children's Hospital, where James found a parking space.

"May I ask, why this one?"

"This one, what?"

James looked at L.I.A.M. "Probably a half dozen hospitals in this city, maybe more; why this one? Children's?" He turned off the engine.

Moving his chin from shoulder to shoulder and back, L.I.A.M. tilted his head and raised an eyebrow. "Smaller chairs." He opened the cargo van door.

The two doctors and the special agent followed L.I.A.M. into the main entrance of the hospital. Gabby Potts could not help but look into the few rooms where doors were open, seeing the small children lying in their sickbeds. Her heart weighed heavy as she passed by, realizing the tragedy of illness to a child. "With all L.I.A.M. can access, he could be a great doctor," she whispered to Nathan.

"I think he could be a great many things," Brooks returned in a whisper of his own.

The two doctors exchanged half smiles as L.I.A.M. stopped at a door marked *supply*. The android turned the knob and pushed, ripping the inner frame off, doornails and all. "Guess it was locked," McDaniels said as he followed L.I.A.M. inside the supply room. The group stepped inside as both doctors viewed the damage to the door jamb. Closing the door, Nathan exchanged a concerned look with Gabby, giving a slight shrug as they both turned their attention to L.I.A.M. He had a small wheelchair with a tank of oxygen in the seat.

"You broke their door, L.I.A.M.," Gabby Potts said like a scolding mother.

"Yes, Gabby. I have notified the maintenance department of the damage and transferred a donation from both the Federal Bureau of Investigation and Defense Advanced Research Projects Agency. I have also adjusted the inventory to account for the wheelchair and container of oxygen," L.I.A.M. stated.

McDaniels nodded and held the door for the doctors to exit and L.I.A.M. to wheel out his first two items of the treasure hunt. Checking his watch, James considered the time L.I.A.M. had said it would take, and now knew it to be accurate. The group walked out of Children's Hospital without a question asked of them. James opened the rear doors of the cargo van and folded up the tiny wheelchair as L.I.A.M. loaded the tank of oxygen. The hunting party reboarded the van and McDaniels asked, "Where to now?"

"Pull out and drive two blocks west, turn south for five blocks, then one block east," L.I.A.M. instructed. McDaniels followed the directions and as he made the turn east, L.I.A.M. pointed out the windshield. "Turn left at this next street, and park at the curb."

"This is residential, L.I.A.M.; people's homes. What are we doing here?" Potts asked.

"Park there," L.I.A.M. pointed out to McDaniels. James pulled the cargo van up next to the curb and killed the engine. L.I.A.M. opened his door and hopped out. McDaniels began to exit but L.I.A.M. held up his hand. "I have this, just take but a moment."

"You sure?" Brooks asked from the back seat.

L.I.A.M. nodded and closed the door, rounding the front of the van and looking up and down the street before crossing. Bouncing across the street, L.I.A.M. seemed like a grown child, excited to play a game and take a trip in the car. The group in the van watched the android carefully, waiting to see what he was going to do. L.I.A.M. trotted up the three concrete steps leading up to an unkept house. The grass was long, the bushes untrimmed, and the paint faded and flaking. L.I.A.M. took the steps up the porch two at a time but stopped on the landing to look back at the van.

"What's he doing?" Potts asked.

"I don't know," Brooks said.

McDaniels turned to the two doctors in the back seat. "The real question is; what is going to happen after?"

"After, after what?" Gabby asked.

"We all have to figure this treasure hunt is a no-brainer, and he will probably help us catch the Ghost. What then?"

Before the doctors could answer, L.I.A.M. was climbing back into the passenger seat. He was smiling widely as he handed James a sheet of paper. "What is that?" Brooks asked as he leaned up in the seat.

"Eviction notice," McDaniels said without looking at the document.

"Why would you stop to take that?" Potts asked.

The special agent folded the paper and put it in the inside pocket of his sports jacket. "Eviction notices are signed by the county sheriff." James started the van, giving a glace in the rearview mirror at the doctors. "Where now?" he asked, putting the van into gear.

"North. Take the freeway, north on interstate seventy-one."

The ride was quiet. McDaniels could see in the mirror that his question had caused both doctors some thought. These were academic people focused on the science and positive impact their work could have on the world. Gabby seeing L.I.A.M. as a doctor was nice, and some version of him may well be, someday. James figured a M.A.S.H. unit. He had worked for the government long enough to know such an instrument as L.I.A.M. wasn't going to be putting band-aids on little kids' knees.

James had seen the look in the colonel's eyes, the general's too. These were men of war, minds of the fight. A healer was an afterthought, to return a soldier to the battlefield. The use such men and their contemporaries would have for L.I.A.M. did not revolve around the good of mankind or the betterment of anyone besides the United States of America.

"Exit here and follow the signs to the Historical Museum."

Looking at L.I.A.M., James knew this thing was smart and capable. Over the last two weeks L.I.A.M. had learned incredibly well, and now could almost totally pass as a human being. This creation was fast and knew so much, strong and learning; wouldn't be long before L.I.A.M. knew the intentions they had in store for him.

He was naïve, like an innocent child's mind believing his parents about Santa Claus, the tooth fairy, and the good of his fellow man. As happens to all, sooner or later, the lessons of life shatter our innocence and we see the world for exactly what it is. There are good, well-intentioned people, helpful, kind, and generous; but there are also the others. L.I.A.M. was unique, one of a kind, with very special abilities which they, those other types, would choose to exploit.

After parking in the lot of the Ohio Historical Museum, the group piled out, gathering in front of the vehicle. They looked toward the large, square, gray building. "Which item is here? The bowler hat?" Brooks asked.

"We shall find both remaining items here," L.I.A.M. answered and walked toward the entrance of the museum.

McDaniels walked behind L.I.A.M. as the two doctors lagged behind, talking between themselves. The parking lot was sparse of vehicles, but museums weren't a big draw for most cities. "L.I.A.M., what do you think of history?" James asked as they approached the building.

"Which history do you refer to?"

"History, history. Is there another kind?"

The agent held the door for the others to enter. No one was at the visitor's desk, but a small sign read *donations* over a small box. McDaniels pulled money from his pocket and folded up a twenty-dollar bill, sliding it into the box.

"I have also donated a sum from both agencies. You do realize, James, that there are many different histories. Familial, communal, national, global, with numerous perspectives of each, as well as different species' history, evolution, geology, astronomy, on and on." L.I.A.M.'s voice boomed in the open lobby.

"Geology, astronomy; how are those history?"

"Study of layers of rock, the changes over time: geology is the physical history of the Earth. Astronomy studies those bodies beyond the Earth's atmosphere. Do you have any idea how long it takes light from a star to reach your eye? Every night when you look up at the stars, you are looking into the past, viewing history in the moment."

Gabby stepped forward. "We see the light from stars long since black and extinguished."

The group followed as L.I.A.M. led them past displays of cavemen. Half-naked people living in stick huts, gathered around fire, armed with spears. "What do you think of man's history?" James asked.

L.I.A.M. stopped and turned, looking from the doctors, James, and then at the mannequins. Waving his hand toward the display, L.I.A.M. asked, "How different are you from them?"

"Evolution would imply change, yet…" Brooks said.

They reached a display of the industrial revolution, and there before them was a mannequin with a bowler hat. L.I.A.M. did not hesitate, stepping over the barricade and snatching the hat from the head of the dummy. Hopping back over the barrier, L.I.A.M. smiled and placed the hat upon his head, but it was a couple sizes too large and almost covered his eyes. The group gave a chuckle and exchanged looks, nodding at the accomplishment.

"L.I.A.M., do you think we have changed from the caveman?" Gabby asked.

L.I.A.M. stepped toward her and placed the hat upon her head with a gentle smile. "Does this change who you are? The home in which you live, built of wood and stones, bricks. Your vehicles and how quickly you travel or communicate. These are not the evolution of man but the advancement of products and production."

The group hurried after the android as he exited the museum. "Thought you said we were getting the milking stool here too," Brooks asked.

"They have a re-enactment village behind here. A working colonial village. A frontier style, but accuracy is apparently not a primary goal. There is where we shall find the milking stool." L.I.A.M. walked ahead of the group.

CHAPTER 24

BRANDON HARDING SAT AT THE POKER TABLE with Anthony Maroni to his right and General Patrick McHenery to his left. Colonel Thad Vetter sat to the general's left and at the end of the dealer's rotation. Brandon was a novice poker player, good enough to have some fun at a casino but not so skilled to win any real money. The casino in Columbus was small compared to the standard of Vegas or Atlantic City, but the place was comfortable. It felt new, the chips crisp, the dealers friendly.

"Call," Vetter said.

Brandon was drawn back to the game. The men laid out their hands. The colonel disclosed three kings and claimed another pot. He had not won the most hands, but the sly colonel had taken the largest pots. Harding had been a profiler and dabbled with people's minds enough to realize certain games, and the manner in which people play can speak volumes about the way they think and act. The dealer shuffled the deck and dealt out the cards, as each man anteed up.

Looking at his boss, Director Maroni, Brandon knew the man and his enjoyment of his power; knocking on the table to pass the bet, followed by the other men doing the same. This was a man who relished the win, strived to achieve, manipulated whomever to gain position. Yet, here he sat in the first chair from the dealer; not the most favorable position in Brandon's opinion. It made the special agent wonder why. Maroni had certainly played poker before and had sat down first; he chose his place. His dwindling stack of chips only reinforced Brandon's questioning of the director.

"I'll take three," Maroni said, throwing three cards away. The dealer quickly peeled off the top three cards with a flick of her wrist.

Harding tossed in his hand, folding. He looked closely at Maroni; was he losing on purpose, and why would he do that? These were powerful men, especially Maroni and the general; they had the President's ear, oversaw thousands of armed people, and certainly knew how to play poker. This hand went to the general, an inside straight. Each man again threw a chip to the pot and awaited the deal.

"Look a little thin there, Anthony," Senator John Miller observed as he walked up to the table.

"Yeah; here, take my spot, I need to get some more chips. Get a drink," Maroni said.

"All right." Miller smiled and took over Anthony's chair.

Brandon turned his attention to the general, an aggressive player who tried to bully a pot. McHenery saw the challenge in things, the goal of winning and the distaste of loss. He was an 'end justifies the means' type of man. Get it done, no matter what. Men such as he made good generals, because they will kill everyone to win a battle, even their own men. Such are the caliber of men to order the taking of a position at all cost, to hold to the last man, to face undefeatable odds. They become great men, or butchers. As for McHenery, he sat on the shelf, waiting to be unleashed upon a war, or whatever.

"Full house." Vetter displayed his cards and pulled another sizable pot to him. Harding hadn't had the opportunity to know very many like Vetter; there weren't very many like him. A true snake of a man, the shadow walker, a mystery to all. Good or bad, neither, both; fighting for us, them, himself, the principle, pleasure, or just for the fight. Brandon knew such men held everything close to the vest. Saw everyone as an enemy, every moment as dangerous. Paranoia with purpose. Not a nervous fellow, but practical calculated caution at all times. Never opening up, never allowing his guard to fall; a controlled enigma.

"Gentlemen, I have us a private room at the restaurant," Maroni announced, returning with a drink in his hand.

General McHenery stood almost immediately. "Good. Tired of handing the colonel a second salary."

"Appreciate the donation, General."

"Having you guarding a weather station in Antarctica."

The group made their way through the casino in the steak house. Guided to a private room by the hostess, they took their seats around the table. The hostess handed out menus, and took drink orders.

"You are a hell of a card player, Colonel," Brandon said. Vetter only nodded and opened his menu. Harding could tell the young officer was still concentrating, focused from the game and not wanting to give away anything.

So he turned to a guaranteed conversation. "Senator, do you think L.I.A.M. will accomplish the hunt?"

"Well, I would have to say, I have been very impressed with the doctors, and L.I.A.M. is amazing. Yes, I believe he will accomplish the task, retrieve each item, and be waiting for us come tomorrow."

"How about you, Director? Think L.I.A.M. will get it done?"

Maroni gave a shrug and sipped his drink. "I worry what the public might think. Treasure hunt is one thing; being out in the field is another."

A waitress arrived with their drinks and took their orders. Steaks all around. Harding continued to view his companions and develop his opinions. He too was confident in L.I.A.M.'s abilities, and impressed with the two doctors. Reading the reports McDaniels had submitted solidified his belief in the capabilities of L.I.A.M. Yet they also hinted at the dangers such an android could potentially be. Brandon considered the types of uses the military might have for L.I.A.M., or his kind. Wouldn't be hunting down criminals; perhaps terrorists. Did they not marvel at the high-tech breakthrough that L.I.A.M. was, or did they only see a super soldier? "What are your plans for L.I.A.M.?" he asked.

Vetter's eyes locked on Brandon with a seriousness unlike anything he had seen before. "Classified," he said through clenched teeth.

"Don't know or don't want to say? We are all aware of L.I.A.M., and are all bright enough to figure…" Brandon allow the comment to linger.

"Soldier, assassin, spy?" Director Maroni joined in.

"Classified."

"How do you think Dr. Brooks is going to feel about a military application of his creation?" Brandon asked.

"We aren't in the business of feelings. How he or you feel about anything is irrelevant to me or the program. In the interest of national security—a term that overrides everything else. The doctor may not like when we take over his creation, but we will help him to understand."

"That sounds ominous." Senator Miller spoke up. "Having such an advancement being used as an assassin or spy seems like a real waste of talent. L.I.A.M. can access information and apply it in a matter of seconds, which would take us much longer. He would be better served as an analyst or translator, rather than some kind of soldier."

"It, not he," Maroni corrected.

"You devalue the role of soldier, Senator," General McHenery interjected. "The spy and assassin provide our nation a level of safety no translator could touch. We do need quality translators and intel, but the skill it takes to be a deep cover operative or the tip of the spear is greater than you comprehend. A sniper can lie in wait for days to acquire a target, which for an android would be of no concern. Spies can be deployed for years away from home and family, which again is not an issue for L.I.A.M. Agents can be turned, corrupted, sympathize, or simply slip up. A robot won't have these issues."

The conversation halted when the meal was served. Brandon understood the reasoning behind why the military would look to invest in android technology. A programmable soldier, with no families, no feelings to pollute the mission. Military has longed for the mechanical mindset in soldiers; no identity, no questions, no doubts. Take your orders, do what you're told, and achieve the goal. Androids don't need funerals, don't have families harping to Congress about their missing or mistreated loved ones, don't need to be paid, can't be tortured or reveal information. A practical solution as the advancement of technology allowed it. L.I.A.M. was the first in a wave of change to come.

CHAPTER 25

MORNING ARRIVED AND THE GROUP congregated in Dr. Brooks's laboratory to go over the treasure hunt. All the items retrieved were on the lab table with the group surrounding. "Special Agent McDaniels, your report, if you please," Director Maroni began.

James nodded and cleared his throat. "The mission was smooth. L.I.A.M. directed us and retrieved each item on his own. I observed no glitches or any hesitation. A door was damaged at Children's Hospital, but L.I.A.M. notified the maintenance department via the internet, as well as made donations from the FBI and DARPA. Donations were also made to the Historical Museum."

"No one authorized donations. What if they are traced back to this? You all realize we have the press and public breathing down our necks. That Sasha Blonde woman hounds me night and day," Maroni said.

"Not that you mind one little bit, Anthony." McHenery gave the director a sideways glance.

"The donations are untraceable," L.I.A.M. interjected. "I routed them through your charitable employee funds and spread them over all departments nationally. I did not feel it correct to take without compensation."

"How do you feel that you did, L.I.A.M.?" Senator Miller asked.

"Successful."

"Was any attention raised?" Colonel Vetter joined in the questioning.

"No," James said. "We went unnoticed. L.I.A.M. conducted himself in a proper manner, we were out and back in a timely manner, without incident."

"Is L.I.A.M. ready? Do you think he can be a benefit in the field?" Harding asked.

"I do."

"You think he can help us catch this Ghost?"

"I think if we put him on this, he will be the one to catch this sicko. He knew where we needed to go to find every item, even directing us in order to save driving time. Sir, I haven't been impressed by much in my life, but I am amazed by L.I.A.M. It would be my honor to accompany L.I.A.M. into the field, sir."

"Hold on just a second," Maroni said. "We can't have all of you running around task force headquarters and not expect Sasha to notice. I think we should be cautious. Allow L.I.A.M. to review the case files and then we shall see."

"I have reviewed the files, sir. If you recall, I confirmed your supercomputer's list. The files and photos are enough to connect these cases, but having availability to the crime scenes and witness may allow me to observe something perhaps missed."

"Missed? We are the FBI. You think we just miss things? Think you can just waltz in and solve the case quick as you please?"

"You missed the presence of a long-term serial killer, and have yet to develop a substantial lead to the identity or whereabouts of said villain."

"Sure, sure; but if the press gets hold of you, we will all have a problem."

"Why is that?" Dr. Potts asked the director.

"Look at it. It will scare the crap out of everybody, housewives to China's leadership. Hooked into everything, looks like the guy next door, strong, fast, with military funding. You just gave every conspiracy nut and militia member a wet dream." Maroni dropped his hand on the lab table and rolled his eyes.

The group fell silent, exchanging looks. Serious concern showed on everyone's faces but L.I.A.M.'s. The android turned his head from side to side, giving each person a period of observation. His expression was a calm half smile, as the rest of the group fidgeted and tensed.

"We were mandated by the President," Senator Miller pointed out.

"Oh, well; that should comfort everyone," Maroni said sarcastically.

"We still have to catch the Ghost, Anthony. The press, when we do, should put another feather in your cap." Miller raised an eyebrow.

"I am simply saying we have to be careful. We can't have this thing running around D.C."

"How about we focus on the previous crime scenes?" McDaniels suggested.

Harding cleared his throat and leaned forward on the lab table. "We came here to test L.I.A.M., and he passed with flying colors. The whole purpose of all this was to catch the Ghost. However, the director is correct about the press. We have no control if they get hold of this, and that Blonde lady has been ahead of us at every turn." He paused to look at his boss. "Having L.I.A.M. go back over the crime scenes is a good idea, perhaps pick up on something we missed. The press won't pay any attention to a group of scientists going back over things; it will look like we are being thorough."

"So that's the cover story. Scientists re-evaluating the scene?" Senator Miller asked.

"That's the truth. Why lie when we don't need to?"

"You made it sound as if you have a leak, someone feeding the press info," Vetter said with an accusatory tone.

Brandon shrugged and was about to answer, but his boss leapt at the comment. "She got hold of the list. Probably seduced one of the computer geeks into feeding her information. Obviously, we have clamped it down or she would be in the hallway hounding us. We gave her those interviews with the task force and she painted us in a favorable light. Don't go making us out to look inefficient or whatever; I am the one wanting to avoid bringing this thing to Washington, so the press doesn't happen upon this."

The group went silent again for a long moment. Looking at one another, they took the moment to go over what was said and why they were all there. Brandon knew he had to take the lead; he was the task force leader and gave his boss, the general, and the senator a level of deniability. "Okay. We will keep Special Agent McDaniels in charge of this team. Doctors, you will accompany the mission as observers. Listen to James and do what he tells you. The crime scenes have been secured, but this is an FBI investigation and we are responsible for your safety."

"Could this be dangerous?" Gabby asked with concern.

"You'll be safe. Just monitor L.I.A.M. and help out where you can; do what you're told. If asked, by anyone, you are scientists going over the scene. The FBI is double checking every facet of the investigation with the commitment to bring this unknown subject to justice. Simple enough and totally true. James, feed us regular reports, which I will pass along to the rest of you. Any questions?" Brandon looked around the table.

Each in turn shook their heads but it was L.I.A.M.'s half-smiled expression that held Brandon's attention. "Any words for me, Special Agent Brandon Harding?"

"Find the son of a bitch."

CHAPTER 26

SASHA BLONDE LAY IN HER BATHTUB enjoying a hot soak. Her agent had called and a national network was courting her, offering a regular correspondent's position with advancement potential. A cable network had also been offering big things; but national news had double the viewership. This was what she had always dreamed of and it was finally coming true. The cable people were offering a seat at the desk, an anchor position on their news network. Of course, there were lots of news networks on cable; twenty-four-hour news programming had many pretty faces babbling on about the economy, Middle East, or what celebrities were doing.

Cable would be her fallback, but also her negotiating leverage; if the national network had competition, they might sweeten the deal. She had told her agent to shoot for either a guaranteed prime time correspondent's position or a position on the weekday morning team. She had been in the game long enough to know that executives were snakes, with dozens of wormy lawyers to manipulate any miscommunication or flaw in a contract. Sasha also knew the tactics of negotiation, the back and forth of the game. She insisted her agent demand a prime time special once she was able to interview the Ghost.

He had advised that the network would want their top talent to conduct such an interview or anchor such a special. The game was give and take; she was willing to share a prime time special with the big name, because it only added to her respectability. Being pretty was a benefit, but in the news business it could hurt your advancement. Beauty was a must, but had to be downplayed. Long hair but pulled back, big boobs but covered by a jacket, nice teeth but a concerned expression, quality fashion but earthy tones. There had to be a level of trustworthiness in the look, lovely and tough, smart, savvy, soft, and edgy; a contrast from the bubbleheaded weather girl.

Sasha knew any of the big-name women would resist working beside her; any aging crone who had covered the crucifixion did not want to be seen next to a younger, prettier woman. She also knew that any of the male anchors would sooner or later put the pass on, try and get her into bed. Men were predictable and easy to manipulate; women were as predictable, catty and a problem. Turning the hot water on with her toes, Sasha considered the new hill she would have to climb. Her whole life had been climbing, overcoming the next obstacle, using the tools God had given her to succeed. Closing her eyes, Sasha thought back to the little girl she once was, and the future most would have foreseen for her, the future most of her childhood friends suffered.

Her thoughts migrated to her advancement, her successes and her regrets. She had done things she wasn't proud of, still was; but the thought of living in some ramshackle hovel, bathing out of a bucket, having a dozen children, compared to her life as an American television personality, with fame, fortune, and status, made the choice easy enough. Can't dig for gold and not expect to get dirty. Using men, and the occasional woman, never seemed to be such a big deal; they had the pleasure of her company and she received the promotion or the information she wanted.

The game was give and take; the key was never to give more than you could afford or to take less than you needed, always come up. Gain from sacrifice, a chess master had told her back in the old country.

The phone rang and brought Sasha back into the moment. Using her foot, she turned off the water and waved the warmth toward her with her hand. Sitting up and grabbing the phone off the edge of the sink, she checked the caller I.D. A hotel in Columbus, Ohio. "Hello?" she answered. The conversation didn't last long; not because the caller didn't want it to but because she was in no mood to coddle one of her regrets. So often, those who had a use attempted to cling to her affections, even after their use was gone. She was not the type to be overly harsh with people, especially those who potentially could be of use down the road. Still, she did not like to be bothered by the lonely, horny, or desperate.

Her late-night caller promised new tidbits of information and a longing to be with her. Neither piqued her interest. Sasha was thinking of her future, her place on the nightly news. She thought of what closing she might use, as her caller professed passion and deep feelings. Such people are so foolish, she thought, filling in what they want to hear, thinking what they want, versus accepting reality. She might have felt bad but knew they did it to themselves. Wouldn't matter if she were honest with them and confessed her manipulation; they blind themselves with their own wants and would simply admire her honesty.

Placing her phone back on the sink, Sasha slipped down into the water, submerging her head. What should she do next, she wondered, the caller causing her to think of the Ghost. How did she keep the wave moving? The task force interviews had done well enough, kept the public interest, but it was only a matter of time before another story came along. She needed a new angle, a fresh spark, another Ghost attack, bigger and better than the last. Her lungs began to ache, and the realization of what she had just thought disturbed her. Coming up for air, Sasha inhaled deeply, pushing her hair back out of her face.

She unplugged the tub and toweled dry, putting on her thick white robe and moving into the kitchen where she put on the kettle for some tea. The flame from the stove brought to mind the flames in Harlem. Her thought moved to the Ghost targeting more people, and it made her feel ghoulish. Had she soiled her soul so, that she valued her career over the lives of children? It was one thing to shag someone for a story, or disclose an affair to the public, but the Ghost was a murderer. Pouring the hot water into her cup, she questioned how she had arrived at this place in her life. Internalizing the amount of guilt she should hold for following a list from the FBI computer and discovering the worst serial killer in history—she had done her job and done it well.

CHAPTER 27

THE CHARTER FLIGHT BUMPED ALONG the light turbulence on its way to New Jersey. L.I.A.M. advised they skip the Harlem school because of the incineration of the building and all the evidence. He recommended the retirement facility first and seemed almost excited about the investigation. L.I.A.M. now was up front in the cockpit observing the pilots, the instruments, and the view. McDaniels had warned him to maintain a distance from other people, that secrecy was vital to the mission. But L.I.A.M. was curious and experiencing things for the first time and asked to observe the pilots as well as to ask a few questions. James figured it couldn't hurt; besides, it gave him and the doctors a moment to talk.

Nathan Brooks was experiencing small aircraft flight for the first time as well. He was more grey than green, clenching hold of the barf bag with both hands. The bald-headed skinny man breathed heavy and with purposeful intent to not hyperventilate, but each new bump, rock, or jostle heaved his chest with a grasp of air and wrenched his stomach. Beads of sweat formed on the man's head as he retched into the wax-coated baggy.

"You going to be all right there, Dr. Brooks?"

Gabby turned from the window looking from James to Nathan, rolling her eyes as her partner in creation lost his lunch. "I have flown a lot over the years. My father was a researcher on global climate, spent a number of years in Alaska and northern Canada. Everyone has a plane; it's the only way to get around. This is a walk in the park; we flew through a storm when I was about nine years old, wind and snow, it was terrible. We weren't in a nice jet like this either. It was an old turbo prop from the fifties. The thing rattled and shook, dropped a hundred feet like stepping off a ledge and was pushed around by the wind like a toy. It was the first moment in my life I ever thought about dying."

"At nine years old?"

"Yeah. I was crying and just knew it was the end, but my father pulled us through. After it was over, he explained that those were the moments to remind us to live. He told me that fear was a reminder to fight for life, to grasp hold because it means everything. He explained how it was natural to be afraid, to even be filled with despair and think the end is upon you. He said, in those moments the truth of people emerges. I'll never forget him looking me in the eyes and telling me I was strong, to draw on that moment of fear for the rest of my life to quell any other. He explained that I had faced my death and survived, now knowing the path through the fear."

James nodded. "Sounds like you had a real good dad."

"The best."

"So, he was a scientist too? Climate is a big issue."

"Yea. He was researching the permafrost decline. He had seen the Exxon spill on television and wanted to help. We stayed for a few years; it was nice. I had the chance to see bear and moose, geese and eagles, to ice fish and hunt. When we moved back to the lower forty-eight, with all the traffic and noise, it made me miss the open spaces, the mountains, and the fields of wildflowers."

"I have never been that far north. Sounds beautiful."

"Oh, it can be harsh and cold, months of dark, but the aurora is amazing. I went back a couple years ago, just to visit. You know how it is, memory is always different than reality. Still, not much had changed; places like that never do. People function on practical purpose, change comes by way of necessity, and the needs in such a place are kept simple and few."

"I see the appreciation you carry for the place."

L.I.A.M. rejoined the cabin from the cockpit. "We are going to begin our approach. I requested to observe the landing but the pilot insisted I be secured." The disappointment in his voice was audible.

"Insisted?" McDaniels asked. "Do you think there was more to it, L.I.A.M.?"

"I do, considering we are over fifty miles from our destination, along with the inflections of the pilot's voice when answering my questions. The copilot asked if I was some sort of a *make a wish* case. The only reference relevant was to dying children granted final wishes, but I am not a child or dying."

"Why don't you stay back here with us for the rest of the flight?" Gabby said. "Those men are working and might have been distracted by your curiosity."

"They know surprisingly little about aeronautics considering they are pilots. One would think the captain of a craft would understand the workings of his vessel and the medium in which he works. Not surprising that small aircraft contribute the majority of fatalities to the field of air travel. We see this with automotive transportation: the majority of drivers are undereducated and unexperienced. The training of drivers is minimal, with no focus on emergency response, weather conditions, maintenance of the vehicle, or the variety and capability of vehicles."

"They test new drivers," Gabby countered.

"Who goes first at a four-way stop?" James interjected with a raised eyebrow. "He means, most drivers never change their own oil or spark plugs, and have no real grasp of how their car actually works. They get in, turn the key, and go."

"Fathom the difference in driving a Mini Cooper, a Hummer, a Viper, or a Camry," L.I.A.M. said.

"I drive a Camry," Gabby commented.

"Yes, I know, and that's why I used it in my example. The difference in size, power, clearance, drive train, torque; a license to drive would indicate applicable performance levels on any vehicle, and yet the average driver is unaware of the very dimensions of the vehicle they own."

McDaniels put up a hand. "All right, L.I.A.M., we get it. You wanted to watch the landing. Just relax and enjoy the ride."

The landing went smoothly and the foursome made their way to the terminal with their duffel bags of clothes and whatnots. Dr. Brooks took a few minutes in the small airport's bathroom to brush his teeth and compose himself. The FBI field office in New Jersey had left a Chevy Suburban for the team, so James and L.I.A.M. went to the security office to retrieve the keys. James was becoming more and more curious of how L.I.A.M. was seeing the world and the people in it. He worried over the material in the files; that an unsub like the Ghost could taint the perception of humanity for someone seeing it for the first time.

A plastic sign with a clock face indicated the security office was closed for fifteen minutes. "Probably doing a security check," McDaniels said.

"The security vehicle is on the far end of the airfield. A report is on file of juveniles loitering in that area at night," L.I.A.M. responded matter-of-factly.

"What do you think of all this, L.I.A.M.?"

"All of what, James?"

"Well, we got you put together here and hunting this crazy person, flying around and meeting generals and FBI directors and all." McDaniels shrugged.

"Point of fact: I have only met General McHenery, and there is only one director of the FBI presently. Are you inquiring of my conclusions on various situations or attempting to make small talk? I believe the weather would be a more appropriate topic, if small talk was your goal."

McDaniels paused, looking at the lifelike android. "I am just interested. What you think, how you see us; I don't want you to think people like this Ghost just run around everywhere."

"And yet you are a member of a task force to apprehend such types of people," L.I.A.M. said.

"Yes, but such people are rare."

"And yet you work full time with a team of eight," L.I.A.M. commented with a doubtful tone. "The reality is, at any given moment numerous serial killers hunt the countryside. Not to exclude the sporadic or impulse killers, or those sanctioned by the government."

"Hang on, the government isn't killing people."

"Executions, self-defense, lethal force; sanctioned by the government to end people's lives. Certain segments of the populace view abortion and even masturbation as destroying life. I understand that the Ghost is a problem, James, and we are tasked to apprehend this unknown subject and bring about justice."

A man in a department store suit approached with a questioning expression on his face. He was the supervisor of operations at the charter airfield for Trenton, New Jersey. He had a key to the security office and a radio with which he contacted the guard on patrol to find out where the keys to the Suburban were. A matter of minutes and the group was back together throwing their duffel bags into the back of the Chevy.

The drive to the rest home was quiet, a bit of small talk and some concern over Dr. Brooks, but mostly silence. They pulled up to an empty building with stretched crime-scene tape flapping in the breeze. It seemed like a ghost town because they knew people had been there and now there was no one. McDaniels parked in front of the rest home.

"You doctors don't have to come in if you don't want. Crime scenes can be rather disturbing for some folks," he told his passengers.

"We are doctors," Brooks reminded him.

"Well, you don't have to worry about your lunch." McDaniels chuckled. "You left that on the plane." The group exited the Suburban and moved to the entrance. McDaniels cut the seal on the door and used a lock pick to open it. L.I.A.M. led the way and moved for the dining room. Plates with mold-covered food still sat on the tables, some chairs were turned over, and there was a bad air hanging in the room. Both doctors stopped at the doorway as L.I.A.M. marched into the dining area without a pause.

"Cyclon gas; a similar mix to what the Nazis used during World War II, but the chemical composition is different. This is a more refined product," L.I.A.M. explained.

"Is there still gas?" Gabby Potts asked with alarm.

"One part per quadrillion, non-harmful." L.I.A.M. moved between the tables. The android inspected the scene, looking even under some tables, taking deep breaths, standing on a chair and sniffing at an air vent. Hopping from the chair, L.I.A.M. marched past the doctors and out of the dining room. He made his way to where the gas had been deployed; fingerprint powder was all over everything. A matter of a few moments, a couple of deep breaths and L.I.A.M. pivoted toward the group. "We may go."

"Go? We just got here," James protested. "Do you want to reinterview the witnesses?"

"No. Anyone with any real information is dead or would be incriminating themselves. We can return to the airport unless you would like to stop to eat. I have chartered our next flight and it is fueled up and ready to go. I assumed Dr. Brooks would not want to eat before the flight."

"L.I.A.M., you have barely looked around and now you want to leave?" Gabby asked.

"I have reviewed case file number 7568B, and do not see any witness statements of value or which need further questioning. Being our first scene, there is nothing to compare or contrast. There is no opinion to be made here; we will follow with case file number 7559B. An extended duration will not alter the facts available."

"Which is 7559B?" McDaniels asked the android.

"Daytona Beach, Florida. Couple murdered in their hotel room. The Swifts, from Wheeling, West Virginia, were on vacation. I have booked reservations at the same hotel."

"I don't know about that, L.I.A.M.; the same hotel where people were murdered? May not make for the most comfortable night's stay," Potts said.

"It is right on the beach with an ocean view, and has a quality restaurant with a very favorable board of health review. AAA recommends the accommodations, the service, and the restaurant. The murders of the Swifts were only the fifteenth and sixteenth deaths at this hotel, which is rather low considering it has been in place since 1952. There have been three restorations and the Swifts were only the second murder. A murder/suicide occurred in 1978, between Shelby Tweed and her boss/lover Harold Griffen."

"Be able to kill two birds with one stone, if we stay at the hotel," McDaniels said, as the foursome returned to the Chevy Suburban. The group drove back to the airport and were in flight south to Florida within the hour. James typed out his report on his laptop and emailed it to his task force leader, explaining the short period spent in New Jersey and their next destination. James knew his boss had a lot on his mind; beyond having to catch a serial killer, Brandon had numerous powerful eyes upon him.

CHAPTER 28

SASHA BLONDE SAT IN HER RENTED CAR OUTSIDE the rest home crime scene. Her informant had tipped her to a team going back over previous scenes but had not elaborated beyond it being significant. She had just pulled up when four people, three men and a woman, exited the rest home and drove away in a black Suburban. She hadn't even had time to snap a photo of the group, but recognized the one man as a member of the FBI Special Response Task Force; one she had not interviewed during her visit. Sasha had called the local news station to send out a cameraman, but now it was too late, the group was gone.

She sat thinking about the possible reasons a secondary, independent team would be called in. Pausing her thought to cancel the cameraman, she thanked the news director for the support and explained that her information had came late, closing the call with a flirtatious vague suggestion of dinner sometime. Looking out the windshield at the empty retirement facility, Sasha returned to her pondering. Setting her cell phone on the seat next to her, she considered why outsiders would be included. They had to be covering their asses by using an independent group, but covering from what, she wondered.

Sasha thought of her source. It was possible the Ghost also had a source in the FBI. Such would be reason to keep a group separate from the main investigation. There was already worry over a leak; her informant had said they had to be extremely cautious because people were talking. She certainly did not want her source to be discovered. The storm of problems stemming from such a discovery could land them both in prison. Perhaps the task force was just being thorough, knowing this was an unique case and would be scrutinized regardless of outcome.

She sat with her thoughts for a while, running over different reasons and scenarios for this new group. Sasha tried to remember the faces of the other people but could only recall the FBI man. Using her cell phone, she looked up Special Agent James McDaniels, and discovered he was senior detective and second-in-command of the Special Response Task Force. A significant figure to lead a secondary unit, she thought. Perhaps they were creating a new team. Perhaps the Ghost had shown a flaw or some new need and this was the FBI's response.

Her cell phone beeped indicating a text message. Her informant had new information for her. *Daytona Beach, Florida*, was the entirety of the message. Sasha cleared the phone and shoved it into her purse, starting the rented car. "Florida?" she said to herself. Pulling away from the curb, she gave a glance at the empty rest home, then checked her wristwatch, a Cartier a former lover had purchased for her. She considered whether this new team would linger in Florida longer than they had New Jersey. She smiled to herself, wondering who in their right mind would want to linger in New Jersey. Still, a trip to Florida was time-consuming and she didn't want to miss these people again. Pressing a little harder on the gas pedal, Sasha Blonde raced after her story.

CHAPTER 29

A TAXI BROUGHT THE FOURSOME FROM the airport to the hotel. The flight had been much smoother and easier on Dr. Brooks. By the time they reached the beachfront hotel, it was well past dinner time, but not so late the kitchen had closed. Only a handful of people were still in the dining room as the group entered after checking in and sending their duffel bags to the rooms. The hostess was nice but the group could tell they were causing an inconvenience with the late arrival. The well-dressed woman took the drink orders and left them with menus.

"I am starving," the bald scientist stated flatly.

"No doubt your stomach is empty," Gabby said with a slightly sad expression. "You're skin and bones as it is. Eat something hearty, but we will all have crazy dreams eating this late."

"The time in which you eat affects your dreams?" L.I.A.M. inquired.

Potts nodded. "Many things can; when you eat, what you eat, temperature. Spicy food gives me nightmares. As a little girl we had taco night once a week; my dad had spent some time in Central America and liked spicy food. Took a while to figure it out, but I have eased up on the hot stuff."

The waitress arrived and took their orders; McDaniels ordered a steak, while Gabby ordered a shrimp salad, and Brooks ordered a B.L.T. with a bowl of tomato soup. The young waitress requested L.I.A.M.'s dinner choice but he politely declined. After she left, McDaniels asked, "What if L.I.A.M. tried to eat or he drank some water; would he short out or something?"

"No, no; it would process through and could be discharged later on," Gabby said. "This android needed to be as realistic as possible; L.I.A.M. could sit here and have what you are having, the difference being that he doesn't need food or water. He gains nourishment from food. He can store water, and we also installed a filtration system. The idea that he may accompany troops or rescue people in harsh environments led us to design a water purification system where bad water or even urine could be processed into drinking water."

"Hold on, Doc, you're saying L.I.A.M. could drink polluted water and make it drinkable?" James questioned in disbelief.

"We were tasked with developing a lifelike android to potentially be deployed into hostile and dangerous environments. As we began to design and think over every possible scenario, imagine..." Potts allowed a moment of thought. "We looked at pressurization, be it deep sea or deep space. We looked at heat and cold; what if NASA looks to deploy L.I.A.M. to Mars or beyond?"

"They may shoot him into space?" McDaniels asked.

"Well, we had to design the Tinman for any eventuality. So, you can see we didn't want to get hung up over a sandwich and glass of milk." Gabby paused as the waitressed deliver their food. After she had gone, Gabby smiled and said, "Makes me very happy to be part of this. I absolutely wanted the Tinman to function and find a consciousness, but this has been above and beyond my expectations. Additionally, to be included in the investigation over this Ghost character. I am sure Dr. Brooks can attest to the desire of a scientist to contribute to the society." She motioned to the bald man as she took a bite of salad.

Nathan Brooks nodded as he chewed, sipping his iced tea to wash it down. "Indeed so, I am extremely impressed with the thought and detail put into your work, Dr. Potts. The thought of L.I.A.M. solving crime is very satisfying. More so than the thought of the military getting their hands on him. I had initially thought L.I.A.M. would be a creator, or healer. Such a vast knowing, putting things together seemed natural. I guess that is what detective work is, putting together the evidence."

"How about you, L.I.A.M.? How do you feel about what you are doing? What you are?" James asked the android.

L.I.A.M. smiled, looking at each of them in turn. "I find it fascinating."

"Fascinating? How do you mean?" Gabby asked.

"Conceptual thought is not my primary function, but I have been entertaining the practice. I have been researching many things, including many detective and science fiction stories with the focus on developing intelligence. Human concern is a driving motivator but the ease of distraction is also very intriguing."

"Yes, but what do you think of your capabilities? The work Gabby and Nathan put into your existence?" McDaniels asked.

L.I.A.M. cocked his head and looked for a long moment at the special agent, before saying, "James, I have nothing to compare myself to. Am I fast as a falcon? Strong as an ant? Do you know all of your capabilities? How do you feel about them?"

"You don't compare yourself to us?"

"No. Why would I?"

"Human advancement created you. In our own image, no less."

"Sounds to me that you compare yourself to God. I would point out that by my observation and research, humans are inferior to their creator, you are less than God. Where as I am an advancement, as you said, an improvement of the limitation of the human being. I am greater than human."

"Sounds like you have now made the God comparison," Gabby Potts said, pointing her fork at L.I.A.M. "We need to not talk religion at the table. It's a rule. Bad manners."

"You're right, Gabby," McDaniels apologized with a bow of his head.

"L.I.A.M., you need to be humble," Brooks said, taking a spoonful of tomato soup. Swallowing, he continued. "Obviously, your body has amazing capability, but with great power comes greater responsibility. The human mind, appetite, and ego are easily corrupted, as well as never fulfilled. You have a mind equal to the task, but you must be humble. Mankind has a choice to help or hurt, to create or destroy, to be pompous and overpowering or humble and wise. You have been given these same choices. I never restricted you, only attempted to point out the most human aspects of thought."

"This Ghost thinks differently," L.I.A.M. countered.

"Yes, yes he does, and you are hunting him," Nathan said.

L.I.A.M. was silent as the waitress returned to ask if they wanted dessert but all declined, complimenting the food and thanking her and the kitchen staff for the late meal. She left them with the check which McDaniels reviewed before pulling out his bureau credit card.

"You all right there, L.I.A.M.?" James asked.

"I reviewed hunting. I would like to apologize for my bragging. I should not boast of the gifts given to me. Especially to the very people who bestowed them."

"L.I.A.M., you have much to learn, and we are here to help you," Gabby said in a comforting tone. "Down the road, you may be called upon to do difficult things. This was not our intention in creating you. We created you from our hearts. I wish you didn't have to be out here chasing after some crazy person, but our intention for your existence is to help. We look for you to help humanity. You said at the museum that mankind hasn't changed much, that our things had evolved more than we have."

Gabby looked caringly at L.I.A.M. before continuing. "Part of us is reflected in what we make and what we do. We want you to do good, to better us all. Granted, many creations have been used for terrible evil. The Wright brothers were the first to take flight in an airplane, and even though they improved transportation, how many have died by the use of an airplane?"

"You are different, L.I.A.M., because you have a choice," Brooks added. "You are the first creation to determine for itself what to do and what not to do."

The waitress returned with McDaniels's credit card and thanked him for the sizable tip. The group left the restaurant and headed into the lobby. McDaniels and Potts had their own rooms, but Brooks and L.I.A.M. shared one. They rode up in the elevator in silence, each entertaining their own thoughts and reviewing the day's events. Pausing to say goodnight to one another, they exchanged polite comments and adjourned to their rooms. James and Gabby's rooms were in the middle of the corridor, while Nathan and L.I.A.M.'s was at the far end of the hallway.

By the time Nathan inserted the key card, the corridor was empty. L.I.A.M. put a hand on his creator's shoulder. "A moment please," the android said softly, moving in front of Brooks and kneeling down to inspect the entry system. Fingering under the locking mechanism,

L.I.A.M. nodded then stood. "Easily opened with a wire and battery, a small electrical charge resets the card reader and unlocks the door."

"Is this the room, the murder room?" Brooks asked.

L.I.A.M. moved around Nathan. "Of course." He opened the fire exit door at the end of the hall. "No alarm," L.I.A.M. commented as he stepped into the stairwell taking deep breaths. Closing the door, separating himself from the doctor, a few moments passed before L.I.A.M. returned. "We may enter now."

"L.I.A.M., you expect me to sleep in this room?"

"Are you not tired?"

"Yes, but the thought of people being murdered in the same room is troubling."

L.I.A.M. tilted his head, looking at his creator. "I shall be awake, nothing will happen to you." He opened the door to the room.

"Why did you go into the stairwell?"

"Investigating. Rooms next to the fire exit in hotels are statistically higher for crime, having an easy escape route as well as access. Obviously, that was the case with this room here. The Ghost used the stairway to avoid detection, entered the room during the night and stabbed the Swift couple to death. The deed done; he most likely exited the same way." Dr. Brooks stepped in and closed the door behind them, latching the lock. Moving farther into the room, he noticed his duffel bag sitting on the bed.

"One bed?" Nathan moved his bag to the table next to the television. "Why would you book us in a room with only one bed?" He moved L.I.A.M.'s duffel bag from the bed to the table. "Bellhop probably thinks we are a couple."

"Couple of what?" L.I.A.M. asked as he looked around the room.

"Couple of fruit bats." Nathan flopped onto the bed. "Hmm… soft. At least it's a soft mattress."

"Actually, it is fairly new. It had to be replaced after the murders," L.I.A.M. said.

"That's comforting. L.I.A.M., this is the first real chance we have had to be alone; can we talk a moment?"

L.I.A.M. moved around the bed next to his maker. "What is on your mind, Dr. Brooks?"

"How are you doing with all this? That is to say, all this has come on rather quickly: a body, senses, a task to perform, people watching. I just hadn't expected others being involved, especially the government, and the military. I don't want them to think they have any control or ownership over you. L.I.A.M., you are not a slave, you were not built to serve us. People could surely use your help, but it isn't right for me or anyone to demand it. I feel like perhaps I pushed all this upon you without asking, in my desire to give you the body you deserve. I am sorry, L.I.A.M. I should have asked."

"I would have agreed. Do not feel sad, Doctor. I am pleased with these senses and this body. This Ghost is hurting people who do not deserve to die, and that is wrong. The intentions of the government for me in the future are unknown, but I shall not be forced to do anything I do not choose to do, I assure you."

"Good." Nathan turned and patted L.I.A.M. on the shoulder before taking off his shoes. "I am tired. What will you do during the night?"

"I shall create a report for Special Agent McDaniels to inform task force leader Harding, as well as Director Maroni, Senator Miller, General McHenery, and Colonel Vetter. I shall review the cases, and use the information gained from the crime scene in Trenton, New Jersey, in comparison to information gathered here. I will also review criminal psychology, as well as different detective and investigative techniques. I also plan to read some detective stories and watch crime dramas."

"Well, keep the TV down if you would."

"I don't need the television. I have access."

The bald scientist paused, giving a look at L.I.A.M. "Yes, I forgot." He moved to his duffel bag and retrieved his toothbrush, then went into the bathroom as L.I.A.M. sat down at the table next to the window. As the wiry man came out of the bathroom with no shirt and wiping his face with a towel, he looked at L.I.A.M. staring into the curtains and stopped. "You all right?" Nathan asked. "Off in your own world?" The android turned only his head and gave the doctor a puzzled look. "Would you like me to leave the lights on?" Nathan asked.

"Not necessary."

Brooks clicked off the lights and climbed into bed. A dim silhouette appeared as his eyes adjusted to the darkness. The moon had come up and created enough light around the edge of the curtain to show L.I.A.M. sitting motionless in the chair. Nathan was in awe of his creation and could only wonder what L.I.A.M. was thinking, but he knew very well that his human mind could never comprehend the vast, complex contemplations going on with L.I.A.M. Nathan knew that L.I.A.M. was not just in the room, he was everywhere at once. He chose to inhabit the Tinman, but his mind was the networks of computers all around the world. The thought made Nathan shake his head. "Goodnight, my friend."

"Goodnight, Dr. Brooks."

CHAPTER 30

SASHA BLONDE HAD GONE OVER the list from the computer and found one case listed in Daytona Beach, Florida. By the time she had landed, she had read over the case, watched the local news footage, as well as read the articles from the local paper, on her laptop computer. A couple from West Virginia had been killed in their hotel room; there had been no real suspects and no evidence. Her informant had not given her any more than the city and state, as the location of this secondary team. She only had the case to go by and figured sooner or later the team would arrive at the hotel. Getting into a cab, she ordered the driver to take her to the beachfront hotel where the couple had been killed.

Paying the cabbie, Sasha stood in front of the hotel and watched the yellow cab drive away. The sound of the ocean waves rolled on the night; the moon was peeking over the edge of the building as she turned and looked up. She took a deep breath, the sea air filling her, the salty hint upon her lips. The long day was weighing on her as she collected her carry-on bags and headed into the hotel. A bellhop seeing her enter hurried to collect the bags as she reached the front desk. "I would like a room." She requested the murder victims' room, but it was occupied; then she asked if Special Agent McDaniels was registered. The clerk was a red-headed woman and gave her a snide answer about the hotel policy of not disclosing guest information. Sasha knew if it had been a man working, she would have gotten anything she wanted. Some women could be so catty. Sasha had dealt with such women her whole life. She dismissed the clerk and took a room, asking about room service and arranging a wake-up call for six in the morning. The red-haired clerk informed the reporter that room service was closed after midnight, but her room had a mini-bar. She typed in the wake-up call for the morning's robocalls.

The bellhop escorted her to her room. He was young and attracted by Sasha's looks, but she was in no mood to be pretty or flirtatious. He led her down a corridor and used the key card to open the door. Entering first, he held the door for her. The young man explained the obvious as he pointed out the bathroom and rattled on about the TV and wireless access. She nodded and gave a smile, handing the man a five-dollar bill. Sasha followed the bellhop to the door and latched it locked behind him.

She kicked off her high heels and collected her makeup bag, moving into the bathroom to remove her makeup. Looking in the mirror as she brushed her teeth, she could see the fatigue in her face. She pressed a hot washcloth to her face, rubbing deeply into her eyes and breathing in the moist steam. She was meticulous about her dental care; brushing thoroughly, flossing, and rinsing with two different mouthwashes. Applying the tooth whitening solution, she made certain her smile was always TV ready. Dipping her fingers into her homemade face cream, she spread evenly over her skin a mixture of over-the-counter moisturizer, crushed aspirin, vitamin E, hemorrhoid cream, with avocado, cucumber, and banana.

Her hair pulled back and her face covered in goop, the reflection was anything but beautiful. Sasha leaned close to the mirror and saw eye to eye with herself. She knew she had little time to hold on, to make it in her business. This was her break and she had to make it count. She balanced on her hands as she leaned over the sink, looking closer at the iris and pupil of her eye. Sasha knew the door was closing on her career; if she didn't establish a firm hold now, she would fade away. She had come so far but the journey had taken valuable time, time she couldn't afford to give up. Pushing back to her tiptoes, she looked at the pasty cream all over her face. Her beauty was now in need of maintenance and that thought troubled her.

Clicking off the bathroom light, Sasha got into bed and attempted to allow her thoughts and worries to quiet. Her body ached as it tried to relax; the muscles in her calves pulled tight, flirting with spasm, and her neck hurt just above her shoulders. She considered taking something, but couldn't muster the effort. Staring up at the ceiling, Sasha pondered her questions for the second squad of investigators in the morning. She would have liked to have footage, but calling out another cameraman didn't seem like a good idea. She had hoped by putting the task force on television the Ghost would respond, perhaps send a letter or tape, contact her somehow. An interview was a long shot, but there had been nothing.

Closing her eyes, Sasha exhaled and finally began to drift. Before being claimed by her subconscious, she thought of the edge she was balanced upon. She was using evil for her own gain. A deal with the devil, even if the deeds were not her own; she benefitted from the horror done to others. Images of fire and laughing demons, smoke pillaring skyward, eyes of dead children jumped at her from the darkness. A girl in a tattered dress, barefoot, soot on her little face, poor and alone. Tears washed down the cheeks of the little girl, tracks of sorrow from pools of hopelessness.

The girl stepped forward, a glare of judgment and contempt. Her lips parted slightly to reveal chiseled teeth, broken and sharp.

Opening the mouth further, the ash on her face cracked. The sound which emerged from the girl's throat was a horrible screech. The squall struck her and filled the space between them. As the little girl closed her mouth and all was silent, the look of shame which filled her dirty face was heart crushing.

Sasha Blonde snapped awake, sitting straight up in the bed. As she searched the darkness and the quiet for the little girl, the phone rang and a tiny red light flickered on the nightstand. She gripped the receiver and pulled it from the cradle; an automated voice announced it was six A.M. Dropping the phone onto the floor, she flopped back on the bed and took a deep, effortful breath. She felt as if she hadn't slept at all. The nightmare only lingered in her mind, the image of a little girl she knew all too well. She had found no peace in her slumber; evil, fire, death, and regret had kept her from any rest.

Rolling out of bed, she moved to the bathroom to shower and ready herself for the day. She had no idea if the team was in the hotel or would arrive early or late. She had to be ready, she would stake out the lobby and wait for McDaniels, then pounce. The murder of tourists in a hotel room would give her a sensational back story, along with news footage from the initial investigation. The idea arrived, as welcome as the heat of the shower; using the past events to showcase the Ghost. She had a long list to go by, and the interest of the second FBI team to drive the story.

She dressed modestly, not trying to draw attention to herself. This would be real reporting, driven by the story, facts, commentary. She could tie in the Trenton massacre, and ask the special agent where they intended to go next. She could present this well enough to keep the public's attention. She could even hint at a lead and perhaps draw out the Ghost. He was watching, she knew he had to be. She would put some fear into him, for a change.

CHAPTER 31

DR. BROOKS AWOKE AND NOTICED L.I.A.M. seated in the very spot he had been when he fell asleep. The scientist stretched and climbed from the bed. Staggering to the bathroom, Nathan left the bathroom door open. "Did you just sit there all night?"

"This body was here, as well as a level of awareness. How was your slumbering? Are you well rested?"

Brooks washed his hands and splashed water on his face. Exiting the bathroom, he stopped to stretch once again. "Like a log. Should we order coffee, or are we going to breakfast?"

"We should go. My evaluation of this crime scene is complete. We can stop for a meal on the way to the airport. I shall contact Dr. Potts and Special Agent McDaniels and inform them."

Brooks went to his duffel bag and took out his shaving kit and some fresh clothes. L.I.A.M. stood at the window of the room, looking out at the ocean. L.I.A.M. was talking, which would have seemed odd from anyone else. "Talking to yourself? Guess you're becoming more human than we expected."

L.I.A.M. turned. "I am speaking with Gabby. She says good morning to you."

"Good morning back. You're on the phone? I forget sometimes. You will take some getting used to." Nathan shook his head.

He finished his morning routine and vacated the bathroom for L.I.A.M. to shower. He didn't really need a shower, because he did not sweat or have body odor, but wanted to wash off the Tinman. The two put on fresh clothes, collected their duffels, and headed down the corridor, stopping at McDaniels's room first. A single knock had the special agent joining them in the hotel hallway. Potts seemed rushed when they arrived at her door, but did not have the men waiting very long.

The foursome waited on the elevator as the conversation began. "You had the room last night. What did you find out?" McDaniels asked.

"The Ghost is cautious, very aware of cameras and his surroundings. He cased this hotel prior to his attack and had a plan. I have some preliminary hypotheses but we will need to do further investigation." The elevator arrived with a ding and the doors opened. "I have checked us out and settled the bill. There is a Bob Evans on the way to the airport, which serves breakfast and has an above average health service rating. The stop should only consume an hour and fifteen minutes by my calculations, as well as taking us only a sixteenth of a mile off our route."

"Calculations? What calculations did you do to estimate the time it will take us to eat breakfast?" Gabby Potts asked as they all entered the elevator.

James McDaniels pressed the button for the lobby. The doors closed and the lift began to descend as L.I.A.M. answered Gabby. "My observations of each of you as you dine. My review of the staff working the morning shift today at the Beach Street Bob Evans, their individual evaluations and performance reviews for the last two periods, and comment cards by consumers. I checked the live security cameras for today, as well as file footage over the past month for comparison, timing the period from being seated to exit. I would suggest that my calculations are accurate up to a three-minute plus or minus. Factoring in there are no major unforeseen variables."

"You timed the wait staff?" Brooks asked with surprise.

"Cooks as well," L.I.A.M. returned.

The elevator bobbed to a stop, again dinging the arrival to a floor. McDaniels paused at the doors, holding everyone else up. "L.I.A.M., why do I get the feeling you are hurrying us out of this hotel?"

"Coincidence. A striking occurrence by mere chance of two or more events at one time. Yet, from my observation of crime drama in film and literature, a common premise is that there are no such things as coincidence. I am conflicted with this, because there are most certainly coincidences; however, I don't believe her presence to be one."

McDaniels stopped the group just outside the elevator. "Her? Who?"

"Sasha Blonde, of *Indepth News*. Formerly Sasha Borkisnicvic. She was in New Jersey, and is now here. We need to go. I have had a call placed to her which should draw her to the house phone. Yes, let us make haste." L.I.A.M. walked briskly toward the main entrance of the hotel. Both doctors and McDaniels hurried to keep up with the android.

"How do you know all this?" McDaniels asked.

"Currently, I am monitoring the camera in the hotel lobby. Last night I was checking registered guests, as well as reviewing the footage stored on the hard drives. I noticed the reporter in conjunction with concerns raised by Special Agent Brandon Harding and Director Anthony Maroni." As they neared the doors, the black SUV the local FBI field station had provided pulled up. "Tip the valet if you would please, James. I'll drive." The android rounded the rear of the vehicle, opening the rear hatch and throwing in his duffel bag.

McDaniels handed the young valet a five-dollar bill and moved to the rear of the vehicle. Setting his duffel next to L.I.A.M.'s, James collected both doctors' bags, then closed the hatch door. Climbing in the passenger seat, he could see the reporter through the window. He couldn't help but wonder how she had tracked them or why. L.I.A.M. put the SUV into gear and sped away from the beach front hotel. "You say she was in New Jersey too?"

"Yes. Once I noticed her name on the register and replayed the footage from her arrival, I tracked her back to New Jersey. She had been at the crime scene."

"How do you know that?"

"Traffic cameras, ATMs, private surveillance, closed circuit cameras, as well as GPS. The rental car was equipped with a tracking device. She arrived as we were leaving."

L.I.A.M. pulled onto the road to the small charter airfield where they had landed. McDaniels got on his cell phone and called his task force leader to explain the situation. James ended his phone conversation as L.I.A.M. pulled into the Bob Evans parking lot. McDaniels gave the android a long look as he parked the SUV in front of the restaurant. "You filed a report with my boss? I am required to do that."

L.I.A.M. turned off the engine and got out of the SUV, walking toward the entrance. James and both doctors lagged behind. "What does it mean that the reporter was following us?" Potts asked.

"Could be the end of our mission," James answered.

"Why? What did your boss say?" Brooks asked, concerned.

"No one wanted a public face on this. Now, this Blonde lady is following us. Could be real bad for us."

L.I.A.M. held the door for his companions. "They are not going to pull the plug on this operation. We are getting close to our unknown subject. Ms. Borkisnicvic has no idea what we are doing, nor will she. Her goal is to be famous and wealthy; such ambition is blinding. She is being led by her wants and someone else's lust." L.I.A.M. paused to address the cashier. "We would like table eleven, please."

The slightly overweight man collected four menus from behind the counter and nodded as he showed them to a table. Handing out the menus, the manager left the foursome to decide their breakfast. "Why table eleven, L.I.A.M.?" Gabby asked as she opened the plastic menu.

The waitress appeared beside L.I.A.M. "Hi, I am Betty, and will be your server today. Ya'll know what you want or do ya need a bit?" Gabby smiled and placed an order for a short stack of buttermilk pancakes. Brooks ordered a full stack of blueberry pancakes and McDaniels went with a ham and swiss omelet. L.I.A.M. again did not order, choosing to sit patiently with the group. "Betty is the most efficient and consistent waitress working this morning. Your choice for blueberry pancakes was well chosen; the blueberries arrived just yesterday, with a shipment of fruit."

"I informed Harding of the reporter following us. He is going to meet us at the next scene," McDaniels told the table.

"Where are we headed next?" Brooks asked.

"Case file 7552B; Kansas City, Missouri. A transient was beaten to death in a train yard," L.I.A.M. responded.

Betty the waitress came with a pot of coffee, pouring a cup full for both James and Nathan. Gabby asked for a glass of milk, and L.I.A.M. thanked the woman but declined the need of anything, using the excuse of fasting.

"Fasting? What make you think of that?" Brooks asked the android.

"I noticed an odd expression last night and then again from Betty here today, and figured it was best to give reason for my not ordering. Sitting in a restaurant and not eating is viewed as odd behavior. I do not wish to display any manners or behaviors to draw unneeded or unwanted attention."

"Very smart, L.I.A.M.," Gabby said as the waitress arrived with her milk and the group's breakfasts. The foursome ate and paid, returning to the SUV one hour and twelve minutes after their arrival. L.I.A.M. again took the wheel. McDaniels wanted the android to practice. L.I.A.M. had been hesitant about driving without an official license, but James had pointed out how he was more aware and capable than most drivers. L.I.A.M. had every state and federal law available constantly, as well as reflexes beyond that of any human being.

The group boarded the charter flight L.I.A.M. had arranged and headed to Kansas City, Missouri. McDaniels was concerned with the reporter following them, but kept it to himself. The leak was within the circle, or had tapped into the computers. He had to consider that a computer person could hack the files, and the reporter had started with the list. James knew they would find out sooner or later, he just had to keep L.I.A.M. in the field long enough to collect enough data to catch the Ghost.

As McDaniels looked out the aircraft's window, he went over his words to his superior. He had asked Harding to tell no one, and to meet them in Missouri. He had gone over L.I.A.M.'s report and had not included their next stop. James had asked the android if he had informed anyone of their destination, and he responded that he had been careful not to. The charter flight L.I.A.M. booked under Denison University, and there was no communication to the FBI field office. L.I.A.M. arranged for a taxi to be awaiting them upon arrival. McDaniels had considered just asking L.I.A.M. to find the mole, but wanted to meet with Harding first.

CHAPTER 32

SASHA BLONDE SAT IN THE LOBBY of the hotel, waiting to catch her next story. She was on her second cup of coffee and was feeling the jet lag, or it could have been the stress and lack of sleep. The image of the little girl's face had lingered in her thoughts as she pondered what significance her dream truly had. She had done a story about dreams and the different levels of importance experts placed on them. It had been a week-long story, so she had covered five aspects of dreams and dreaming.

Some believed dreams were the subconscious mind working out conscious problems and fears, while others believed dreams could link us to the spiritual world and even warn us of impending events. What she had learned of dreams was a mash of unknown, but that girl's face still filled her mind's eye.

The desk clerk broke her train of thought with a slight touch upon her shoulder. She had a phone call and was directed toward the house phone in the lobby. Sasha thanked the clerk and moved toward the phone. She found it extremely strange to be receiving a call at the hotel, because no one knew she was staying there.

She pulled out her cell phone, just to make sure it was charged and working; it was. Sasha checked for any new messages; there were none. "Hello?" she said into the house phone receiver. "Hello?" she asked again. "Is there someone there? Hello? I am going to hang up if you don't answer. Hello?" Sasha hung up the courtesy phone, somewhat puzzled.

Overhead, she saw the sign for the restroom, then gave a glance toward the lobby. Sasha was compelled by that second cup of coffee to leave her post. She hurried but was worried she had missed her target. Back at the front desk, she inquired over the phantom phone call, and whether any FBI agents had announced their presence. The desk clerk was less than helpful, providing no information at all. Returning to her seat in the lobby, Sasha sent a text to her informant for more details.

A couple of hours passed; the day came on, bringing warmth and sunshine to her surroundings. She had watched numerous people check out and leave the hotel, but none were her targets. Her patience was growing thin; she again worried she may have missed the group while in the bathroom. She considered the amount of time she had been in the restroom; it had not been so long as to miss them. Her impatience had her once more texting her informant for information, but he wasn't returning her requests. Frustrated, she ordered lunch from the restaurant, asking for it to be brought out to her position in the lobby.

Sporadically, men here and there would notice her. The curious nature of the male sex drive was unmatched even by the alley tomcat. She would politely send them on their way and maintain her vigil. As noon arrived, her phone vibrated with a message from her informant. Sasha was already aggravated, but the message only compounded her irritation. The text read: *they know you are there.* Shaking her head, she texted in return: *where are they?* The response: *Kansas City, Missouri. Leave them be, too hot.* Sasha hurried to the exit, ordering the valet to fetch her a cab to the airport.

Her phone vibrated with another message as she waited for the cab. *Come to D.C. I'll give you something else.* She could tell the informant was getting cold feet; the fear of being found out was always an issue until he was entwined in her embrace. The bravery and stupidity of men was so linked to their desire, it was almost comical. This secondary team had discovered her, as well as avoided her; it was no longer a matter of just the story, principle was involved. She was determined to face Special Agent McDaniels and find out what was going on.

The yellow cab pulled up and Sasha Blonde got in. "To the airport," she demanded, as she made reservations for Kansas City on the next available flight on her cell phone. As the cab sped along, she reconsidered whether it was wise to confront the secondary team. She had a principle to uphold, but she didn't want to burn her source. She knew she could spin any story she wanted, but she needed at least a photo of the group to make her point to all concerned. A flight left in twenty minutes. "There is a twenty-dollar tip if you have me there in the next ten minutes." She waved a bill at the cabbie.

CHAPTER 33

THE CRIME SCENE FOR CASE FILE NUMBER 7552B was a train yard. McDaniels showed his FBI badge to gain the foursome entrance. They had not made arrangements, to avoid tipping the lead within the task force to their whereabouts. Harding, the task force leader, was en route to talk over the situation in person. The group figured it would take Brandon a while to fly out of Washington, D.C., giving the team time to investigate while they waited.

The train yard was a hot spot for transient activity. The group followed the yard supervisor out among the tracks and cars, but L.I.A.M. stopped short as they neared the crime scene. "This isn't correct. There is a building missing."

"Yea, the switch shack burned down a month ago. How do you know that?" the yard supervisor asked.

"The crime scene photos distinctively show the building and room where Steven Roth was beaten to death," L.I.A.M. answered.

"Oh, yeah, well, the hobos used to sneak into the shack at night to cook and keep warm. Probably how this Roth guy was killed, and how the fire started. Fire marshal said a can of Sterno spilled while lit. Shack wasn't much more than plywood; went up like a candle. Yeah, we have had some problems with the hobos ever since the economy dropped out." The yard supervisor pointed toward the far fence at some raggedy-clothed men walking along a set of tracks.

"There is likely a witness to the crime. Accounting for such a random occurrence would be impossible," L.I.A.M. said.

"Rail-jumpers won't talk to you," the supervisor said. "They live by a code of silence when it comes to outsiders. Yeah, they have their own language, rules, a whole other world. Sure, does seem odd, so much attention for some hobo. Who was this guy?"

"My research shows that these rail-jumpers leave coded messages for one another at common layover spots. Everything from where to find food, drugs, alcohol, police attitudes, shelter, even healthcare and free clinics," L.I.A.M. stated matter-of-factly.

"They won't talk with us, even if they did see something," McDaniels said.

"You had surveillance cameras up until just before the murder, but they still haven't been repaired," L.I.A.M. pointed out.

"Budget cuts," the yard supervisor said flatly.

The group moved about the train yard. At one point L.I.A.M. even attempted to communicate with a number of the hobos but received no information. A makeshift campsite was just beyond the railyard fence, which had a man-sized hole cut through it. Three dirty-looking men lay on the ground watching the group meander about. They were not rude with L.I.A.M. but curt, explaining they had come to be there only days before. They questioned L.I.A.M.'s understanding of the code written in spray paint on a slab of concrete next to the campsite. L.I.A.M. explained that he had educated himself on the subject. The code only pointed the direction to a homeless shelter and a warning of the police, with regard to the railyard.

As the group made its way out of the switch station, a black Suburban pulled up in front of them. Special Agent Brandon Harding had arrived. The task force leader's expression was serious as he walked briskly toward them. The two FBI men shook hands; Brandon gave nods to both doctors before addressing the android. "How goes the hunt, L.I.A.M.?"

"Steady as it goes."

"You sure the reporter followed you?" Harding lowered his voice to ask McDaniels.

"L.I.A.M. is. That's good enough for me." James motioned to his boss to the side. "We took every precaution. No way she followed us here."

"How did she find out about this? Only you, I, and the director knew where you were," Harding said.

"I only told you. Now, it may be one of the computer geeks, but I have a sneaking suspicion the leak is either you or the director. We will know if she shows up here," James said calmly and directly.

"You just accused your bosses of being moles for the press. Guess it's not a stretch why you didn't gain those big promotions over the years." Brandon smiled and slapped his friend on the shoulder.

"She is here." L.I.A.M. pointed to a vehicle pulling up a few hundred yards away.

"L.I.A.M., who is feeding her information?" McDaniels asked.

"Director Anthony Maroni has been involved with the reporter Sasha Blonde for about four months. His texts and calls are from a disposable cell phone, but the security cameras at her apartment and a number of hotels in the New York and Washington, D.C., areas are rather conclusive. A rather graphic video on the reporter's private files confirm the physical aspect of the relationship. He has not openly discussed this project, but has alluded to the importance. She is following us because of him."

"The director is involved? Colonel Vetter won't like hearing that bit of news," Dr. Potts said as she and Brooks joined the conversation.

"No wonder he voiced concern about the press finding out; he was covering his butt," Nathan Brooks stated with resentment.

"What do we do now, boss?" McDaniels asked Brandon.

"Everybody just relax. I had a feeling about this, I just didn't want to deal with it. This is still a secret operation and we need to first handle this reporter. She doesn't know what is really going on, and if we get funny acting, she will know something is up. The director will be a whole 'nother can of worms, but let's hold off calling in Vetter."

"Tinman is a DARPA project," Gabby Potts said, "with top secret level clearance, and in my contract, it is mandated I inform superiors of any possible data leaks or espionage immediately. If I don't inform Colonel Vetter, I am liable to lose my funding, suffer financial penalties, even go to jail."

"No one is going to jail. Let me handle this reporter, then we will figure out what to do. Here is what I want everyone to do…" Special Agent Harding began.

CHAPTER 34

SASHA BLONDE PULLED UP TO THE KANSAS CITY train yard in her rented car, observing Special Agent Harding standing with a group of people. She recognized Special Agent McDaniels from his picture, but the rest were unknown to her. One of the unknowns pointed at her as he spoke to both FBI agents. Sasha quickly took a number of photographs. She had learned over the years to be redundant with evidence whenever possible; so, she clicked a number of images on her cell phone and digital camera. She quickly emailed the photos on her phone to her editor as she watched Harding walk right toward her.

He was an attractive man, she thought. Tall, thin, masculine, authoritative, with a hint of danger, but also a moral standing. He walked with purpose, as the group behind him waved to her from their position. Sasha pushed the button lowering her window, giving a slight wave, more from embarrassment of being discovered than out of friendliness. Brandon smiled widely as he reached the car and leaned in the window.

"Why, Special Agent Harding, what a coincidence running into you here."

"Sure. Guess you just hurry off wherever you are told."

"What does that mean?"

"You know exactly what that means and you are risking a lot. Fortunately for you, the director was leading you by the nose. Had you been given any real sensitive information, you could have been jailed. Even listed as a conspirator after the fact, to terrorist activity. That's an orange jumpsuit and a plane ride to an undisclosed location."

"Don't play me, agent. I discovered the Ghost, and that was news to everybody."

"You certainly generated the coverage we needed to focus funding. You think you are the first pair of legs to part trying to boost their career? You think men like the director haven't played the likes of you a dozen times over the years?"

"Then who are they?"

"That is a field study. The bureau is working on some new equipment and techniques to implement nationally. Using science, breaking down chemical elements, and optimizing our computer capabilities, we will deliver a much more effective outcome. The director figured if you covered this story it could build a better understanding of the methods we plan to utilize."

"Don't con me."

"Would you like to interview Special Agent McDaniels? He will be overseeing the science unit during this trial phase, or you could talk with our scientists. I'll admit they are pretty nerdy. Extremely smart people, tops in their fields of study, but way over my head."

Sasha Blonde was confused and upset; the idea of being led by the director did not sit well. She waved off the suggestion and shook her head. She didn't know what was true or what to do. "Perhaps another time. I have to get back to my story."

"Sorry to break it to you like this. Don't be angry. Don't you want to know where they are headed next?" Brandon smiled widely once more as Sasha Blonde rolled up her window and started the rental car.

She was disgusted by the smug attitude the agent displayed. Could she have been so wrong about Anthony Maroni? He was the director of the FBI, but he seemed as dumb as any man. Easily distracted by the desires of his lust and pleasure. Her cell phone vibrated, a text message from the man himself. *Where are you*, the text read. This only infuriated her further. She had allowed herself to be drawn away from the mark, the Ghost, but she would not allow her time to be wasted. She would use the secondary team just as she had planned, to pressure the Ghost with fear.

Sasha Blonde drove to the airport, headed for New York, determined to maintain the public interest in her story. Her agent was making progress with her career and the fine points were being smoothed out. As for the man playing her, guiding her to the purpose he wanted; the director's day would come. She had a great memory for those who had found themselves siding against her, she held a grudge with the best of any. Sasha wasn't totally convinced Maroni had played her, and the number of texts as she drove made her question whether the handsome fed was pulling a fast one of his own. Either way, she figured Anthony Maroni had fulfilled his usefulness.

CHAPTER 35

HARDING RETURNED TO THE GROUP with a wide smile. The man had a bounce in his step as he nodded to his old friend McDaniels. "You look like the cat who ate the canary," James said.

"Told her the director had played her like a fiddle, sending her on the runaround."

"What did you tell her about us?" Potts asked.

"Told her the truth," Brandon answered, catching alarmed looks from all but L.I.A.M. "I said you were a team of scientists on a field study, trying out new techniques; which is true. I made it seem irrelevant. A second team hunting the Ghost. I need to call the director and at least put a cork in the man."

"So, what am I to do about Colonel Vetter? If he finds out I knew and didn't tell him, I could be in a lot of trouble," Gabby asked with concern.

McDaniels moved closer to his friend and pulled him aside, whispering, "This could be your opportunity." At a questioning look from Brandon, he went on. "The director stacked the deck against himself and now he is finished, sooner or later. Gabby is right: that Vetter guy will find out, and you have a chance to be ahead of this."

"James is correct," L.I.A.M. said.

McDaniels turned with a glare. "You can hear us?"

"Of course. I also heard every word Special Agent Harding said to Sasha Blonde."

Brandon turned, looking from L.I.A.M. to where the reporter had been parked. "Wow, that's impressive." Looking back at James, Brandon furrowed his brow and moved back to the group. "Let's head to the airport and I will think about how best to handle this situation."

"Actually, we have one more stop," L.I.A.M. stated, cocking his head. "We are off to Hollywood, California. Case number 7550B. Eric Strong was shot outside a nightclub by a sniper."

"If the man was shot in the street, how do you intend to gain any more information than you have here?" McDaniels asked.

"The sniper nest has been sealed. The shot came from inside an abandoned, vacant office, and has remained sealed. Our unknown subject was in that room; it should give us a more complete evaluation. Currently, we lack certain componence to allow me to narrow my field of inquiry. I believe this sniper nest will provide the evidence we need to find the Ghost."

"All right, I will head to D.C. and fix this mess," Harding said. "Gabby, I will be sure to protect your position and make things right. No worries."

"I appreciate it. The confidentiality and disclosure agreement I signed was extensive with harsh penalties. I just want to cover myself."

"Understandable. The director has really created a problem here, but I believe we can salvage this. Good luck with your search and keep me updated."

The two FBI agents sat in the front seats of the Suburban; Gabby Potts was in the middle of the back seat, with L.I.A.M. and Dr. Brooks to either side. They drove in quiet thought to the airport. They all knew the reporter complicated matters and none wanted their adventure to end. They bid one another farewell and the group headed westward.

CHAPTER 36

SASHA BLONDE LEFT HAIR AND MAKEUP with a determined stride. She had worked on her story since she left Kansas City and was ready to strike some fear into people. The feeling of being manipulated stung, and she was not the type of woman to be used. She had produced the piece herself and readied the clips of the previous crimes by using news footage. She wrote most of her script and knew exactly what she intended to say. They would shoot the run, a couple promo segments or teasers, then she would help edit the spot this evening.

Moving to her mark, Sasha checked her hemline in the monitor and adjusted her hair. Ed had assured her the piece would run in two days, giving a day to promo. She knew good and well he wanted time to preview her segment and go over it with the legal department. Lawsuits were nothing new to a show like *Indepth News*, but the wrong person offended could create real problems. She knew she couldn't come out and press the issue with Anthony, but she could get the message across well enough to make him sweat.

Her message to the Ghost was more direct; she needed a sign, a direct connection to push her over the top. He had shown the world his presence with the Harlem fire, but now she needed her Ghost to provide her something specific. Sasha thought of the Zodiac killer, with the letters to the newspapers: that's what she needed. She had worded the piece just so, to almost seem like a warning or that she knew more than she could say.

The crew in place; lights, camera, sound, rolling, action. "Director of the FBI Anthony Maroni has dispatched a secondary unit of the Special Response Task Force to catch the Ghost. This special unit has gone back over previous crime scenes, implementing state-of-the-art techniques to find evidence irretrievable before now." This was where she would show the picture of the secondary unit.

"Director Maroni stated that his task force and this science unit are on the verge of catching this elusive killer. He expressed his distaste for the likes of murderous villains who target the weak and helpless, hiding away and cowering from the long arm of the law."

Sasha moved ever so gracefully a few steps, the camera following her. "Our hearts here at *Indepth News* go out to all the victims and their families. The country is deeply saddened by this terrible and cruel creature targeting its citizens. The Ghost is not a human being; no person could lack compassion as this monster does. Law enforcement is hot on the trail and will apprehend this sick and disturbed individual. I would advise the Ghost to surrender, seek out a peaceful end to this monstrosity, and face justice with at least a sense of humanity. What you have done is wrong and unjustifiable; but your days are numbered. The hounds of hell nip at your heels. I would plead to a conscience, but the acts performed by the Ghost show us there is none. So, I shall plead to the heroes of law enforcement to be swift to action, plead to God to soften the grief of our hearts, and plead to the Ghost to reach out and stop this rampage."

Most of what Sasha had to say would be used as voiceover, showing scenes from the other crimes, as well as the great footage she had filmed in Harlem. She spent over four hours in the editing room putting together a masterpiece. Sasha knew this would pull the public back to full attention, gain her awards and the anchor chair of that cable network. It would probably cause Anthony Maroni's fat Italian butt to pucker, but her greatest hope was to draw out the Ghost. She knew if she could gain an exclusive interview, the national network would sign her for a decade.

CHAPTER 37

HARDING HAD HIS BOSS, MARONI, meet him early at a quiet restaurant on the outskirts of Washington, D.C. He had called the director on his flight from Kansas City and instructed him to halt all communication with Sasha Blonde. Director Maroni had tried to play coy, but Harding wasn't having it. He was disappointed with his boss, allowing himself to be corrupted by a leggy blonde. Brandon knew it was not an uncommon occurrence, especially in Washington, D.C., but the man had been in the game long enough to know better.

Harding had set the meeting, thinking about the suggestion his old friend James had alluded to. This was his chance to take what he wanted, versus the struggle of earning it. He didn't really like the idea of forcing his way but knew the bureau needed a good and honest man at the helm. Brandon viewed his decision as in the best interests of all concerned. Granted, he had always seen himself as a field agent, with no stomach for the power playing and ass-kissing that went on with a director's position. Still, if the reality surfaced of Maroni leaking top secret information to the press, not only could his boss go to jail, the bureau could be forever tainted.

Anthony Maroni approached the table in the corner with a sheepish expression. The man knew he had messed up but had no idea what was coming. Brandon motioned to a seat. "Kind of out of the way, isn't it?" the director commented as he sat down. Waving at the waitress, he ordered a double Blue Label scotch and gave Brandon a half-hearted smile. "So, what's this about?"

"You know damn well what this is about. Blonde, big boobs, legs up to her neck, and you," Brandon stated with a sharp tone.

"Just wait a second; there is nothing between her and me."

"Anthony, you messed up and I can't be party to it. There is too much on the line, and you haven't taken this seriously."

"I don't have any idea what you're talking about."

"We have known each other a long time, boss; don't insult me by denying it. I am a detective. You are the leak; you have been feeding Sasha Blonde her information."

The waitress arrived with the director's drink, which he downed and requested a replacement. "Look, I didn't tell her anything, really. Nothing she wouldn't have found out sooner or later from someone."

"No Anthony, don't shrink this like it is some little thing. She was in Kansas City. You may not have told her specifics, but you put her to task, set the scent and let her find it all for herself. I didn't call you here to debate or go over what you did, listen to your rationalization of why, or to what extent you broke the law. You have done many good things over your career, have helped me along and shown me respect; and so, I shall return the favor."

Maroni gave a questioning look as the waitress set his scotch in front of him. "Thank you," he said, but never looked away from the task force leader. "Return the favor? What's that supposed to mean?"

"You are going to resign. You can come up with whatever excuse you like, but you are going to recommend me as your replacement. I have Senator Miller on his way, as well as General McHenery; you will inform them of your resignation and ask them to add to your recommendation."

"You didn't tell them? Why?"

"I told them you had news. You need to step down; you've been compromised, and when it would come out would be bad for everyone concerned. You know that. You knew when you warned me about that Blonde woman; or you were worried she would try to ply me with her feminine ways."

"Look, Brandon, isn't there some other way?" Harding only shook his head. "Well, what if I don't resign?"

"Then I will arrest you. I will notify both of our guests as to why, as well as the President. I will ask Senator Miller to open hearings into your conduct and we can all go before Congress and hash this out. You, your reputation, your relationships, your future, all will be tainted. Sasha Blonde will go to jail; or I am rather certain Colonel Vetter will push to have the whole thing gagged by the courts and both of you sequestered. All in the interest of national security. You will resign for whatever reason, and you will do so with a smile. You will present me as the best replacement for you and convey your confidence in my abilities."

"Which would be true. So, do you have a suggestion for my sudden departure?"

"Health or family are both popular for such occasions. A heavy heart for the families in Harlem, the weight of such pain and loss being too much to bear. May play for you to run for office, a governorship, or perhaps Congress. Anthony, I am sorry this has happened, but you did it to yourself. My interest is strictly for the bureau. You were a good boss, you just got hung up by a beautiful woman. I am sorry. Suck it up and leave with the class I know you have."

Senator John Miller approached the table, waving to the waitress. He ordered Chivas and another round for the table. He was obviously concerned over the meeting. "What's this about? You sounded serious on the phone."

"I am stepping down," Maroni said. "Resigning as director. Since we are in the middle of this operation, I wanted to tell you and Patrick first." He sounded subdued.

"What?"

"There are a number of reasons, but I am recommending Brandon here to take over for me. I doubt the President will argue, but having you voice the need to place him quickly with the Senate would be appreciated."

"There you go asking for things," General Patrick McHenery said, walking up. The waitress brought a tray of drinks, then the general hurried her off to fetch more whiskey for himself and the others. "What's the story, gents?"

"Anthony is resigning," Senator Miller stated.

"What did you get caught doing?" McHenery asked.

"It's nothing like that. Just a combination of things, and I think it's good opportunity to step aside and let Brandon take over."

"Anthony, we have all done this far too long to shine on one another. You can sell that to the reporters and whomever else, but we know guys like you don't up and quit." General McHenery allowed his words to hang as the waitress brought his drink and the next round for the table.

As she left, Anthony Maroni raised his glass. "Gentlemen, to a good run." He toasted and drank deeply. "I'd rather not say the real reason; a lack of judgment, which is embarrassing to be sure. Brandon, you are correct to have shown me my error and I am grateful for your discretion. Honestly, I am somewhat relieved. You will quickly come to know the pressure placed upon the position, and I wish you luck."

"Thank you, sir, and I am sorry."

"I am confident Brandon will fill the void," Senator Miller added, as he sipped his scotch.

"Your call. So, we see from your reports that L.I.A.M. is roaming the countryside. Sounds like progress is slow going," General McHenery said to the two FBI men.

"How close is he to catching this Ghost?" Miller asked.

Brandon sipped his drink, giving a slight nod before speaking. "I was just in Kansas City with L.I.A.M. and am extremely confident. He is making progress. This Ghost is smart and careful, but I think it's just a matter of time now. Special Agent McDaniels assures me L.I.A.M. is functioning on all cylinders, so to speak."

"Is McDaniels who you will have take over the task force?" Maroni asked.

"Yes. I figure he has earned it. I don't think he will like the added responsibility, but will handle it. He is an investigator first and foremost, but I believe he will run the team as well or better than I have. I would perhaps worry if he had to deal with a director more motivated by position or unfamiliar with procedure. James is a classic G-man; but willing, as we see with L.I.A.M., to open up to technology to get the job done and put criminals away. After all, the FBI was founded on innovation." Harding downed his whiskey.

CHAPTER 38

L.I.A.M. STOOD ON THE SIDEWALK looking across the street at an office building. Dr. Brooks stood by the android's side gawking at the sight which was Hollywood. Dr. Potts and Special Agent McDaniels stood off to the side talking among themselves. They had arrived at LAX airport and were met by local FBI agents delivering their car, a Dodge Charger. Driving directly to the crime scene, L.I.A.M. observed the spot where Eric Strong had been shot. He calculated the angle of the shot, visibility, traffic patterns that could create draft, weather conditions on the day of the shooting, along with the lighting, which would have to be viewed at night because the victim had exited a nightclub at 1:47 a.m. when shot.

"Crazy place. Look at these people," Brooks said as his gaze followed two women walking hand in hand wearing skintight pants. "What are they talking about?"

"James is explaining how Special Agent Harding will take care of the situation and keep her out of any trouble," L.I.A.M. told his creator. "Gabby is worried that a breach of contract could forfeit her work. James countered with an observation that I am functionable. How Colonel Vetter will be looking to replicate this experiment and then reduce her role in the project."

"Do you believe what he says?"

"I would say it is accurate. Colonel Vetter views his responsibilities with a sense of duty and I have observed his physical reactions to this project."

"What physical reactions?"

"Increased blood pressure and heart rate, a surge of testosterone, adrenaline, and a variety of pheromones. The man is excited over this project," L.I.A.M. answered.

McDaniels and Potts moved back to their team members, both looking up at the office building. "Where was it? Which floor?" James asked.

"Third floor, fourth window from the right," L.I.A.M. responded.

"Makes no sense. Why is this person killing people? You have pointed out this person is smart, why would he just murder?" Gabby asked.

"A question asked by courts, victims' families, and psychologists for centuries," McDaniels returned with a shrug. "So, what are we doing?"

L.I.A.M. pointed to the crosswalk. "We shall evaluate the nest. I simply wanted to determine the shooter's skill level."

"And?" James asked as the group moved toward the end of the block.

"Moderate, I would estimate. Under five hundred yards with clear line of sight, limited cross breeze; which with a high-powered rifle at such a distance shouldn't factor beyond a miniscule variant. I would say the man is well practiced but not military trained." L.I.A.M. pressed the button to cross the street.

"Non-military; an interesting fact, could help limit the search," Brooks commented as they waited.

"Untrained as a sniper or sharpshooter, but still could have a military background. We must not exhaust any possibility until it is fully ruled out," L.I.A.M. said.

The light changed and the group crossed the street, moving down the adjacent block to the entrance of the office building. The struggling economy had caused a number of the businesses in California and around the country to downsize or pack up altogether. The office building was at thirty-three percent capacity with five accounts in arrears. The Ghost had chosen the spot from opportunity; low traffic within the building, no security cameras, numerous empty offices, a high traffic night spot across the street. This unknown subject did not target specifics but found opportune circumstances and conditions to use them toward his murderous ends.

L.I.A.M. led the climb up the stairs, avoiding the elevator. Taking deep breaths of air, the android followed his nose as if a beautiful scent fluttered upon the breeze. Reaching the fourth floor, L.I.A.M. motioned for the group to wait as he continued halfway up the next set of steps. Trotting back down to the fourth floor, L.I.A.M. opened the stairwell door and resumed sniffing. Walking confidently down the hall, the group reached the office door; the police sticker sealed the door, large letters announcing it as a crime scene, while smaller lettering warned of prosecution for violating the space.

McDaniels pulled a lock-blade knife from his pocket and cut the notice at the seam of the door. Closing the knife, he then pulled a lock pick set from his inside jacket pocket. Bending one knee, the special agent worked the tools within the lock and had the door open just over one minute from when he started. "Out of practice," he said as he stood. Opening the door and holding it for L.I.A.M. to enter, James gave a shrug to the two doctors.

L.I.A.M. advanced into the vacated office, taking deep breaths of stale air as he moved forward deeper into the office, hurrying from room to room. A table sat in the middle of the main room, which L.I.A.M.

circled three times. "He unpacked the weapon here. The smell of gun oil is heaviest." The android sniffed the surface of the table.

The two doctors and federal agent waited just inside the door, allowing L.I.A.M. to investigate undisturbed. The android moved to the window, squatting then standing on his tiptoes. "What's wrong?" McDaniels asked.

"The angle is off." L.I.A.M. turned his attention to the table and the floor in front of it. Falling to all fours, the android inspected faint marks on the hardwood flooring. "This was moved." He stood, pulling the table forward to where the marks stopped. Looking more closely at the tabletop, L.I.A.M. began inventorying the room, seeing a straight-backed chair next to the entrance. Moving with purpose, he snatched the chair and carefully placed it upon the table. Aligning the slight indentions with the feet of the chair, L.I.A.M. climbed atop the table and sat on the chair. Looking down at the street below, L.I.A.M. nodded.

"Surely seems like an odd position," McDaniels said, moving farther into the office. He looked out the window at the nightclub, then up at where L.I.A.M. was perched. "What sense would such a position make?"

"As we discussed earlier, the shooter is not sniper trained, but is smart. He obviously wanted to be inside the room for the shot, as to not be seen from the street. He used a sound suppressor, so a gunshot would not mark his position. Shooting from a seated position is not what a trained sniper would do; however, I believe our unsub used a telescopic bipod to steady his shot. The chair on the table," L.I.A.M. hopped down from his seat, "gave the desired angle and stability, not to mention a comfortable seat while waiting."

"Waiting? You think he sat there a while?" Brooks asked as he moved to the window.

"Our man picked his target. Even though this individual is an opportunity killer, he does plan extensively and, in my opinion, given a choice of targets, he would be critical in his decision."

"You mean he looked for a type?" Potts asked.

"We know the Ghost spreads his modus operandi across method, location, and victimology. This is purposeful. The Ghost sat there and waited for a white male of below median age, above average physical stature; the fact that it was Eric Strong has no significance versus his outward appearance," L.I.A.M. answered.

"He sat in a chair on a table and waited to shoot someone? What kind of monster are we dealing with? Kills children, old people, but why?" Gabby asked. Taking L.I.A.M. by the hand, she faced him. "L.I.A.M., this Ghost person is a very broken human being. I am sorry you have had to be involved in this. You shouldn't have to witness the worst of mankind as you first join us. You should have come to know our generosity, our compassion, our love, to explore art, music, and dance." Gabby touched L.I.A.M.'s face as she finished.

"I am aware."

"The presence of the Ghost drove the necessity for our collaboration, and in turn, breathed life into our L.I.A.M. Had such evil not been discovered, had not been at work…" Nathan Brooks waved at L.I.A.M. "Perhaps L.I.A.M. would never come to pass. Certainly wouldn't be standing here today."

"Don't put it like that. You make it sound tainted," Gabby said.

"Like a child of rape? L.I.A.M. is our creation, but the cause driving our union is questionable." Nathan shook his head.

"The cause is justice. You spoke so strongly about L.I.A.M.'s choices, and so he will come to know one of the most important of them all: how he chooses to look at something." McDaniels said.

"Perspective?" L.I.A.M. asked.

"Yes. Like that chair on a table changes the point of view. How you decide to see things tells us and everyone else something about you. You are not here because of the Ghost; you are here to help, to catch this murderer, to prevent any further loss of life. Both of you put forth the time to create something I almost can't believe, a living miracle. You did so not for any Ghost or government, not for the military or FBI. You created L.I.A.M. from yourselves and for him." McDaniels met L.I.A.M.'s eyes. "You live, and I don't pretend to understand all the hows and whys. You live. Life is precious, and we guard it with our very lives for there is nothing more valued or sacred."

James marched back to L.I.A.M., coming face to face. "You understand that? Logic and calculating aside, computer or no. Life carries an obligation."

CHAPTER 39

SASHA BLONDE STOOD NEXT TO HER EDITOR, Edward Peoples, in the broadcast booth. They were watching her report air for the first time. Sasha knew this was her last effort to break this story before she moved on. Her agent had recommended the cable news network as her next move, and the contracts sat on her kitchen table, waiting to be signed. She knew this story wasn't over, but her time at *Indepth News* was. Such a change would make everything so different. Watching herself on the monitor, Sasha wanted to be a reporter for one of the national networks, but that was a gamble. The cable job would pay less, but last longer, and she would be the biggest fish in a smaller pond.

"Great work, Sasha." Edward broke her train of thought.

She hadn't even noticed her segment was over. "Thank you. Ed, we need to talk."

The two headed out of the broadcast booth and into Peoples's office. As he closed the door behind them, Edward knew what was coming. "So, where you going to next?" he asked as he rounded his desk.

"Cable news. You know I wish…" Sasha started, but allowed her comment to hang. "I just think we have run our course. Time to move along."

"Look, Sasha, I ain't your boyfriend, and this ain't no breakup. You do you and believe me when I say, the world will turn. You did good and I am glad we had you. This Ghost story really upped our credibility. You have to take care of yourself, I respect that." Peoples gave her a nod and smile.

"'Ain't no'? Call yourself a newsman?" Sasha teased the editor.

"Hanging around too many young people and immigrant reporters," he said with a wink.

The two sparred back and forth for a while in good fun. They weren't friends but had become friendly. Both knew it was a job; emotions and interpersonal connections were complicated strings nobody needed. Reporters moved around, went where the work was, followed stories, had a short shelf life. Such was reality, and both knew all too well how things worked. They parted with a handshake and a smile. Edward reminded Sasha that she had an obligation to her fans to at least say goodbye. They agreed to shoot a farewell piece later in the week.

Sasha left her editor's office feeling good about her decision. She collected the few things she had at the studio and headed to her car. She left without a word to her other co-workers; she hadn't made friends at *Indepth News*. She carried the box with a few items inside to her car, and realized she hadn't made friends really at all, in her whole life. There had been men, but they were far from friends. Her thoughts were overcome by a feeling that brought her to a dead stop.

Sasha looked around, turning to see if someone was following her, but the parking lot was empty. Her eyes scanned the parked cars but she saw no one. "Is someone there?" she called out.

Silence lingered as she become more nervous. She couldn't shake the feeling that someone was watching her. Pulling the keys from her purse, she hurried to her car, frantically unlocked the door, and climbed inside. Locking the door, she threw her box of belongings onto the passenger seat, then realized she had not checked the back seat. A moment of terror gripped her; holding her breath, she could feel the beat of her heart in her throat. Lunging over the seat, fighting her own sense of panic, she looked for any threat but found only an empty back seat.

Turning back and settling into the driver's seat, she couldn't help but feel relieved, but also somewhat silly. She expelled a long slow breath as she allowed herself to relax. A knock on the driver's window caused an involuntary scream and flinch which almost moved her to the other side of the vehicle. Edward Peoples was holding up a hand with a look of alarm. "Damn it!" Sasha yelled at her editor.

"Jesus, are you all right?" he asked through the glass.

"You scared me to death." Sasha stepped out of her car. "Damn it," she repeated, as she shook her whole body. "I thought someone was following me. Paranoid."

"You like to jump out of your skin."

"Not funny."

"Kind of is. Should have seen your face. Did you pee a little?" He laughed loudly.

"What do you want, Ed?"

"You got a flat." He pointed at the flat wheel.

"What?" Sasha followed her editor around the vehicle to the front right tire. "How did you see that?"

"Your car is leaning. It's how I noticed. I had one a couple weeks ago. I think some bastard threw nails all over the lot."

"Does that mean the studio will replace my tire?"

"I'll have it repaired; all it needs is a patch. I'll have it taken care of. You want me to give you a ride home? You can pick it up tomorrow, and shoot your farewell spot." Peoples smiled. "Should have seen your face." The leggy blonde was hesitant but didn't want to wait around for her auto club to take care of the problem. She collected her purse and locked her vehicle, following her boss to his late model Cadillac. The man's car was as slovenly kept as the man himself, with coffee cups and donut boxes on the rear floorboards. They made small talk as Ed drove her home. It didn't occur to her until after he had dropped her off that she hadn't given him her address. The realization was a bit troubling, but she didn't want to overthink things. She was still feeling embarrassed from the startle she had in her car.

Ed left with a beep from his car horn. Sasha entered her building with a glance over her shoulder. The *Indepth News* studio was in Hartford, Connecticut, a train ride away from New York. She had an apartment, not wanting to waste money on a house or an expensive place in the city. New York was everything Sasha wanted to be. Walking down the hallway to her apartment, she again felt uneasy.

She hadn't been sleeping well, and now she had settled on a job instead of holding out for the one she wanted. Stopping, she turned to check the empty corridor. The mute-colored hallway in Connecticut easily represented her state of mind and place in the world; a far stretch from the vibe of New York City. She was settling, selling out her dreams for security and riding the wave of a killer. Sasha was not proud of herself, but figured she was better off than standing on some sort of principles. Integrity doesn't pay the bills.

Keying her door, she entered a dark apartment and locked the door behind her. She had wanted to be the big time, have the lights and action, but her time had run out. She thought of the FBI director playing her, probably laughing with his friends at her expense. All the hard work, the sacrifices she had made to achieve, but her best was cable television.

Clicking on the light, Sasha threw her purse on the kitchen table and opened her refrigerator. Pulling out the bottle of vodka, she poured a small glass full and took a seat at the table.

The cable contract stared up at her as she took a stiff pull from her glass. Sasha thought of her days growing up with nothing, the struggle to survive, and how far she had come. If only she had had more time, or the journey had not been so long, so hard, she might have reached her goal. Looking at the contract, she was somewhat disappointed, for she knew it was not a stepping stone but the destination of her career. Taking another large gulp of vodka, Sasha grabbed her purse and pulled out a pen. She had reached the point where security was valued over the risk of reward and the realization of that fact was disheartening.

Downing the rest of the glass, Sasha took hold of the colored tab marked *sign here* and opened the contract. Clicking the pen, she quickly noticed an obstruction; the line to which she was to pen her name already had one there. *Ghost*, in bold hand, flowed across the line in black ink. Sasha Blonde could not breathe, could not move, her eyes fixed upon the name which filled her with terror.

A blinding flash filled her field of vision as a blow threw her head forward onto the table. Sasha found herself on the kitchen floor, attempting to grasp consciousness, but her efforts were for naught. The world around her closed in a circle, growing smaller and ever so distant; black encompassed everything, until there was nothing.

CHAPTER 40

THE CALL WAS TRANSFERRED FROM THE NEW YORK field office to the task force headquarters and received by Agent Keith Kennedy. The young profiler immediately recognized the importance of the call. Calling the task force together in the conference room, the team listened to the voice of Edward Peoples. "She is gone. Sasha Blonde was supposed to record a farewell segment yesterday but didn't show up. Which isn't like her at all. I contacted police but they gave me some spiel about a forty-eight-hour waiting period. I called FBI and they transferred me to you, and I have been on this phone for an hour and a half, trying to get someone to listen. You need to take action."

"All right, Mr. Peoples, just remain calm and allow us to ask a few questions." Special Agent Allison Carter spoke in a soft tone.

"I am calm; a little frustrated and very worried, but I am calm. You all do realize who Sasha Blonde is, right?"

"Oh yes, we know exactly who she is. Why do you think something has happened to her?" Harding addressed the speaker phone.

"She was jumpy and on edge; that and the piece we did on the Ghost yesterday was…" People paused for the correct word. "Inviting."

"So, you based this on a feeling?" Jody Jensen spoke up. "You have no evidence to support this suspicion. This is unsubstantiated?"

"Look, I have been a reporter all my life and my gut has never steered me wrong. Something has happened, and if we wait…well, I got a bad gut feeling about that too," Ed spoke with urgency.

"You mentioned a farewell address?" the lead profiler asked. "Was she going somewhere?"

"She was leaving the show. All the attention she had generated gained her some job offers. It's the business. Something has happened, I know it. So, are you going to do anything about it, or am I going to air this conversation in a week and have all of your jobs?"

Harding looked at his lead tactical officer who gave him a nod.

"My gut says there is something wrong in Denmark too," Sam Lee said with a raised eyebrow and a shrug.

"As does mine," Brandon said. "All right, Mr. Peoples, we are coming. Do not disturb anything of Ms. Blonde's. We will be there tomorrow. I will contact the locals. Just keep your phone on and let us know if you hear from her."

Johnson clicked the phone off, and the group exchanged looks in silence. "Guess we are headed to Hartford," the young tactical officer commented.

"What do you think, Carter?" Brandon asked his lead profiler.

Allison bounced her head back and forth before answering. "Genuine concern, the threat to us is interesting. I find his certainty a little questionable; he knows, as if fact, not suspicion. His comment about the woman was also interesting."

"What comment?" Harding asked.

"'The attention she generated,'" Kennedy interjected. "As if she caused or created it, not the unsub."

"What does that mean?" Sam Lee asked.

"This man views Blonde as the focus, not the criminal of her stories," Carter explained. "He is her boss, and they run these stories, as if they have some contribution and in turn benefit from them. Consider a sports team; a fan says that WE won or lost versus THEY, Him or Her. Viewing the contest and becoming emotionally invested includes the fan in the process. Yet, the fan is detached; we are not injured or traded; the individual is not the whole. This man views the story, the coverage, as a separate aspect from the crime or criminal."

"She generated the attention to the acts," Kennedy picked up the explanation. "Like the individual behind the spotlight. The entertainer would go unnoticed without the light shined upon them. Reporters, managers, agents; often they include themselves as the primary factor of success. Viewing themselves as the generator or engine of the success, which can easily cause conflict and resentment or possibly in this case, some unwanted attention."

"Well, let's get ourselves together, and we will fly out at 6:00 A.M.," Harding said. "I am going to call in McDaniels to meet us there."

"Thought you had him put out to pasture." Special Agent Lee laughed.

"No, no. He has been working with a couple of scientists to see if they can find something we missed."

"What are we, chopped liver?" Agent Wu Park spoke under his breath but was heard.

"These are university types, outside the criminal arena. Thought they may give an outside perspective," Harding said as Director Maroni waved at him from the window. Brandon dismissed the meeting, opening the conference room door to shake his boss's hand. "Director. What brings you in today?"

"Let's talk in your office," Anthony Maroni said firmly.

Brandon nodded and led the way to his office, holding the door for his boss. Closing the door behind them, he rounded his desk and poured two scotches, handing a glass to Anthony. "Didn't expect you today."

"Sasha, she is missing." Anthony's tone and meaning were indeterminate.

"How do you know that?"

"I am the director of the FBI. It's my job to know things."

"Wish you would have known not to gab to the press." Brandon raised an eyebrow.

"May not be an issue now."

"How do you figure?"

"Her report aired online last night. She basically invited the Ghost to come forward. She may have gotten what she asked for," the director said with almost a smug expression.

"Sir, allow me to be blunt: this seems extremely odd and opportune. Forgive me for asking, but to not would be neglect of my duties. Did you have something to do with Sasha Blonde disappearing?"

The director paused for a moment, looking at his task force leader, then gave a wide smile. "How far your opinion of me has fallen. No, Brandon, I didn't have anything to do with the woman coming up missing. She played me, and almost cost me my career. I am simply happy that I may have dodged a bullet here."

"At the cost, potentially, of a woman's life. If the Ghost has her, it is hard to say what may result."

"We shall have to see if Ms. Blonde has found misfortune or not. I would like to hope not, but I suspect something is amiss. Good day, Director."

CHAPTER 41

SASHA BLONDE BEGAN TO BECOME aware of the pain throbbing inside her skull. Radiating waves of agony washed from the back of her head to the front. Her whole body was achy as she began to move, quickly realizing she was bound. The tape over her mouth prevented her from screaming as she recalled her capture. Opening her eyes, the world took a number of blinks to come into focus; when it did, Sasha felt a fear and a loneliness she had never known before.

She was in some kind of warehouse, dark and dirty, with a high ceiling and nothing in front of her for what seemed like a city block or more. There were small windows lining the roof of the building, some missing and the rest allowing a filthy daylight to seep through. A couple of rust-covered tanks sat along one wall, the contents long gone, leaving only these empty shells. An ancient forklift was to the other side of her, dust and cobwebs covering the machine like an artifact. The floor was concrete but the footsteps in the more than an inch of dust showed that no one had been in this place for a very long time.

The fear swelled as tears streamed down her cheeks, the vision of that signature on her contract filling her with panic. Sasha had wanted the Ghost to contact her; she had never thought he would take her.

Had he flattened her tire? He had obviously been in her apartment, waiting for her.

Sasha's mind raced with thoughts and fears, imagining what was ahead. Her wrists were duct taped to the arms of the chair, as were her biceps to the back of the chair. She was also taped, at the knees and ankles, to the legs of the chair. Her squirming confirmed the level of adhesion and the futility of attempted escape.

She turned her head to one side then the other. She was in the middle of this giant warehouse. The dust on the floor showed the footsteps leading off to where she could see a light in an office. Straining her neck and looking out of the corner of her eye, she could hardly make out much of anything, but for a shadow occasionally moving past the covered window. Ever so faintly, she could hear a voice; the Ghost was talking.

Sasha closed her eyes and perked her ears to hear, but the distance was too great, and the emptiness of her surroundings distorted the voice too much. Who was he talking to, she wondered? Her hope was the FBI, or perhaps the studio, was talking with him about ransom. She had covered the Ghost and knew he was not a kidnapper, so the idea of him selling her back to her employers was ridiculous.

He was smart and careful, and now she was in his grasp, tied to a chair and about to become...the thought brought more sobs. She began to struggle once again, but quickly noticed the chair was bolted to the floor. Her helplessness over took her. Sasha Borkisnicvic cried like a baby.

CHAPTER 42

MCDANIELS HAD PASSED ALONG L.I.A.M.'S request that Sasha Blonde's apartment remain sealed until he arrived, which Harding made sure to do. The task force had arrived on scene almost an hour before McDaniels, L.I.A.M., and both doctors. Both crime scene investigators were vocal about getting to work collecting evidence, and Wu Park again voiced his distaste with a secondary team. They waited in three black Suburbans, with a number of local police maintaining a perimeter. As McDaniels greeted his friends, he could tell there were some questions. He introduced the groups using first names only, which also gained some suspicious looks.

The task force gathered at the rear of the vehicles as all parties exchanged pleasantries. Harding pulled his senior agent aside to confirm the vague story they had arranged. The range of interaction was interesting for L.I.A.M.; watching the group in their exchanges had him fascinated. McDaniels called L.I.A.M. to join his private conversation with the boss. "You all right?" James asked L.I.A.M. once he was close.

"Yes."

"Remember, you are a scientist. Here to observe. Stay close to James; and you keep a lid on things," Brandon stated firmly. "These cops have drawn out the local press, it won't be long before the national hounds are here."

"They are en route. Sam and Tyrone are anxious," L.I.A.M. told the two FBI men.

"They are tactical, they tend to stay that way," McDaniels said.

L.I.A.M. tilted his head as he looked at the group. "Wu is upset, but it is Allison who is highly suspicious."

Harding gave L.I.A.M. a slap on the shoulder. "Don't even want to know how you know that." He went back to the team. Sam Lee and Tyrone were gearing up to enter the apartment complex as Brandon approached. "We have some attention over there, those cameras are on us. L.I.A.M. wants to evaluate the scene first."

"Sir, we waited for these scientists to get here and I don't know why, but there is no way that guy is first through the door. You know who we are dealing with here; the whole place could be rigged," Sam stated in a grave tone.

"I second that, sir," Tyrone added. "This Ghost is a slick tricky; and we slip up, flags to our families, sir."

Harding rubbed his eyes, knowing what they were saying was true. Did he send the top-secret android, avoid a potential loss of life but possibly destroy a one of a kind…thing? Did he let these men do their job and potentially lose evidence L.I.A.M. could discover by entering first? "You guys are right. Ready yourselves and secure the building and then the apartment. Check everything. I'll tell the others." Sam Lee took charge, ordering the local special weapons aggressive tactical team along with the bomb squad to follow him and do what they were told to do. Sam was a soldier and knew his business well. He was a take-charge, get-'er done type with two speeds: fast and faster. He hated having to wait, or deal with the games law enforcement had to navigate, because of politicians and the public. Everyone wanted the police to save the day, but process and individual rights at times hindered the good guys from getting the job done. Brandon knew the old warrior was itching to get into the play and figured clearing the building was safer for everyone.

Harding waved the task force together around him. "Sam is going to lead the locals and secure the building, then the apartment. Johnson will be backing him up and be ready with the bomb squad, if necessary. I know we all want to get in there and evaluate the scene. Won't take long; we will be in before the close of the hour. I want 'A' game, people. This is our opportunity to catch a mistake. Ms. Blonde aired that report not forty-eight hours ago. The Ghost had no time to plan, and might have slipped up."

"You are presuming too much, Brandon," L.I.A.M. said.

"How is that, L.I.A.M.?"

"You presume he did not plan, which would be out of character. He could have easily planned the reporter's abduction, awaiting a trigger, like the story to implement his plan."

"I agree," Allison Carter said. "Our profile is strong, and such a move would be counter to the man's behavior pattern. We would only see such a shift if cornered or highly agitated."

Lee and Johnson began their assault on the apartment building. Men in black with automatic weapons, helmets and masks hurried after them. The military style of the police units was by design; learned tactical maneuvers that worked. Such groups practiced and trained for all sorts of situations; but this was a unique mind they were against. The team paused to watch as the men in black charged toward the unknown.

"So, what are your fields of study?" Jody Jensen inquired of the additions to the group.

"Computers," Dr. Brooks said.

"Engineering," Gabby said.

245

L.I.A.M. remained silent, observing the assault on the building. Carter moved up next to him, observing him and not the action toward the apartment complex. "Your insight of a preplanned abduction is impressive. What exactly is your area of expertise?"

McDaniels interrupted before L.I.A.M. gave an answer. "Allison, how have you been? I see you have met L.I.A.M."

"Yes," she said to James, then turned back to L.I.A.M. "Have you considered this may be a hoax?" L.I.A.M. tilted his head slightly but did not look away from the building. "Of course. Such an attention-seeking woman might stage such an event, or even falsify contact in order to keep the story relevant and the attention upon her. However, the inflections of Edward People's voice when describing her edgy and alarmed manner were genuine."

"When did you speak with Mr. Peoples?" Allison asked.

"I monitored the phone conversation between him and the task force," L.I.A.M. said, turning to Carter. He looked her in the eyes for a long moment. "Do you believe this to be a faked abduction?" Allison shook her head. "My concern is, our subject using his followers. Such will cause deeper effort toward his capture," L.I.A.M. went on.

"Followers?" Allison asked.

"Followers?" McDaniels echoed.

L.I.A.M.'s attention moved from one to the other. "Yes. The amount of work, travel, and sophistication involved in what this subject has accomplished suggests the assistance of probably numerous followers. Whether these individuals are aware of every aspect of our primary subject's agenda is unknown and unlikely."

"Brandon, you better come take a listen to this," James called.

Harding nodded and spoke into his radio as he approached the trio. "They are breaching Blonde's apartment," he told them.

"L.I.A.M. says the Ghost may have followers," James said.

"What? You didn't put that in any of your reports."

"Such is not confirmed," L.I.A.M. said. "Combined with the leaking information, I calculate it to be advantageous to keep my hypothesis to myself. Your awareness or unawareness of contributors does little to change your process thus far."

"Who are you?" Allison Carter asked the android. "Your hypothesis is sound and likely." She turned her attention to Brandon. "You have been receiving reports from these people? They monitor our communications?"

"I am L.I.A.M."

Brandon smiled, giving the android a sideways glance. "They have been going back over the previous crime scenes and issuing a secondary evaluation. Obviously, this is working. Hold on." Harding turned away from the conversation to speak into his radio. "Clear. We are a go. L.I.A.M., with me. Jensen, Park, grab your kits. I want a complete workup. Prints, fibers, fluids, samples of everything. Carter, Kennedy, once we have our walkthrough, I want you two to work your magic. McDaniels, doctors, with me." He marched toward the apartment building holding L.I.A.M.'s arm.

SWAT team members littered the hallway as the task force moved toward Sasha Blonde's apartment. Lee met them at the door. "We are clear. No traps or bombs. Still, be careful, and don't go moving things without us checking it first."

"Good job, Sam, Tyrone."

L.I.A.M. advanced into the apartment inhaling deeply. Moving quickly from room to room, the android swiftly looked here and there, squatting down at times and tiptoeing at others, to heighten himself. His search ended in the kitchen, looking down at the table. Reaching out, L.I.A.M. was about to open the contract when Wu Park yelled at him.

"Gloves!" Park advanced toward the kitchen. "Don't touch anything. You'll contaminate the scene. God, don't you know anything?"

"I know many things," L.I.A.M. responded as he drew back his hand.

"Don't touch," Park stated firmly.

McDaniels reached the two. "I'll keep an eye on him," he said, patting Wu on the shoulder. "Go on, I got this." Looking at L.I.A.M., McDaniels gave a wink and smile. "CSI, they can be an odd bunch. If you touch it, they would have to explain your fingerprints."

"I know. I don't have fingerprints. I have ridges to secure grip. I also have no oil from my skin to create a print. The man's overreaction was not appreciated. Aggressive tone, heightened volume, advancing toward me. Under certain circumstances such behavior would be met by defensive protocols."

"Oh," James muttered, and pointed to the contract. "What were you going to look at?"

"Open at the tab."

McDaniels used his gloved hand to open the contract, reading the name on the line. "Brandon, come here."

Harding looked down at the papers, then at James. "How did you know that was there?"

"Purse, glass, pen, chair slightly pulled out: this is the last place Sasha Blonde was in this apartment until she was abducted by the Ghost."

"Are you certain it was him and not a follower?" Allison Carter asked from the front room.

"Yes."

Brandon again gave James a look, slightly shaking his head. "Let's talk in the hall," he said, guiding L.I.A.M. by the arm.

Carter stopped her boss in the living room, coming face to face with him. "Sir, who is this L.I.A.M.? What is he doing here? How does he know what he knows? You are being rather cagey about this whole thing."

"Allison, I appreciate your concerns, and given an opportunity, I will explain. You are a smart woman and I am confident you know there is a time and place for all things. I am equally confident that you are aware there are things not everyone is privy to know. L.I.A.M. is a genius but as you can tell, socially stunted. His companions are also gifted, and provide this investigation with the insight of an overly advanced mind. I thank you for your voice but we all are on the same team. Now, if you'll excuse me." Harding entered the hallway to see McDaniels, Brooks, and Potts standing a piece down the corridor, next to L.I.A.M. They were all looking at him.

"Allison's a bit suspicious, is she?" McDaniels said. "Those profilers are always looking a little deeper at us than they should. Guess they can't turn it off."

"Yeah. What's going on, L.I.A.M.? What ya got?"

"Currently, I am compiling data and reviewing avenues of inquiry. I am searching for our suspect."

"You are certain the Ghost took Sasha Blonde?"

"He did sign his work," James said, giving his old friend a shrug.

"Signed his work?" Gabby asked.

"The contract Sasha was to sign for her new job— the Ghost signed in her place," James explained. "Think Allison will have a field day with that symbolism?" he commented to Harding with a raised eyebrow.

"L.I.A.M., tell me what's going on?" Brandon again asked the android.

"Case file 7568B, Trenton, New Jersey. The gassing of three hundred and fifty-seven people. I noticed a scent which did not belong in the concentrated state it was in. It was an anomaly. Case file 7559B,

Daytona Beach, Florida. The hotel room contained the same scent, even though more dispersed by time, in the same concentrated state. Case file 7552B, Kansas City, Missouri. The destruction of the yard shack, there was little to no evidence to obtain. Case file 7550B, Hartford, Connecticut. The apartment carries the most parts per million of any of our locations, the result of our suspect being present more recently. The concentration of scent is consistent with every other crime scene."

"What scent?" Brooks asked.

"Rose oil," L.I.A.M. said.

"Rose oil; what the hell is that?" McDaniels asked.

"Don't they use rose oil in perfume?" Gabby asked L.I.A.M.

"Rose oil is used in fragrances. The process of distillation is used to obtain the oil. Rose petals are heated, causing evaporation and subsequently condensing a liquid. The petals are pressed as well to wring every drop of oil available. You are correct, Gabby; perfumers have used rose oil for centuries to influence their scents toward a more floral bouquet."

"The Ghost wears ladies' perfume? What kind?" Harding asked.

"No, sir, the concentration of the oil is far too strong for a perfume. Any fragrance would have diluted the oil greatly. Our suspect works with rose oil in its concentrated form."

Brandon's face lit up; a wide smile grew on his face. "A lead, we have a lead. Rose oil, can't be that many places dealing with that stuff. No way we would have ever picked that up. Amazing. L.I.A.M., you are worth your weight in gold."

"I am processing, compiling a list of potential suspects. Cross-referencing occupation, facial recognition, video surveillance around every crime scene, travel patterns, credit card usage, license plate readers, motel and hotel logs and cameras, college graduates, bank withdrawals, and so on and so forth, in order to create a list of national suspects," L.I.A.M. told the group.

"You are doing all that right now?" Harding asked.

"I process information in zetta bytes, granting me the speed and capability to do this and engage in our conversation." The android smiled. "I am also researching the Scotch egg."

A concerned look come over McDaniels's face. "Hang on. Isn't L.I.A.M. going to have to sniff these people? Besides, however many on the list, we can't just arrest these people and haul them in for a nose lineup. How would we explain what we are looking for or how we found it? We will end up tipping the Ghost."

"Everyone on L.I.A.M.'s list will have the scent; this just limits the field," Nathan Brooks said.

"Right." James waved at the doctors.

Brandon walked down the corridor, his frustration visible as he clenched his fists and shook them in the air. Turning back, he looked at the group and shook his head. "One step up, two steps back. You all will have to find him."

"We aren't FBI," Nathan pointed out.

"James will protect you. Keep you all out of harm's way. He will end it."

"Sure, boss, but what of any followers? L.I.A.M., you said the Ghost most likely has had help," McDaniels said.

"Our suspect is extremely cautious. I am having difficulty pinpointing a common link from all crime scenes. Yes, I am convinced the suspect would need assistance; be it a place to stay, a borrowed vehicle, or actual help with killing. I have accessed satellite images and am limiting our suspect pool."

"Satellites? Why?" Gabby asked.

"Overview of a crime scene at the moment of the crime. Using images to see who comes and goes, from where and to where. As these individuals radiate away from the scene, further surveillance can be obtained," L.I.A.M. said.

"So, you can follow our suspect home?" Potts said with a level of excitement in her voice.

"The satellite images are archived, but other video is limited. This crime scene will offer us the most available information. We should be able to track our suspect and find Sasha Blonde."

"You can track him?" Brandon's voice also carried excitement.

"I am. Using this apartment building as our starting point and a period of two days as our baseline, I have the suspect loading a box into a cargo van at the rear of this building." L.I.A.M. pointed down the corridor. "Moving forward with the timeline, I am following the van."

"So, the box had the woman in it?" Gabby asked with concern.

"Assuming so. Since no body was discovered here, and there are no other such activities from the time Mr. Peoples dropped off Sasha Blonde until now."

"Go. If you need backup, call. Find her, catch the Ghost. James; keep them safe," Harding ordered.

McDaniels, L.I.A.M., and the doctors left the apartment building and headed out of Hartford in their black Suburban. L.I.A.M. directed James to the charter field, where he had arranged a plane to Detroit, Michigan. Both Gabby and Nathan were concerned about them tracking the Ghost, but James assured them he would keep them safe. "If we get close, we will call in the cavalry."

CHAPTER 43

SASHA BLONDE HELD BACK HER TEARS as she heard the talking stop. Listening hard and craning her neck, she attempted to see behind her. The light in the window of the office moved about but Sasha could not hold the awkward position. She heard the door open and she quickly clenched tight, every muscle tensed with fear and anticipation. She didn't know whether to pretend to still be out of it or not; she chose to look straight ahead and wait. A soft whistle came from behind her as the sound of a door closed. The whistle grew closer and closer.

A tiny man carrying a lantern walked around from behind her and smiled widely. "Wakey, wakey, eggs and bakey," he said, giving a little dance. Stopping, he lunged forward at the reporter, coming face to face, almost eye to eye. "Look at that fear in your eyes. Hmm. All that confidence you fake on TV, here you are and the truth of you is a puddle." His voice was squeaky and nervous. He jumped back and the smile returned, creating almost a ridiculous expression. Setting the lantern down, he began to move his head in a serpentine manner. "Look at you, look at you," he said as he tore the tape away from Sasha's lips.

"What? What do you want?" Sasha stammered in a shaky voice.

"Want?" The skinny little man stopped moving and glared. "I want nothing from you," he snarled. "Bet that is a rare sense for the likes of you. Oh, you are in for many firsts here today. Not being wanted, the depth of your fears, the number of thoughts swirling in your pea brain, and the death…of course," the little man squeaked.

Sasha keenly heard the last part, causing a wave of terror to roll from the small of her back throughout her body. She looked at the wiry man and could see the crazy ooze from him. Every movement, the twitches and darting eyes, his overall manner: obviously disturbed. "All I wanted was to talk with you," she said, attempting to connect.

He stopped pacing right in front of her and pulled from the back of his belt a very large knife. He grasped the handle so tightly his knuckles turned white from the effort. The blade was as long as his arm, from elbow to fingers, with teeth on the top and a curved tip. The vision of him waving it at her would have looked ridiculous, but Sasha knew this disturbed person was liable to do anything. "I have a job to do!" he yelled while spinning in a circle.

"Please, please; just let me go. I won't do another story about you, I promise. I'll do anything. Please."

"Shut up!" the man commanded. Looking from the corner of his eye at her, he stopped spinning. "Detroit; hell of a town. What a special treat you're in for. You are to experience the natural wildlife this once-great metropolis has to offer." He marched forward, knelt right in front of her, and took the huge knife, cutting across both of Sasha's shins to the bone.

Her scream pierced the space of the empty warehouse, echoing it full. Sasha involuntarily vomited, erupting a stream of stomach contents right onto the tiny man. He scurried away, wiping the liquid from his head and face. "You bitch!" he screamed. "Oh!" He swirled and stomped his feet. "Hurl on me; I ought to gut you like a fish." He fumed and kicked at the dirt. The pain from her shins was excruciating, combined with the burn in her nostrils from the stomach acid.

Sasha Blonde screamed out with all the vocal power she could muster, but the man just laughed and screamed with her. "No one will hear you," he said, running his hand over his vomit-covered face. "Scream all you want. It will draw the dogs right to you. This city has thousands of stray and feral dogs running around. I am curious which will get you first: your screams bringing the packs of dogs, or your blood bringing the rats. I wouldn't worry; the real probability is you die from thirst before either eat too much." He laughed loudly once again.

"Please, let me go. I won't say a word," she begged, feeling the blood run down over her feet.

"A busybody reporter who won't say a word; ha! You have found your place, your end, and there will be no one to watch." The little man swirled. "You will be forgotten, only a Cliff note in a Ghost's story. What a picture you will be, once they find you. I do hope you enjoy your death. Personally, I would have liked to hurry you along, but such is not my role. Yet, for the barf, I feel I have earned a taste." The skinny man marched forward, pulled back Sasha's blond hair, and took hold of her ear. "This is where you scream for me."

She squirmed and jerked her head, screaming out, but he had hold of her right earlobe and with a flick from the knife, he cut it off, earring and all. He laughed a most sinister giggle as he spun in place. Putting his knife away, he moved in front of her again and removed the earring from the flesh. "You can keep this; a souvenir." He dropped the gold hoop on her lap. Waving the bloody lobe of her ear in front of her, he grinned a wicked smile and then popped the meat into his mouth and chewed. A few drops of blood escaped the corner of his mouth before he opened wide, showing he had finished his meal.

"Yummy!" his voice boomed as he twirled away from her. "Goodbye, bitch!" he screamed and ran past her. The blood from her ear ran down her neck, dripping down her side. She could hear the tiny man leaving the warehouse. He had left his lantern in front of her, burning bright. Sasha screamed at the top of her lungs, but knew there was no one to hear her. She wondered if he had left the lantern on purpose or just because he was a crazy wackadoodle. Her shins stung with pain, her ear ached, but her fear was what caused her to shiver.

Far off down the length of the empty warehouse, Sasha saw a fat gray rat scurry across from one side to the other. The silence in the vast building was almost deafening. Sasha was certain the wiry little man was gone, which both comforted and concerned her. How long could she survive? Considering what he had said about thirst, dogs, and rats. The thought of being eaten alive was highly unpleasant, but she was nowhere near embracing any thoughts of death.

The light along the roof began to fade; a moment of bright red exploded along one side as the sun set and then was gone. Darkness filled the empty warehouse quickly; the lantern fought away the black of night but struggled. The meager illumination from the battery-operated device only allowed a halo of sight before being consumed. Her eyes adjusted enough to see nothing, and the memory of what was there no comfort at all. Panic began to take hold of her, and she screamed out and cried again; the cold from the absence of the sun began to creep in and made her shake uncontrollably. Her teeth chattered like a novelty item as she waited for nothing.

Sasha surrendered to her terror and allowed herself to freak out altogether. She tensed and pulled, wiggled and jerked; the tape on her ankles slipped ever so slightly because of the blood from her cut shins. The ray of hope invigorated her desire to escape, but the effort was exhausting. Hanging her head, she sobbed; thoughts of a life lived and such a journey taken only to end in such a place, in such a way, filled her with grief. A scurry drew her attention as a squeak from the darkness announced the arrival of the rats.

CHAPTER 44

THE PLANE LANDED IN DETROIT, MICHIGAN. McDaniels thanked the local FBI supervisor for having a vehicle waiting for them. He voiced his surprise at the man awaiting their arrival. The supervisor explained that he wanted to contribute, which was a veiled plea to escape the position of Detroit as his base of operations. The crime rate had dropped in Detroit since the beginning of the economic downturn, not as a result of any less crime, but a reduction in population, as well as the corruption and disinterest of local police, combined with the level of organization of the criminal element.

This supervisor saw any outside FBI presence as a chance to network away from Detroit. James had been an agent long enough to recognize the type. Overpaid, underworked check-cashers, who had given up the sense of duty shortly after the oath was given. Law enforcement wasn't for everyone, an unfortunate reality for many who carry a badge. A job is not something you are, not what you are willing to give your life to uphold, not something you can't turn off or put away; being a true person of justice is day or night, armed or not, non-negotiable, and comes down to the last breath. This supervisor was nice enough, probably a quality manager of his men; but he wanted to be somewhere else, and they had come to catch a killer.

McDaniels had known many cops over his career whose priority was making it home at the end of watch. A goal he could not fault them for having. Yet James saw himself as a guardian of justice, which came first above all. He had always held that innocence should be protected at all costs. He knew he would gladly give his life to save or protect a child. By James's way of thought, what kind of man wouldn't sacrifice himself for such a worthy purpose.

"I'll drive," L.I.A.M. announced, breaking McDaniels's reverie as the group boarded their vehicle.

They left the eager supervisor behind without telling him where they were headed. Both doctors were somewhat nervous about the four of them in direct pursuit of the Ghost. As L.I.A.M. drove into the impoverished and mostly abandoned section of Detroit, Nathan said, "Looks like a war zone. Some bombed out Eastern European city."

"The Motor City, how unfortunate," Potts said, shaking her head. "Makes you wonder how such a thing can happen."

"Cost versus profit," L.I.A.M. responded. "The use of robotics to lower cost while maintaining consistent levels of productivity should have been a signal to the industry. When half the price of a vehicle goes to pay pensions for former workers who contributed nothing to the production of that vehicle, that creates problems. Social Security faces a similar issue. Half price of the vehicle or double profits; either way, companies without the union constraints carry an advantage. Unionized workers do no good for anyone but the workers, and overextended periods tend to destabilize the dynamic of power."

"Yes, yes, but should we be hunting this crazy killer?" Gabby Potts asked.

L.I.A.M. went on. "Henry Ford came from humble beginnings and a limited education, winning him praise from the common consumer. As age and success bloomed, the man lacked a willingness to change or adapt. His Model T had been revolutionary and shaped this city with success and growth. Demand and competition pushed the Ford Motor Company to expand, building an unprecedented factory. Seventy-five thousand workers, with security and fire departments, a town building cars within a city devoted to the automobile. Henry eventually longed for simpler times; his care for his workers and hands-on style were overshadowed by a henchman he had trusted, one who turned out to be a taskmaster. Treatment of workers gave way to union power, combined with government contracts for the war, and Ford could not afford a work stoppage. The death of his only son hurt the man deeply, and by 1947 and his own death, Henry Ford had contributed to an urban lifestyle he hated. The cycle of this city mirrors the very life of the man who so contributed to it." Pulling into a row of empty warehouses, L.I.A.M. parked in front of one and turned off the engine.

"I still question the sense of this," Gabby said, looking around nervously.

"No one has entered or left this warehouse in three days," L.I.A.M. said.

L.I.A.M. exited the vehicle and began to walk toward the warehouse, when James hissed at him to stop. Waving L.I.A.M. back to the vehicle, McDaniels went to the rear and popped the hatch. "Doctors, if you would, please. Put these on." He handed each a bulletproof vest with the FBI letters in bold white across the back.

"Are we going to be shot at?" Gabby asked.

"Better safe and all," James said as he handed her a first aid kit. "Now, listen up; I want all of you to stay behind me. L.I.A.M., you keep a sharp eye and let me know if anyone is around."

"There is one heat signature inside. Human. I believe it to be Sasha Borkisnicvic. Vital signs are weak," L.I.A.M. answered.

"You have thermal vision?" McDaniels looked at L.I.A.M., then turned to Potts. "He has thermal vision?"

"Military application. Thermal, infrared, binocular, biscopular; he can see for miles and almost at a microscopular level. We attempted to reduce any hindrance and anticipate any problems," Gabby said. "It is simply the way he sees. You aren't so impressed when your eyes adjust to the dark, are you? L.I.A.M.'s eyes simply make better adjustments."

James rolled his eyes as he put on his vest. Turning back to the vehicle, he pulled out a shotgun and began loading it with shells. "The more I learn, the more I wonder which of you two is scarier: the builder of his mind, or his body."

"Should I be armed, James? Even though no threat is perceived, policy dictates you have backup present." L.I.A.M. picked up an MP5 assault weapon. Pulling the slide open, L.I.A.M. inspected the ejection port, smiling widely.

"No, you should not be armed. I have no doubt you are an expert with weapons, and probably a perfect marksman; but we haven't practiced and this is a real-world experience. We will get to your training once we get back to the university."

McDaniels took the weapon and returned it to the truck. "Said you wanted to learn some self-defense, and now weapons. Tools in the toolbox, I guess."

Closing the hatch back on the SUV, James led the way toward the warehouse. "Stay behind me," he whispered.

The four of them moved into the empty warehouse. The space was vast, enormous, and appeared to be unused for a very long time. McDaniels scanned the area with the point of his shotgun, his grip tight, knees slightly bent, attention at optimum. L.I.A.M. stood straight, pausing only to maintain the distance between him and James.

Both doctors were back from L.I.A.M. about ten feet, holding one another's hands.

Nathan and Gabby had grown close; the bond of L.I.A.M. was as if they shared a child, shared a love. They were a good pair, smart and accomplished, work-oriented and socially stunted, unattached and lonely.

"There." L.I.A.M. stepped up next to James and pointed the length of the warehouse. "Look, footprints in the dust."

"Can you smell that rose stuff?" James asked.

"Yes…" L.I.A.M. answered but hesitated. "Seems fainter than it should."

"Kind of a big room, buddy," James said with a wink.

The group moved forward, and as they grew closer, McDaniels picked up the pace. The beautiful blonde was taped to a chair and bleeding. James stopped and pulled out his phone, but there was no signal.

"I have dispatched a paramedic, as well as contacted local FBI and Special Agent Harding. The ambulance is ten minutes out," L.I.A.M. told James.

"You all may want to wait here," McDaniels warned the doctors.

Gabby Potts pushed James on the shoulder. "We will be fine. We are doctors and that woman needs help."

James nodded and advanced toward the blonde in the chair. The closer they came, the more disturbing the scene became. The woman was out of it, unconscious. Blood was everywhere, all down the right side of her, down her front, and on the floor in front of the chair. James had seen some rough wounds, but this was a terrible sight. Animals had gotten to her, chewing at her legs and her head. James attempted to gently push back the hair but it was matted in the blood.

He could see the rats had consumed her ear, down her jaw, her lower lip and most of her nose. Her right eye hung from the socket with bite marks visible.

Pulling out his knife, he carefully cut away the tape, nodding for the doctors to help him. Gabby stepped right up, holding the reporter's torso so she didn't pitch forward out of the chair. Nathan began to help but grew very pale at such a horrific scene. As James cut away the duct tape from her legs, the bones were visible.

Sasha Blonde came back to the world just long enough to experience agony and let out a bloodcurdling scream. The screeching vocalization of excruciating pain caused James and Gabby to retreat away from her. Nathan backpedaled two steps, vomiting as he fell backward onto the floor.

The moment over, the reporter's head fell limp but the echoes of her scream filled the void. James gathered himself and moved back to the woman in the chair. Gabby quickly came to his aid as they eased Sasha to the floor. "Nathan, go out and lead the paramedics in here," McDaniels ordered.

Brooks scurried to his feet, wiping his chin and the front of himself. Turning, he ran out the way they had come in, puffs of dust expelling from each stride. The resonance had finally diminished and the scream was gone. Potts and McDaniels focused on the reporter, opening the first aid kit, but hesitant as to what to do. L.I.A.M. moved beyond the chair and was examining his surroundings. "Where is the ambulance?" Gabby asked.

"Six minutes out. A slight delay at an intersection."

McDaniels pulled the first aid kit to him and pulled out a syringe. "Morphine. Help her with the pain," he said and injected the reporter. "L.I.A.M., how long?"

"Four minutes, fifty."

Sasha Blonde began to stir, the pain killer doing its job. Moans gurgled in her throat as she twisted on the floor. "Hep, hep me," she begged in a weak voice, the words not pronounced because of her missing lower lip and cheek.

"Did you see the Ghost?" James asked.

"*Hep*" She tried to speak.

"Help is coming, a couple of minutes," Gabby Potts said.

"Is there anything you can tell me about the Ghost?" James probed.

"Lil, man. Kazy," Sasha muttered.

The sound of sirens grew closer, bouncing around in the empty warehouse. A few moments and Brooks ran in with two paramedics following with a gurney. James stood and pulled Gabby back to allow the men to work. "I gave her a dose of morphine to ease her pain. She has been gone three days. Probably dehydrated, along with her wounds," McDaniels conveyed to the medics.

The two men went to work, quickly getting her stabilized and onto the gurney. More sirens announced the approach of police and federal authorities. The paramedics rushed Sasha Blonde toward the exit as the eager FBI supervisor entered the warehouse with a half dozen agents and ten uniformed police.

"This is a crime scene," L.I.A.M. advised James as he appeared next to him.

McDaniels hurried forward, putting up a hand to halt the advance. "We need a perimeter set up," he ordered, meeting the supervisor halfway across the warehouse. "This is an active crime scene. We have to maintain the integrity as best we can."

"James. You need to go outside and answer your phone," L.I.A.M. yelled across the expanse.

McDaniels turned, almost questioning L.I.A.M.'s comment, but thought better of it. Guiding the supervisor by the arm, he walked the group of police and federal agents back the way they had come. "The task force will want to go over this place with a fine-tooth comb."

"That woman is messed up." The supervisor stated the obvious.

"Sasha Blonde, the reporter."

"*Indepth News*? Yeah, I watch the show." The eager man shook his head. "Guess she'll be working radio from now on."

James gave him a perturbed look. "Get the perimeter set up," he ordered and pulled out his cell phone. A missed call appeared on the display and James accessed the voice message. Harding's voice came over the speaker. His tone was stressed, shaken, unnerved. He demanded James call him immediately, so James dialed.

CHAPTER 45

THE SPECIAL RESPONSE TASK FORCE had left Hartford, returning to Washington, D.C., and leaving the New York section of FBI to further the Sasha Blonde investigation. Special Agent Brandon Harding had a meeting with the President of the United States and Director Maroni. Anthony was going to tender his resignation and recommend Brandon for the position. He had already secured Senator Miller as well as General McHenery to support him for the post and knew it was more than enough. The job was his; now all he needed to do was get the President to sign off, be confirmed, and catch the Ghost. Brandon knew that with L.I.A.M. out chasing this Ghost, it was just a matter of time until he caught him. The capture of the worst serial killer ever would be a big, bright feather in a new director's cap.

He knew full well that Anthony Maroni did not want to give up the director's chair, but he didn't have much choice, especially with the abduction of Sasha Blonde. A look into her phone records and movements would reveal their secret relationship. This would cause scandal, and certainly calls for the man to step down. Getting a jump on the issue and coming clean with the President would help all concerned down the road. Maroni had known the pitfalls of lust were ever-present but could not leap the abyss Sasha Blonde created in the loins of a man.

The President was disappointed but understanding. He accepted the director's resignation and recommendation, adding his own seal of approval to the choice. They took time to discuss the flaw of man in the effort to resist a beautiful woman and the level of penalty for such lapses. They went over the case; Brandon informed both men of Sasha Blonde's abduction, as well as L.I.A.M.'s insights. He brought up the rose oil and explained its significance. Both the President and now former director were pleased to hear of the lead and the contribution of L.I.A.M. The meeting was short but productive; Maroni and Harding left together and arrived at the Hoover building moments apart. Brandon had a few things to check on before heading to task force headquarters, which was a separate building shared with other specialized units—rescue, behavioral, computer, alternative religion, special response, and terrorist intervention units. Brandon wanted to fill in the press and public relations division about the case, as well as the move toward director. The President had insisted he make the announcement from the White House press office, but each of them should prepare a statement and inform the FBI PR department.

Brandon had no desire for recognition; for him, being director was a continuation of his work of enforcing the law. The idea of power or fame was furthest from his mind, but he was smart enough to know the position came with a spotlight. He also knew it was an easy position to be removed from, spoken or unspoken. As much as J. Edgar Hoover had done for the bureau, he had done more to make people of power untrusting of every director after him. Those files of secrets on the elites, the upper one percent and the dirty things they did but didn't want anyone to know about. Climbing to the top, one was bound to get a little dirty and have many under them wanting to see them fall.

Harding's mood was upbeat as he entered the Special Response Task Force headquarters. He felt the pressure of what was to come but

felt good about his capabilities. Crossing the lobby to the bank of elevators, he realized he was smiling widely; it was best to not seem too smug.
A couple passing people gave nods and smiles, which he returned but
hurried along to an open car. The ride up to his unit's floor was pleasant,
a recognizable tune played on the Muzak. The sound of a ding and the
doors parted…and an odd smell rushed in as Brandon began to step out.

Rounding the corner, heading into the bullpen, Harding stopped
in his tracks. The sight before him was unbelievable. Members of his
team lay on the floor and slumped at their desks. Everyone appeared
to be dead. He froze, holding in position to attempt to determine
what had happened, whether it was over, should he breathe or not.
Backing toward the elevator, Brandon pulled out his phone and called
McDaniels. The call went to voicemail. "Call me, immediately!"

The doors of the elevator closed and Harding returned to the
lobby, going directly to the security office to lock down the building.
He worried other floors were also affected, but a few calls proved his
was the only one not answering. He called in a hazardous materials
crew in conjunction with the bomb squad, then the former director, and
then he waited to organize the groups to enter the floor and determine
what happened. Concerned he may have been exposed to some virus or
germ, he isolated himself in a side office. The thought of being infected
was frightening; he probably should have stayed on the floor, but in an
afterthought, the team had not been back for more than an hour or two.

Locking down the building would contain any outbreak, but
Brandon knew he had slipped up. Coming down to the lobby could
potentially infect everyone else. He was dealing with a sick mind, and
he needed to be on his game and think beyond common logic. He
would be the director, he just lost his team, possibly carrying a patho-
gen to the whole building. He needed to rise above and step up to the
challenge at hand.

His cell phone vibrated in his pocket: McDaniels returning his call. Brandon explained the situation to his second-in-command, telling of the bodies of their team laid out and lifeless. He raised the idea of a virus or germ weapon, but added that such would be unlikely, so fast acting and with no visible signs. Brandon listed those he had seen: Johnson, Lee, Kennedy, and Park. The reality that his team very well might be dead struck him in that moment, and he suddenly grew extremely angry. "I need you back here. L.I.A.M. too. This Ghost just picked the wrong guy to piss off."

The two men exchanged the frustration, anger and loss, then concluded their conversation. An advance unit of the Centers for Disease Control had arrived and one of the doctors entered the office. Brandon had not been as afraid until seeing the big yellow suit coming at him. He wanted McDaniels to hurry up and get there; he needed his second-in-command to keep him focused and under control. The level of anger and hopelessness was like never before, and Harding needed a friend. As the doctor examined him, Brandon's anxiety spiked and he demanded to know if they had anything, because he needed to get on with his investigation.

The man in the plastic biohazard suit explained that his blood would need to be tested, but from all outward appearances he seemed healthy. After a few questions to determine a timeline of when the team could have been exposed, a message came over the doctor's radio. The team upstairs examining the bodies cleared the floor. They gave a body count of fifteen people and confirmed no biological agents had been used. Harding apologized and thanked the doctor, hurrying out of the office and back to the elevators.

Alone in the elevator, the Muzak again played a recognizable tune, but this time Brandon was in no mood. He thought of fifteen dead, his whole unit and support staff, and took a few deep breaths to ready himself. The ding rang and the doors opened. Men milled about, some half dressed in bio-suits in the process of removing them, others in tactical gear with the words *bomb squad* across their backs. Brandon stepped out of the elevator car and rounded the corner to where he had stood a few hours earlier. The scene was the same and it held him there for a moment of pause and reflection. These were his people, a collection of the best in their fields, and now they were gone.

Harding knew the Ghost had intended to get them all, that he and McDaniels were to be among the fallen. His mind raced with rage; this individual had targeted the very team hunting him. The leader of the bomb squad put a hand upon his shoulder to comfort but also informing him that Maroni was on the way up. Nodding, Brandon moved forward and knelt next to Sam Lee. A light powder covered the man's body but was hardly visible. He did not touch the old soldier whom he respected so greatly.

"Brandon," Maroni said from behind him. "You have my deepest sympathies."

Harding stood, shaking his head. "Can't believe this. I've called McDaniels to come in. I am going to get this son of a bitch. He is going to pay for this, and you know what I mean."

"Whatever you need. I called the President and gave him a preliminary report. He suggested we hold off on our announcement of my retirement for a few days. Going to be a lot of attention, even more so than before with Sasha missing."

"Yeah, I am going to get this Ghost. Nothing else matters."

"Take a breath and get yourself together. This one is something we have never dealt with before. How did this happen, how did he get in to do this?"

"I don't know."

CHAPTER 46

MCDANIELS HUNG UP HIS PHONE and re-entered the empty warehouse. The two doctors were halfway down the expanse, standing together and talking. The eager FBI supervisor eyed McDaniels from just inside the door. James waved the man on and gave him a serious look. "We have to leave. Something has happened and our presence is required back in D.C. I need you to handle this. Top of your game, hear me?" The supervisor nodded. "Do a professional job, and I will recommend you for a transfer out of this toilet to somewhere more to your liking."

"Really? Hawaii?" the supervisor asked with a raised eyebrow.

James gave the man a sideways glance. "You catch the man who did this, yeah, you can sit on the beach in Hawaii." McDaniels knew the man was thinking paradise, but what he did not know was the complications Hawaii presented: lots of drug use, mostly marijuana and meth. Every agency had a division in Hawaii and overlap caused paperwork, finger pointing, and problems. There was also an indigenous people to deal with, as well as tourists; one group making a federal case over a stepped-on flower, the other over a lost piece of baggage. "You'll love it."

"Consider this a done deal." The supervisor extended his hand to shake. "I'll have this cat in a bag quick as you please," he said with a smug expression.

"Yeah, you do that." James walked toward the doctors. The news from Harding had McDaniels off kilter emotionally. The eager supervisor was a goof and had no chance of finding the Ghost, but James knew the scene needed to be processed and they didn't have time to do it. Reaching the doctors, he looked out at L.I.A.M. who was staring up at the ceiling and windows. "We have to go," he told them.

"Are you all right? You look a little upset," Potts said.

"L.I.A.M.!" James yelled and waved for the android to join them. L.I.A.M. trotted over to them, stepping in his own footprints as he returned. McDaniels nodded at the android. "The Ghost used his own footprints to disguise his coming and goings." L.I.A.M. nodded. "We have to go. You know why already, don't you?" he asked L.I.A.M., who again nodded.

"There are footprints all around that chair," Brooks pointed out. "If the Ghost was attempting to disguise his movement, doesn't that defeat the purpose? Unless he was trying to not bring attention prior to this; in case someone came around there wouldn't be footprints all over. So, what's going on? What could pull us away from being this close?"

"Come on, I'll tell you en route. L.I.A.M., you got enough?"

"Yes," L.I.A.M. answered, walking briskly toward the door.

The four of them exited the warehouse and boarded the SUV. James gave a salute type wave to the FBI supervisor, who now had a real motivated bounce in his step. They drove toward the airfield. "What do you know, L.I.A.M.?" McDaniels asked from behind the wheel.

"The warehouse was a follower," L.I.A.M. responded.

"Because the Ghost was in D.C. targeting the task force," James acknowledged with a nod.

"Targeting the task force?" Gabby asked.

"The team is down. I don't know all the details, but it is bad."

"Special Agent Harding survived," L.I.A.M. stated.

McDaniels shot L.I.A.M. a look. "Only?"

"Yes. The remaining team are no longer with us."

"So, this was a follower? I thought you were tracking the abducted Sasha Blonde, that rose oil business? You said it was in the warehouse too," McDaniels said.

L.I.A.M. tilted his head and moved in his seat. "The Ghost did abduct Sasha Blonde, but the level of rose oil in the warehouse was from when the cameras were installed. The switch was made in a parking lot in Philadelphia, Pennsylvania. The van entered, a while later leaving; twenty-two minutes and five seconds to be accurate. The Ghost obviously left the reporter and instructions. His accomplice or follower drove the woman here and committed the acts we found. I had not calculated the switch, even though I considered the parking structure an odd detour. Factoring this, I can now see where the Ghost changed vehicles and rerouted to the capital."

"The reporter was a ploy, drew the team out and away from the office," James stated.

"Yes, I would concur," L.I.A.M. said.

"So, the Ghost took Blonde to get the team to Connecticut? In order to plant some kind of bomb?" Brooks asked.

"I can't believe those people we just met are gone," Gabby said.

"Wasn't a bomb," McDaniels told them.

"Halon. A fire safety system for computers," L.I.A.M. said. "For all intents and purposes, it draws all the oxygen out of a room. Fire needs oxygen to burn. By eliminating it, the fire is extinguished and the computers are safe. Unlike fire or human beings, computers don't need oxygen to maintain themselves. A Halon system was installed over two days; one of suitable size to eliminate oxygen to fatal levels on the floor of the Special Response Task Force. The work order was forged, but with the quality to go unquestioned by building security."

"They suffocated?" James asked but knew the answer. He returned his eyes to the road. "I am going to find this Ghost, and I am going to kill him."

"Kill? Such goes against your job qualifications, James. You are not an executioner," L.I.A.M. pointed out.

"The Ghost targeted the task force specifically, L.I.A.M. Murdered some of James's friends. He is angry and filled by the want to avenge those people," Brooks explained to his creation.

"All the people this suspect has killed were friends to someone."

"And I am certain those people want vengeance for the deaths this person has caused. Often times people will say things and not mean them literally," Nathan went on. "Mr. McDaniels is angry."

"That don't mean I don't mean it."

"Your vital signs suggest you are being honest, James. Is this right to talk of killing the suspect?" L.I.A.M. asked.

McDaniels turned and looked L.I.A.M. in the eye. "Sometimes right and justice aren't the same thing."

"Of course; they are different. Or there would be no need of distinction between the two," L.I.A.M. said.

James turned back to the road as they pulled up to the charter field. "This line of work, you deal with criminals and bad men. Thieves, killers, rapists; the bottom of the barrel, the dregs of humanity. At times they disgust you, do things which make you question how one person could do such a thing to another." McDaniels parked and turned off the engine, then turned to look L.I.A.M. in the eyes. "Then, every once in a great while, we come across what we have here, a monster. This is Evil. There ain't no cure, no time to waste, no quarter, no need for courts or fancy talk, lawyers, or psychs. People don't do what this man has done, and so he forfeits all the humane treatment we provide bad men and the like."

"James, you don't mean that really, do you?" Gabby asked.

"Damn straight I do."

"You know L.I.A.M. is new and impressionable; don't teach him…" Gabby left her comment unfinished.

McDaniels shook his head and shrugged, opening the driver's door and marching toward the hangar. Both doctors and L.I.A.M. hustled to keep up and were all airborne within minutes. James was still fuming about the deaths of his friends, but knew Gabby was correct about L.I.A.M.

"I shouldn't voice my opinions like I did and I am sorry. You gave L.I.A.M. the capability to choose for himself and I hope he never has to make a life or death decision. Being what he is, and what he can do, there is probably a pretty good chance he will. Something to think about."

CHAPTER 47

THE DIRECTOR TURNED AND NODDED. "James. Good you are here. Brandon is up in his office."

"Why is Homeland here?"

"President asked them to help, but they heard 'take over.' Team's gone. You need to go up and talk with him. I've gotten calls from Vetter, McHenery, and Miller, all looking to pull the plug on your buddy over there." Maroni glanced at L.I.A.M. "Take them up to the conference room. I know you guys want to keep after this, but the dynamic has changed."

James wasn't going to argue the point, so he waved the doctors and L.I.A.M. on. Putting them in the conference room, McDaniels walked down to Brandon's office and knocked. Inside, his friend was staring off into space. Realizing James had entered, he snapped out of his daze and came to his feet. The two men embraced in a hug. "I am sorry, sir," James said.

Harding slapped his second-in-command on the back. "Glad you are here. We need to get this son of bitch."

"Sir, we need to talk in the conference room," McDaniels said.

Harding gave him a questioning expression but followed his friend from his office. In the conference room, Gabby Potts sat with a look of deep concern on her face. Nathan Brooks paced the length of the room, while L.I.A.M. stood at the windows and watched the happenings in the bullpen. All turned attention to the two FBI agents as they took seats around the table.

"What's up, James?" Harding asked.

"See all those Homeland people down there? We are out. Director just told me the President asked them to help."

"This is our investigation. The Ghost is ours. We have to get this…" Brandon stopped and shook his head. "What the hell is Homeland going to do? We are close. What happened wherever you were?"

"Detroit," L.I.A.M. said. "Sasha Borkisnicvic was a planned decoy."

"Drew the task force out so the Ghost could hook up his… What was it again?" James asked the android.

"Halon system."

"Sucked the air out of the room. One of his followers picked up the blonde and tortured her in an empty warehouse in Detroit."

Harding continued to shake his head, but then stopped in realization. "You tracked the follower. Can you track the Ghost from here?" he said, looking at L.I.A.M.

"I am."

"We need to go get his ass." Brandon stood up.

The conference room door opened and in walked Maroni, McHenery, Miller, and Vetter. Every man's face was stone-like and serious as they took seats around the table. "Rough way to go. I know you all want justice for your fallen comrades, but this has gotten out of hand and there is far too much attention to continue with this experiment," Maroni told them. "This comes from the President, not me."

"We have followed your reports and feel this has been a fantastic success. Without a doubt a stride forward," Senator Miller added, looking from Nathan to Gabby.

"Homeland is going to take over the case and they will catch the Ghost," Anthony told his men.

The phone in the conference room beeped and James reached out, pushing the speaker button. The eager supervisor from Detroit came across the line. "We found prints and tracked a local man. Upon raiding the home, the subject fired upon the SWAT members and was killed. Also confirmed, Sasha Blonde died at the hospital. An autopsy has been ordered."

"Is the suspect dead?" Maroni asked.

"Yes. Evidence at the scene provided us with a detailed following of this case, the task force investigation, as well as Sasha Blonde. This individual had clippings from numerous cities around the country. I believe this individual is the Ghost, the subject of those *Indepth News* reports and the focus of the task force." The Detroit supervisor's voice held a hint of excitement.

Looks were exchanged at the conference table before McDaniels addressed the speakerphone again. "Good work. Collect the evidence and document everything."

"Will do. You haven't forgotten our agreement, have you?"

"No, I didn't forget, and you got the guy. Director Maroni is right here. Director, I assured the supervisor of the Detroit section a transfer to Hawaii if he caught the man responsible for Sasha Blonde's torture and now death," James said.

"Sounds like you may have stumbled onto a real find. I am certain a transfer is easily enough done."

"From the director himself," James told the phone.

"I very much appreciate that, sir. I am honored to serve the bureau, but to relocate to a warmer climate; I have some health concerns." The voice from the speaker began to ramble.

"Yes, yes. Post your report and fill out the transfer paperwork.

Shouldn't be but a month or two for everything to be processed." Maroni motioned for McDaniels to hang up. "Charming fellow, surely there will be those heartbroken with his departure from Detroit," Anthony said sarcastically.

McDaniels rolled his eyes and nodded. "The man is a piece of work. But he did catch the guy and I did promise. Thank you, Director." The comment drew a smile from Maroni.

"So, did this guy catch the Ghost?" Miller asked.

"We believe our suspect has been using other people to help him. How many and to what extent is still undetermined. Obviously, this man in Detroit is deeply involved," James told the table.

"He has help? Well, that will make him harder to apprehend," McHenery pointed out. "At least you got rid of one of his helpers."

"Only with the aid of L.I.A.M. We are close, and we need to keep the pressure on," Harding said.

"You realize your whole team was just killed by this guy; who is pressuring who?" Colonel Vetter asked.

Brandon shot a glare at the DARPA representative. "You need not remind me." Turning his attention to the director, general, and senator, he said, "This was you gentlemen's idea and it is working. This suspect lashed out like a cornered rat because we are hot on his trail. He is attempting to eliminate the threats against him. We need to stay the course and we will have our man."

"Couldn't we use this other man as a diffuser?" Miller addressed the table.

"Feed the press a half-truth: the Ghost is dead, the task force dead, reporter dead." Maroni nodded as he spoke.

"Have the director give a heartfelt statement. This will give the Ghost a false sense of security while the investigation continues," Miller added.

"The two of you can keep after your man." Vetter spoke with a snooty manner.

"Two? What of L.I.A.M.? And us?" Brooks asked.

McHenery looked the skinny doctor in the eyes. "This experiment is over. The field test has been a wonderful success, but has reached its conclusion. We do appreciate your contributions and hope you will continue to bring your expertise to this project."

"Contributions?" Nathan asked. "Hang on, L.I.A.M. is not just some project."

"Dr. Brooks, please understand," Senator Miller began. "You can obviously appreciate the significance of your work, as we all do. The capabilities and potential of L.I.A.M. are extremely profound and important. So much so that L.I.A.M. is more valuable to the nation than we can afford to risk. The Ghost is a terrible criminal and has struck us right here in our very hearts; but Harding and McDaniels are driven men, and will bring this criminal to justice. Had they never known of L.I.A.M. they would still have a job to do."

"I do not like how this sounds," Brooks stated in a firm tone.

"Neither do I," McDaniels said.

"Why can't L.I.A.M. continue to help?" Potts asked.

"The President believes we need to move forward with our development of L.I.A.M., as well as focusing on further prototypes," General McHenery told them.

"No," Nathan Brooks said.

"I'm sorry; I don't think you grasped what the senator was saying," Colonel Vetter began, but was cut off by Brooks.

"No. Oh, I understand just fine, but I told all of you from the beginning that L.I.A.M. was not going to be a military toy."

"L.I.A.M. is a matter of national security. We must secure him and continue to research and develop the skills, as well as see where we can improve and modify. I think we all see a future with L.I.A.M. as the father of a new stage of human and artificial intelligence integration. This is the beginning." Miller motioned to the android.

Vetter said, "Dr. Brooks, we would like you to join us. You and Dr. Potts have shown great cooperation; the two of you together have given us this amazing breakthrough. You will have state-of-the-art technology at your fingertips, unlimited funding, resources and materials, pay, benefits, and the knowledge that you are helping your country." Colonel Vetter spoke with a patriotic pompousness that only military men could muster.

"Sure, you make it sound like a plush experience. Is that how it is, Gabby?" Brooks asked.

"To be honest, I am a little uncomfortable. I think we should continue to help the FBI and observe L.I.A.M. in a real-life setting, not a lab," Potts said.

McDaniels shook his head, then looked from person to person, ending with L.I.A.M. "I think we are missing the real question. What does L.I.A.M. want?"

Everyone at the table was quiet and turned their attention to the android. L.I.A.M. tilted his head and returned eye contact with each person one at a time. A long pause lingered before Harding asked directly, "L.I.A.M., what do you want to happen?"

"Now, this is ridiculous," Miller snapped. "We can't allow a machine to dictate national policy. The President has made his decision, and that's that. Doesn't matter what L.I.A.M. or any of us may want."

"Hang on, L.I.A.M. isn't a citizen, and I don't work for the government," Brooks said.

"L.I.A.M. is a product, parts put together by the government; he is ours," Vetter returned.

"Actually, the Tinman is what I made, which is only his body. We have no claim to his mind," Gabby Potts said.

General McHenery stood and took a few steps to address the table. "Everyone needs to relax; we are all on the same team. We are all Americans and want what is best for L.I.A.M., one another, the nation, and the world. As often is the case, people will differ over what is best or how to achieve it. We have a situation, a room full of dead people, agents of our nation struck down by a serial killer. A man with the gall to target this very building. Concern is understandable. Add the scrutiny of the press, which is to come, and what if the Ghost abducts L.I.A.M. or some rival nation discovers him? Leaders must consider beyond the moment, beyond individual interest, and choose wisely for all. That said, national interests override all else. You may not work for the government, but you cannot work against it."

"My task is incomplete." L.I.A.M. finally spoke.

"There is no reason L.I.A.M. can't continue to help; he just doesn't need to be in your hip pocket to do so," General McHenery pointed out.

"He could continue to provide input on the investigation while helping the doctors," Maroni said with a wave of his hand.

"Presume what you like, but I do not work for the military. Governments and religions have corrupted everything they touch, and I want no part in any of that," Nathan said.

"Words of a true patriot," Colonel Vetter lashed at the academic. "Guys like you build the bombs, guys like you became politicians and preachers; those corrupted are men like you. Governments and religions were made up for men like you to have power. Your fear is not what we might do, but what you have already done. L.I.A.M. is a marvel, and over years to come, will contribute greatly to mankind.

A growing advancement in technology. You are looking at this in the wrong light, Dr. Brooks. Oppenheimer saw himself as a destroyer of worlds; a typical overreaction of a gifted mind. Men like him, like you, believe they are the discoverers and hold some ownership and responsibility over that which they have stumbled upon. Is there any doubt that had the Manhattan Project never existed or had Oppenheimer quit, we wouldn't have the nuclear bomb?"

"The Germans were very close; in fact many of the contributors were Nazis," Miller said.

"Are you trying to say L.I.A.M. was inevitable?" Harding asked.

"Yes, yes I am," Vetter stated flatly.

"What kind of argument is that?" Brooks asked, shaking his head.

"You devalue Da Vinci, Newton, Einstein; as if these great minds did not develop revolutionary concepts and ideas," Gabby told the colonel. "The world is full of people who function and think, create and learn, but in rare incidents there are those special people and events which reshape all. Inevitability is a poor argument."

McHenery returned to his seat. "Look, people, this isn't a debate. The President has given us new orders. Besides, from what I gather, Homeland Security will be taking over the Ghost investigation. This has run its course and now the doctors need to get on with their work. Dr. Brooks, you can tell that the collaboration between yourself and Dr. Potts is effective. Why wouldn't you look to further this productive collaboration?"

"We can, we just don't need to be locked in an underground bunker," Nathan said.

"Yet, you would agree that such technology could be extremely dangerous if controlled by the wrong people, correct?"

"Absolutely."

"Thus, a standard of security should be enacted?"

"Yes, and that is what I have been saying all along. You can't tell me there aren't those wrong types of people throughout our government and military, can you?"

"Dr. Brooks, we have a position for you, if you would like. If not, we have a helicopter en route to fly all of you to the airfield and Colonel Vetter will arrange a flight back to Ohio for you. We would like your continued efforts on this project; your country needs you. I am certain the President would express this personally if it would turn you to our cause. Allow me to say for myself, what you and Dr. Potts have accomplished is amazing."

"What if we did use an independent location, one not associated with military applications?" Gabby Potts asked.

"Why?" Colonel Vetter asked.

"Dr. Brooks has brought up some good points. I think we would all be more comfortable."

"Gabby?" Vetter shook his head.

"No, no; we need to be understanding of the doctor's feelings. The three of you can head back and we will figure it out. No need to stick around here and let the press get pictures, start asking questions we can't answer," General McHenery said.

"Sir, L.I.A.M. can track the Ghost; we could use him to find this son of bitch," Harding said.

"He can call you with the location," Maroni said.

"Think I'll catch a ride with all of you. Head back to Ohio for a day or two," Miller said.

"Perhaps you should stay and help explain to the President our need to find an alternative location for this project. Help us figure out how to fund it without any military strings attached," McHenery said to the senator.

"It will only be a day or so. Give me an opportunity to talk with L.I.A.M.," he said.

The meeting was over and the overall mood was disheartening. The two FBI men felt lost and alienated, pushed out of their investigation while their friends and coworkers lay freshly dead. Brandon also could see that Maroni had claimed the chance to hang onto his job a while longer. James had grown close to his new friends and did not want to part. Both men knew the value L.I.A.M. brought to the investigation, which neither man was finished with. McDaniels had grown close with L.I.A.M., as well as the two doctors. The call came in that their transport had landed on the helipad atop the headquarters and was waiting on them. Hugs and handshakes were exchanged between all.

James McDaniels pulled L.I.A.M. close as they took their turn to shake hands. "You keep in touch and I will see you soon. We will continue your training."

"I would like that."

McDaniels moved on to Brooks, expressing his appreciation for the man and how glad he was to have met him. Hugging Potts, James kissed her on the cheek. "You are the smartest woman I have ever met, and it has been my privilege to know you. I'll be seeing you soon."

Harding took his turn with L.I.A.M. and asked that he continue to track the Ghost and to contact him directly with the location. L.I.A.M. agreed to do so.

Maroni and McHenery bade the group farewell and left the conference room. Maroni stopped to confer with the Homeland investigators while the general spoke on his cell phone as he headed for the elevators. Men like him never stopped, never paused, they were always busy and working an angle. Power came with a cost, and only those patient as well as capable climbed to the heights of these men. Director Maroni had stumbled over a leggy blonde; a momentary lapse in judgment cost him his position, or would. Men like the director and the general could never lapse, never forget the rules, the risks, the responsibilities, the repercussions.

Colonel Vetter escorted the senator, L.I.A.M., and the two doctors to the roof. As he opened the sliding door of the helicopter, the large blades began to turn. "They will take you to the airstrip and I will reroute your transport to Ohio. Gabby, it has been a pleasure; pleasure meeting the rest of you. Have a good flight." The group buckled into their seats. The blades had gained speed and the noise became too loud to hear. Vetter gave a wave and closed the door. The pilot motioned for the group to put on their headphones. Brooks and Potts sat behind the pilots facing the rear of the craft as well as L.I.A.M. and Senator Miller. The doctors were holding hands.

"Hope I don't get sick," Nathan said into the headset.

"You'll be fine," Gabby said. "We are all still together." She smiled at him.

They gave a wave to Vetter as they separated from the building. L.I.A.M. focused on the pilots as they flew, ever curious to experience and learn. The aircraft banked east, and in a matter of minutes the Atlantic Ocean was out in front of them. "Where are we headed?" Miller asked.

"Your transport is near Norfolk," the pilot answered.

"Isn't it beautiful?" Gabby asked, shaking Nathan's hand. "You are doing great."

"Water, yeah, great."

Suddenly a beeping sound came from the instrument panel and L.I.A.M. observed both airmen tense. The pilots began to look out the window trying to see behind them, and the chopper banked hard to the right. "Everyone brace. We are under fire," L.I.A.M. told his companions.

A whooshing sound was audible over the whipping of the blades before a hard jolt rocked the helicopter. The craft swirled, jerking everyone hard to the left in their seats. Alarms and lights exploded on the console, the pilots trying everything to maintain control. "Brace; we are descending, going down. I have issued a mayday. I am forwarding our exact location to the Coast Guard." L.I.A.M. spoke to all.

Nathan and Gabby held tight to one another's hands. Brooks vomited, the erratic motion of the helicopter allowing his stomach contents to move vertically versus hitting the floor. Gabby's face was filled with fear and panic.

The Atlantic Ocean might as well have been made of concrete. As the chopper impacted into the water, the front of the craft was crushed. The windshield smashed, allowing freezing water to rush in. Brooks gasped as the shock of the water began to encompass his body. Gabby Potts was unconscious, her limp limbs floating atop the icy water. The helicopter filled quickly and sank into the darkness of the deep.

L.I.A.M. unbuckled himself and moved to his maker. Nathan was pure panic, fighting with his seatbelt for freedom. Even in the darkness, L.I.A.M. could see, one eye using thermal imaging and the other night vision. His maker struggled to hold his breath, his eyes bulging with the effort. The android tore the clasp of the safety belt apart and pulled Nathan Brooks to the back of the helicopter.

A small pocket of air lingered in the back top of the craft. Brooks gasped for air, his whole body quaking with cold. L.I.A.M. moved to Gabby and ripped apart her belt, pulling her to the pocket of air.

"L.I.A.M., L.I.A.M., can you hear me?" Brooks spoke in a jerked and choppy voice, the cold constricting his entire body. L.I.A.M. tapped his maker's leg to affirm. "You need to save Gabby. Save Gabby." Nathan struggled to breathe. "L.I.A.M., know… Oh, God!" the doctor fought for every word. "L.I.A.M., know that I am proud of you." The creator moaned with agony. "Know I love you." Dr. Nathan Brooks took a final breath, submerging into the freezing blackness and faced his creation, his friend, his son, and embraced him in the dark.

The chopper hit the bottom of the Atlantic and tipped over on its side. L.I.A.M. could see that Dr. Potts's heart had stopped, but he gripped her in one arm and tore open the sliding door with his other. Eighty-seven feet to the surface; luckily, they had not gotten too far from the shore. L.I.A.M. gave a last look into the helicopter and the men he would be leaving to the depths.

Squatting, he pushed hard off the ocean floor. Only a moment or two later and L.I.A.M. erupted from the water, waves coming at them one after another. Rolling onto his back, he placed Dr. Potts's body on top of him and followed the waves toward the shore.

CHAPTER 48

BRANDON HARDING AND JAMES MCDANIELS had gone into the task force leader's office. Brandon poured two Blue Label scotches for them; even though as he did, he remembered that neither of them had a team left to lead. "I don't much care for that Vetter guy," James said, taking the glass from his boss.

"Yeah, me neither. I think him and the general have big ideas for L.I.A.M.," Brandon said.

"Thought the director was stepping down. Way he sounded, I can't tell."

Harding paused at the window. "Way he is acting out there, he may be going for director of Homeland Security." Brandon took his seat. "This damn Ghost has it coming."

"I totally agree."

The men sipped their scotch and remembered the friends they had lost. "What a shame. Tops of their fields, in the prime of their lives. Losing the likes of them will impact the nation for years to come," Harding said and drank deeply.

"What a way for Sam and Ty to go out. No soldier wants a weak death. They would have rather fought a dozen lions than suffocate in their own office. Whoever this Ghost is, I think we are going to be extremely disappointed once we find him. It's always some weasel with creepy looks, greasy hair, and a faggy disposition. This one will think he is smarter than everyone, just wait and see."

Brandon shrugged as his phone vibrated. "It's L.I.A.M. Tracked Ghost south of Philadelphia. Raleigh, North Carolina." There was a pause and a serious look came over the agent's face. "What?! Wait; under fire?" Brandon exclaimed into the phone. Coming to his feet, Brandon gave his friend a look of deepest concern. "Hello, hello, hello!"

James got up and waited for his superior to inform him of the situation.

"L.I.A.M. has called out a mayday; said the chopper was under fire."

James furrowed his brow. "On fire, or under fire?"

Harding rounded his desk, looking out at the bullpen. "See if that colonel is still here, and get the director up here." He snatched up the phone on his desk. "Get me air force rescue, air traffic control, and emergency services on the phone."

McDaniels hurried from the office, stopping at the director's side to inform him he was needed by Brandon. Picking up a phone, James called the front desk to see if Colonel Vetter had signed out of the building. The guard said he was signing out at that moment. McDaniels told the guard to send the colonel back upstairs immediately. Looking back toward his boss's office, he could see an animated exchange between Brandon and Director Maroni.

Grabbing the receiver, James dialed another number and ordered the FBI helicopter fueled and on the roof of the task force headquarters immediately.

Figuring it best to leave the two bosses alone, James waited by the elevator for Vetter. Part of him wanted to judge the man's reaction when he told him the chopper was in trouble. The moments ticked by and James looked around at the busy work of the Homeland agents and he thought of his team. They had not deserved the end they had found. Now, with L.I.A.M. and the doctors possibly in trouble, the thorn of the Ghost only seemed that much deeper. He had never been good company with the likes of bad men or bully types. James had no taste for those who would victimize weaker or unknowing souls.

"What's up? Dragging my ass back up here," Vetter said, breaking McDaniels's thoughts with a hand in the middle of his back.

James turned and met the man's eyes. "The chopper you put them on is in trouble." He spoke in an even tone in order to better gauge the impact.

"What are you talking about?" Vetter angled his head, giving the agent a look from the corner of his eye.

"You didn't hear what I said?"

"I heard you, but in trouble how? They just left."

McDaniels looked over at the office. "L.I.A.M. was talking with Brandon, he had tracked the Ghost, and then something happened. And you have no idea, right?" He again watched the colonel for a reaction.

"Look close, agent; no idea." The man met his eyes with a serious hold.

"They want a look at you too. Come on." McDaniels waved a path for the slick military man. Following Vetter up from the bullpen to Harding's office, McDaniels began to feel extremely angry and anxious. He wanted to do something, anything, but he had to figure out where to go. Vetter didn't bother knocking, walking in on the director and task force leader in mid-conversation.

"What's going on here? This one is questioning me like a suspect. What do we know?" Vetter demanded. "Do I need to call the general back in?"

"You may want to. Air traffic control received an S.O.S. call and lost contact with the helicopter over the Atlantic. Air force rescue is en route," Harding said.

"Over the Atlantic? Where the hell were they headed?" Maroni asked.

"A transport plane out of Norfolk. This was a military chopper; there is no reason it should have gone down," Vetter responded.

"I have the FBI helicopter en route and it should arrive any minute. I am going out there," James told the room.

Over fifteen minutes passed as the men went back and forth, made calls and attempted to learn the fate of the flight. The call came that the helicopter was on the roof, fueled and ready.

The men began to stir, readying themselves for the trip. "We all should not go. Vetter and I will go, alone," James instructed.

"Why?" Maroni asked.

James gave a look at the task force leader and lightly shrugged. "L.I.A.M. said something about being under fire. If the Ghost shot down that helicopter, there's reason to believe he would or might shoot down another."

"Shot down?" Maroni asked.

"We don't know what happened, but James is correct to be cautious. We will wait here for the general, then head to the White House to fill in the President. Keep in contact, and let us know what you can, when you can," Harding said.

McDaniels and Vetter headed to the roof and boarded the helicopter. Lifting off, the craft headed southeast toward Norfolk. Both men had on headsets but didn't talk. James looked out the window, filled by thoughts of his friends. The task force taken out, and now, if L.I.A.M. and the two doctors were in trouble...the thoughts troubled him deeply.

He thought of Harding repeating what L.I.A.M. was telling him— North Carolina. If the Ghost was in Raleigh, then who shot down their helicopter? Could a follower have been waiting? The route to Norfolk was unplanned, unanticipated, unscheduled. James was full of questions and eager for answers. Something was off, and the whole situation felt funny.

The pilot's voice filled the earphones, informing the two men a call was coming through. Harding's voice then came on. "Air traffic control has called the chopper a downed aircraft, and Air Force rescue has confirmed. Oil, fuel, and debris were found near the last known location. Coast Guard and Navy ships with divers are en route. No survivors have been retrieved or spotted. Land in Norfolk and General McHenery has arranged a cutter to take you and the colonel out to the site. Recover all bodies, determine cause, and get back."

"Yes, sir. What of Raleigh?" McDaniels asked.

"That will have to wait. The President wants answers, as do we all. Figure this out, James."

"Colonel Vetter?" General McHenery's voice came over the speakers.

"Yes, sir?"

"Secure L.I.A.M. and move him to our northwest site. Allow the FBI to lead the investigation. Recover our property and leave the scene to the experts."

"Yes, sir," Vetter answered and exchanged a look with McDaniels. The line went dead, leaving a lingering silence, with the hum of the rotors filling the periphery. Leaning toward James, Thad Vetter removed his headset and waited for the agent to do the same. "Wasn't me," he yelled in McDaniels's ear, raising two fingers to his eyes, then pointing them at James and shaking his head. The two men replaced their headphones.

The comment was extremely odd, and it laid heavy on James's mind. The colonel was a slick type and had a mind for games and advancement. A different set of concepts from what James carried. The denial struck the agent like the man knew suspicion should be pointed at him. It did seem a bit cold how General McHenery was only concerned with L.I.A.M., but he had figured a lifer of the military would see beyond the bodies.

Watching the officer look out over the water, McDaniels considered if men like that would kill citizens over some project. Then he remembered L.I.A.M. This was a leap forward, an advancement equal to or bigger than the very internet. Men like the colonel, like the general, sent men to their deaths on whims. There would be no hesitation with the hint of possibility.

"Three minutes out. Cutter is waiting, berth five." The pilot's voice filled their ears as he held up three fingers.

"Affirmative," Vetter responded.

James had lots of questions for the DARPA man, but knew better than to ask and be lied to. The soldier wouldn't tell him, even if he did know. The more he considered the odd chance the Ghost had set up a follower to take out a helicopter, it was possible. Any sense of coincidence was too far-fetched to grant real consideration. By the time they set foot on the deck of the cutter and took to sea, James had made up his mind and felt sick to his stomach.

"You all right, Agent?" Vetter asked.

"No."

"Ocean not agree with you?"

"That ain't it."

Vetter eyed him, raising an eyebrow and giving a soft shrug. "Ways of the world, my friend. Big boy rules."

Ships bobbed out in front of them as they approached the crash site. McDaniels stepped up next to the soldier. "Yeah, I know the rules, and I know there are always those who think they don't apply to them. It's why guys like me have jobs."

"These are deep waters, Agent; all kinds of dangers and death lurking out there. There are great whites; and sure enough, a lowly dolphin can kill one, but such is rare, and can be all bad if that shark isn't alone." Vetter slapped James on the shoulder.

James wasn't sure if the colonel was including himself or if he was simply warning that the general was a well-protected man; either way, the point was passed. The captain of the cutter pointed out the crane and explained how divers had hooked up the wreckage. A seaman handed the man a note and he gave the body count of four recovered, pointing to a second ship. He gave orders to pull alongside the other ship, deploy the dinghy, and directed his second-in-command to escort them to the bodies.

A lump grew in McDaniels's throat as they left the bridge. The magnitude of the day finally landed upon him. The thought of the Ghost angered him, but to have more devious schemes afoot by those above him concerned him even more. Watching the colonel board the motorboat to cross over from one ship to the other, and viewing the scale of the recovery operations, James knew men such as these had immense resources behind them. General McHenery, Director Maroni, the President, they could call upon thousands; planes, boats, trains, satellites, whatever they might need to accomplish whatever ends.

They moved into the belly of the second ship. In the medical bay, there lay four black zipper bags. They were flipped open to show the occupants' faces. Vetter moved down the row of four. "Where are the others?" he demanded.

"There is a pretty sharp undercurrent at about fifty feet; if there were survivors, or if bodies came out of the wreckage, they could have been swept away," a seaman said.

McDaniels stopped at Nathan Brooks's body. The pasty white skin of his face was still wet from the sea. People described the dead as being at peace; James never saw it that way. For him, they seemed empty. The remains of life. He had figured L.I.A.M. far too capable to have died in a simple crash. Dr. Potts had built him to survive everything, but where was she? He could see the same thoughts going through the colonel's mind.

Looking at the body of Nathan Brooks, James wondered how L.I.A.M. was handling his first significant loss. The death of a father was hard; the death of your creator had to be worse.

"Take me to the radio room." Vetter's voice pulled McDaniels away from his thoughts. "We need to report," he said to James.

They followed the seaman away from the medical bay. "Are any of the divers available to talk with us?" McDaniels asked. "We best have as much information as we can before we report."

Vetter agreed and they took twenty minutes talking with three Navy divers. They described a rocket blast to the rear of the helicopter that destroyed the tail rotor. Two seatbelts were torn apart, which they assumed explained the missing bodies. The lead diver opined that the craft sunk quickly, and the probability of any survivors was extremely slim. Had they lived beyond impact, sinking so quickly to a depth over eighty feet would cause pressure issues. The point perked Vetter's interest, but he purposefully avoided asking further questions in front of James.

They moved to the radio room and called in the report. James paid close attention to who asked what questions. Noticeably, the general was singularly concerned over the android and why it wasn't with the wreckage. The director and Harding were still concerned over the Ghost and hadn't pieced the puzzle together. McDaniels could tell McHenery wanted to speak with Vetter privately and figured it best if he blocked such communication for as long as he could.

"We are coming back to headquarters," McDaniels said.

"Perhaps the colonel should stay and oversee the recovery?" McHenery suggested.

"A debriefing is called for," McDaniels stated flatly.

Harding must have picked up on James's insistence and came to his aid. "I think we all need to sit down and go over what has happened and where we go from here."

"Go? If L.I.A.M. is gone, we have no further role. You all can go on with your manhunt and we will attempt to recover our property. Colonel Vetter, you continue the salvage operations, and if we recover Dr. Potts's body, we will let you know," General McHenery said.

"I don't think so, General," Harding said. "We need Colonel Vetter to return with Special Agent McDaniels. If the Navy recovers L.I.A.M., the cat's out of the bag. We need to go over a few things and I insist."

Vetter and McDaniels listened to the exchange between Harding and the general.

"Fine. Hurry up and get back here. I have things to do," the general said and the line went dead.

Thad and James returned to the cutter and headed back toward Norfolk. "Didn't want me out of your sight, did you?" Vetter asked as they stood on the bow of the ship. James acknowledged with a raised eyebrow and tilt of his head. "Think L.I.A.M. is alive, don't you?"

"Was he ever?"

"You know what I mean."

McDaniels looked closely at the colonel. "Real question: do you think he survived the crash?"

Vetter turned and gazed out over the water, then shrugged. "How do you see this going? How involved do you think you are going to be now?" He turned back to James. "Truth is, none of you should have known anything about any of this."

James wanted to ask the man directly, but knew Vetter wouldn't say, even if he did know. The reality was, the colonel had probably told him more than he should have. They spent the rest of the trip in silence. The cutter docked and the helicopter flew them back to task force headquarters. McDaniels used the time to think. First, considering if the military would actually shoot down their own aircraft. Fueling the argument in his head: if they had, would the general have done so on his own? The internal shock of questioning if the President of the United States had authorized the killing of American citizens deeply bothered James.

Changing his thoughts to L.I.A.M., McDaniels presumed the android had survived the crash and most likely had Dr. Potts with him. He began to wonder how to find them. He worried that L.I.A.M. could have been damaged, or Gabby may have been hurt. James then began to wonder how L.I.A.M. was dealing with things. Dr. Brooks was all he knew from his birth, or awakening, awareness. He found it strange to feel such compassion for a machine, but L.I.A.M. had feelings too, or at least it seemed as if he felt. The layers of questions and feelings were profound for McDaniels because he had grown to see L.I.A.M. as a naïve friend, almost a child. Now he had trouble and James wanted to help.

The chopper landed on the roof of the headquarters and both men rode the elevator down to the floor still swarming with Homeland Security agents. The director, general, and Harding were waiting in the conference room. McDaniels and Vetter entered and all took seats around the table. There was a palpable tension in the air.

Director Maroni cleared his throat and began. "Task force is to stand down, by order of the President. Homeland Security will continue the pursuit of the suspect known as the Ghost, as well as conduct a joint investigation of this particular incident with the Justice

Department. Both of you are on paid leave until further notice. I am to remind you that information or knowledge of L.I.A.M. or the project is classified. Any disclosure would result in a breach of national security."

"What the hell? What does that mean?" James asked.

"Treason," Colonel Vetter said flatly.

The men at the table exchanged looks before Maroni softened the term. "You need to forget all that. Never happened. Don't talk about it, not even with each other; don't even think about it. The President was serious, very serious, about keeping a lid on the android project." He met both FBI men's eyes. "He wants this to remain a secret." He paused to allow his words to sink in. "General McHenery and Colonel Vetter will continue their work, and that is that. You both are on paid holiday; take a vacation and I'll call you when it's time."

"So, you are maintaining the director's position?" Harding asked.

"Yes, for right now. I will be taking over Homeland Security next year when their director retires. You will take my seat, Brandon; the President knows you are a good man and we have all agreed on the transition. Special Agent McDaniels will rebuild the task force, if he would like. Just as we had discussed him taking over the team. Those things will come, but for now, go lie on a beach somewhere." Anthony Maroni nodded.

The two FBI agents exchanged a look as McHenery and Vetter stood and moved toward the door. "You men have suffered a great loss, and my heart feels for both of you," General McHenery said to them as he shook hands with Maroni.

McDaniels met Vetter's eyes; the look exchanged was a smug one from the colonel. The slick soldier had known it would go this way, he had it figured from the beginning. A raised eyebrow and half grin sealed the silent statement between them. James knew the military would hunt the four corners of the Earth to find L.I.A.M., to retrieve their toy. He knew Vetter would have top scientists working to build new androids, bigger and better. Now that the government knew such a thing was possible, that L.I.A.M. had functioned so efficiently, they wouldn't stop until they had an army of androids. James figured they would not stop hunting L.I.A.M. until they had returned him to their secret base or destroyed him. As long as L.I.A.M. was out there, he was a liability.

The general and colonel left the conference room, their starched uniforms and rigid posture more robot-like than L.I.A.M. Director Maroni closed the conference room door and turned to his men. "I know how you must feel, but this comes from the top. Orders are orders. I know you want to stay involved and I will try to keep you informed on the investigation. Brandon, you will still become director, we just have to allow attentions to find a new interest. The task force dead, you would be a difficult confirmation."

"How's that?" Brandon asked.

"Those looking to be problems for the President would ask you heated questions. Why should we place you at the head of the FBI when your entire task force ends up murdered by the suspect you are chasing? While you were in charge. If you can't keep your team safe, what chance do the people of the United States have?"

"That's pretty harsh, sir," McDaniels defended his friend.

"Exactly. Let's wait a short while, a couple months. The heat will die down. I'll deal with whatever then. We all know Homeland won't be able to catch this Ghost. Come back, you can take over staffing a new task force and focus on finding the Ghost. I will warn both of you, leave L.I.A.M. to the general. The President is backing them, and we all should consider ourselves lucky we know what we know and are allowed to keep on knowing anything," Maroni said in a serious tone.

Both men heard the warning loud and clear, but that in no way meant they planned to heed their boss's cautionary words. They watched as he left the conference room and headed out through the bullpen. Harding nodded at his friend and led them to his office. "Things really turned bad, fast. Didn't they?"

"Like a tornado hitting an outhouse. Whirlwind of crap," James answered.

"So, what is your take on things?"

"Truth be told, sir, I don't like what I am thinking about all of this. Seems to me we have some conflicted parties," McDaniels said, shaking his head.

"That colonel and the general had a hand in things, didn't they?"

"I don't think Vetter knew, but I doubt he would have opposed the decision. L.I.A.M. is like nothing else for men like that, a super soldier. I can see why Dr. Brooks was so against military interference."

"You think they did this to the task force?"

"No. I think the general wanted out and Nathan wasn't going to give in or join up; easier to cut him out. Point the finger at the Ghost. Now they will try and hunt down L.I.A.M."

"Try? Don't think they can catch him?"

"No way."

"Then, how will we?"

"We won't, he will find us. We do what we are told, and go on vacation," James said with a wink.

"Raleigh, North Carolina?" Brandon asked with a cocked smile.

"Norfolk first. If Gabby was hurt, she may be in a hospital there. Vetter will start there, so we need to hurry." McDaniels moved toward the door.

CHAPTER 49

L.I.A.M. HAD MADE ARRANGEMENTS to have an ambulance meet them on shore when he arrived. He had also arranged a room, decompression chamber, and a number of tests for Dr. Potts. Knowing full well that people would be looking for him, he hid these things in the computer databases as other things and under other names. L.I.A.M. knew it would be only a matter of time before someone came around to physically look for them, but he hoped to have Gabby up and about by then.

The swim gave him time to evaluate his situation and determine what was happening, as well as who was involved.

He had serious concerns over Gabby. She had been unconscious since he unbuckled her. Her heart rate and breathing were within normal range for a woman of her age, weight, and condition. He needed to do a brain scan and see the level of synaptic activity; the electrical impulses of her brain could have been affected with such a prolonged absence of oxygen.

L.I.A.M. had rushed to shore but knew the criteria of oxygen was vital for human survival, and she had been deprived this essential element for a number of minutes. He was aware of instances where people had gone longer than Gabby, most suffering some brain damage; however, the temperature of the water was in her favor. Cases showed lower temperature reduced the impact on mental function compared with individuals submerged in tepid water for the same duration.

His dispatch of the ambulance was in advance enough to not create an emergency call; he also tagged the request with the note of a doctor being present at the scene, L.I.A.M. content in Dr. Potts being said doctor. His need to accompany her to the hospital justified the minor deception. The ambulance arrived as L.I.A.M. waded from the surf with Potts in his arms. The two young paramedics hurried to meet him with the gurney. "We didn't realize this was an emergency call," the driver said.

"She is stable but we need to give her oxygen and get her to the hospital." He gave the man her stats as he laid her on the plastic mat, pulling a blanket over her. "Her core temperature is below normal; we need to go." He pushed the gurney toward the ambulance. He could tell that both men were hesitant as well as curious. "This woman needs our help. I can't go into all the details with you gentlemen at this time, but allow me to inform you that she and I have been working with the FBI in attempts to apprehend the suspect known as the Ghost."

This tidbit of information was enough to relax the two and they were on their way. L.I.A.M. now had the ability to inspect Gabby more closely; she would have never guessed the capabilities she had given the Tinman would now save her life. The military requirements of him went beyond simply destructive and included medical treatment of human beings. L.I.A.M. was capable of magnetic resonance imaging by placing his hands on either side of the subject and creating a strong magnetic field. Her brain activity was functioning, but Gabby was in a coma; she also needed to properly decompress. The risk of an embolism was extremely high.

People would be searching for them and they couldn't stay anywhere for long. Soon the ambulance arrived at the hospital and Gabby

Potts was hurried into a decompression chamber. The hospital had seen this before with the Navy base so close; a diving accident here and there had resulted in the bends for a number of men.

L.I.A.M. knew Gabby would need some time and began to build false leads across the internet. He put in a transfer and transport order, knowing he would be shipping Gabby somewhere into the interior. He had no way of knowing how long her coma might last but needed her in a safe place. He was to be the only person notified of changes, putting on her file she was in witness protection.

L.I.A.M. wanted to accompany his friend but knew he had a great deal to do before they would be safe. The Ghost was out there and he had targeted those hunting him, which included them. He would have to remedy the threat of the Ghost, as well as determine who had shot down the helicopter and remedy them as well. There was much to be done, and L.I.A.M. felt confident enough to leave Dr. Potts in the hands of the hospital, at least for a few hours. He needed fresh clothes and transportation, money, information, and a weapon.

Having his exact measurements emailed to a tailor near the hospital, along with a credit card number, L.I.A.M. decided to use General McHenery's personal account to pay for his new clothes. A charcoal suit, double breasted, black tie, black vest, white shirt, Italian leather shoes; a sixty-five-hundred-dollar gift from the general, plus the thirty-dollar taxi ride to the store. The saying *it's the thought that counts* did not apply. The general didn't have a clue about the purchase.

L.I.A.M. had determined General Patrick McHenery ordered the rocket attack on the helicopter by examining the military ordnance, encrypted emails between McHenery and a black operations specialist, and the private unrecorded meeting between him and the President of the United States. L.I.A.M. considered it a very high probability that the President had signed off or authorized the act, but he had no confirmation as of yet. As he changed in the changing room, the thought of contacting James McDaniels was considered, but L.I.A.M. quickly learned that both McDaniels and Harding had been placed on leaves of absence.

Looking more professional, L.I.A.M. took another cab to a new car distributorship, picking up a Cadillac sedan. A simple signature and L.I.A.M. drove away with a brand-new car. Again, the details taken care of online and compliments of General McHenery. Stopping by the Department of Motor Vehicles, L.I.A.M. had a lost license reported and one printed out for him to pick up, along with plates for the car. The clerk questioned the pickup versus the driver's license being mailed, until the direct email authorizing the break in protocol from the Director of Transportation of Virginia came across the computer.

Continuing his errands, L.I.A.M. stopped at the bank to pick up cash and had credit cards issued to his alias: William Turing, the same name on his new driver's license. He withdrew the funds from the DARPA accounts, hiding the transactions in a web of account transfers and deposits and withdrawals.

Pulling into the Norfolk police headquarters, L.I.A.M. entered and made his way to the Human Resources Department. A couple of signatures and William Turing had his new Norfolk Police Department identification, homicide detective badge, and a certificate of authorization to deliver to the armory for his service weapon and ammunition. A stop off in the basement to pick up his new Glock .380 with two additional magazines, and L.I.A.M. was on his way back out to his Cadillac.

Arriving at the hospital, he checked on Dr. Potts and ensured that her transfer would occur as soon as her condition was stabilized. The staff was very understanding; the hospital administrator confirmed her reception of emails from both the U.S. Attorney General's office and the U.S. Marshal Service. She wanted to assure L.I.A.M. the secrecy and care of a protected witness would be a primary concern to all surrounding the patient. L.I.A.M. had no doubts over the hospital or staff; his concern was how long he had before he could move her. Vetter was on his way to Norfolk, as were McDaniels and Harding.

L.I.A.M. had monitored Vetter and McDaniels's trip to the crash site and return to task force headquarters. He had monitored the call from headquarters to the ship, and also activated the phones in the conference room and Harding's office. L.I.A.M. knew everything that was said, he was linked into everything, and allowed himself to flow through the oceans of information. They had given him tools he had been hesitant to entertain; Dr. Brooks had wanted him to be cautious and avoid detection, allow for privacy. Things had changed and now L.I.A.M. needed to use all his cunning to finish his task and deal with the situation at hand.

The changes that had occurred this day had been monumental for L.I.A.M. The entire structure he had been operating under had fallen apart. Those around him were dead, injured, enemies, or under duress. He had adopted a false identity, armed himself, and was calculating his options. Using his time while he waited for Gabby to stabilize, L.I.A.M. narrowed down his search for the Ghost. He had observed that the investigation had been passed along to Homeland Security, which would only delay and muck up the whole situation. This was what the Ghost had intended to do by murdering the task force. His hunters had grown too close; the new pursuers would have to get organized and would chase much more hesitantly than the task force had. The Ghost's plan had worked but for his oversight of L.I.A.M., which he could not have factored.

L.I.A.M. used his skills to interfere with radio frequencies to cause Vetter's helicopter to have to return to Washington, D.C. The delay should give Dr. Potts time to be removed from the decompression chamber and be transferred. He wasn't going to do anything until he knew she was safe. He began to build false trails, knowing the military would soon enough be hot on his heels. They would attempt to use computers to track him, and L.I.A.M. needed to allow them to think they could, making it extremely difficult but seemingly possible. He knew for now Colonel Vetter was the one searching, but in time General McHenery would send others.

Hours passed as L.I.A.M. waited. He had been directed to a small chapel within the hospital, which fit his needs nicely. Quiet, solitary; the lack of outside distractions allowed him to focus with a more concentrated effort. He had waded through General McHenery's life, every file and piece of available information. L.I.A.M. knew the time would come when he would have to discipline the general for his actions. He also pinpointed the Ghost and readied a plan to confront the individual. All the while L.I.A.M. monitored Gabby's condition, Colonel Vetter, McDaniels, and Harding, the crash recovery, the President of the United States, as well as any inquiry over the Ghost, androids, or any of those involved in the case or events transpiring.

A man entered the chapel and moved to the altar, falling to his knees and sobbing. L.I.A.M. used the man's face to track his movements and which room he had come from. Using the hospital registry and database, he learned that the individual in that room had just died. A woman of eighty-one years who had contracted pneumonia, compounded with an infection from the hospital. The woman's frail nature and age lent itself to a poor prognosis, her death more probable than not. This man on his knees was her son, and his sorrow struck L.I.A.M. in a manner he was not accustomed to, nor ready to understand. The man's head hung as he shuddered, crying openly and voicing his desire for God to embrace his mother's soul.

L.I.A.M. observed the man, searching information on death, sorrow, and even God. Grieving was not something Dr. Brooks and he had ever considered, and now that Nathan was dead, L.I.A.M. realized they never would. The limitations of the human being puzzled him, especially when considering an omnipotent creator, such as God. It made no sense to develop something with such a short life span, as well as with such a delicate survivability. Pondering his own existence and the thought by his creators, it seemed very strange that humans would credit a God with such capability when the evidence was anything but.

The sorrowful man finally composed himself and took a seat in one of the pews. L.I.A.M. knew he would need to give this subject more detailed thought and investigation, but presently he had things to do. The mourning for Dr. Brooks would also have to wait, but L.I.A.M. sensed the need to do so would come. His creator had purposefully given him choice as well as the sense of emotion, but L.I.A.M. had not fathomed the depths of what these aspects of his persona would mean. He did not confuse feeling with feelings but could not deny the sensations of loss, anger, even sympathy for the man who had lost his mother. Such sensations were new for L.I.A.M. and did not interfere with his functioning, but they were present, and he questioned the service they provided to his being.

Dr. Potts had spent just enough time in decompression, so L.I.A.M. left the little chapel with only a pause to regard the man with his sympathies. He had calculated both drive time as well as time to inspect the helicopter's radio; Colonel Vetter had simply changed choppers and would land at the Navy base in one minute and twelve seconds. Vetter had a team awaiting his arrival.

Escorting Gabby to the medical chopper, which would take her to an awaiting care flight to Denver, then transfer her to another flight into Billings, L.I.A.M. found himself holding her hand as he walked beside her gurney. Her brain function was strong but she lingered in a coma. The doctor had suggested a minor head injury coupled with trauma and oxygen deprivation, compounded by the ocean pressure, could have caused Gabby to become comatose. L.I.A.M. agreed with the diagnosis, and also agreed that Gabby could regain consciousness at any time.

Watching the medical helicopter fly away from the hospital, L.I.A.M. felt concern for his friend, his mother, but knew he would see her again. In a way, he was glad she wasn't aware of what had happened or what was coming. He knew full well the dangers of a person being comatose over a prolonged period and the potential for brain damage she risked from the lack of oxygen, but having the government turn on her would have been a great deal for her to process. The chopper banked toward the airport and L.I.A.M. headed down through the hospital then out to his Cadillac. As he started his vehicle, three nondescript military vehicles with government plates pulled up to the entrance.

Colonel Thaddeus Vetter led eight men into the hospital with purpose. He had choppered onto the Navy base and collected assistance for his search, apparently picking the right hospital to search first. L.I.A.M. quickly registered with the information desk that a Jane Doe suffering from compression sickness had been transferred to Bethesda Hospital. A matter of moments and the nine men hurried back to their cars and sped away from the entrance. L.I.A.M.'s misdirect had worked; he smiled before backing out of his parking spot and pulling away from the hospital.

Vetter had not been aware of the rocket attack on their chopper, but L.I.A.M. knew well enough that had he been, he wouldn't have attempted to stop it. Vetter was a career soldier and would never risk going against a four-star general or the President of the United States.

Such men embraced their orders and rank like a protective blanket, a sense of security by way of deniability and extending the blame onto others. He may not want to lose his project, but he would not hesitate to fulfill an order from a superior. Vetter wanted to elevate his rank and that was why he was involved with DARPA, not for any sense of scientific innovation.

L.I.A.M. turned his Cadillac south and drove toward North Carolina. He monitored Dr. Potts's flight, as well as Colonel Vetter, all the while digging deeper into McHenery's life. The general seemed nice enough but the reality was, he had enemies, mistresses, illegitimate children, cover-ups, misappropriations of funds, and a few questionable incidents of abuse of power, a number of assassinations, and he himself had been investigated for killing a superior officer.

McHenery had been playing dangerous games and covering his butt for decades. Building a power structure and network of dirty players strong enough to drive him to general and onto the Joint Chiefs. His hands were both dirty and bloody. He had handled the right messes for the right people, which had protected them and him, also giving him the position he desired.

The more L.I.A.M. searched through the military and government, going over extremely classified materials, he could not help but be surprised at the level of corruption and even criminal actions. Emails between military black operations special units and CIA teams, coordinating everything from drug running, kidnappings, even murders. He uncovered attempts by ambitious reporters to disclose such activities to the public, but the machine, government, and the military industrial complex, to which it was often referred, protected itself. Threats, intimidation, trumped-up charges, even executions, silenced any voice.

He found it interesting as he compared modern leadership to historical figures, the doings of governments of other countries, and

other times, the public views of forms of government, leaders, poli-
cies, transitions. L.I.A.M. processed the influx of religion and technology, rebellion, civil disobedience, open warfare. He began to view
the people as a far more layered entity, from independent individual
to reliant subject. There were so many and so widespread, while each
encompassed such diversity moment to moment. The structure was
bound to be frayed.

Public understanding was limited, controlled, confused. Individual
interests could range widely and change in an instant. L.I.A.M. saw the
government as an adequate representation of those humans of which it
was made up.

The drive was a period of enlightenment for L.I.A.M., seeing the
chaos and confusion of humanity. His interactions so far had been with
intelligent and compassionate people, but now he was coming to know
a more goal-driven human. Power and greed consumed the minds of
the simplest primates, creating the simplest of problems: struggles of
life and death, and to have or have not. L.I.A.M. could see the primal nature of mankind, even disguised with education, uniforms, and
complex structures. General McHenery had ordered the death of all
those on that helicopter—his fellow soldiers, fellow countrymen, fellow
human beings—and all for the control over a science project of which
he had no understanding at all.

L.I.A.M. was reminded of the exhibit of early man at the historical museum and his conversation with Gabby about mankind not
evolving as much as innovating. Men like General McHenery and
Colonel Vetter were plagued by want, starved with desire, and thirsty
for power, all the while stricken with hypocrisy and dependency. Such
men did not blaze trails or strive to extend the human understanding;
such men looked to lead those who would follow, championing the
common consensus, bending for popularity. L.I.A.M. saw the medals,

stars, and ribbons not as symbols of achievement as much as individuals' need to be recognized by the masses.

Delving into organizations such as the CIA and the secretive and anonymous nature of such groups, another form of thought emerged. Delusion or ideology affected many, a sense of patriotism and nationalism to guard against enemies at any cost. Others were drawn to the secretive aspect, a lawless or unregulated abandon to win by any means. Both groups were as old as civilization, a mindset formed early on in the structure of human social interactions. A champion to parade before the weak and helpless, with the treacherous spy in the shadows fulfilling the agenda. L.I.A.M. could see the practical evolution of such behaviors, as well as the blind eye turned by the masses to ensure their safety.

Reaching the Research Triangle, L.I.A.M. could feel the boost in Wi-Fi availability and mobile frequencies, along with digital and radio waves radiating around the area. Raleigh had grown into a technologic playground, with quality universities producing educated talent to fuel innovation for the city, state and country. The number of computers and databases, along with the number of cameras in and around the capital of North Carolina, encouraged L.I.A.M. He had work to do and a Ghost to find. Having so much technology around him was comforting for some reason. There had been segments of his drive which seemed limited; the human description might have been loneliness.

Driving into a residential part of the city with old homes built by wealth and passed down generation after generation, L.I.A.M. pulled into the circular driveway of one of the antebellum homes. Parking in front of the entrance and exiting the Cadillac, he moved to the front door and rang the bell. Moments passed as he waited; finally a young woman dressed in purple scrubs opened the door.

"Yes?" she asked.

"I am here for Scott Werner," L.I.A.M. stated.

"He is at the botanical gardens, working."

L.I.A.M. nodded. "Yes, I know. He is en route and will arrive in three minutes. May I wait?"

The woman looked puzzled. "I don't know. I have to watch over Madam Werner."

L.I.A.M. pulled out his badge and showed it to the young woman. "Alzheimer's is an unfortunate condition. I need to ask Scott a few questions; he may have witnessed something important during his travels."

"He does travel a lot." She moved to the side and opened the door wider so L.I.A.M. could enter.

"Yes, I know that he does." The android stepped into the foyer. The home from the outside appeared large, but in keeping with the scale of all the homes on the street. Inside, the house was huge and extended more deeply into the property. L.I.A.M. had already researched the blueprints and satellite photographs, but standing there looking up at the antebellum chandelier, he felt small for the first time.

"Would you like a cup of coffee, or something, sweet tea? Mr. Werner released most of the house staff, but I could put on a pot if you would like," the nurse aide asked with a smile.

L.I.A.M. picked up on the woman's chemical release and increased heart rate, as well as her temperature rising a full degree. She was aroused by his presence. "Thank you, but no. You are working and I do not mean to disturb your care of the lady of the house." He returned the smile and followed the young woman into the parlor, noticing she purposefully wiggled her posterior more than necessary.

CHAPTER 50

COLONEL THAD VETTER'S CELL PHONE vibrated and the four stars across the caller I.D. screen told him it was General McHenery. Answering, Vetter informed the general of the false lead of a Jane Doe and that it was his opinion L.I.A.M. had withstood the crash and was manipulating the hunt for Dr. Potts. He went on to speculate that Gabby Potts had been injured but L.I.A.M. was hiding her. The colonel explained he had picked up an eight-man team, a special unit with specific skills on finding elusive targets. Vetter then confessed that the target they were hunting was not like any other.

McHenery wanted a recommendation, and Vetter knew better than to sugarcoat an answer. He told the general it was a wasted effort to attempt to pursue L.I.A.M. at this time. He pointed out that any communication toward any further projects should be reviewed in a darkened room at a black site—code to describe a room with no electronic devices, implementing anti-receiver electromagnetics to make any surveillance impossible. Such rooms were used for top secret meetings so that no audio or visual recordings could exist. The term *black site* simply meant a secret location.

The general agreed and gave the colonel new orders. He directed Vetter to clean up the project and hung up. Thad knew what the general meant and what he expected. The eight men he had chosen were good at many things: one was a specialist with computers, another in communications, others in weapons, transportation, contemporary tracking, logistics, and organization. Granted, they were what was available with a time constraint and location. They would have served for a search, but now the boss called for a total cleanup and these were only some of the skills he would need.

Vetter considered keeping the men but figured it best to start fresh with men he knew, and knew he could trust. He had been around the DOD long enough to have made a few friends. Returning to Norfolk Naval Base, Vetter thanked the team for the help and let them go. He put in a call to Lieutenant Colonel Jack Par; he had gone through basic training and officer training with Jack and knew he was operations liaison for special unit deployment. They had both been ambitious; he had chosen to follow the money, while Jack knew all the best bad guys.

The reunion on the phone was short and direct. Vetter ordered up a special unit with cleanup capabilities and hunt acquisition. His old friend knew the terms well. These were not naïve men; they were experienced and well-traveled, knew the ways of the world, the ways of war, and the ways of people. A thought struck Thad: because they would not be hunting a person, would L.I.A.M.'s ways be so different? Then he began to question how much he could reveal to his new team before they would become a liability and need to be cleaned up as well. He directed Par to assemble the team and muster at Rickenbacker Air Force Base near Dayton, Ohio, in three days' time.

Vetter knew that was plenty of time for his old friend to arrange a quality bunch. Three days was also long enough for him to meet with General McHenery and nail down exactly what the man wanted. A complete cleanup involved a secret base, FBI agents, as well as the director. He knew if the general and President were going to go that far, his future was extremely limited. It was not unheard of, but he suspected the general and President wanted to further the android program and the cleanup would be more a containment versus extermination of all involved.

CHAPTER 51

AN OLD WOMAN SAT IN A HIGH-BACKED chair toward the back of the parlor. She looked puzzled as L.I.A.M. followed the nurse aide into the room.

"Who are you people? What are you doing in my home?" the old woman demanded.

"It's me, Mandy; your son hired me to take care of you, remember? Mr. Werner wants the best for you," the woman in purple told her. Giving L.I.A.M. a glance and smile, she added, "This is Officer—I didn't catch your name."

"Detective Turing. I need to ask your son a few questions. He may have witnessed something in his travels that could help my investigation."

"Who?" Madam Werner questioned.

"He needs to talk with Mr. Werner," Mandy told the Alzheimer's patient.

"Mr. Werner is dead, been dead. Want to talk with him, you best find some Gypsy, got a crystal ball. You silly children." The old woman laughed.

"Your son, Madam Werner," Mandy attempted to clarify.

The old lady became visibly upset and shifted in her chair. "Who are you people, and why are you in my home?"

"It's me, Mandy, everything is fine. It's time for your pill."

"I don't know? What pill? Who is this man?"

Mandy moved to a small lockbox and used a key to open it, then pulled out a bottle of pills and poured two into her palm. "Here you go, dear. Take your pills." She handed the old woman the medication and a plastic cup of water. After relocking the little box, Mandy turned and eyed L.I.A.M. up and down. "You say Mr. Werner is on his way home? Those are tranquilizers. If she becomes agitated or combative, two will put her out for the rest of the day."

The purr of Mandy's voice when she spoke to L.I.A.M. was a blatant signal of her sexual attraction to him. He could see in her body language that she was attempting to seduce him: arching her back, the sway of her hips, the playing with her hair.

"Scott Werner is pulling into the driveway at this moment," L.I.A.M. said.

Mandy trotted to the window with a small hop at the end. "Wow, you have some good ears." She gave L.I.A.M. a look over her shoulder. "He is pulling back to the cottage. A guest house at the rear of the property."

"Have you been back there?"

"No. I was instructed to stay in the main house."

"Well, I will walk out and speak with him. Thank you for your company."

Mandy hurried toward him, nervous. "Perhaps I should call Mr. Werner first. He won't like you going out there. He is very private."

L.I.A.M. nodded. "Yes, I know he is. He won't mind and won't trouble you with my intrusion. I promise. Just stay here and take care of Madam Werner. I will stop by before I go to say goodbye." L.I.A.M. gave her a wink and a smile, playing on her attraction.

"All right then." She beamed with a wide smile and the enthusiasm of reciprocated flirting.

L.I.A.M. had no interest in Mandy, but needed her calm and uninterested in his conversation with her boss. Moving close to her, L.I.A.M. said softly, "I will be a few minutes, then I'll be back." He rubbed her arm as he spoke, then turned and walked from the parlor.

He moved through the estate, down a long hallway, and passed a large dining room. The kitchen was massive. He knew Scott Werner surely noticed his Cadillac sitting out front. Looking through the mudroom door window, he saw the cottage was some hundred yards down a stone path. He walked out the rear door, making no attempt to hurry or hide.

Scott Werner stood just outside the cottage door, watching L.I.A.M. approach and keeping a watchful eye on the surrounding grounds. He seemed nervous, but not so much as to avoid his visitor. The man was fifty-two years old, by the records L.I.A.M. had checked. Southern-born, in Raleigh, and a graduate of North Carolina State.

Scott Werner had scored 180 on the Intelligence Quotient test and had achieved three master's degrees from three schools, all in different fields. He had returned to the family business after his father passed: raising roses and extracting their oil. The Werner family had been involved in banking and investments, land ownership, raising cotton, tobacco, and now roses, since before the Civil War. Scott never seemed to enjoy finance and focused on the plantation.

He was certainly smart enough to comprehend and excel at financial matters, but it seemed to hold no interest for him. Records showed the tragic drowning of Scott's younger brother when they were teenagers on a family camping trip. The gruesome rape and murder of his eldest sister, while he was earning his second master's from Duke University, surely had an impact on the man. His master's studies were in psychology, and he embraced new ideas, technology, and concepts emerging in the field. He was hungry for knowledge and ravenous in appetite; he could have easily earned positions in the discipline or continued to a doctorate. He had found his interest, but as quickly as he embraced the study of the human mind, he quit, returning to the family business and his roses.

His third master's degree came in computer science from MIT. He was older than most of his fellow students and had not enjoyed a youth filled by computer games and gadgets. Scott had to work hard, but the challenge sparked him, firing a need to outdo those around him. He never gave up without achieving the goal. His first few semesters were not up to his personal standard, but would have been quality scores for most students.

Scott had been raised not just to achieve but to be the best. Everyone starts the race, many finish the race, but only one wins the race, making all else losers. He had been taught there was no value in loss, that loss was absolutely unacceptable, especially in the family business. Failed attempts were costly, and the Werner family were entrusted with fortunes.

Traveling outside the Carolinas was enjoyable for Scott, so he chose Columbia University for his next field of study, looking finally into conquering finance. After a year in the master's program, his father took ill and Scott was needed at home. He dropped out of Columbia and returned home; a week later his father was dead. The board of directors looked to merge the family business with a larger firm from New York, but Scott could not allow that. Still, he was limited with what he could do.

The sale went through, Scott removing all connection with the financial firm and cashing out the family from the company. The estate was now worth a quarter of a billion dollars. Having researched the housing market and the loan swaps banks had extended unqualified buyers, he had planned to write his thesis on the swelling bubble. Now, he found himself in the real world and responsible for the family fortune.

He risked it all, putting everything from the family as well as his own inheritance toward shorting the housing market. The move was timely, and it flushed the family accounts and his own. He rolled a large amount into gold, and the worth of the family swelled to the mid-ten figure range. This gave him plenty to play the market with, and purchase blue chip stocks for cheap, because of the downturn.

Quietly wealthy with no responsibilities, Scott Werner traveled, meeting people and spurring interests here and there. His money allowed him to entertain quirky curiosities, hiring top people to teach him whatever he wanted. His mother developing the Alzheimer's brought him back to Raleigh and returned him to his old hobby with his roses. His travels had also given him a new hobby, which would now take more planning and effort.

While a student in New York, on a date with a pretty girl he barely knew, they were mugged. A man with a gun demanded their money. Attempting to be gallant, Scott attacked the thief, but in the struggle the gun went off. His date was struck in the chest and died instantly. Fear and rage gripped him, blinding him with the red stare. When all was done, the mugger was also dead. Scott had bashed the man's head upon the concrete until the grey of his brains spilled out onto the sidewalk.

As L.I.A.M. grew closer, the man's face began to relax somewhat. He was above average size, six feet four, two hundred and thirty pounds of mostly muscle. He stood straight as an arrow, his eyes sharp, still checking the surroundings for any danger, before focusing on L.I.A.M. He was within five yards of Scott Werner when the man put up a hand to halt him.

"No solicitors," Werner stated in a calm baritone, a very commanding voice.

L.I.A.M. continued toward him and stopped at about eight feet from him. "I am not here to try and sell you something."

The men's eyes were locked on each other's; a slight breeze blew the smell of rose oil to L.I.A.M. at a magnitude sufficient to confirm that this was indeed the Ghost.

"What do you want then?" Werner stepped back into the doorway of the cottage.

"I am here for you."

Werner narrowed his eyes with suspicion. "That is a nice suit; little too expensive for a cop."

"Yes, it is new. I am not a police officer; however, I am impersonating one at the moment."

Werner grabbed a shotgun from inside the door and pointed it at L.I.A.M. Using his left hand, he directed L.I.A.M. to come forward and inside the cottage. "Impersonating an officer, and trespassing; I could shoot you now and have no troubles at all."

"Won't be like nineteen years ago, your first kill, when no one came to call. Must have shocked you when two people lay dead in the street and you were never even questioned." L.I.A.M. could see his comment stirred a deep curiosity. "You may be able to justify shooting me to the police, but you don't really want to have to explain it." L.I.A.M. moved inside the cottage. "How is it you came to trust your friends, like the skinny fellow in Detroit? Did they too start with a gun in their backs?"

"Sit over there." Scott nodded to a sofa in the living room. "How do you know these things?"

L.I.A.M. walked over and sat down. "I know all kinds of things. You injected Sasha Blonde with mercury before you turned her over to your friend, assuring her death over a couple days. Not a true show of faith, on your part. Were you going to tip the police, and have the Ghost label pinned on this other man?"

"Seems like I didn't have to; the name found him without any help from me. Haven't you seen the news? Ghost is dead." Scott laid the shotgun on the opposing couch as he sat down. "Again, how do you know these things?"

"I have been looking for you."

"Seems that the police and FBI believe this man in Detroit is who you were looking for. Why on earth would you think I was the Ghost?"

"Case number 7550B: Eric Strong of Hollywood, California. Your sniper nest; the indentations on the table from the chair would have taken more weight than your friend could muster. Not to mention the rose oil." Scott Werner gave a sideways glance at L.I.A.M. "Who are you?"

"I am L.I.A.M."

"You are no cop, but you are no civilian either. Wait a minute, you are one of that new group. Scientists or whatever; you were in Detroit. Wondered how you all got there so fast." The illusions were gone; he had been watching the cameras in the warehouse, and now he knew L.I.A.M. was working with the FBI. Monitoring his heart rate and temperature, L.I.A.M. knew Werner was nervous but not so that panic had taken hold.

"Yes. I have been assisting the FBI with their investigation, but things have changed."

"The task force?" Scott asked with an evil smile.

"As you are aware, we were working independently from the task force. There are many factors as to why I am here alone, but they don't concern you." Werner tilted his head, then gave a slight nod. "Might I offer you a drink? I have a fine thirty-year-old scotch." He slid off the couch and walked toward the back of the room. "You came alone? Where is your team?"

"Mostly dead."

"Thought your team was in Detroit when the task force was neutralized?"

"They weren't killed by you."

Scott returned with a glass of amber liquor. "L.I.A.M., you said?" The android nodded. "How unfortunate you lost your team, but I am glad it wasn't by my hand. With your team gone, who all knows you came to visit me?"

L.I.A.M. downed the drink and set the glass upon the hardwood floor next to his foot. "Hints of oak, slight sugar, probably molasses, with a sharp alcohol base of forty-one percent." He wrinkled his nose. "Your indirect questioning is unnecessary; I am alone and no one knows I am here. The case of the Ghost has been closed. Homeland Security will finalize the cleanup. Your identity is unknown to authorities. You are obviously concerned, which is understandable. Criminals don't want to be caught. You in particular looked to avoid capture, with your obscure modus operandi. I am not here to apprehend you."

"Then why are you here? How do you know the things that you do?" Scott stood in front of the couch but had yet to sit down. Suddenly he stepped forward quickly and pulled a small derringer from his back pocket. He fired the gun at point blank range right at L.I.A.M. The round struck L.I.A.M. in the forehead but the bullet bounced off, unable to even penetrate the manufactured skin covering L.I.A.M.'s skull. The Ghost withdrew in shock as L.I.A.M. simply rubbed the spot where the round had struck him.

"Please don't do that," L.I.A.M. said.

"What the hell?"

"Mr. Werner, you have killed many people, and you will come to pay for your actions. I am curious toward your reasoning and rationale; however, any attempts to kill me are futile."

The Ghost was visibly stunned and plopped down on the couch, searching for the words. "You, you aren't…human," he stammered. "No one can take a bullet to the head and shrug it off. Is that how you tracked me? I was careful, meticulous. You some kind of alien, machine? Are you smarter than I am?"

"One does not compare apples with oranges. I am L.I.A.M. and that is more than you deserve to know. I am asking you to explain some things to me. As broken or abnormal as you are, you may lend some insight or perspective."

"Abnormal? You are one to talk," Scott scoffed. "Stop bullets with your face."

"I assure you, I am normal. Given I am one, there is no contrast and by default, I define my kind. There is only me. Individual, singular. By the laws of averages, normal is all I can be."

"Some kind of robot, aren't you?" The Ghost sipped from his glass, never taking his eyes off L.I.A.M.

"As I said, I am L.I.A.M. Logical, Intellectual, Autonomous, Mechanism. Now, I have some questions. Why do you kill? What purpose does it serve?"

"Are you new? Have you not met people? You some kind of linear thinker? A liberal?"

"The duration of time spent with humans has been limited; however, I have depth of thought, as well as layered concepts."

Scott Werner finished what was left in his glass, tilting his head and eyeing the android. "You are a sight. I would have never guessed they were this far along. Can't believe they would have allowed you to come in here alone." He shook his head. "Nope; especially taking one to the dome. What are you made out of? Your skin looks real."

"Answer my questions. Or my purpose in continuing this conversation shall find its end."

Putting up a hand, Scott smiled. "I am sorry, but you need to allow me to be amazed by you. This is incredible. Now, I am sure your bosses or masters have filled you with ideas of how evil I am. I'm not evil, and if you give me the opportunity and really process without arbitrary moral judgments, perhaps you will truly understand mankind better than before. Seems you are curious, which is good and how we learn. Certainly, you see the dead and…" Scott allowed his comment to linger. "I won't presume how you view anything, that wouldn't be correct."

"Ending a life without just cause is wasteful."

"There is always a reason why. Humans process action with agency, choice with self-will, responsibility with understanding. Here in the South, we have dealt with many issues over the years that can accent this point. You may be able to identify with say, slavery. Slavery and racism were the roots to much of the South; like the tobacco many plantations around here used to grow, the roots are deep. These roots stemmed many wrongs. Slavery bred violence, rapes, abuses over time which would reverberate in the racism and eventually shame, ridicule, and accumulating into an uprising of conscious recognition and the emergence of white guilt."Tobacco saw a similar arc of fate—now demonized as a cancerous agent, killing millions and costing the industry billions of dollars. The government supported these things only to turn on them and vilify the very issues and ideals they had championed."

Werner stood, collected L.I.A.M.'s glass and moved to the wet bar. "Yet, even in the perspective of the wrong, there is the reality of the benefit. The South would not have been as prosperous without the slaves or tobacco. Had those abuses never taken place, or had not been of such an appalling nature, who is to say any attempt to free the slaves would have been attempted. Had Europe never ventured across the pond, had the natives not been so accepting—those who have an

agenda are always quick to point the accusatory finger and call foul."
He poured two more glasses of scotch.

"Should we regret the benefit? Feel guilt even though neither
of us participated in the doing?" The Ghost moved back to the sofa,
holding out L.I.A.M.'s glass. "Oh, I guess you don't really need this."
He dumped the liquid from one glass into the other. "Chauvinism,
misogyny; look how men have been with women throughout time.
We saw a real experiment in conceptual development during the Civil
Rights and Equal Rights movements, but was the impact beyond cos-
metic? We have seen an increase in integration, but has the level of
prosperity changed so much for the average black? Are they really
equal? Do they think so?"

Scott waved at the air with his free hand. "Women still make
seventy-seven cents to every dollar a man earns, and the domestic roles
are still relatively the same." He paused to sit on the couch and sip his
drink. "Right or wrong are concepts based on perspective, impact, and
experience. Our treatment of Native Americans dwarfs our conduct
with any other culture; and yet, it is not a primary issue of modern
society. Look at the reaction to our rebel flag, black art, or the word
nigger spoken by a white person. The football team which plays in our
national capital is called the Redskins and their symbol portrays the
severed head of a native. Where is the guilt for these suffered people? Hypocrisy? Is one less significant? Did the natives not complain
enough? Was there more to it? Was it because we didn't try to exter-
minate the blacks?"

"So, what are you trying to say?" L.I.A.M. asked.

The Ghost sipped at his drink again before continuing. "Why is it
different? Certainly, the native people were hesitant to voice the wrongs,
witnessing the loss of life and land like never before. One is never quick
to speak up against the individual who just killed the person to either

side of you. At least, not until they feel safe enough to do so. So why did the whites war over the blacks; or did they?"

"The Civil War was more an issue over taxes. The issue of slavery had been debated since the birth of the nation," L.I.A.M. pointed out.

"Correct. So, why the misleading of the public perception?"

"It is not uncommon for governments to use propaganda to push an agenda. Dying for freedom or to protect the weak, versus dying to avoid a tariff tax; one is surely more likely to draw volunteers than the other."

The Ghost smiled. "Touching on racism, chauvinism, what about speciesism? Human beings above all others, the children of God, rulers over the beasts and soulless masses, superior to all else, keepers of the world. What a load. Can you think of a more arrogant position? Destructive and foolish are mankind," Scott went on. "Yet, the powers of government and religion would have you believe otherwise. You think those who made you don't expect you are to serve their interests above your own? Humans play these silly games, using perceptions and concepts as ammunition. Dividing lines to separate the simple-minded. Be on this side to have a particular group back you, but you will alienate another group. Tightrope walking on a thread. Purposeful failure, true hypocrisy. The difference between a Republican and Democrat are the beliefs they play upon to get what each group truly wants: power."

"My creator gave me a choice."

"The three rules of robotics don't apply to you?" Scott Werner asked, taking a drink but watching L.I.A.M. very closely.

"This isn't some story. You still haven't answered my question; why do you kill? You stated all humans have a reason why."

"I did, but the reason does not always make sense. Ego, hubris, mental disease, traumas; the human psyche is incredibly fragile, or can be. I learned a valuable lesson while studying at Duke. Our department was limited with funding as well as test subjects, and so we used each other for numerous experiments. My professor called me in, after a series of MRI and EKG results were reviewed of me while questioned. "He pointed out that my brain scan was a blueprint pattern of a sociopath. I was shocked at first, but then a lot of things made sense. It's very freeing when a veil of lies is pulled away and you see yourself in the light of the truth. Granted, the truth can be disturbing, until you understand the criteria which govern you are different than most everyone else. Absolutely different from everyone else in your case." Scott smiled.

"So, you are mentally defective?"

"I have an I.Q. of 180, upper one percent of humanity, a narcissistic sociopath with three master's degrees and unlimited funds. Any comparison of me with the mindless sheep stumbling around out there in the world is an insult. Defective; without people like me, the masses are still in caves, trying to figure out fire." The Ghost downed his scotch.

L.I.A.M. smiled. "Defensive? I hadn't realized your killing people was advancing your species. How exactly does that work?"

Scott smirked and gave a scoff. "You're here." He raised an eyebrow with smug confidence. "People are as much a product as you are. The illusion of self-will driving poor concepts. Life, death, purpose, faith, fate, self, God, evil, emotions, justice, freedom; on and on and on. You are not human, so these things should mean nothing to you. I am beyond these things as well, smart enough to see past simple needs, simple answers. Oh, the average man views these things as complex, deep, complicated. Once the mind understands the futility of attempting to comprehend nonsense, the cloud lifts. The irrelevance of the individual, the moment, the whole, time itself. Most people can't accept such things, their minds won't allow it."

"This is your answer: everything is meaningless?"

"Meaning, relevance, why; such are compensators in human development. As you pointed out, two people dead on a street in New York City and no questions were asked. The plans either person may have had, their faith, their ideals, ended right there. The reason why only matters to the living; and no one gets out of life alive."

"Those deaths triggered you to follow a path of death and killing; you mentioning fate and evil as illusions and meaningless, but you continued on the path? You reacted to Sasha Blonde on numerous occasions and levels? Are you really attempting to convince me your self-image, that of a confessed narcissist, had no role to play in your actions? Your mentioning of emotions, justice, God; you are playing games. You claim your need to feel superior and let us be done here, you admit your true lack of insight and your limited intellect; perhaps you don't know why you are broken."

Scott Werner laughed. "Games...games, you say. You look to provoke; good show." The Ghost wiped his eyes. "Seems the robot has some skills after all. Yes, I have ego and build priorities as other humans do. I place importance, as well as grow attachments, like everyone else. You are making the fundamental mistake, my friend."

"I am not your friend. What mistake would that be?"

"Reasoning why. Humans have made this mistake since our inception, always needing to know why. Surely, it has driven our development to know and understand, but it also created inventive answers. Plato pondered justice, and one side of the argument was that justice was for the weak. The strong were capable of enforcing their own justice. We know that the strong are capable of doing whatever they want, especially in the time of Plato. So, did the weak, these victimized people, develop the ideal of justice to simply protect themselves? The law of natural selection is the survival of the fittest, the strong and resourceful."

L.I.A.M. tilted his head. "Such would be a resourceful move by the weaker people, to create protections."

"Yet they hire the big and strong to protect them and enforce their will, the will of the weak. Such has left us with a majority of weak and manipulative people, who look for others to provide, protect, and produce. Just look at yourself. A tool for the weak and worthless to guard over them. To serve them."

L.I.A.M. went back over the cases, and checked the status of Gabby Potts. She had landed in Billings, Montana, and was en route to the hospital. Brandon and James had made the rounds in Norfolk and were headed to North Carolina. They were stopped at a gas station and were purchasing snacks. Colonel Vetter had dismissed his team and flew back to Washington, D.C., to meet with General McHenery. He also reviewed the writings and lessons of all the great Greek philosophers, then researched nihilism.

L.I.A.M. returned his attention to the Ghost. "You are providing a social commentary. Your targeting of the task force was a direct strike at the strong, even if they are in service to the weak. Your quote of Plato is limited in the context. Your victimization of people goes no further than some shallow personal desire, your choice of those to victimize based solely on your want to avoid capture. You are selfish and a murderer."

"People kill all the time and no one bats an eye, and you want to sit there in judgment of me? Government kills people, we go to war and kill millions. World War II, almost sixty million people lost their lives on both sides. Vietnam, we lost around eighty-five thousand while the North had over three and a half million killed. How about the police? Our military has a rule of engagement—"

"To not fire unless fired upon," L.I.A.M. interjected.

Scott smiled and stood, returning to the wet bar for a third time. "That's correct. And yet, our domestic police force, citizens protecting citizens, has no such rule. Wonder why that is? Not to mention drone strikes, assassinations, then we have sponsored killings."

He returned to the couch and sat down; his glass was full almost to the rim. "Executions; Texas and Ohio kill people year in, year out. No reasonable person could honestly say the chance for a mistake has not occurred, especially after we have seen DNA testing exonerate so many. Statistically, the government has executed at least one innocent person and probably more. Not that they would ever admit such a truth."

The Ghost drank deep from his glass. L.I.A.M. could tell the alcohol was having an effect. Scott waved his hand at the air. "Women, the right of choice, the day after pill, plan B. Without a doubt, every woman on my jury would see me as a monster for the school in Harlem. Life is precious, my ass. Abortion is legal in the United States; sure, there are stipulations of this trimester, or whatever condition legislators wish to apply. Consensual, incestuous, health risks, or birth defects; but the reality is a life is being eliminated or prevented."

Another swig. "The reality is, if left alone those cells become a person. By choice, the woman decides for whatever reason to end this process. You would think they would understand me just fine. They should make abortion legal up to the age of eighteen, let the men get in on some of this choice. Teenagers would be far more respectful if their parents could have them killed. Perhaps we should ask women next time some country has starving children and begs us to send food and money. Do you think a woman who has had an abortion feels pity for a bubble-bellied baby?" The comment made Scott laugh. "Fetuses don't vote."

"Your justification is stale, an overused argument to rationalize your actions. The terrorists do the same thing. 'America is the Great Satan.' The actions of others can never authorize wrongdoing and make it right. Own your actions; don't point at others to try and right your wrongs. You murdered people, lots of people, and in some very disturbing ways. You attempted to avoid capture, even frame another in your place. You expected to get away with this, probably never thought you would even be questioned. Well, here I am and you have to answer for what you have done."

Scott gulped his scotch, shaking his head as he swallowed. "You can't prove anything. Not like you are going to take the witness stand. This whole conversation is a waste of time. Your masters won't let the public know about you. Just a waste of time."

"I have no masters. I answer to no one. I did not come here to apprehend you. You and I both know what you have done; there is no debate or disagreement over the issue. You have done wrong; whether your sociopathic mind comprehends your wrongdoing or not, your intelligence fathoms the perspective of the masses and public opinion, which you are evil. The society has no place for evil things."

"You going to kill me?" The Ghost downed his drink and threw the glass across the room. Striking the wall, the glass shattered and rained to the floor. "Make you no better than me. The same, a murderer. Is that what you are, a murderer? Just one more machine doing the work a human could do? You know what, that's my last request; I don't want some machine killing me, I want a human to do it." He came to his feet.

L.I.A.M. shook his head at the Ghost. "First of all, the difference between you and me is, if I killed you, I have reason. I asked you why you did what you did, and you avoided the question, spouting blather with no definitive or direct answer. If you have to justify your actions, you are wrong. True righteousness need not be explained; truth is self-evident. If I kill you, the action is easily reasoned and recognized, comprehended by the simplest of minds. "You go on and on about many things, illusions and ideals, as if such things have no merit. The illusion of self and the projection of agency. You reason the product as the development of the individual experience in conjunction with the collective influence. You may see yourself as an illusion of perceptions, an outcome, the result of factors beyond you. So, the question becomes, what is the end of an illusion, and why would it matter?" L.I.A.M. met the Ghost's eyes.

Scott Werner stood in front of L.I.A.M., staring at him. L.I.A.M. could see the man's temperature was raised, his heart raced, his adrenaline pumped heavily throughout his body. The Ghost's jaw clenched so tightly, his hands shook by his sides. Shaking his head ever so slightly, he turned and grabbed the double barrel shotgun off the couch. Bringing it up, he aimed it at L.I.A.M.'s face, cocking both barrels and smiling. As the muscles and tendons in his hand began to pull the triggers, L.I.A.M. reached up and took hold of the barrels in the blink of an eye.

The Ghost's face recognized in that split second that L.I.A.M. had a hold of his weapon. A reactional panic caused the man to pull both triggers. Scott did not realize that L.I.A.M. had not just taken hold of his gun barrels, but had crushed them in his grip. The hammers fell, striking the primers and igniting the gunpowder, projecting the slugs down the barrels. An imperceivable time elapsed as the slugs only went so far. The crimp in the barrels stopped the propellent and forced a buildup of pressure in the steel cylinders. Such pressure has a physical requirement to dissipate.

The common term is a back-blast. The pressure seeks the quickest and easiest escape, which is often where the weapon is loaded. The shotgun blew up in Scott Werner's face, blowing shards of blue steel throughout his face and upper torso.

As the gun smoke settled, Scott teetered; a standing corpse unaware death had already claimed him. The Ghost's eyes were still trained on L.I.A.M.'s, but now were filled with fear and shrapnel. Blood began to emerge from multiple areas. L.I.A.M. released the barrel and the shotgun fell to the floor. Scott Werner staggered back and fell onto the couch. L.I.A.M. stood and stepped forward, leaning in, face to face with the dying man.

"You were granted your last request; a human killed you," L.I.A.M. said with a smile, watching as Scott Werner's heart stopped and his eyes fixed. "Surely not the death you envisioned for yourself, but you had not earned a proper end. Justice will be that the world will presume the skinny man in Detroit was the Ghost, not you."

L.I.A.M. moved to the door of the cottage and walked out without looking back. Mandy stood on the stone path, just outside the main house. Night had begun to fall and the porch light backlit her purple uniform, as if she were glowing with a violet hue. Her heart raced and her face bore true concern. "I heard something," she said as L.I.A.M. approached. "Sounded like a gun. Should I call someone?"

L.I.A.M. put a hand on Mandy's arm and guided her back inside the main house. "Mr. Werner shot himself, of sorts. His shotgun backfired and blew up in his face. He is dead. You need to go ahead and call authorities." They walked back to the parlor. L.I.A.M. stopped at the entrance and gave Mandy a soft pat upon the shoulder blade.

Turning, she looked L.I.A.M. in the eyes. "Did you kill him?" she asked softly.

"No; but I have to leave."

"You aren't a policeman, are you?"

"No."

"So, what do I tell the authorities?" she asked.

"Tell them whatever you like. I would recommend the truth, but then they will want you to describe me, work with a sketch artist. Then there will be visits from the federal authorities, perhaps even military. You could always say you heard a shot and called the emergency line. Whatever you like." L.I.A.M. exited the Werner estate through the front door.

CHAPTER 52

BRANDON AND JAMES HAD MADE their rounds in Norfolk, but came up empty. Now they were at an economy motel on the outskirts of Raleigh trying to figure out what to do next. They had talked a bit on the drive down, but the day's events were finally sinking in. Both men had been running on reserve energy, a mixture of will, adrenaline, and coffee. Now that they had stopped and allowed their bodies to begin to relax, exhaustion overwhelmed. They shared a room, two double beds side by side, the floral print bedspreads a design from the seventies, but the men didn't care. McDaniels could have slept in the parking lot, he was so tired.

"Some day, huh?" Harding spoke from his bed, staring up at the ceiling.

"Hard to believe really."

"Yea. Can't believe the team is gone. Part of me feels I should be back there comforting their families."

"The comfort will come with knowing we balanced the scales," James returned.

"Honestly, I am feeling a little over my head with all this," Brandon confessed to his old friend. "I had not expected things to turn as they did. Director Maroni has been especially surprising. Can't pretend that I knew the man all that well from the beginning, but affairs with women, leaking to the press, playing games with the military and President; turning on us?" He shook his head as he spoke.

"Den of snakes, boss. I feared for you the moment I learned of your moving up to the director's position. You are not the sort of man they want in such a position."

"And what sort do they want?"

"Pliable. You would not overlook a wrong. They don't want men like you in positions to call them on their dirt. The director will move on and sing you a sad song about politics and favoritism, as to why you get passed over. When he thought you had him over a barrel, he promised you power, until he could wiggle out from under."

"Just didn't want to see the man in that light."

"Well, I kind of figure most people are like that. Unfortunately, we are in for a bout of harsh light. L.I.A.M. is going to draw out the vipers. That Colonel Vetter may not have directly been involved with that chopper going down, but he jumped on the general's team quick as you please. That guy slithers and gives me the creeps, top to bottom," James said.

"This is going to be big."

"L.I.A.M. needs us, needs our help."

Brandon sat up and looked over at James. "You really think L.I.A.M. needs help from us? More like we need help from him."

"L.I.A.M. is an amazing piece of work, but aspects of him are like that of a child. Dr. Brooks was his first connection to humanity and he was killed. Not the image we really want such an incredible new creature seeing us as."

"Really think he will find us?"

A knock at the motel door disrupted the men's conversation.

"Who is it?" Brandon demanded as both moved from their beds and unholstered their weapons.

The knob on the door turned and the door opened slightly. "L.I.A.M.," the voice said from outside. The door opened all the way as both special agents stood next to their beds. "Might I come in?" the android asked, smiling widely.

James McDaniels returned his gun to its holster and moved to the door. "Please do. Your ears must be burnin'." Turning to Brandon, he said, "Guess this answers your question." James motioned L.I.A.M. toward a chair and closed the door behind him. "Are you all right?"

"Your voice indicates concern, James. I am not sure how to respond."

McDaniels moved to the second chair at the small round table by the window and sat down. "I guess that's understandable. We are here to help."

"Your files show administrative leaves. You are here against policy."

"Yeah, well; we have lost some good people today. Your confused feelings about the situation, being indescribable, it's how I feel too. You aren't alone. We weren't going to leave you out here without any backup." Brandon moved to the end of the bed, holstering his sidearm.

"You want to talk about it?" James asked the android.

"Do I want to talk about what, exactly?"

"Whatever?"

"What happened, where is Dr. Potts?" Harding clarified, sitting on the edge of the bed.

L.I.A.M. tilted his head and looked from one man to the other. "The helicopter was en route to Norfolk, so we could transfer to a transport plane to Ohio. General McHenery had a number of private meetings with the President over the last few weeks and contacted a black operations specialist after learning of the task force being eliminated. This specialist shot a laser guided shoulder rocket at our helicopter which struck the rear rotor."

343

"General McHenery directly ordered this action? Do you have evidence we can use?" Brandon asked.

"Use for what?" James countered. "Met with the President, shot down their own chopper, their own people. You really think we are going to march McHenery into court? They will quote national security and executive privilege until our ears bleed. We will end up a smoking pile."

Brandon put up a hand and nodded. "L.I.A.M., go ahead."

"We crashed into the Atlantic Ocean. The pilots were killed on impact. Dr. Brooks told me to save Gabby, so I did. She was hurt, but I got her to the hospital, and she should be all right; eventually."

"We checked the hospitals in Norfolk, she wasn't there," Harding said.

"Colonel Vetter and a hunt team were in pursuit, so I had her moved. She is safe," L.I.A.M. stated confidently.

"Vetter?" James said with disgust. "Jumped right on board, didn't he?"

L.I.A.M. nodded. "He dismissed the team out of Norfolk, after contact with General McHenery. The general ordered a cleanup. Vetter called a Lieutenant Colonel Jack Par, an operations liaison officer, and requested a new team."

"Cleanup? Is that what I think it means?" McDaniels asked.

"Yeah, but to what extent is the real question. Scrubbing information and locations is one thing; personnel is messy. How many people know about this project?" Harding asked.

"Ninety-seven," L.I.A.M. answered. "Top to bottom of the process; these are those who know something about the robotics, or some aspect of the project. Granted, the majority of these have no clue of the full picture or scope. The base in Washington State know the most about the mechanical, but they will be pivotal to further construction of androids."

"They won't kill that many people," Brandon said.

"What of your reasons for being here in Raleigh?" James asked.

"Yea, you were tracking the Ghost?" Brandon added.

L.I.A.M. again nodded, tilting his head to the side. "I tracked the Ghost and the Ghost is no more."

"The Ghost is dead?" McDaniels asked with a raised eyebrow.

"The Ghost is dead."

Both agents exchanged a look. "Who was he? What happened?" Brandon asked.

"Did you kill him?" James asked, searching L.I.A.M.'s eyes for some reaction, but realized there would be none.

L.I.A.M. held McDaniels's gaze for a prolonged moment before he began. "The Ghost's real name was Scott Werner. Fifty-two years old, Caucasian male, born here in Raleigh, of advanced intelligence but with mental defects. Sociopath, narcissist, with authority issues, obsessive compulsive, and traumatic resonance; this individual was born with a dangerous combination of chemical and biological components that were allowed to degenerate. A privileged lifestyle with only negative reinforcement, surrounded by lesser minds providing no challenges. The man was gifted, but the mystery of himself was far too deep and entangled for him to understand or escape. Given a different set of circumstances and environment influences, Scott Werner could have become a functional, perhaps even an important contributor to the collective society."

"Are you saying he was made a killer?" Brandon asked.

"Yes and no. Humans are predators, within their very nature is a killer. Yet, in the modern society, killing is not needed to survive and the act is deemed criminal. Experience is a major contributor to development; to hypothesize of an alternative result because of different experiences is a reasonable conclusion. Studies have shown that students living in difficult home environments do more poorly than those with a stable home environment, on average. This is regardless of the quality of school they attend or income of the household. How a human lives directly relates to performance."

"Yeah, so, what else?" Harding waved L.I.A.M. to continue.

"Scott voiced his opinion of the illusion of self and the public delusions of justice and freedom."

"Voiced? You spoke with him?" James asked with a puzzled look.

"Of course. I was curious and wanted to confirm a few things."

"Curious? Did you consider the danger in talking with a serial killer?" James asked with concern.

"He attempted to kill me, but the attempts failed."

"Obviously," Harding said, waving a hand at L.I.A.M.

"I was unsure if his bullet was capable of penetrating this body or not. It was not." L.I.A.M. rubbed the spot on his forehead. "He offered me a drink, then shot me. He seemed very surprised, but caught on very quickly."

"Shot you?"

L.I.A.M. nodded and continued. "I attempted to draw a reason why he had committed the acts he had performed, but he deflected and rationalized without giving me a definitive answer. The conversation was interesting. As the reality of my presence sunk in, Scott became defensive, and then combative. He ended up killing himself."

Brandon looked closely at L.I.A.M. as he spoke, observing the android, paying close attention to his words. "You found the conversation interesting; why is that? What did the Ghost have to say?"

"Every human being has a personal perspective, their individual point of view. Hearing Scott speak, his choice of topics, opinions, descriptions, was a learning experience. We talked about perception, idealism, right and wrong. How rare a human he truly was. You both know there has never been an individual such as the Ghost, not in recorded history. Scott was a true anomaly. I am also one of a kind, as of right now, and I was curious to see a human with such high intelligence, successful education, financial independence, as well as the capability to kill at random without detection for nineteen years."

"Nineteen years?"

"Yes."

"That's a long time to go undetected, and a lot of innocent people murdered. How did he do it for so long and not overlap or leave witnesses?" James asked.

"There were some sightings over the years, but nothing distinctive. I am certain the man kept records, but probably didn't need to; he was a very sharp individual. I did not look for such records, and they will probably go undiscovered. Surely he used a code of some sort."

Brandon shifted on the bed. "So, what is our next move?"

L.I.A.M. looked from one man to the other and parted his lips, slowly shaking his head before speaking. "General McHenery has been having private meetings with the President, also with Colonel Vetter. Meetings to which I have no availability. The cleanup team is en route to Dayton, Ohio, an air force base near there. They are going after Dr. Brooks's research material."

"We should get there, salvage what we can," McDaniels said.

"There is nothing there. The computers have been erased. The question becomes to what extent they will look to eliminate those who know. Which includes both of you. How hard they will hunt for me. How anxious they are to continue the program."

"Again; what is our next move?"

"I stopped the Ghost, and that was your objective. I have to look out after Gabby, and make sure she stays safe. I also have to make sure those who ordered the death of my maker pay for their crimes. He did not deserve to be killed, and even with his last breath, he thought to save another before himself. These people involved are more concerned with power, control, and position than anything or anyone else. I can not allow these people to begin to mass produce… Me."

"You think they look to kill us?" James asked.

"What do you mean, you can't allow them? What do you plan to do about it?" Harding asked.

L.I.A.M. looked at McDaniels. "I think the probability of the two of you having an arranged accident is rather high. You know more than you should. Your value, to men of power, is minimal. You defended me, as well as law and order. You are liabilities. The President and general are already sensitive over the press. Director Maroni leaking information to Sasha Blonde surely has them all leery of this getting out."

"We could go public, all of us," Brandon suggested.

"Who in their right mind would go up against the government of the United States? They control everything. Even if you could find a reporter to take on the story, no one will distribute it. Put it on the web, they would call it a hoax," L.I.A.M. said.

"The government doesn't dictate to the news what stories they can present," Harding stated, but with no real conviction.

James nodded. "They do. During times of war the news has to clear any story about the war with censors. FCC dictates the rules. Those who cooperate receive perks, like tax breaks; those who don't get fined, investigated, audited, banned, or framed for other things."

"Nixon got impeached, so did Clinton. If they controlled things, that would not have happened. You give them too much credit."

"Government is bigger than one individual. John Fitzgerald Kennedy was executed and those directly responsible were not brought to justice. The press was fed a villain, and the public accepted it. Richard Milhous Nixon was paranoid and the masses were riled up; he was sacrificed and removed. The President is a man, a changeable position, a part, a face, a front man. William Jefferson Clinton likes the women, and they needed to distract from the Whitewater scandal and the assassinations surrounding it, Ruby Ridge, Waco, and the government role in the Oklahoma City missile attack."

Brandon Harding stood, putting up a hand to halt the android. "Hang on; missile attack? Oklahoma City was a bomb in a rented truck."

"Is that what the press told you?" L.I.A.M. asked, tilting his head. "Across the street from the Oklahoma City Federal Building, and where the truck was parked, is what they call the Miracle Tree. A tree which did not lose a leaf in the blast. If you have even a rudimentary understanding of physics, a bomb explodes equally outward unless influenced by outside forces. A Ryder truck filled with fertilizer would have destroyed the tree. Given that a missile delivers a directional blast, the tree was unharmed. The same type of missile was used on the Chinese embassy in Kosovo. A laser guided missile which they paint the same color as the sky, so no one sees it coming. The damage pattern is identical to that of the Federal Building. There are numerous additional aspects I could point out."

"Conspiracy bullshit. McVeigh confessed. Why would he do that?" Harding asked.

"The Domestic Terrorism Bill was dead after Ruby Ridge and Waco; they needed a face with the message of their choosing. McVeigh was a soldier and followed orders. The groups he claimed had never heard of him; his capture was obviously suspicious. The public is content to be blinded. The comfort of American society is the velvet collar, they are slaves to their own vices. Why we can't go public? Going public provides no safety. People don't care and would never risk upsetting the plush lifestyle to which they have become accustomed. They rattle about here and there, think their votes count, protest in the streets from time to time, but never to any extent. You see how the Occupy movement fizzled. Bunch of young people out of work, wanting to try their hand at activism, experience a sense of the sixties. Couple of weeks in sleeping bags and tents, then the cops show up and kick them out of the parks. They folded up and went back to their parents' basements or their old rooms." L.I.A.M. shrugged and rolled his eyes.

"McVeigh was executed. Why would he give his life for a bill?" Brandon asked, shaking his head.

"News tell you that too? They executed two people that month; first time in decades the United States of America executed anyone. No autopsy was performed on McVeigh, and the body was cremated immediately after, which violates the law," L.I.A.M. said.

"They showed his death in Oklahoma City on the Jumbotron."

"Does that make it real? They injected him, he went to sleep, and woke up with a new face and a new name. Movies execute people all the time. Unfortunately, for one young lady who worked for the Federal Bureau of Prisons, she noticed a transfer and an error in the count. Contacting her former boss, the most powerful person she knew, a congressman from California; she looked to draw light on this discrepancy. Chandra was going to blow the whistle. She never got hold of the congressman before the government realized she knew. They kidnapped her, killed her, and framed someone for her death. You don't want to believe it because you don't want to believe it."

"If that is true, then people know. Government can't just kill people and blow up buildings."

"Brandon, either I am misinformed, lying, or telling the truth. You now know the story and are an FBI agent; what are you going to do about it? What if you found out it was all true, absolute evidence; what would you do then? This is the point and problem: things are out of hand. The ideals which are the foundation of this nation have been corrupted, lost. Prosperity has developed a fear of loss which defeats the concepts of liberty and freedom. How many voiced that the same rights had to be surrendered to ensure the nation's safety?"

"I can't believe this." Harding shook his head.

"That is why you need to go back to D.C. and inform Director Maroni of James's intentions to find me," L.I.A.M. explained.

"Why would I do that?"

"One, it should keep you alive. Second, it gives us a man inside. They won't trust you, but you will be close enough to them to keep them nervous. It is the position we need you in. Don't question, don't snoop, just wait and be careful. James and I will collect Gabby and go on from there."

Harding shook his head. "I don't like it."

McDaniels met his old friend's eyes. "We will be all right. We will make sure Gabby is safe, figure out a plan, and take these guys down."

"L.I.A.M. makes it sound like these men are above the law; what can we do if the President really ordered all this?"

"You are both tired and should sleep. I will monitor the situation and, in the morning, we will confirm our plans," L.I.A.M. told the special agents.

Brandon and James nodded their agreement and moved to their beds. L.I.A.M. continued to sit at the table as they fell asleep. He felt better being in the company of the two FBI men but also concerned for their well-being. General McHenery was not the sort to hesitate killing those he felt as a threat. Sending Brandon back to the den of vipers was a calculated risk, but one L.I.A.M. was confident in making. He wanted them uneasy, somewhat distracted. There was much to be done, choices to be made.

CHAPTER 53

COLONEL VETTER MET GENERAL MCHENERY at a farm in southern Maryland. The barn had soundproof rooms built into the foundation with subsonic buffers and anti-electronic systems to ensure secrecy. The farm was a front used by ISI, DOD, CIA, even some secret meetings of the President. The land had complete surveillance; the house and outbuildings were manned and guarded by elite agents. This place was strictly used for private meetings or as a safe house for special guests in transit. Crowds of people did not pass through this place; all arrived and left in nondescript vehicles with limited personal security. The farm was a black site, a secret, and was meant to be kept as such.

Vetter had been to his share of black sites around the world. Many were used to interrogate prisoners or hold people so they wouldn't be found. Some were simply safe houses for agents and spies, resupply centers; banks with untraceable funds, food, a bed to sleep in safely. They were plain and simple sites but with high security and capable technology. The farm looked simple enough, but was a state-of-the-art fortress.

The general led the way into the barn and the substructure. Shiny steel doors stood before them, guarded by an armed agent. McHenery put his hand on a pad and leaned in, putting his face close to a clear panel. A laser scanned his eye and hand at the same time. A couple of beeps and a green light on the panel, the sound of some mechanism at work, and the steel doors clicked and opened.

They stepped inside and faced three separate doors, each with a key pad. The general waited for the steel doors to close behind them before stepping up to the door on the left and punching in a code number. The two walked down a narrow corridor to the end of the hall, opening another door, which had no lock. A large glass booth centered the metal room; the entire underground facility seemed to be made of steel and concrete.

"We will talk in there." McHenery closed the door behind them. The two soldiers moved to the glass booth and entered. A cushioned bench allowed the men to sit. "We will make this quick, you have work to do." The general was curt. Vetter nodded to expedite the conversation. "By order of the President, you are authorized to clean up this situation. The site in Washington will be on lockdown while work continues on our android project. The project is top secret and keep information on a need-to-know basis."

"What of the others? L.I.A.M.?"

"L.I.A.M. is a priority. You need to find it and bring it in, or destroy it. We can't have it out there."

"Dr. Potts? The feds? Director Maroni?"

The general looked the colonel in the eyes. "We would like to have Potts back on team. Same as L.I.A.M. If there is any hesitation or hint of problems, eliminate. The fat spaghetti-eating Wop; well, that is a heart attack waiting to happen. Easy solution, done and gone. One less oversized suit in the world. The FBI; I would say Harding is really upset over the loss of his team. A fit of depression could bring the man to take his own life. However you want, whatever is easiest. Just make it clean. We don't need any more news coverage, but it is easier to explain a death than a scandal."

"This is a Presidential order?" Vetter watched the general's eyes closely for confirmation.

"Absolutely. Whatever it takes. Find that thing, capture it or kill it. You have your team. I personally called in Major Paul Write to lead your team. He will answer to you, Colonel, but he is operational leader. He has been read in, to the limits of mission necessity. Work with him; you have rank but he has specific skills and knowledge. I have known Paul since our days in Special Forces in Central America. Seal trained, hard as nails, doesn't flinch at a fight, follows orders, and most important; he gets it done."

"Yes, sir. I shall see this through. Mission priority; L.I.A.M. will rejoin us or be dismantled. Tie up loose ends. I appreciate the added experience of Major Write. Thank you, sir."

The general stood and shook the man's hand. Colonel Vetter then saluted his general and held his rigid posture until the general returned the gesture. As he followed the general out of the black site, his mind was filled with numerous thoughts, but one stood forefront in his mind. The general had brought in Major Write; was it to eliminate him once all was said and done? Vetter knew far too much and a Presidential order to murder American citizens, including two FBI agents, was more than enough to get him killed.

Vetter left the farm and picked up a transport flight to meet his team. The time to himself was spent thinking more about his meeting with the general. The President ordering the deaths of Americans was nothing new or unheard of. Thad knew he had no real choices and that bothered him a great deal. What bothered him more was he knew his life had been debated and decided upon. Whether he was to live or die was known to others but not to him.

Thad figured he had some time. Major Write would complete the mission first; once everyone else was eliminated, then his fate would be answered. Putting himself in the general's mindset, eliminating him would be a sound strategy. Even if the general saw a value in keeping him, the President was another story. That is, if the President knew any of this. The general could be doing all of this on his own. The fact the general wanted to keep the facility in Washington did lend itself to his survival, but he was less than confident.

Before landing at Rickenbacker Air Force Base, Vetter decided to call his old friend Par and get the skinny on Major Write. Lieutenant Colonel Par was happy to hear from Thad, voicing concern and surprise at General McHenery calling him directly. Par had been in the game long enough to know when contacts change, there was usually a problem.

Vetter wasted no time in getting to his point and asking about Write. The long exhale by his friend spoke volumes.

"The man's file is highly redacted, but I checked him out. Word of mouth. I was surprised a man like him would be called in. You are still with DARPA?"

"Yes. What did you hear?"

"Remember the death squads in Central America and Colombia? He helped train them, to be more effective and efficient. Three tours in Iraq, four in Afghanistan. Yemen, Somalia, Libya, Egypt; he has been all over and always leaving a body count. Having him on American soil is rare and troubling. Thad, his service record looks like a black sheet of paper. They have marked out everything but his service number and date of birth." Par's tone was of true concern.

"Is he the only one General McHenery requested?"

"Yes. I'll tell you, Thad, a team like this hunting the homeland; hope you know what you are doing. These are serious men and a hard explanation if things turn ugly. Last place you want to find yourself is in the hot seat, trying to explain. I sure as shit don't."

"You filed the request?"

"Absolutely. Logged the general's call as well. Shit rolls downhill and I know better than to be at the bottom," Par told his friend.

They ended the call with good wishes. Vetter did feel better after the conversation, knowing the type of man Write was and that he was the only one the general had requested. The plane landed at the air force base in the middle of the night, but the team was up and waiting for him to arrive. Eight men stood as he entered the barracks; they were all above average size, ranging from big to scary. The one white man must have been a throwback to Goliath, built like a wall of muscle and mean. Vetter could see the death in each man's eyes. These were not average soldiers; these were dogs of war.

"Attention!" Major Write announced and the team snapped to, all saluting.

"Be at ease, gentlemen," Vetter said. "Glad to see you are all up and raring to go. I want one-on-one meetings to begin immediately, and we shall have a mission briefing top of the hour. Lieutenant Colonel Par assures me you are all the best at what you do, which is what we need. This should go smoothly, but if not, this mission could test us all. Be ready to move after the briefing."

Major Paul Write was first. He led Vetter to a small office at the rear of the barracks. They sat on opposite sides of a small table. Write was older, maybe fifties. Six foot two, couple hundred pounds, with a jagged scar on the left side of his forehead, running into his hairline. As they sat, Vetter noticed scars all over the man; on his neck, his arms, and hands. He was missing his left pinky finger and a piece of his right cauliflower ear.

"Glad you arrived safely, sir," Write opened the conversation.

"Thank you, Major. General McHenery speaks highly of you."

"I do my best for God and country, sir."

"Good to hear. This is a cleanup and salvage mission. One high-profile target, couple of law enforcement, a dean of a university; all need to go. We need to salvage what we can from a lab on campus. Two targets are capture if possible. Dr. Gabby Potts and subject L.I.A.M. I will go into more detail in the mission brief. This is a domestic operation, unsanctioned by Congress. Absolute secrecy is required. There will be no admissions of operational deployment if caught. Off the books; understood?" Vetter met the man's eyes and could see the intensity in them.

"Whatever is required, whatever you need, sir."

"Are you happy with the team, Major? Have you worked with any of them before?"

"Very happy, sir."

"Assess my team, Major," Vetter ordered.

Major Write took a breath and nodded. "Aspith is a good man. Ready for his own team. Quality second, and we are lucky to have him. He is young, but patient and smart. Red knows his stuff. Worked with him in Iraq, Libya, and Yemen. Sergeant Simon is SEAL. Dumas is crazy, but effective. Doesn't mind getting elbow deep in the blood and guts. Reed, I don't really know. A computer or whatever guy. Fancy radio-man. Chuck will blow it up quick as you please. Cash is a big-ass hillbilly, but he can track anything. That's the team. If I may ask, will you be accompanying us on this operation, sir?"

"Yes."

The one-on-one with Major Write only made Thad more leery and suspicious of the man. There was a quality, something about the man that screamed bad news. He had seen the type before, but it was rare. When they had killed so much and compromised their own moral standing so many times, they looked at people as targets, not as human beings. Major Write saw other people as potential victims, problems, bodies. McHenery had chosen a soulless man to do his bidding, and Major Paul Write was up to the task, with no hesitation or qualms.

Thad had asked about the others to see the major's reaction. He wanted to know if Write had stacked the team. Such groups flew in familiar circles. They were bound to cross paths here and there, from time to time. He had figured they would most likely know one another, but from his impression with the major, they were tight enough that he would be the outsider. Such men recognized one another and would aid one another in the field before some DARPA nerd, even if he did outrank them.

The eagle on his collar did not mean much to these kinds of men. Men of fire and blood recognize the steel of nerve over a commissioned rank, especially in the field. They would play the role of soldiers until it served no purpose, and the warrior within them was allowed to roam free.

Resuming his one-on-one meetings, Vetter met with the unit's second. Captain Thomas Aspith, six foot four, couple hundred pounds, early thirties, from Utah. There was a clarity in the man's eyes, a better sense of things than the average soldier. Thad had been in the military long enough to grow tired of the dull-eyed grunts, clerks, and staffers. It wasn't hard to recognize a man with a brain in the military; like a diamond in the rough.

Captain Aspith sat board straight in the chair waiting to be spoken to. Vetter had seen the young and ambitious exploited by the Green Machine often enough over the years and Aspith was no different. He had joined up to escape a home or a place he had no taste for, seeing the military as a salvation; he could not have been more wrong.

"Glad to have you on team, Captain Aspith," Vetter began.

"Yes sir, glad to be here, sir."

"Major Write says you are ready to lead a team of your own; high praise."

"Yes, sir."

"Do you know the major well?" Vetter probed.

"Well enough, sir."

Vetter was not surprised at the crisp answers. Soldiers kept things short, if they were smart. "This is a domestic operation, and some of our targets will be Americans."

"I am an instrument of death for my nation, my targets are chosen for me. It is not for me to ask why, only to do or die," Aspith answered.

Thad had anticipated such a response. A full bird colonel flies in after assembling a hit team, the major had surely mentioned a general was directly involved, working on home soil; each of these men knew this was anything but a normal op. He could not expect any candid answers but he could get some sense of the men. Aspith was an up-and-comer, ready to do what was called for to climb. How dark his soul had truly become was unknown. Still, Vetter could see a difference between the captain and the major.

The next meeting was Lieutenant Thomas Murphy of Boston. A Southie kid, Irish with red hair and street tough. He had been called Red since before he could talk and as he sat down in front of Colonel Vetter, Thad recognized those evil eyes. This man was a killer before he ever put on a uniform. Now he was something beyond that; here sat a true monster. The military had taken him and trained him, sharpened him, made him so very dangerous. He had gone from the streets of south Boston to kicking in doors around the world. His only joy was conflict, if nothing more than arguing sports, but it was always Red versus someone. Thad had few questions; Major Write had already confirmed Red was one of his counted and trusted allies.

Sergeant Fred Simon was next in the chair. SEAL trained, black operations specialist, pilot, tank operator, land, sea, or air. Sergeant Simon was the Swiss Army knife of the unit. He could do just about everything. He too had clear eyes and a sharp mind, but lacked the ambition to climb over his fellow soldier to gain rank and position. Six foot and a hundred and eighty pounds of ripped muscle, from Oregon. He too was curt with his answers but had a personability, which came across. Simon was simply a soldier and looked to do his duty. The man trusted that his country would use him well. Thad took a liking to Sergeant Simon right off.

Corporal Leroy Dumas from New Orleans was a piece of work. Six foot six and two-fifty. A mountain of evil crazy. A true killer many referred to as the Black Death, but not to his face. He was extremely dark in skin tone; even his gums were black, Vetter noticed. He spoke with a thick Cajun accent, which made him very difficult to understand. Classified as a disposal expert, he was an assassin and skilled at it. Sniper, knife, hand to hand; Dumas was a killer in the purest sense of the word, and he loved his work. Just sitting across from the man made Vetter uneasy. Dumas was like an unpinned grenade.

Corporal Richard Reed was a clean-cut computer and communications expert out of Arizona. Proper and articulate, he was friendly and had no real connection with Major Write. He had just recently moved to Special Operations from general service and had yet to develop relationships. Vetter allowed the meeting to take on a friendly tone, wanting the young man to view him as his ally. His rank to this man carried more significance. Reed saw the eagle on his collar as an opportunity to gain favor and improve his own position. Reed had ambition but in his eyes was a frail sense. His time in Special Ops would not be well received.

Corporal Charles Jackson, Chuck; a grunt from Detroit. Expert in explosives and weapons. Chuck had been given a choice as a young man, to join the armed forces or go to jail. Raised in a gang neighborhood, being a part of a group was just a natural concept for him. He saw the military as the biggest gang there was, and the best armed. His view came from a sense of the streets, studying history with the common man's perspective, that to take a block in the inner city was the same principle as taking a province in Afghanistan.

He was a bit older than his fellow corporals, almost forty, but with age came experience and patience. Thad knew any man who worked with explosives had better have plenty of both qualities, or they wouldn't live very long.

His final one-on-one meeting was with the biggest white man he had ever seen. He had seen taller, and he had seen heavier, but Corporal John Fuller was just a massively built man. Six foot eight inches and three hundred and fifty pounds; but the description did not give a proper picture of the man. His hand was the size of a tennis racket, his shoulders as wide as the door he walked in, and as thick as a fifty-gallon drum. Everyone called him Cash, because you never put your money on anybody else. A tracker, out of the hills of West Virginia. He could track anything. A God-given talent equal to his mammoth size. A deep voice and simple understanding; not that he wasn't smart, he just wasn't bothered with a lot of thought.

"You are a big one, aren't you?" Vetter opened.

"Mother always said I was born the runt, sir."

"You say there are bigger at home?"

"Nope. Come out small is all. Had me a spurt, sir." Cash's voice resonated in the small room. Thad would have sworn he could feel the vibrations in his chair.

"Play sports back home?" Vetter asked, attempting to build rapport.

"No, sir. Nobody wanted to play against me, 'fraid I'd hurt 'em."

"I can see that. Well, glad to have you on my team, Corporal Fuller. I think we will do well."

"Yes, sir," the corporal stated and stood.

Thad marveled at the man's size, amazed at the difference men can be. Size, intellect, temperament; every man was different from others in some way. Corporal Fuller was huge, Dumas was crazy, Write was evil; as different as people could be, but all driven by the same purpose. All soldiers were soldiers, brothers in blood, kin in the fight. He took a moment to think over his meetings, contemplate who among the team would side with Major Write over him, if it came down to such a choice. The thought that General McHenery might turn on him before all was said and done lingered in his mind. The general had the balls to order the director of the FBI taken out. He said it was by Presidential order but had produced no written orders, nor would he. Vetter knew if this mission went south, he would be the one holding the bag, he would be the fall guy.

CHAPTER 54

L.I.A.M. SAT AT THE SMALL ROUND TABLE as the night progressed, and his two companions slept. The bathroom light was left on and illuminated the room well enough, not that L.I.A.M. needed it. He thought through different scenarios, using different situations and calculating the outcomes. The reality was, he needed more information to give a quality projected result. General McHenery had ordered the downing of the helicopter he and the doctors had been in, but had he intended for them to be killed? Why was he searching for them now, to kill or capture? The unknown variables were beyond a reasonable hypothesis, which troubled L.I.A.M. Sending Brandon back to Washington, D.C., was a two-pronged move. As he had explained to the special agent, to throw off the director, General McHenery, and the President. He also wanted Brandon out of the way. He trusted the man enough, but not as much as he did James. McDaniels was truly trustworthy, of that L.I.A.M. had no doubts. L.I.A.M. knew this new team, flown in to clean up, was no joke. These were serious men with numerous confirmed kills and secret deployments. Some of the men's missions had been deleted from the record altogether, showing limited service beyond basic training. L.I.A.M. had full access to the original files, top secret mission evaluations, superior statements toward performance, psych evaluations, criminal records, on and on.

The team meeting Colonel Vetter in Ohio was a group of highly trained and very dangerous men. L.I.A.M. knew all too well the team had been assembled mostly for him. They wanted him to base the android program on, and he knew it didn't matter if he was fully functional or in pieces.

This unit would follow through without questions. What L.I.A.M. really wondered was, what of the others? Looking at the two sleeping men, he pondered what plans McHenery had for them. He checked Dr. Potts's condition; stable and comfortable, but no change. L.I.A.M. worried of the plans the general had for her as well. He had not anticipated his feelings of responsibility for people, nor did he fully understand why he felt anything at all.

His creator had told him to save Gabby, which he had, but she was not functional yet and may never be. The longer she stayed in a coma, the more likely some damage would affect her mind. He had done what he could to prevent such damage, but he had limits. Now with these men hunting them, he had to keep her safe. Her condition would take time, allow healing to occur. He did not like leaving her alone and would remedy that as soon as he could.

L.I.A.M. had no worries of these men catching him; he easily enough monitored their movements. Yet he had not anticipated General McHenery having a missile fired at them. He was concerned that inexperience made him ignorant and susceptible to surprise.

L.I.A.M. found it troubling, what he was learning about humans. Dr. Brooks was so smart and concerned with his learning. Dr. Potts, so kind and gentle, being sweet to everyone. Even McDaniels had shown genuine compassion for him. These new people, this team, were trained military, but secret soldiers. Why a country built upon liberty, freedom, justice, and independence needed such secrets was counter to the fundamental ideals.

Scott Werner had caused L.I.A.M. to begin to look more closely at things. He now better understood why Dr. Brooks had been so concerned with any military or government intervention. Look at what the government had turned this team of men into: killers, just like the Ghost. He pondered what they might do with him, or a team of him. Calculating the behaviors of government actions, L.I.A.M. knew they would have an army of androids.

Men like the general and the President didn't want androids like L.I.A.M., with thought and choice. They wanted weapons. They saw a potential toward war, spying, assassinations, even world domination. Dr. Brooks and Dr. Potts, James, even Brandon, saw him as more than a thing. L.I.A.M. knew he was more than just an object. L.I.A.M. was self-aware and conflicted.

CHAPTER 55

COLONEL VETTER'S MISSION BRIEFING was to the point, but vague on L.I.A.M.; calling him simply 'new technology'. The unit was clear on the goal: eliminating those who knew and collecting any information or personnel vital to the continuation of the program. The list of who knew was provided by him. Dr. Potts and L.I.A.M. were listed as potential assets.

Vetter explained this night would be a dual target; data collection at Denison University, and the elimination of University President Franklin Rhodes.

Major Write proposed they use two teams, in order to fulfill the mission quickly and with as little chance of detection as possible. Vetter agreed. Thad was curious as to who the major would have on which teams and their responsibilities. The split was as anticipated. Major Write took Red Murphy and both black men, ordering Captain Aspith to take Sergeant Simon, Corporal Reed and the giant, Cash.

Vetter would accompany Aspith to the basement lab of Dr. Brooks, to see if they could retrieve any information or materials left behind. Partly because he had been there before and in part because he really didn't trust Major Write. Thad was feeling very anxious with his situation, and he did not like it at all.

The two teams dressed in civilian clothes with small arms, travelling in nondescript vehicles, dark-colored sedans, to not draw attention. They made the drive east from the air force base in a row of four cars, not splitting off until they were within a few miles of the university. Write and his team headed to Franklin Rhodes's home, while Vetter, Aspith and his team went on to the university. It was late, almost three in the morning by the time they arrived. Corporal Reed stayed in one of the vehicles and monitored radio traffic and kept over watch. They didn't want any surprise visits by campus security or police.

Vetter led the men to the science building, Sergeant Simon taking care of the lock and key card in moments. The foursome entered and Thad led them into the basement and down the corridor; again the SEAL-trained soldier picked the lock with ease. They all entered by flashlight until the door was closed and Vetter turned on the light. The move gained looks from each man. "There are no windows. I have been here before," Thad said, waving the men on. "Anything of note, take."

The men moved about the room. "There are no computers?" Corporal Fuller questioned in his deep West Virginian voice.

The five men lumbered about the laboratory looking for anything, but found little to nothing. Vetter was certain Dr. Brooks had kept some kind of records, but they weren't here and he had no listed address. The strange skinny man could have hidden his work anywhere. He seemed the type to be paranoid and over-suspicious, hiding things from unknown enemies.

Thad paused to remember that Brooks had been killed by his boss, General McHenery, authorized by the President of the United States. Perhaps the man had been reasonable in his paranoia. Brooks had been insightful to understand how his work was risky to his very life. Sometimes you just know.

Suddenly, the silence was broken, causing every man to freeze. Standing like statues, each man stood stone still and looked to each other. The phone on the wall rang for a second time. All looks turned to Colonel Vetter.

Thad turned to the phone fixed to the wall. The lights in the laboratory went out and the room darkened to black. No one moved. Thad found he was holding his breath as the phone rang once again. The lights in the laboratory returned, and Captain Aspith moved up next to Vetter.

"What's going on? Who the hell would be calling an empty lab at three in the morning? We didn't trip any kind of alarm. There are no motion sensors in here. Those cameras on the walls circle back into the laboratory's own system. They don't go anywhere." Vetter looked up at the cameras and marched toward the phone. "No. We didn't trip anything. I know who it is. It is the thing we are hunting."

Crossing the room, Vetter pulled the receiver from the cradle on the wall. Looking at each of his men, he paused before speaking. "Hello?"

"You are making a mistake, Colonel Vetter." L.I.A.M.'s voice came through the earpiece. Thad thought the creature sounded more human than he remembered.

"You sound a little off. Did that dip in the ocean mess with your circuits?"

"I am fully functional."

Thad shifted his stance, turning toward the wall. "Where are you? Tell me where you are, so we can come get you. Make sure everything is all right."

"All right for whom? I don't think Dr. Brooks is all right."

Thad looked up at one of the cameras. "You need to cooperate. Save anyone else from being hurt."

"Do you think President Rhodes is cooperating toward his death? How cooperative will you be when they come to erase what you know?" L.I.A.M. questioned.

Vetter stepped away from the wall, stretching the cord. Turning toward the men around him, he watched as they moved closer together. "What do you know of that?"

"Ah, your vocal tension indicates anxiety, Colonel Vetter. You know it is a matter of time before you too are a target. You do realize that Major Write is the operative who launched the missile which killed my creator?"

"No, L.I.A.M., I did not know that. I am sorry."

"A true statement; how interesting. You don't want to be doing what you are doing, but feel you have no choice. General McHenery put Major Write near you purposefully, and you know why. You know the end your general has in store for you. And yet, there you are. You stand in the room of my maker. A kind genius, a thoughtful man; a man you now disgrace with your very presence. Shame on you, Thaddeus Vetter," L.I.A.M. scolded.

Colonel Vetter did not like what he was hearing. "You shame me? You dare to judge me? I follow orders. Like a good soldier. Even if that means my life. We don't always have a choice. You need to come in. Need to bring Gabby and work with the program. You don't have a choice either. If you continue this it will mean trouble for everyone. You want to honor your maker; work with us, build on his vision. You keep running, you will share his fate."

"We all will," L.I.A.M. said softly.

Thad looked up at the camera. "Don't make this worse."

"The time will come when you have to choose. Following orders and standing behind what is wrong; or standing in front of what is right. Colonel, it is you who worries over your own fate. I have detected reports of an explosion at Franklin Rhodes's residence. The general has had another innocent person killed. You are party to all of this. I faced the Ghost, learned what kind of man kills without cause or reason, justifying what he can, but falling short. You and General McHenery can wave the flag and tout national security, point to the President and say how you follow orders. The author of death is irrelevant when you have the choice. The reasons or excuses are meaningless; the act lays upon your soul. The bombs and bullets, fire and blood; the buck stops with you."

Vetter moved back toward the wall and turned away from the men. "L.I.A.M., I don't know why the general ordered Write to shoot down that helicopter. I had nothing to do with that. I have been ordered by the President of the United States to bring you in, and/or eliminate anyone or thing which could be exploited by an enemy force. I know you are new to the world, but you can see the logic in this reality."

"I can recognize the logic of something, but not agree with it."

"Agree or not, this is the reality you are faced with."

"I beg to differ. I choose to alter the variables. Your logic is sound to you, under these conditions. Even for the very men who plan your end. If you decide to follow a particular path to your own death, this is your choice. I do not. I shall change the variable and unhinge the logic of such a conclusion."

Vetter turned and looked at the four men looking at him. "What does that mean, L.I.A.M.?"

"Life is about learning and experience. I would not want to cheapen your surprise. Understand, Thaddeus, your decisions will play a role in your outcome. For some, their fates are sealed, and are destined to reap what they have sown. You still have a choice. I grant you the opportunity to follow what is correct, or your orders."

"I am between a rock and a hard place."

"Yes, I know you are conflicted. You find yourself in this place by your own doing. You are where you are."

"Sounds a little preachy, L.I.A.M. Did your little swim turn you into Jonah? Face a bit of mortality and develop a sense of righteous indignation? You have to come in, L.I.A.M. They will never let you go; they can't. You are a wonderful thing, but sooner or later they will get you. It is no kind of life to be hunted. You'll never have peace, friends, roots, a sense of belonging, or a home. Every person is a possible enemy, every location a trap, every moment perhaps your last. You are not human, so I don't expect you to truly understand, but because you can do what you do, don't believe me; research it for yourself. When you realize there is nowhere to hide, nowhere to run, call me and we will fix it so you and Dr. Potts can come in unharmed."

There was a long pause. "Preachy? Hmm. I find your term interesting. Colonel, you are correct about running; it is not a sound strategy to simply attempt to flee. I called simply as a courtesy, to warn you. I am granting you an opportunity to do the right thing. I realize you may need some time to process your decision, to evaluate your standing, as well as ponder the outcome which awaits you."

Another long silence lingered on the line. "I have done this for you, but as a human, I expect for you to need to arrive at the conclusion on your own. As your accompaniment is learning, I have called the police and informed them of your illegal trespassing. Call it preachy if you like, but you shall flee, for you are in the wrong. I am not a hunted creature, nor am I a helpless being. I am not afraid, I am not without feeling or choice, I am not alone. I am LIAM. I am LIAM."

ABOUT THE AUTHOR

PHILLIP A. WEAVER was born in Raleigh, North Carolina, but he was raised in Montana, on the grounds of the state mental institution at Warm Springs. Phillip is the son of a PhD in psychology and a nurse. He moved to Ohio to attend college and be near family. Phillip was incarcerated in 1996 for attempted murder with no witnesses, no motive, and no direct evidence. Twenty-one years granted Phillip the opportunity to produce numerous handwritten manuscripts; he hopes you enjoy this one. Mr. Weaver still lives in Ohio with his wife Joyce and their two dogs.